STEALING

CHASTITY

Devon Hartford

COPYRIGHT NOTICE

Want to get an email when Devon's next book is released and receive a FREE Bonus Story?

Sign up here:

http://eepurl.com/B7crf

or go to **devonhartford.com**

and **SIGN UP**

DEDICATION

To Elle Casey, friend and fellow story-TELLER.

If you hadn't given me the perfect advice at the perfect time, I might have shelved this book permanently. Thanks to you, it lives.

Now I owe you twice.

Stealing Chastity

Every GOOD GIRL wants a BAD BOY to steal her virtue...

CHASTITY

My new neighbor Lance McKnight is rude, crude, and totally irresistible.

My mom hates him. She says he's going to corrupt me.

Lucky for me Lance doesn't care what Mom thinks. From day one, he makes it clear he's going to have his way with me no matter what Mom says.

Works for me.

I'll do whatever Lance tells me.

No matter how bad it is...

LANCE

I get what I want from women any time I want.

That pisses you off, doesn't it?

Deal with it.

That's the hand life dealt me. I'm just making the most of it.

What you don't know about me is, from what I've been through, it doesn't make up for much.

That's all about to change. Because my new neighbor Chastity Shields is some kind of something else. Mmmm, mmmm.

I don't know what to make of her.

But I want her.

And I'm gonna take her.

Every last way I can think of...

WARNING: Just when you think you know where this book is going, it doesn't. Lance McKnight is a real bad boy. At first you'll hate him. But in the end you'll love him twice as much.

Recommended for ages 18+

Stealing Chastity is a scorching hot standalone with an HEA

Prologue

Age 8.

"Daddy?" I shake his arm. It's night time. He sits in his big chair in front of the TV. The TV is really loud. "Daddy? Wake up. I can't find Mommy." I feel dumb calling him Daddy. If I call him Daddy, he yells at me for being a baby and tells me to call him Dad because I'm a big kid. I'm scared, so I forget. "Daddy? Where's Mommy?" I turn off the TV sound so it's quiet. "Daddy? Wake up."

He doesn't.

He likes to sleep in his chair with his beer cans.

He doesn't sleep in bed with Mommy anymore.

Not since I was seven. But they still yell at each other every single day.

I shake his arm again. "Daddy?"

"Get offa me, God damn it!" He throws his arms around like tree trunks. He's still asleep.

I jump back and fall down hard on my butt. "You hurt my ear, Daddy." I rub it. "Wake up. You're having a nightmare. Daddy?"

He snores loud.

I cross my legs and stare at him.

Maybe Mommy will come home if I think about it really hard for a long, long time.

She doesn't.

"Daddy, wake up!" I whisper loud but it's not yelling because it's whispering. "Daddy?"

After forever, he opens one eye. "Go to bed, Lance."

"Mommy's gone."

His other eye opens.

"She's gone, Daddy."

Both his eyes open real big. "What?"

"Mommy isn't in her bed. I had a nightmare. I was scared so I wanted to talk to her. She isn't in the house anywhere."

He sits up in his chair like it's really hard to do, like he weighs a million pounds. "Where is she?"

"I don't know. I'm scared, Daddy." I'm afraid he'll yell at me for not calling him Dad or hurt my ear again. He's always hurting my ears.

He doesn't. He stands up like he's dizzy and walks to Mommy's bedroom.

I follow him.

He stands in her doorway. "Where did she go?"

"I don't know." I'm whispering because it's night time.

He turns on the light and walks into her room and looks in the closet. "Her clothes are gone. Where are her clothes?!" He stares at me.

"I don't know!" I didn't take them but his angry face doesn't believe me.

BAM!!

He punches a hole in Mommy's closet door. "Where the fuck did she go?!" He's yelling at me with his beer words. "Where did she go, Lance? God damn it, where is she?!" He stares at me like I'm invisible.

I *feel* invisible right now. Like I disappeared like Mommy. Oh, no. Did I make her leave? Or is it because she hates Daddy? I don't know. Does she hate me too? I don't know.

I start to cry.

Daddy is crying too. "She's gone, isn't she? Why did you let her leave? *God damn it, answer me! Why did you let her go?!*"

"I didn't!" I run to my room and close the door and crawl under my Batman blankets, all the way until I disappear.

I cry and cry.

Daddy cries too. In the hallway.

We both cry until forever.

++++8++++

LANCE

Age 16.

Valentine's Day.

I'm in love with Marissa Rodriguez.

Today is the day I show her how much.

I've got it all planned out. I hope everything goes the way it's supposed to.

I walk down Tropicana Avenue sweating my ass off. Not because of the Las Vegas heat. It's winter and it's barely 62 degrees. I'm sweating because I'm so damn nervous. In one hand I've got the bouquet of roses I five-fingered from the VONS around the corner. In the other I've got the box of chocolates I also stole.

Marissa lives in the cheap ass brown apartment building next to the cheap ass orange apartment building where I live with my dad. Both are a few blocks away from the UNLV campus where Marissa is a college freshman. The chicks at the University of Nevada Las Vegas are easily the hottest in the state. I know because I see them every day at the Del Taco across from campus.

Marissa is by far the hottest of the hot.

And she's mine.

I'm the luckiest dumbshit on the planet.

In my back pocket I've got the poem I wrote for her for Valentine's Day. I've been working on it for two weeks and it's awesome. She's gonna love it.

The armpits of my UNLV football T-shirt are soaked by the time I climb the steps to her apartment.

I knock on her front door.

My heart is pounding.

I've got my poem memorized, but I want it handy, just in case. I stuff the bouquet under one sweaty arm and pull the index card out of my pocket so I can read it:

Before you was nothing
The world dark
The blue sky too high
For me to touch
To hold
To kiss

After you was everything
The world bright
The blue sky mine
Your touch divine
Your kiss
Your lips

All mine

Will you be my Valentine?

I know it's corny. But it's true. It's how I feel about her.

Marissa still hasn't answered the door.

I knock again. Her doorbell is broken, just like mine.

She should be home. She doesn't have class on Tuesdays. I do, but I skipped school to come here and give her all this stuff. One more day of Saturday School won't bother me any. Marissa is worth it.

I wonder where she is?

Maybe she went out to get something. I walk down the steps and go around behind her building. Her car is in her carport. That means she's home. I walk back across the red lava rocks and stop below her bedroom window. It's closed. I walk back the other way and notice her bathroom window is open.

I could climb through it.

But I don't want to scare her.

Maybe I'll go knock again.

"*Ay, Papi!*"

I frown.

Was that Marissa? I listen closely.

Words drift from the bathroom window. "*Right there, Papi! Right there!*"

It sounds like Marissa. But she wouldn't...

"*Yes, like that! NNNnnnn! Yeah Papi! Fuck me harder, Papi! Harder!*"

I'm getting a hard on. That's normal.

But that can't be Marissa. She never calls me *Papi*.

Maybe it's her roommate Sarah?

"*Fuck yeah, Marissa. Come on my dick, bitch!*"

"*Oooooh, Papi! Fuck me, Papi!! Ay!! Fuck me!!!! Ay yi yi!!!!!!!*"

My face burns.

It's her.

"*Fuck yeah, bitch! Fuck yeah!*"

He's calling her a bitch.

I see red.

Blood red.

I drop the box of chocolates and throw the roses onto the rocks. I stride around the building and my poem spins from my hand, forgotten. I take the stairs three at a time and throw my boot through the front door like it's not even there. The door slams against the wall inside and I storm into Marissa's bedroom.

I'm shocked to a stop.

Some naked fuck is pounding away at my girlfriend on her bed. Our bed.

"Lance!" Marissa squeals.

"What the fuck?" the naked fuck grunts, spinning off her.

My jaw drops. Words tumble out of my mouth like dropped rocks. "You're... Brad Wheeler. You're a linebacker... For the Rebels..." That's the UNLV football team. Those guys are heroes around here. Except for this fuck. He's about to be a dead legend.

His heavy brow knots. "Yeah. That's me. And would you quit staring at my dick? And get the fuck out of here, kid."

"You called my girlfriend a bitch."

He smirks, "Fuck off, kid. She's not your girlfriend. She's mine." He flicks a look at Marissa.

Her eyes are huge.

His eyes go big too. "Did you fuck him?" His face burns bright red.

Not as red as it's gonna be when I'm done punching it.

"Fuck you, Brad," she scowls pridefully, her nose in the air.

He turns to me. "Did you fuck her?"

Now my eyes are big. "No! I—! we—!" *made love*. Why can't I say it?

"You fucked her, didn't you?" He jumps up from the bed, his dick waving in my face as he marches toward me. I know the look in his eyes. I see it in my dad's eyes all the time. Brad is going to take a swing or three at me. That's usually not a problem with my dad because he's always drunk. But Brad is twice his size.

I swallow hard, my mouth all cotton.

"*I'M GONNA KILL YOU, MOTHERFUCKER!!*" Brad roars, charging toward me like a rodeo bull.

The microsecond before he tackles me, I spin to his side and clock him across the jaw.

He goes down.

But gets right back up again.

"You shouldn't of done that, kid," he growls.

Marissa watches.

She just fucking watches.

Is she enjoying this?

She whispers, "Show him how much of a man you are, *Papi*."

Does she mean me? Show Brad?

Brad tackles me, slamming me against the bedroom wall.

The building shakes.

I fall to the floor.

"Show him, *Papi*," Marissa hisses. "Show him!"

My heart drops out of my chest and my fight goes with it.

Brad starts punching.

I don't even notice.

My eyes are on Marissa the whole time.

Slowly, Brad stops punching. He stares at me.

Marissa whines, "Why did you stop, *Papi*?"

Brad spins around. "Shut the fuck up, Marissa! He's a fucking high school kid!"

"Show him, *Papi*! Show! Him!" Her eyes are on fire.

"Are you crazy?! I'll get kicked off the team if I get arrested for beating up a kid, you dumb bitch!"

He called my girlfriend a bitch. Again.

My fist explodes up into Brad's balls. He falls like a redwood tree.

I stare at Marissa.

Her eyes are pinned on Brad and her mouth droops open.

I want to kill her.

She smiles huge, like it's her birthday. "You killed him, *Papi!*" She bites her lower lip. "Oh, *Papi!* Do you know how much that turns me on?"

I thought Brad was *Papi*.

None of this makes any sense.

Brad groans, curled around his balls, cradling them protectively.

Marissa stands up on her mattress.

She is the most beautiful woman in the world.

She walks over to me, her perfect breasts swaying. Her pussy is already wet. With Brad.

I hiss, "Fuck you, Marissa."

I push myself up to my feet and stumble out the front door.

"Lance! Come back, *Papi!* Come back!"

I nearly fall face first down the steps outside.

When I make it to the bottom, my eyes land on my index card.

It sits scuffed on the cement walkway at my feet.

My upper lip quivers with hatred.

I hate everything on that index card.

I work up a wad of spit in my mouth as I swallow back tears.

"Lance! Baby! Where are you going?!" She's at the top of the steps. Naked. Ready to fuck.

I spit on the index card and run down the street as fast as I can.

That's the last time I do anything nice for a woman.

They don't deserve nice.

My heart closes to all women.

Permanently.

Chapter 1

Age 26.

PRESENT DAY.

"Watch where you're going, dumbshit!" My dad growls as I jump our U-Haul truck over the curb of the new suburban shit hole we're about to call home. He spills the whiskey hidden in his AriZona Iced Tea bottle onto his wife-beater. Yeah, my Dad is a miserable fucking cliché. "Jesus, Lance, were you drunk when I taught you how to drive?"

"No, but you were." It's the truth.

His eyes narrow. He's thinking about hitting me.

I goose the gas and the U-Haul lurches up the driveway.

"God damn it!" Dad bounces around the cab, almost falling out of his seat because he refuses to wear a seat belt. He's so focused on saving his stealth whiskey he forgets to punch me.

That's a good thing for two reasons. One, he hits like bricks and always leaves a mark. Two, I wasn't paying attention to what I was doing because the finest piece of ass I've ever seen is bending over the trunk of the Toyota parked next door, pulling something out.

Hole. E. Fuck.

Look at that ass...

Priceless.

A sliver of pink shines between the legs of her cutoff denim shorts like a beacon. Neon pink bikini bottoms. They're so tight they look painted on. Fuck. My dick missiles in my pants. All I can think about is peeling that bikini off and jamming my face in her pussy. You know it tastes as good as it looks.

Dad is busy yelling at the whiskey soaking into his wife-beater like it's a silk fucking shirt

I'm busy staring at Pink.

Tan smooth caramel legs and arms. Too bad a baggy white shirt covers her from the waist up. But a tease of side boob and neon bikini top shows through the arm hole. Her surfer blonde hair is a mess of golden tangles. Perfect for grabbing while I hit that shit from behind. If my damn Dad wasn't sitting next to me, I'd throw the E-brake and rub one out right here.

Pink pulls a big pink box out of the trunk of the Toyota.

The kind of box cakes come in.

Shit, all I want to do is come in her pink box.

But I still haven't seen her face under that mop of gold. She better not be a butter face. With an ass like that, you know I have to fuck it.

"Stop the god damn truck, Lance! You're gonna hit the garage!"

I stand on the brakes and the U-Haul skids to a stop inches from demolishing the garage door of the rental house. Good thing I'm quick.

"You idiot! Look what you almost did!" Dad bitches about shit long after it's a non-issue.

Sudden movement in the corner of my eye shocks me into motion and I twist my shoulders instinctively, just in time to miss getting my jaw clocked. I slide out of the cab before he can take a second shot.

"Get the fuck back here, dumbshit!" he growls.

I ignore him.

Pink walks toward the front door of her house with her unreal ass bouncing under her cutoffs in a way that knots my balls. At this point, she could have three eyes and a beak and I'd still have to fuck her before the night is over. If I don't, I'm never gonna sleep.

"What the fuck are you smiling about?" Dad grumbles as he walks around the front of the cab. He can't see Pink because she's already hidden by the big bush standing between us and her porch.

Fucking bush. Speaking of bush, all I can think about is fucking hers. "Nothing," I say casually.

"Then quit fucking around and let's move this shit in."

His ass-i-tude rolls right off my back. There's no way he can possibly ruin my day today because this dreary shit hole suddenly got all kinds of sunshine.

The hot pink kind.

Fuuuuuuuck YEAH.

+++++8++++

CHASTITY

"Mom!" I holler, standing on the front porch. "Can you open the screen door please! I've got the cake!" My birthday cake, which I just picked up from Sweet Lady Jane's on Melrose, is gigantic. Despite the fact we're always broke, Mom insisted we buy a nice cake for my eighteenth. Not for my sake, but for appearances. So people won't *know* we're broke. "Hey! Mom?! Where are you?!"

She's inside getting the house ready for my pool party tomorrow night. She isn't one of those moms who lets you "use" the house for a party. She has to host it and chaperone it so everything will be her version of perfect.

For a moment, I consider opening the screen door latch with my pinky. A vision of the cake box tumbling to the ground followed by me lifting the lid to discover a smear of lavender flowers and frosting glued to the top stops me.

"Mom!!"

"You need help with that?" a strange male voice says behind me.

Startled, I spin around and see…

Goodness!!

The hottest guy ever. Tall, scorching hot smile, broad shoulders, narrow waist, and muscled arms wrapped in tattoos. On a rough looking guy like him, I expect to see studs or tapers in his ears, but instead his ears look mooshed. Both of them. They're the only part of him that *isn't* perfect. Somehow it makes him more real.

Where did he come from?

Not from around here. All of our neighbors in this mediocre slice of suburban paradise are families with 2.5 kids or silver-haired old people. This part of the Valley is Boring Central.

Mr. Hot Sauce eyes me like he wants to sprinkle himself all over me and take a bite.

An instant heat wave hits my face. I would hide behind my hair but a U-Haul truck in the driveway next door catches my eye. A trailer holding two motorcycles is hitched to the back. One looks like a racing motorcycle and the other looks like something from Sons Of Anarchy, which I only know about because I secretly watch it at my bestie Lark's house. Why? Because my mom won't allow us to watch any worldly programming at home. But who needs TV when you have a real live gorgeous bad boy moving in right next door?

I say, "Are you my new neighbor?"

"Yeah," he grins, his lush lips relaxing into a devilish grin. "What's your name?"

"People call me Chaz." I hate telling people my given name. It sounds *SO* stupid.

"That's a cool name. Is it a nickname?"

"Yeah." *Please don't ask.*

"For what?"

I roll my eyes and sigh, "Chastity."

He chuckles, "That's not gonna last."

"What's that supposed to mean?!" I demand. Does he think I haven't heard that before? Of course I have. But from someone as hot as him? Never. Because I've never *met* anyone as hot as him.

He shrugs, still grinning.

"What's your name?" I sneer. "Virginity?"

"No. Virginity is a girl's name. My name's Virgil. But people call me 'The Virgin'." He winks at me. "Never had sex. Saving myself till marriage."

I laugh. "Yeah, right." There's no way this guy is a virgin. "Come on, tell me your real name. I told you mine." I stare at him defiantly.

"You show me yours, I show you mine?"

"No!" Could he be any more obvious? "What's your name already?"

"Lance." His eyes smolder for a second then boldly drop to my breasts. His eyes just sit there, parked on my chest.

I'm about to ask him if he's getting a good look, but I realize I *like* him ogling my breasts. Usually I don't, but gosh, he's so frickin' hot.

His devil's grin curls. "Let me hold your pink box for you."

My eyes gawk. What the *Eff* did he just say?

He takes the cake box from my hands. His boldness is overwhelming.

I'm powerless to resist him. My heart thuds in my chest.

"I'd offer to shake your hand…" his eyes glimmer wickedly, "…but I've got both my hands all over your… *box*."

I snort a laugh, but I'm literally speechless. Oh. My. Goodness. Is he kidding? I can't believe he just said that. But my lady parts believe every word. They're literally shaking between my legs. In fact, my knees are shaking too. It's a miracle I can even stand up right now. I hope this Lance stud doesn't notice. I'm usually much more composed than this, but I've never had a guy come on to me this hard before. Emphasis on hard and coming. Geez, what am I thinking?

"I'd offer to get the door for you," he grins, "but I can't do that either, because—"

"Because your hands are full! Got it!" I am *totally* blushing from head to toe. Even my lady parts are blushing.

"What's in your *box*, anyway? I'm thinking cherry *pie*…"

"It's cake! Regular cake!" I blurt as I spin and rip the screen door open.

He glances at the threshold.

Why am I suddenly thinking about that vampire thing where you have to give them permission to enter your house otherwise they can't come in? I know. Because Lance looks like the sexiest vampire ever. But that's just kids' books.

"Can I *come* inside?" His devil's grin is preposterously cocky.

"You did *not* just say that," I giggle.

"What, that I wanted to come inside *your*..." He trails off.

Hot sexy images of thrusting naked bodies flash through my brain at ten million miles an hour. Despite what my strict mother believes, I've seen internet porn. More than once. Ahem. Meanwhile, my mind is screaming, *Come inside my WHAT?! Come inside my what and WHEN?! Now?! Right here on the porch?! Please do!! Right NOW!!!!* Of course, I say none of these things. Rather, I smile demurely. And blink guiltily and repeatedly. *Come inside, come inside, come, come, come inside my—*

"...house." he finishes, his voice nearly silent as he mouths the word like it's a kiss.

My half-open lips quiver as I try to snatch that word from the air. Who knew the word *house* from this man's mouth could be such a turn on? When I realize how desperate I must look, I bite my lower lip. I also lock my knees together for good measure. Otherwise I'm going to jump into his arms and beg him to do whatever he wants to me right here on the front porch.

In full view of the neighbors.

His eyes trap mine.

I can't look away.

His are dark brown with a fiery ring around the deep black pupil. They are literally enchanting.

I know because I'm losing my mind and all control over my body as my heartbeat throbs in my nipples and between my legs. I am one hot throbbing... gulp.

Yup. This is it. This is the moment when I tell the sexy evil vampire he can *come inside* my house and do whatever the heck he wants with me. I'm game. I open my mouth to speak. "Yuh—"

"Chastity? Who's this?" Mom barks behind me.

Every muscle in my body tenses as motherly guilt stomps all over the arousal coursing through me. Geez, how long was she standing there watching? One thing's for sure: having sinfully sexy thoughts about sexy vampire Lance with my mom standing right behind me makes my nipples shrivel.

"Is this your sister?" Lance blurts.

"No," I grumble. "She's my mom."

Way to ruin the moment, Mom.

++++8++++

LANCE

Score!

Fine Ass Chastity's mom is as hot as she is. Total MILF.

I can't decide who's hotter, Chastity or the mom.

"Do I know you?" the mom asks, her face all hard like she's tough. I bet she's a bitch in bed.

Me like. "Not yet..." I say it like the next thing she's gonna get to know is my dick.

The mom is a slightly older but equally hot version of Chastity.

Fuck, I'm hard for both of them.

It wouldn't be the first time. Mrs. Schneider and her blistering hot daughter Kayla back in Vegas would blow your mind. And your dick. They did mine.

The mom frowns at me, totally checking me out.

Damn, I bet this is the hot bitch face she makes when she comes. I can't wait to find out if I'm right. I ask, "What's your name?"

"I'm Mrs. Shields," the mom says, emphasizing the Mrs. part like I should show her some respect.

I ignore it and cock my chin at her like I would with any random babe I want to bone. "Lance."

She glances over at the U-Haul. "Are you renting the house?"

"Yeah."

"Just you? You seem terribly young."

I sigh, "My dad's around here some fucking place. Probably moving shit in already."

Silence.

The two of them look like I just dropped a flaming bag of shit on their doorstep.

"Pardon me?" Mom has that bitch thing going again. She puts her hands on her hips, which are housed in the hottest mom jeans I've ever seen. If she thinks they're gonna hide what she's got, she's fooling herself. She stares at me like nobody says no to her.

Am I missing something? I glance between them. "What?"

Mrs. Uptight Panty Shields glares, "Please don't curse in front of me or my daughter."

I snort. Is she serious? I'm gonna be doing a lot more than *saying* fuck to these two soon enough.

"Mom..." Chastity whines.

"Cool it," Panty Shields barks at Chastity.

Chastity rolls her eyes like she's heard this noise a thousand times before and she's sick of it.

If I was Mom's daughter, I would be too. But I'm not. I just wanna fuck the both of them. "Yeah, whatever. What do you want me to do with Chastity's... *box*?" I wink at Chastity, holding up the cake.

Chastity's eyes blow up the size of soccer balls.

"I'll take it," Mom grumbles, trying to pull the box out of my hands.

"I've got it," I say calmly, holding on. "I'll bring it inside for you. Where do you want me to… Put. It." We all know which IT I'm talking about. And where.

Mrs. Shields' slits her eyes and tips her head to the side. She's acting like she doesn't know what I just said, but she knows. It's all over her fuck me harder face. She totally wants my IT. She snarls, in a hot way, "Please hand me the cake, young man."

"Stop being such a fuckwit, Lance—" Dad suddenly growls behind me. "—and let go of her box."

I repress a laugh. There's no way I'm ever letting go of Panty Shields' pink box. Not till I'm done with it. And I never do anything Dad says when he's sauced, on principle. Besides, I'm sure he noticed these two honeys were hotties the second he laid eyes on them and rushed over here to make his own play. It's not like all the booze broke his dick.

"Give it to her, Lance," Dad grunts.

Now I do snicker out loud. He better believe I'm gonna give it to her. Why did he have to show up now? Right when I'm getting my game on? Pain in my ass is what he is.

Mrs. Shields gasps and folds her arms over her frilly no-cut top. No-cut, as in zero cleavage showing. You can barely even see neck. Are you surprised? I'm not. But I'm dying to see what she's hiding. If her cans are anything like the ones filling out Chastity's T-shirt… fuck. Boob heaven.

"I said give it to her, Lance," Dad growls.

Chastity snorts and sneaks a smile in my direction. She's wise to the comedy.

I wink at her. Something tells me I might have to make a choice between her or her mom. They don't look like best buds. Or I can do them one at a time. Whatever works.

My dad stares at Mrs. Shields, a blurry smile on his face. He holds out his hand to shake hers. "I'm Rod McKnight. You can call me Rod."

What a tool. I can tell his whiskey courage is making him think he's George Clooney or some shit when he's *all* Adam Sandler. Dad never passes up a chance to wreck my game. But he's gonna have to try a lot harder than that.

Mrs. Shields smiles at Dad like it hurts. "Faith Shields. Pleased to meet you, Rod." She shakes his hand like it's dirty.

Man, she is a *total* fucking bitch. I love it. Do I *have* to pick between her or the daughter?

She looks at me and Dad thoughtfully. "I detect a family

resemblance between you two. Rod, are you Lance's—"

"Dad?" Dad throws an arm around my neck and yanks me against his side. "Damn right I am." He spews booze breath in my face.

I wince, trying not to gag. I've been to town dumps that smell fresher than him.

"Rod," the mom says, "Can I ask that you watch your language in front of my daughter and I?"

"Sorry, what?" He's clueless. As always.

Mrs. Shields laughs nervously. "It's just that we're not used to that kind of four-letter talk around our house."

Dad frowns like the clown that he is. "Oh. Sorry. I guess I'm a little rough around the edges with strangers. Won't happen again."

What a pussy. And he wonders why I don't respect him.

"I completely understand," Mrs. Shields says to Dad, beaming at him and running her fingers through her hair and tossing it like she's Farrah Fawcett or Jessica Simpson or some shit.

What... *the* FUCK? She did not just do that. My eyes volley between her and Dad.

Oh shit.

They're *in* to each other.

Why, I have no fucking idea. Maybe Panty Shields sees something about him I don't. But no doubt Dad can tell Panty Shields is a hot fucking bitch.

Fuck.

I toss a look at Chastity.

She grabs it out of the air like a love sick puppy.

She's gonna be easier to bag than I thought.

Maybe it's time I cut bait with the mom and focus on stealing Chastity's V-card. Her eyes might scream DTF, but you know an uptight girl like her still has her cherry. I'll make sure to break her in easy and let her down just as soft. By the time I'm done with her, she'll think she's the one breaking up with me.

I glance over at Mrs. Shields who is busy flipping her hair like she's ready to drop her dress.

Who am I kidding?

I want Chastity *and* the mom.

Just to piss off Dad.

Together or separate doesn't matter. But I'm gonna bag 'em both.

Game on.

Chapter 2

CHASTITY

"Would you two like help moving in?" Mom asks Lance's dad. "I'm sure my daughters and I could lend you a hand."

"We can handle it," Rod says confidently.

"It's no bother," she titters.

What the heck? I can't believe my eyes. Mom is *flirting*. Mom does not flirt. Ever. I thought she'd sworn off men after she and Dad got divorced. Then again, Rod McKnight looks like an older version of Lance. The only difference between them is the sprinkle of grey in Mr. McKnight's equally unruly dark hair, and his minimal wrinkles (which of course look good on him). Like father, like son. This is bad. Don't ask me how I know, but I know.

Mom says, "I'm sure you two men are more than capable of handling... things, but as the Good Book says, do unto others as you would have them do unto you..."

Oh. My. Gag.

I'll bet she'd like Mr. McKnight to do unto her.

Mom has never been this shameless. Yes, Lance's dad is almost as sexy as he is. But seriously, I can't believe the man is wearing a wife-beater. I want to say: *Hello! Mom! What about Mr. McKnight says upstanding or God fearing? He's probably never set foot inside a church! And whatever happened to sins of the flesh? You're openly lusting after him!*

The look in her eyes says she's lost all sense. She giggles. Yes, giggles. Mom does *not* giggle. "I imagine you two had a long drive. Can I offer you something cold to drink?" Her index finger twirls absently through a strand of her blonde hair.

"We just came from Vegas," Lance says impatiently. "It was only four hours. We're fine."

"Never mind that," Mom says. "You need to stay hydrated if you're going to be moving furniture all day. Come inside, I'll fix you men a drink."

Men? Oh, boy. Mom has lost her mind.

And like that, she gives the father-and-son sexy vampires permission to come into our house. We all know disaster is soon to follow.

Standing in the kitchen, Mom whips up a batch of ice water with two kinds of fruit. As always, everything has to be perfect. She gets out the good crystal pitcher for the hunky men like she's throwing an impromptu garden party for the ladies from church. That move is *so* Mom. I doubt Rod and Lance care what sort of pitcher she uses. No, she couldn't just fill two glasses under the tap and drop a few ice cubes in. Not Mom.

Her eyes are glued to Mr. McKnight as she chops fresh basil. "The secret with basil is that you have to crumple it to release the flavor. Without it, the strawberries and lemon don't quite live up to their potential."

No wonder she went for the flavored water. It means more time for her to flirt. I roll my eyes and grumble. This is nauseating.

Mom pours two glasses of fruit flavored water and hands them to the men.

"Thanks," Rod takes a swallow. "This is terrific. Whaddya think, Lance?"

Lance gulps down the entire glass. "Damn good."

"Careful, son. Mrs. Shields here—"

"Faith. Call me Faith." Mom beams like it's prom night.

Rod raises his glass like he's toasting. "Faith it is. Like I was saying, son, Faith here doesn't want language like that. You think maybe you could keep it PG while we're in their house?"

"Pee *Gee*?" Lance snorts. "You're kidding, right?"

Rod gives him a look. "Let's just keep it clean, okay?"

Lance scowls at him, but it's the cutest scowl I've ever seen.

Mom says, "And speaking of PG," she turns to me and eyes my shirt, "could you please change into something more… appropriate?"

"What are you talking about?" I blurt, instantly defensive. *What is inappropriate about a V-neck shirt and cutoff shorts over a bathing suit?*

"I can see your…" She can't bring herself to say it but I know what she means.

My bikini top. It's vaguely visible through my white shirt. It's not like it's a bra. I swear, Mom is living in the 16th century. I want to say: *Are you serious? It's a frickin' bathing suit!* But this is my mom we're talking about, which means I can't say *frick* in the house, and yes, she's completely serious. I glare at her.

"Where did you get that swimsuit, anyway? I don't remember buying it for you." Mom has radar when it comes to rule breaking.

That's because she didn't. I bought it last week with my own money because it was on sale at Mermaid Mafia when I went there with Lark and it was the last one and it fit me perfectly. I guess I should've kept it under wraps until tomorrow at the pool party when I'll be eighteen and she can't say anything. Well, she would totally say something, but she wouldn't be able to stop me from wearing it.

She waves her hand. "It doesn't matter where it came from. We have guests."

I hate it when she does this. Eighteen can't come soon enough. It was bad enough she had to approve everything I wore all through high school, but it's summer and I graduated and I should be allowed to wear whatever I want. "Mom..." I groan.

"Please go change." It's an order.

"What do you want me to wear? A turtle neck?! It's boiling hot outside!"

"Don't get defiant with me, young lady." Wow, way to make me sound like I'm twelve. "I will not tolerate your—"

"Fine! I'll put a jacket on. And a scarf. If I die of heat stroke, it'll be all your fault."

She smiles politely. "Don't be flip, Chastity."

I feel my face quivering like I'm going to explode. If we didn't have guests, we'd be screaming at each other. Like always. But I don't want to look like a brat in front of Lance, so I rein it in. "Then don't make me dress like a nun," I grumble.

"I'm not making you dress like a nun." She smiles like we're old friends exchanging sewing tips.

What a laugh. "Could've fooled me." I barge past her.

I am *so* embarrassed right now. I can't believe she started lecturing me in front of Lance. Then again, I can't believe I lost it like a child. Tomorrow is my eighteenth birthday for heaven's sake. After that exchange, Lance probably thinks it's my eighth birthday.

"Pardon her," Mom whispers in the kitchen. Does she think I can't hear her? "She gets like this when—"

"I can hear you!" I holler.

"What's going on?" my younger sister Charity asks, sticking her head out of her bedroom. She's fourteen. The song *Dark Horse* by Katy Perry drifts out.

"Mom. As usual," I growl.

"Oh. What'd you do this time?"

"I broke the dress code."

"You always break the dress code," she says smugly.

I scowl, "Do you want me to tell Mom you're listening to Katy Perry?" Mom considers Katy Perry a whore, Britney Spears a slut, and Lady Gaga the Anti-Christ.

Charity's eyes bulge and she whips her door closed. Without slamming it of course. Otherwise Mom would be down here yelling at both of us.

I swear, if it wasn't for Charity, I would move out of this heaven hole tomorrow. Yes, *heaven* hole. Because the stench of religion around here is enough to make you gag. But I would never forgive myself for leaving Charity behind to fend off Mom's righteousness on her own. If I could, I'd take Charity with me, but Mom would never let that happen.

I close my own bedroom door behind me and stand in front of my closet. What can I wear that won't make me look like a prude in front of Lance? It's a tough call because half my clothes are prudish, thanks to Mom. The other half of my wardrobe is merely boring, again thanks to Mom. She didn't use to be this uptight. Religious yes, but after the divorce she turned into a puritan. I'm convinced Dad left because Mom has always been a bit too righteous for her own good. He was never into church like she is. I really don't blame him for leaving. If I could divorce Mom, I would've done it when Dad did. I wanted to live with him but the court had other ideas.

++++8++++

CHASTITY

FOUR YEARS AGO.
My world is ending.
I'm fourteen.
I sit on the edge of my bed, my dad beside me.
My curtains are closed, muting the bright California sun, drenching my room in gloom. It feels like someone is ramming a jackhammer through my stomach. All I can manage to choke out is one word:
"Why?"
"Because we have to do what the judge ordered, Chaz." Dad says it with potent sadness. His arm is around my shoulder as he explains the details of my family's destruction in a tired voice. "The judge said that you and your sister will live here at the house with your mother during the school year, but you get to live with me in my new apartment all summer long. We'll get to do all kinds of fun things. Isn't that terrific?" He doesn't sound like he thinks so. He sounds like it's the worst thing ever because it is. He's just putting on a brave face. Too bad I can see right through it. At least he's trying.
"Do I get to see you during the school year? Like, at all?" My voice is shaky with low grade terror. The idea of being imprisoned with my mom for nine months at a time scares me to death.
He smiles half-heartedly, "One weekend every single month."

"One weekend? That's it?"

His face cracks, his silent sadness pouring out like a bursting dam. "That's all the judge would allow. I'm sorry, sweetheart."

"No, Dad!" I whine. "I want to live with you!"

He stares at me, his eyes wet. "I'm sorry, princess. I tried. I really tried. But we have to do what the judge says."

"No!" Tears stream down my face. "I don't want to do what any stupid judge says!"

Defeated, he whispers, "We have to, princess. We don't have any choice."

I smear tears with the back of my hand. "This is Mom's fault, isn't it? She made everybody think she was a saint and you were the devil, didn't she?"

I wish I could've been in court to play videos of how she really is. Mom is the insane one. She couldn't talk to Dad without turning it into a fight. She's the same way with me most of the time. But I never have fights with Dad. It's all her.

Dad opens his mouth to speak. "I—"

"*Nooo!!!!*" A shrill scream erupts from across the hall, piercing my heart. Charity. She's ten. She sounds like someone is murdering her. Mom is telling her the bad news in her bedroom. "*Nooo! I hate you! Hate you!! Hate YOU!!!! "I!!!! HATE!!!! YOU!!!!!!!!!*" Charity shrieks so loud it sounds like she's going to rupture her vocal cords.

My hands start to shake as her panic bleeds into mine.

Dad jolts against my side, sucking back a silent sob. His voice shivers, "Everything'll be okay, princess. I promise. Everything will be okay."

I don't believe him.

The sad thing is, he doesn't believe himself either.

++++8++++

CHASTITY

PRESENT DAY.

I shiver as I stuff the memory back down in my stomach where I keep it and others like it. At times like this, my body copes by turning everything down to a low hum, but it's a foggy dentist's drill hum in my stomach.

Whir.

Not pleasant, but better than freaking out at the old memory.

Since that time four years ago, Dad has sadly become more distant. Not emotionally. Emotionally he's always there for me and Charity. But he had to take a management job in Illinois because he couldn't afford to pay alimony *and* child support *and* his bills on what he made here in California because Mom doesn't work. She never has and still doesn't. She's so lazy.

When Dad first moved away, I didn't understand why. Now I do. For the past two years, I've had an after school job dishing up ice cream at Marble Slab Creamery and I know all about budgets because I make so little.

I don't blame Dad for leaving.

I blame Mom for making him leave.

No matter what she thinks, Dad is normal. He doesn't tell me I have to dress or act a certain way. He's not overly protective but he's not overly permissive either. Believe me. He proved it the time I was visiting him two summers ago, the time we spent the day at Foster Beach out at the lake. When Charity and I were playing in the water, I met a cute boy named Ethan who had a great body and tattoos and little nipple rings. When Dad waved us in from the water, I told Ethan I was going to Chase Park that night to watch *Sixteen Candles.* I didn't mention Dad and Charity would be there too.

Chase Park has outdoor movies every summer and you can bring food. Dad bought hot dogs, which he wouldn't let us put ketchup on. It's a Chicago thing. Anyway, that night at the park, Ethan walked up to where we were all sitting on our picnic blanket. He wore a Chicago Bulls sleeveless jersey and ratty shorts. His tattoos were so obvious. He smiled at me with the cutest grin and said, "What up, Chaz?"

"Hey, Ethan," I giggled, already blushing. I didn't think he'd show up.

"Who's this guy?" Dad asked.

Ethan ignored him and grinned at me, "Hey, Chaz. You wanna go sit with me and my boys?" He nodded toward the other side of the huge crowd.

He was so cute, all I could say was, "Ummm..."

Dad said, "Why don't you sit with us, Eeth?"

Ethan did, but he and I were both totally uncomfortable the whole time because Dad sat between us. Amazingly, Dad acted reasonably casual and didn't try to scare Ethan off. After that night, I never saw Ethan again. But at least Dad let him sit with us. If it had been Mom, she would've embarrassed me to death by either yelling at Ethan until he ran off or talked about God until he ran off.

The thing I like about Dad is he never talks about God and he never asks me about church. Ever. He's a reminder there's a whole world out there that doesn't obsess about your eternal soul every second of the day. Don't get me wrong. He expects me to be a good person and work hard at school. But whenever I visit him, it's like I can breathe again.

Being around Mom is suffocating. It's gotten to the point where I don't even know if I believe in God anymore. It's not like the guy ever talks to me. Mom says "He" talks to her all the time. I don't know if I believe her. But if he is real, I can't imagine he'd want me to live in the prison of fear Mom built around us after she drove Dad off. It just seems… wrong.

Whir.

No matter how many times I asked Mom if Charity and I could go live with Dad in Illinois during the school year, she said no. She would get so angry when I asked, all red in the face and shaking, I started to worry she was going to explode or have a stroke or whatever. It didn't help that Charity would always start crying and screaming when Mom said no. So I stopped asking.

Whir.

The good news is, I'm only trapped in this house for two more days. There is a light at the end of the tunnel. For me, anyway. Charity has four more years of this business. I worry about her. I don't want her turning into Mom. Sometimes, she sounds just like her.

Whir.

I don't want to think about it.

More importantly, I need to pick out something to wear.

Something Lance will like.

I stand in front of my closet mirror in a clean white bra and my cutoffs, holding up two different shirts on hangers, trying to decide which one looks better on me.

My bedroom door opens quietly.

"Get out of here, Charity," I grumble, not bothering to look.

When she doesn't respond, I turn and nearly have a heart attack.

Lance.

I gasp and hold the two shirts protectively against my nearly naked chest. At least I haven't given him vampire permission to enter my bedroom. So I'm safe.

He steps over the threshold and closes the door behind him.

Oh. My. Gosh.

This can't be happening. But it is

I'm quivering all over once again. All I can think about is Lance and the lance in his pants. I bite my lower lip. If anything *sinful* happens in my very own bedroom, I blame Mom. She was the one who let the vampires in.

"Get out of here!" I hiss. "If my mom finds you in here, she'll cut your bean bags off!"

"Bean bags?" Lance's slow grin spreads like warm butter.

It makes me desperately want to spread my legs so he can spread himself all over me with his hot butter knife… gulp.

"At this point," Lance smirks, "I don't think your Mom remembers her own name."

"What are you talking about?" I whisper frantically, still cowering behind the shirts. If Mom walks in and sees Lance, she will kill both of us.

"She's all over my dad in your kitchen. I think they're gonna fuck."

"What?! You are lying. My mom would never…" Would she? Not with me and Charity in the house for sure. But… is it possible? I mean, I'm pretty sure Charity and I didn't get here by immaculate conception. But still. We're talking about Mom. After Dad, I seriously thought she would never date again. I suppose miracles do happen from time to time. "Seriously?"

"Go see for yourself."

I'm half tempted. But there's a ridiculously hot guy blocking my way. And I have no shirt on. I could put one on, but I'd be exposing myself to Lance. I could just hold the shirts in front of me, one in front and one in back, and poke my head in the kitchen. But if I did that, Mom would… Same thing: early grave. R.I.P. Chastity Shields. It doesn't help matters that Lance is not being a gentleman and offering to turn around so I can dress. I hiss, "What are you doing in here?"

"I told them I had to take a leak. Your mom said the bathroom was down the hall."

"Does this look like the bathroom?!"

"It looks like my lucky day…"

My jaw drops. My panties are about to follow.

His eyes drill into my soul.

Does he want to kiss me? The look on his face says he wants more than that. Oh gosh. My heart hammers in my chest and my pulse throbs between my legs. I completely forget where I am. Whatever Lance has in mind is fine with me, but he needs to be the one to start this ball rolling. I may regret it for eternity, but I'll worry about that later.

Lance is so gorgeous it hurts.

I will *totally* sin for him…

The sound of Mom's muffled laughter drifts through my bedroom wall. It shocks me back to reality. I haven't heard her laugh like that in forever. Maybe ever.

This is impossible.

Lance McKnight and his father Rod dropped into our lives and upset the balance of the universe.

I can't imagine what's going to happen next.

There's a *squonk!* in the kitchen as chairs shift around on the hardwood.

"Lance?" Rod's voice booms. "Where'd you go, son?"

Now my heart really stops. I can hear Mom and Rod walking out of the kitchen and heading toward my bedroom, which is like two seconds from the kitchen.

I hiss, "*Ship!!*"

Lance smirks, "Did you just say ship?"

"*Shut up!!*" I whisper.

I'm practically topless in my bra.

Lance is staring at me like he's hungry.

Mom is going to crucify me and drive a wooden stake through Lance's heart if she sees us like this!

Unholy crap!

Chapter 3

LANCE

"What are you two up to in here?" Dad asks, all smiles.

Mrs. Shields stands beside him in the open doorway, eyeing me and Chastity suspiciously.

Chastity threw on a white T-shirt before the door opened, but she looks like a squirrel frozen in the middle of the road right before you run it over.

"This is not the bathroom," Panty Shields says to me.

I grin, enjoying all this juicy family drama. "I got lost on the way."

She narrows her eyes. "In a three bedroom house?"

I shrug. "Tried the first door I found."

Panty Shields' eyelids flutter at me like she's trying to make me disappear just by thinking about it. "The bathroom is *that* way."

"Show me the way?" I wink like I'm asking Panty Shields for a bathroom blowjob. Just to piss her off.

All the skin on her face peels back in horror.

I almost laugh because I'm picturing fire shooting out her mouth like a flame thrower.

She says: "The. Bath. Room. Is. Right. Be. Hind. Me."

I'd like to be right behind her because she sure is a feisty bitch. When was the last time this woman got laid? Poor thing. "Pardon me," I say all polite as I shoulder between her and Dad where they're blocking the door. It's such a tight squeeze it almost seems reasonable when I turn to the side and brush my cock through my jeans across her thigh at the last second. Yeah, I'm still hard from staring at Chastity with her perfect tits nearly popping out of her bra.

Mrs. Shields makes this strained "uhnck" sound when my dick touches her mom jeans. She hates me.

I love it.

Dad's too drunk to notice.

With any luck, he'll be passed out by this afternoon and I can raid this place.

I find the bathroom and close the door behind me. As expected, it's a frilly pink girlie paradise. And the toilet seat is down. You know no men come through this joint. I toe the seat up with my grimy boot and start pissing in the bowl.

I can't get over all the pent up pussy under one roof. The question is, do I need to pick between Chastity and her mom? It's pretty obvious there's no way I'll get a three way with those two. They hate each other. I could bag them separately, but what's the fun in that? Truth is, I have too much on my plate already. Getting in Panty Shields' pants would be a shit ton of work. No matter how hot she is, she's not worth the effort. Right now. I need an easy lay, not a full-time occupation. The decision is simple. Chastity obviously wants me.

I'll fuck her first.

Who knows what the future'll hold.

For now, since Panty Shields is drooling over Dad and he has a boner for her, he can run interference for me. That'll be a fucking mess. I can't wait to watch the fireworks. In the mean time, I'll be busy popping Chastity's cherry. Nobody will be the wiser and I'll come out on top. And inside Chastity. Preferably bareback. I just need to get her on the pill first. Virgins like her are never on the pill.

No worries.

I'll convince her.

I smile to myself as I shake my snake and flush the toilet, not bothering to lower the seat. I hope Panty Shields notices I left it up and gets all worked up about it. If she does, it'll only be one tenth of how worked up she's going to be when she finds out I'm fucking her daughter under her own roof.

Because I can't *not* let her in on it.

What would be the fun in that?

++++8++++

CHASTITY

"Who are these people?" Charity asks, leaning her head into my bedroom after Lance is gone.

"Sorry, sweetie," Mom says. "Charity, this is Mr. McKnight. Our new neighbor. His son Lance is in the bathroom." She says it like he's a criminal. Somehow, that thrills me. I mean, he obviously wants to steal my virginity, so it's somewhat accurate. But is it a crime if you give it away?

Mom flashes her eyes at me. Her look says, *I will burn you at the stake if I find out you did anything inappropriate with Lance in your bedroom before I showed up.*

"Nice to meet you, Charity," Rod says to my sister.

"Hi," she replies.

"You look just like your mother." He glances at me. "In fact, I'd say the three of you were sisters," he winks at Mom, "if I didn't know better."

Mom blushes and flicks her fingers through her hair. "Oh now stop, Rod."

Eye roll. She's loving this.

"I mean it," he says earnestly.

"Thank you, Rod," Mom giggles. "Charity, please put some shoes on. We're going to help the McKnights move into their house."

I frown. Between Charity and Mom, I won't get a moment alone with Lance. Mom is a total chaperone.

The five of us head outside. Nobody can unload the U-Haul until the trailer with the motorcycles is moved.

"Who's motorcycles are these?" I ask as Lance rolls the racing one off the back of the trailer.

"This is mine. The other is Dad's."

Mr. McKnight is busy untying the blue nylon wheel straps from around the chrome and black Sons Of Anarchy motorcycle. Up close, it's obvious the bike needs some TLC. The paint is chipped, the chrome faded and dingy, the leather seat cracked.

By contrast, Lance's motorcycle is clean as a whistle.

"Do we have time for a ride?" I ask Lance.

"Sure," he grins.

"You're not riding on that," Mom chuckles. "It isn't safe."

Maybe not today. But tomorrow when I'm eighteen you can bet your bottom dollar I will. Then I can run away with Lance and let fate decide our destination. Mom would totally kill me. But she can't kill me if she can't find me.

"It's safe," Mr. McKnight says to Mom. "Lance is a great rider."

I lift my eyebrows. "See, Mom?"

She shakes her head. "No. You're not riding on that... thing." She's milking the fact I'm still seventeen until the very last second.

Lance pushes the motorcycle into the garage. I follow. He mutters, "Don't worry, I'll take you for a *ride* later." What kind of ride is he talking about? Sounds like both kinds.

"Really?" I whisper, glancing back to make sure mom isn't listening.

"Yeah," Lance grins. "What're you doing tonight?"

"I'm busy."

"No you're not."

I huff, "Who do you think you are, my dad?"

"Is that how you wanna play it?"

"Huh?"

"You have a daddy thing?" He winks at me.

"No!" I scowl. "Are you some kind of pervert?" Wow, I sound like a total grandma.

"Yup." The look burning in his eyes suggests that his form of perversion is well worth the consequences.

I really need to change the subject to something else, otherwise he's going to out me as the prude that I am. "How old are you, anyway?"

"Twenty-six. How old are you?"

Holy cow. He is *way* older than me. The idea gives me sinful shivers, which I hide. Now I really don't want to tell him I'm seventeen. It sounds so teenagery. "Eighteen," I lie. Even though I'm only adding a day to my age, something tells me I'm going to burn in eternity for fibbing. Something else tells me it'll be worth it.

Lance's devil's grin eases onto his face. "My favorite age."

Why do his lips have to be so lickable? I'm about to stand up on my tiptoes and start licking when Mom and Mr. McKnight wheel the other motorcycle into the empty garage. Well, Mr. McKnight does all the work but Mom prances around him like a lovesick pony.

"You guys ready to start moving boxes?" Mr. McKnight asks, toeing the kickstand with his boot and leaning the motorcycle on it.

Lance pins me with his eyes. "I'm all over the boxes. How about you, *Chastity*?" He licks his lips like he's thinking about kissing me. "I think there's a *box* in that truck with your name on it..."

You mean the box with your prize inside, I almost blurt.

Picture this: me in the back of the hot sweaty truck sitting on top of moving boxes with my legs wrapped around Lance's face. He devours me while I melt in his mouth and moan.

Goodness!

"Something on your mind?" Lance drawls.

Mom is staring at me.

"Nope!" It takes everything in my power to push the sinful images out of my mind. I swear, I wasn't this dirty when I woke up this morning.

Maybe it *is* good that Mom is right here, because otherwise I don't know what I'd do. Lance is literally making me stupid. Not that I mind. I suddenly realize that guys aren't the only ones who think with their private parts. I need a cold shower. Or an exorcism. Which begs the question: can you be possessed by a hot guy? Duh.

"You guys," Charity demands, cradling a moving box in her arms, "are we going to stand here all day or what?"

"No, sweetheart," Mom says. "Chastity, help your sister."

Why is everyone ruining my moments with Lance today?

++++8++++

CHASTITY

The McKnights barely have any furniture and everything they own looks like it came from a thrift store or a swap meet. Rod and Lance move the big stuff including a threadbare couch and a ratty recliner while me, Mom, and Charity move the small stuff like the black plastic garbage bags full of clothes and the chairs, all of which are folding or junky.

Back at the truck, Mr. McKnight hands me a dusty guitar case.

"Is this yours?"

"It was. Now it's Lance's. You can put it in his room."

"Cool." I pass Mom on my way through the garage.

A hopeful smile flashes across her face. "Who's guitar is that?"

"Lance's."

"Oh." She looks disappointed. For the past two hours, she's been laughing and giggling at everything Mr. McKnight says like he's the funniest man alive, which he's not. He's not *not* funny, but he's no Dane Cook. I'm sure Mom was hoping Mr. McKnight would serenade her later with this guitar. Too bad. Looks like Lance will be the one serenading me. Mom has also managed to somehow never let me be alone with Lance for more than thirty seconds. Talk about buzz kill. When Mom can't interfere herself, she sends Charity to do her bidding.

Charity comes walking out the door to the kitchen and goes right past Mom and me, heading for our house.

"Where are you going, Chair?" Mom asks.

"To the bathroom," she grumbles without looking back.

Mr. McKnight leans his head out of the U-Haul. "Faith? Can you help me with this?"

Mom's eyes light up like a giddy teenager.

Much like myself whenever Lance calls *my* name.

Gross. I'm nothing like Mom.

"Coming," Mom coos at Mr. McKnight.

Gag.

The good news is, while she's busy with him and Charity is back home…

I make a beeline inside the McKnight house. It's a mirror image of ours. I already know where Lance's bedroom is. I *love* that I know where Lance's bedroom is. Even better, his bedroom is the same as mine, only it's flipped. It's so romantic. Every night when I go to bed, I will be thinking about how he's sleeping in a mirror image of my room. He even has mirrored closet doors like I do. Somehow, they connect our rooms. I can't explain it. When I step over his threshold, I feel the familiar thrill that I've felt every time I've walked in here. It's like I'm allowed to come and go from his bedroom whenever I please. I know the feeling won't last after today, but I want it to last forever. I wonder when I'll be in here again? Tonight? Tomorrow?

Hopefully.

Will I sit on the edge of this bed—*his* bed—our knees touching as we kiss for the first time? I hope so. Will I lose my virginity on this mattress, lying on a blanket of rose petals? A girl can dream.

The thought makes the butterflies in my stomach go crazy.

"You're trapped," Lance says behind me.

Startled, I gasp.

Lance is so tall he fills the doorway. There's no doubt about it, Lance is not a high school boy like the guys at North Valley. He is a man. *All* man. A lock of hair dangles over one dreamy eye as he curls his grin and shakes his head. It's the sexiest head shake ever and it promises naughtiness. "You're not going anywhere," he murmurs.

"I'm not?" I set his guitar case down.

"No escape."

"None?" I swallow loudly. Not that I want to escape from him. I hereby do willingly imprison myself in Lance's bedroom. They can throw away the key so I can never come out. All I need is food, water, and Lance. He can be my jailer and I'll live out my remaining days doing whatever he tells me. No matter how dirty.

His eyes drink mine.

This moment is so magical I expect Mom to blunder in any second and ruin it. She's managed to do it every time before this. But the house is silent. She must be trapped in the truck with Rod doing who knows what. Charity is still back home in the bathroom. Which means Lance and I are all alone for precious seconds.

He walks toward me.

My heart starts to pound louder than drums.

My entire chest tingles with electric anticipation.

He stops right in front of me, inches away.

I shiver noticeably.

He slides the backs of his fingers up my naked forearm. My skin fizzes pleasantly and the sensation floats up to my shoulder and spreads across my chest. My nipples harden instantly. I'm so glad I'm wearing a bra right now.

Lance's eyelids relax and his dark fiery eyes burn into me. He lowers his face toward mine.

His lips part slightly.

He's going to kiss me.

I've never been kissed by a guy.

That's why I'm transfixed. In the past, I always had it in my head that Mom would somehow know if I ever did anything naughty, so I avoided boys like the plague. So I have zero experience in the kissing department. That's why I can't move. But it's okay because I want Lance to slay me. I mean kiss me. I'm not making any sense. But everything about this moment makes perfect sense.

Strong fingers trace the contour of my jaw. I moan softly. My thighs are quivering like crazy. Wetness pools between my legs. How did that happen so fast?

Wow, this boy, I mean *man*, is incredibly bold. Not that I'm complaining. I couldn't even if I wanted too.

His mouth is one inch from mine...

I smell leather and musk. I don't know if it's cologne, Axe body spray, or his natural scent, but the mixture is making me high. Not that I've ever been high. But whatever I'm feeling right now is what I imagine getting high is supposed to feel like.

My eyelids flutter as Lance's mouth approaches mine. I can feel his body heat against my face.

Footsteps in the kitchen.

Mom.

My eyes pop open.

Her mom ESP must be telling her something sinful is about to happen.

Lance is a millimeter from kissing me. With Mom walking down the hallway, it may as well be a mile. Lance withdraws slowly. *Without* kissing me. The look on his face is total contentment.

No!

You didn't kiss me!

A sweet ache clenches every muscle in my body. His fingers fall away from my jaw.

No!

He takes a step back just as Mom walks into the room holding a moving box with a small keyboard poking from the open top.

Go away Mom!! You're ruining my moment!! Again!!!!

"Is this yours?" Mom asks Lance, clearly irritated.

"Yeah," Lance says casually.

Did she catch us? I don't think so. Somehow Lance managed to move all the way across the room a split second before she walked in.

I knew it.

He really is a vampire.

As if trying to make a point, Mom drops the box between me and Lance like a challenge. The contents rattle. I hope she didn't break anything.

Lance scowls at her, only this time it's not so cute. I don't blame him.

I sigh. This is going to be the theme today: people barging in at the perfectly wrong time to ruin my moments just right.

My luck better change before the day is over or I'm going to do something drastic. Sneaking into Lance's bedroom later tonight crosses my mind. I just need to figure out how to sneak out of my house without waking Mom. If I were to wake her, I don't think I'd make it to my eighteenth birthday.

Something tells me it would be totally worth it.

That something is the hungry look Vampire Lance is aiming at me right now...

++++8++++

CHASTITY

"That was quick," Mr. McKnight smiles two hours later when the U-Haul is empty. "How about I buy everybody pizza?"

The five of us stand in the living room of the McKnight house, surrounded by scattered boxes.

"No need for that," Mom says. "I can make sandwiches for everyone. It'll only take a jiffy."

"How long's a jiffy?" Lance prods. "I'm starving. Isn't there a Domino's a few blocks from here?"

Mom frowns, "I will not have you eat cardboard for lunch."

"How about Subway?" he offers. "I saw one next to the grocery store two blocks from here."

"I won't hear of it," Mom smiles in a commanding way.

Lance gives me a *"Can you believe her?"* look.

I give him a brief shrug that says *"She's like this every day and you never get used to it because it's so annoying."*

Lance grins at me.

I blush.

"I'll make sandwiches," Mom reiterates. "Let's all go next door and have a proper lunch together."

"Sounds like a great idea," Mr. McKnight beams.

Forty-five minutes later, I'm sticking red plastic swords into the triangle sandwiches Mom is just now cutting. You wouldn't think five sandwiches would take forty-five minutes, but with Mom? You already know.

"Has it been a jiffy yet?" Charity groans from where she sags on the window bench at the kitchen table. "I'm starving!"

Lance sits next to her "Yeah," he chuckles, "how long is a jiffy supposed to be, Faith? I thought it was quick."

Mom frowns because he's not calling her Mrs. Shields.

I try not to laugh.

Charity giggles and smiles at Lance, "Mom's jiffy is at least an hour."

Lance winks at her, both of them smiling like besties.

Mom glares at him.

Charity openly laughs, obviously egged on by Lance's approval. "Today I think it's gonna be more like two hours." She's never this disrespectful with Mom.

Mom snipers a warning grimace at her. "Chair-i-teeeee…"

Lance mimics Mom's singsong tone without actually saying the word. It comes out as "Mmmm-mm-mmmmm." He doesn't do it loudly, clearly intending it only for Charity's ears, but it's not like this is a mansion kitchen. It's a standard suburban kitchen and everybody hears him.

Mom steps back from the cutting board, resting her wrist against her cocked hip, the kitchen knife dangling from her fingers. Based on the black look darkening her face, she wants to throw the knife at Lance, but she would never risk hitting Charity with it, or Mr. McKnight. The impending drama in the room is suddenly thick enough to cut with Mom's kitchen knife.

Lance's eyes flicker wickedly as he meets Mom's gaze dead on. He doesn't look away.

I'm not brave enough to stare Mom down when she's this mad. Even with my back to her, I can feel the anger pouring off her. I keep myself busy sticking red plastic swords in the sandwiches. If Mom suddenly snaps and goes horror movie with the big kitchen knife, I'm not sure what I'll do because we all know sandwich swords are useless against serial killer knives.

Lance erupts into rude laughter and leans against Charity like she's in on the joke with him.

Charity is mortified, her eyes white saucers.

Mom hisses at Lance, "Do you want this sandwich or not? Because you don't have to eat it, you know. This is my house and my food, and nobody is making you stay."

Lance smirks, his eyes glimmering. "Gee, Faith. Let me think. I offered to buy Domino's or Subway an hour ago for everybody. Now

I'm way past hungry." He stands up from the bench, angling toward the doorway.

"Sit down!" Mr. McKnight bellows. His booming voice freezes the room. Even Lance looks surprised. "Show Mrs. Shields some respect."

I tip my eyes up and meet Lance's, begging him to stay. Having him here is a wonderful thing. For the first time in my life, I feel like I have an ally against Mom. Sure, Charity is my ally, but she's more like a sidekick. Lance is the kind of man who can actually stand up to Mom for real.

Lance's devil's grin returns. "My apologies, Mrs. Shields." He's looking at me as he says it. "I guess I'm getting hangry since I'm so hungry."

"Hangry?" Charity says.

Mom turns to the counter and resumes cutting sandwiches. "That's quite all right, Lance." Not from her tone it's not. "We've all been working hard helping you move everything into your house." Notice how she's running a guilt trip on him already? "I should've offered you chips earlier. I'm a terrible hostess today. Charity, can you open a fresh bag?"

"I'll get it," Lance says.

"No," she presses, "I asked Charity." She's trying to regain control of her kitchen.

"I'm already standing up," Lance says. "Where are they?"

"They're in the cupboard next to the refrigerator," Charity offers.

Mom shoots Charity a look that says *"Traitor."*

Lance smiles victoriously and winks at me as he opens the cupboard and says, "Charity, you want Ruffles or Sun Chips?"

"Ruffles," Charity giggles, loving all of this.

Lance opens the bag and holds it out for Mom. "Chip, Mrs. Shields?" It's not a peace offering. It's more like Lance is the king and he's offering his ring to Mom so she can kiss it.

"No, thank you. I'm not quite finished with the sandwiches." She doesn't even look at him.

"Suit yourself." Lance walks over to the table and offers the open bag to Charity.

She gladly shoots her hand into it, crackling the plastic as she claws for chips like a starving person.

Whack!

Mom slams the side of the knife down on the cutting board. "At least put some on a plate, Charity. There's one right in front of you," Mom grumbles. "Other people have to eat from that bag too."

Charity rolls her eyes and obeys, withdrawing her empty hand.

Mom is the only person I know who doesn't like people putting their hands in her potato chip bags. It's not like Charity didn't wash her hands in front of everybody before setting the table twenty minutes ago.

"Let me," Lance says while shaking chips onto her plate, smiling at Mom the whole time. "That enough?"

"Yeah, thanks," Charity grins.

Then Lance brazenly reaches into the bag with his hand and pulls out a chip and eats it, chewing slowly while staring Mom down. I don't remember Lance washing *his* hands before sitting down at the table.

Mom is ready to blow her top, but she holds it in. She's on the verge of a nervous breakdown.

I'm loving it.

No one has ever shown Mom up like this.

It's about freakin' time.

Chapter 4

CHASTITY

"So, Lance," Mom says, "Do you work or go to school?"

Lance is obviously irritated by her question and jams the rest of his sandwich in his mouth. "Neither," he grumbles.

"You don't have a job *or* go to school?"

Lance smirks, "No. I don't have a job. Or go to school."

Mom sets her sandwich down. "Well then, what *do* you do?"

"Whatever I want."

Mom takes it in, staring at Lance. "To each their own." As she bites a nibble off her sandwich, the look on her face says, "*I suspected you were a lazy bum based on your disheveled clothing and your total lack of respect for your elders and your absence of common courtesy, but now I know for sure.*" That's Mom. Nice to your face, a witch behind your back. She fits right in at our church. I hate that place.

Lance's phone jingles and he pulls it out of his pocket.

"Please, Lance," Mom says. "No cell phones at the table."

Lance reads the screen intently, ignoring her.

Mom rolls her eyes and sneaks a glance at Mr. McKnight who is too busy chewing to notice.

"Lance?" Mom says. "Your cell phone?"

"Yeah," he says absently, still chewing on his sandwich.

"Must you talk with your mouth full?"

He stands up from the window bench. "I have to go."

"Are you leaving?" I ask, disappointed.

"Yeah. It's important."

"Can't you deal with it later?" Mr. McKnight asks. "We're all having lunch. Like a family or something," he chuckles nervously.

Mom says nothing. She wants Lance gone.

Lance glares at his Dad. "It's important."

"What could be so important, son? We just got into town. Relax a little."

"Sorry. I gotta go."

I almost panic, but remind myself Lance lives next door. I'll see him again. And again and again. I hope. Because something about his tone has me worried. What could be so important? A girl? A crime spree? It's impossible to tell with a guy like Lance.

"Thanks for the sandwich, Mrs. Shields," Lance smirks at her. He barely means it.

Her mouth is full of food. She hastily grabs a napkin and covers her lips, chewing as fast as she can and swallowing loudly before speaking. "You're welcome." She's irritated but trying to hide it.

"See you guys later," Lance says, walking out of the kitchen, his boots thudding on the hardwood.

I jump from my chair, "I'll show him out!" I follow Lance to the front door. I have seconds before Mom hollers for me to sit back down and finish my lunch.

Lance opens the front door before I get there.

"Is something wrong?" I whisper.

"Nope," he smiles from ear to ear. It's a fake smile.

I knit my brows. "Then what's the hurry?"

"I'll tell you some other time."

And like that, he's gone.

I sigh and return to the kitchen, disappointed to say the least. I'm surprised to see Mr. McKnight is gone too. "Where's Mr. McKnight?"

"He had to use the bathroom," Mom says.

I sit at the table and pick up a triangle of sandwich.

Mom leans toward me and says in a low voice, "Can you believe how obnoxious that Lance is? I've never met a more impolite young man. He's rude, crass, disrespectful and downright—"

"What are we talking about?" Mr. McKnight asks innocently, suddenly standing in the kitchen doorway.

Mom smiles at him like she wasn't just trash talking his son. "I was just telling Chastity how lucky we are to have two wonderful men like you and your son living next door. Come sit down and have another sandwich."

Mom is so two-faced.

What else is new?

++++8++++

LANCE

I stride across Chastity's front lawn toward my house, kicking up divots with my boot heels. I half expect Panty Shields to stick her head out the window and yell at me to keep off the grass. She can suck my dick.

She doesn't do either.

I don't know what I was thinking earlier about trying to bang that woman. She's a total cunt. Fake as fuck too. I don't know how Chastity and her kid sister put up with her shit because I can't take another second of it. If I hadn't gotten that text just now I would've bailed anyway.

The Shields' house is a prison underneath the pleasant suburban facade.

Inside my garage, I jump on my Gixxer and turn the bike around. The second the rear tire hits the street, I crank the throttle and blow down the road doing a half-wheelie. The primal scream of the engine is music to my ears.

When I'm pissed like this and I don't have a wet and willing pussy handy to take my mind off the bullshit, riding my bike like a maniac is the only thing that helps. Gliding the edge of sudden death on a crotch rocket makes everything else bleed into the background.

I hit fifty before I reach the stop sign at the end of the block. At the last possible second, I hit the front brake hard and the rear wheel lifts a foot off the asphalt in a controlled endo. The tail of the bike floats as I do a slow California roll across the white line at the intersection. I don't even slow for the two mom mobiles waiting to go through the four-way. I goose the gas and lunge between them.

They honk.

Fuck them.

Other than them, nobody notices me blowing the stop sign because they're all locked up inside their cookie-cutter suburban dwelling units doing who the fuck knows what. Playing xBox? Jerking off to the Home Shopping Network or Reality TV bullshit? I don't care. This place is a plastic wasteland. Every house looks the god damn same. The people inside are probably no different. You know nothing ever happens here. I'm half tempted to leave my shit behind and haul ass someplace with more action than this cemetery.

I already hate this place.

I doubt I'll be here long.

Well, long enough to fuck Chastity.

Something about that girl won't let go.

++++8++++

CHASTITY

By the time I climb into bed that night, I'm beyond bummed. Lance never came home.

I spent the entire evening in the living room watching The 700 Club with Mom, Charity, and Mr. McKnight. I couldn't decide what was weirder, that I was watching The 700 Club, which I never do, or that

Mr. McKnight was watching it with us. He doesn't seem like the type, but he seemed happy to sit with us and watch while sipping on his AriZona Iced Tea.

Tonight was the first time there has been a man in the house with Mom. It's not like they were doing anything, but you could tell they had something going on, even with Charity sitting between them on the couch. Mom was glowing. It was so weird.

Charity thinks Mr. McKnight is totally cool. He is, but my mind was elsewhere. The whole night I snuck glances out the front window looking for Lance until Mom finally asked what I was doing. I made some excuse but I kept listening for Lance's motorcycle until Mr. McKnight left and everyone went to bed.

Now I roll restlessly under my bed sheet. It's too hot for blankets. I should be falling asleep, but I can't stop thinking about Lance and our almost kiss.

I'm staring at my clock when it clicks over to midnight.

A smile lights up my face.

I'm officially eighteen.

I don't have to do what Mom says anymore.

I can leave this house whenever I want and never look back.

I sigh.

Charity. I can't leave her with Mom.

But I'm already making plans about moving out. I'm sure I can find an apartment close by. I just need to find a better job because it's expensive around here. My part time job at Marble Slab Creamery isn't gonna cut it. But I'll figure something out.

I can worry about that tomorrow.

Right now, all I want to think about is Lance.

The house is quiet. Mom won't barge in here unless there's a fire or an earthquake. Just to be safe, I lie silently for several minutes, listening.

When I can't stand it any longer, I squeeze my thighs together and my core quivers pleasantly. I slide a hand under the sheet and drag my fingers across my slick seam, spreading my wetness around before circling my clitoris in slow strokes. I bask in memories of Lance's naked desire, picturing his burning eyes and that hungry look of his. When he saw me in my bra earlier I desperately wished the house had been empty. If it had, I wouldn't have covered up. I would've let him look. I would've let him touch, I would've let him do whatever he wanted…

I try to pretend my fingers are Lance's strong hands. What would it feel like if he was touching me? Would he be rough? Insistent? Demanding? Would it hurt just a little bit, but in a good way? Would he put his thick finger inside me? How deep would he go? Sliding in and out? What would it feel like if *he* was inside me? If he thrust hard and steady and grabbed my hips and squeezed my breasts as he took my virginity and came inside me for the first time?

A kaleidoscope of feelings and images flash through my mind as a warm orgasm drizzles through my body. I bite my lip and stifle a moan as I come, wishing Lance was coming with me.

I breathe shallowly and quietly as the orgasm fades.

Before I know it, I slip into sleep and fall into a dream.

I'm in church. The pews are packed like always. I'm squeezed between Mom and Charity. It's summer so it's hot. My church dress is stifling and I'm sweating. Every time I try to fan myself with a thin book of hymns, Mom hisses for me to stop. I'm going to melt in this dress before the sermon is over. The priest is droning on and on at the podium about I don't know what. I'm not paying attention. I rarely do.

"Are you listening, Chastity?" the priest asks, his voice dark chocolate.

I jump in the pew.

Mom elbows me and hisses, "Sit still."

"Chastity," the priest says, "you should really pay attention to the sermon. You might learn something."

That's when I look up and realize Lance is the priest. He looks incredibly sexy in a black suit with a dark red tie. I've never had a thing for priests. The ones at my church are all old and gray and dull.

I also realize that everyone in church is staring at me.

And I am naked.

What happened to my stifling summer dress?

Lance asks loudly, "Were you thinking about me while you touched yourself in bed last night, Chastity?"

The crowd of parishioners gasps. The old ladies with the hats and the Sunday gloves cover their mouths in shock.

Mom hisses in my ear, "Where's your dress, Chastity?! You're naked!"

"I don't know!"

Lance says, "Perhaps you'd like to confess your sins to the entire congregation?"

My eyes pop. Is he insane?

Lance walks down the steps in front of the altar, heading toward me along the center aisle, his eyes locked on mine. He starts unbuttoning his shirt collar. "If you aren't ready to confess your sins, perhaps we should show everyone what you did."

Embarrassment burns through me. I want to run out of there or duck under the pew, but I can't move. I'm frozen in place.

Lance stops in front of me. His suit jacket is gone and his black button down shirt is open, revealing his hard abs. "We can show them the sinful thoughts you were thinking."

"I wasn't—"

"Don't lie in church, Chastity. It will only make things worse." Lance squeezes into the pew, now wearing only black slacks as he worms past the other parishioners. He stops in front of me, his crotch at eye level, an obvious bulge inside. The embers of his eyes glow. Even weirder, the bulge in his pants glows too, red orange through the black material. His dark red tie hangs around his neck like a tail. That's when I realize he has cute little horns poking out of his unruly hair.

"You're the devil!" Mom gasps.

Lance grins, "That's right, Mrs. Shields. But you let me into your house, so there's nothing you can do about it now. I'm taking your daughter." He leans down and scoops me into his muscled arms. "And there's nothing you can do to stop me."

"No!" Mom cries, reaching out to grab me. "Give me back my daughter!"

Lance twists, pulling me away. "She's mine now."

Huge red leathery wings unfurl behind Lance's back and there's a lurch when they beat swiftly downward, lifting us out from the pews. We float above everyone and somehow the church roof is gone and Lance flies us up into the summer sky.

As the church shrinks below us, I feel something coil around my legs and slide between my thighs. I look down and see his barbed red tail on the verge of invading me. The tip of it is glistening with—

I gasp and sit up in bed.

I realize my fingers are inside me. I quickly yank them out and clutch them into a guilty fist that I jam into my armpit.

What? The *eff*? Was that?

And should I feel weird that I'm entirely turned on right now?

I am not right in the head, that's for sure.

But I'm smiling as I lie my head back on my pillow.

Holy crap.

I almost laugh out loud, then I remember Mom, who I do not want to wake right now.

I want to lie here in private and mull over that crazy dream for a while. In a way, it made perfect sense.

Lance really is the devil. As far as Mom is concerned, anyway.

Why does that turn me on so much?

++++8++++

CHASTITY

Eventually the allure of the dream fades and I drift into sleep.

This time, all I dream about is the sound of motorcycles.

Motorcycles...

I wake gently. The clock says 3:33.

Did I actually hear Lance's motorcycle, or was that part of the dream?

I can't say for sure.

The sheer curtains over my window billow inside my bedroom. My window is open because it's so hot outside from the summer weather. For a second, it sounds like someone or something is outside in the backyard beneath my window. I pull my covers up to my chin. I hold my breath, trying to listen for another sound, but all I hear is my heart pounding in my ears. Once again, the curtain billows and I realize it was just the breeze. I close my eyes and try to relax. Now that I'm awake, all I can think about is Lance.

Lance, Lance, Lance.

I wish he was here right now.

A soft zipping sound at the window startles me. Every muscle in my body seizes. Somebody really is outside my window. I'm so scared I don't know what to do. Something pointy traces down along the inside of the sheer curtain as the zipping continues. Someone is going to climb through my bedroom window and kill me any second. I take a deep breath, ready to scream.

A hand pushes through the curtain.

Am I still dreaming this?

I can't tell if I'm awake or asleep.

Lance sticks his head through the curtain.

I'm definitely dreaming. It can't be Lance. Late night rapists are never the hot guy who lives next door.

I whisper, "Lance? Is that really you?"

"Yup." He cracks his devilish grin.

"Am I awake?"

"Seems like it." He pushes himself up on the sill, both arms flexing as he hops onto it like a cat. Then he lowers his boots to the carpet. He's holding a knife. The knife he used to cut through the window screen.

"Are you going to attack me with that knife?"

"I was thinking I might attack you," he whispers. "But not with my knife." He folds the blade into the handle and slides it in his pocket.

"Um, what are you doing in my bedroom at three in the morning?"

"I needed to see you."

"Couldn't it wait?"

"No."

"Did you have to cut a hole in my window screen?"

"I'll buy you a new one. You shouldn't be leaving your window open at night anyway. Never know who might break in."

"Are you serious?" I giggle.

"Very." He sits on the edge of my bed and rests a heavy hand on my thigh.

We stare at each other.

What is he going to do?

His hand strokes my thigh and I shiver. He whispers, "Do you have any idea what you're doing to me?"

"I have no idea." But I'm freshly wet. Does he have any idea what he's doing to me?

"You're driving me fucking crazy. All day long I couldn't stop thinking about this hot little body of yours and all the nasty things I want to do to it."

"So you cut a hole in my window screen with a knife and forced your way into my house in the middle of the night?"

"Since you weren't waiting for me in my bedroom, I thought I'd come to yours." If it wasn't for the impossibly gorgeous grin on his face he would come across as a total psycho. But with that smile of his...

What am I thinking? This is crazy. "Maybe you should go. My mom is in the next room and she's going to hear you. If she finds you in the house, she'll call the cops."

"I'll be gone before they get here."

"Yeah, but she knows where you live."

"She won't call the cops."

"How can you be so sure?"

"Because. I always get my way."

"You're not getting your way with me." I fold my arms over my chest, covering my hard nipples.

His hand strokes further up my thigh, coming dangerously close to home base. The only thing stopping him is a single sheet. It takes everything I have not to sigh with pleasure.

"You are turned on right now," he says it like it's a foregone conclusion.

"So?" Why did I have to admit that? I clamp my legs together.

He smiles. "If you let me, I'll do dirty things to you."

"You are completely crazy!" I hiss. "I'm not going to fool around with you in my bedroom with my mom in the other room!"

"Yeah you are."

Lance peels his T-shirt over his head. Every muscle in his body flexes with the promise of paradise.

The wetness collecting between my legs drips out.

"Take the sheet off." He tugs at it.

"No!" I bunch my arms around it, holding tight.

"No worries. I'm more interested in what's going on down here." He pulls the sheet out from the foot of the bed and slides his hand up under the covers.

"What are you—"

He tickles the sole of my foot.

I slap a hand over my mouth, holding in a laugh. I cackle noiselessly into my palm as he goes to work on the other foot. I kick my legs trying to evade his tickling attack, but with the sheet over my feet, it makes so much noise I stop, afraid Mom will hear us. He continues to tickle. Strangely, the sensation works its way up my legs to my... I let out a little moan. I didn't realize tickling could be such a turn on.

Before I know it, one hand of his has snuck up past my ankle and is massaging my calf muscle. "What are you doing?"

"Loosening you up."

"I'm not loose." I clamp my legs together again and straighten them hard.

He resumes tickling my feet and I go all wiggley again.

"Stop! You're gonna wake my mom up!"

"Then relax your legs."

In the darkness of the room, I have no desire to resist. I relax and his hand climbs past my knees and pries between my thighs. A finger brushes up and down the slick wet slit of my opening through my panties.

"I told you you were turned on," he grins. "Your panties are fucking drenched." He sounds surprised. "Did all this happen just now?"

Embarrassed, I look away.

"Were you playing with yourself before I *came* in?" He narrows his eyes. "You were, weren't you?"

"No!"

"That's what I thought. Were you thinking about me?"

"No!!"

"Yeah you were," he grins. "Were you thinking about fucking me?"

"You haven't even kissed me, jerk. You had the chance earlier, but now it's too late."

"No it's not." He shoots his other arm under the sheet and yanks my panties down. The elastic waistband scrapes pleasantly across my butt.

"Hey!" I should be telling him to stop what he's doing and get the heck out of here, but I'm not.

He holds my panties up to his nose and inhales. "Mmmm. Cherry pie."

"You're foul."

"You love it." He tosses the panties aside and rests his hand on my mound, massaging it with his huge palm.

I explode with sensation. When his thumb trails over my clitoris and lingers, spiraling slowly, I moan. We're alone. I'm powerless to resist him. I have never been touched by a man. It is overwhelming to say the least, especially coming from a man like Lance. Pleasure races through me like a summer storm. I'm leaking freely when his finger slips inside me. It's much larger than mine.

Outside my bedroom door the house creaks. "My mom!" I gasp.

Lance doesn't care. His thumb continues to swirl. It feels wonderful. I feel an orgasm beginning to build. The contractions come on stronger and sweeter. Lance's finger slides in and out of me like an electric eel. His thumb jitters like a human vibrator.

I'm going to come.

I can't come, not with Mom outside my bedroom door. The guilt would kill me. But I don't hear anything now. I guess the house was just settling. So I reach down with both hands and grab his wrist and squeeze tightly, pulling him into me as my body convulses with pleasure.

"That's it," he mutters as he massages his whole palm against me. "Feel it. Fucking come, Chastity. Come on my hand."

I bite my lip and whimper, arching my pelvis up into his hand as the final wave of the orgasm hits me.

When I come down, I'm breathing hard.

That was... the best orgasm I've ever had.

And he wasn't even trying.

What would happen if he *did* try?

I shudder pleasantly.

"More?" he asks.

"You should really go. We probably woke my mom. She's a light sleeper."

"I'm not going anywhere." He stands up and unbuckles his belt and pushes his jeans down to his knees. He bulges in his boxers.

"Put your pants on!"

"No." He hooks his thumbs in the waistband of his boxers and pushes them down slowly, revealing a light dusting of trimmed hair.

I'm dying to know what's under those boxers. His waistband creeps lower until it springs out.

It's beautiful.

I'm mesmerized. I want to touch it, hold it, examine it.

I have no idea what he plans to do now that he is out and I'm wet and ready. I know one thing. I'm not ready to have sex. This is all happening so fast and we haven't even kissed.

"You want my cock." He starts to stroke the shaft, fisting it in the middle and working it slowly.

For a moment, I'm hypnotized by the snake charmer in my bedroom. But thoughts of my mom are nagging at the back of my brain. "You really need to go."

"I'm not going anywhere until I'm finished with you."

His words should scare me but instead they thrill me. Does he mean he's going to have sex with me? Like, a bunch of times until we can't possibly have any more sex in a single night?

He kicks his boots off and sits back down beside me, still stroking himself. His hand moves up and down, rolling the foreskin up and down over the swollen head.

I'm completely turned on all over again. He touches me with his free hand. More waves of pleasure course through me. I want to have sex with him. I don't want to lose my virginity this way. I want to have sex with him anyway. But I shouldn't. Not like this.

He releases himself and holds his palm under my mouth. "Spit on it."

"What?"

"Don't ask questions. Spit on my hand."

Not sure what to do, I spit. A fat drop of my saliva falls to his palm.

He rubs it around the head of his penis. "That's more like it." He strokes himself for a while then suddenly slumps. "Hmmm."

"What?"

"I thought your spit would do it for me. It didn't."

"Oh." I'm not about to offer a blowjob. But the thought does cross my mind.

"This'll do the trick." His fingers scoop into my wet folds until they're completely soaked. Then he smears my wetness all over his penis. He closes his eyes and moans. "Fuck yeah. I don't know why, but pussy cum is always better than spit. It's like my dick knows the difference."

"That's gross."

"But true."

He lays down on the bed next to me, one hand on his penis, the other up above his head so he can stroke my hair. I turn to face him.

We are nose to nose.

We still haven't kissed yet.

But I've come once already and his pent up heat strains between us, his hand bumping gently against my stomach.

"Look at me," he says.

His fiery eyes are gorgeous and captivating.

His breath is sweet. Minty.

His lips brush mine and I'm in heaven.

We're kissing and he tastes like sin.

Slow and soft at first, in contrast to his rough nature. I knew he had a gentle side. But it isn't exactly innocent kissing when his erect penis is hot and hard against my stomach and his hand is covered with my fluids.

He breaks the kiss. "Touch yourself. I want you to come when I do."

"I don't know if I can again. I'm kind of nervous right now."

"Do it."

I do. It feels wonderful. But not quite as wonderful as when he was doing it.

We kiss again.

My whole body is electrified. Somehow, touching ourselves while we kiss is incredibly intimate. We're masturbating together. But that's something you're supposed to do in private. By yourself. So nobody knows. Because no one is supposed to know. And because it's supposedly a sin and definitely shameful. But, for the first time ever, I don't feel guilty about touching myself. It's a total turn on.

He whispers between kisses, "I've been thinking about you all damn day." *kiss* "I wanted to fuck you the moment I saw you." *kiss* "I wanted to bend you over the back of your car and rip those shorts off and fuck you right out in the open." *kiss* "Tangle my fists in that golden fuck me hair of yours." *kiss* "When I snuck in your bedroom this morning and saw you in your bra, I almost did fuck you." *kiss* "You have perfect tits, I'm telling you." *kiss* "And your hips?" *kiss* "Fucking forget it." *kiss*

I am going crazy with lust. But I have just enough brain power left to remember that he hasn't even seen my boobs out of my bra yet, so how would he know they're perfect? He's just telling me what every girl wants to hear. But his dirty words thrill me all the same.

"If your house wasn't so damn crowded, I'd be fucking you right now on this bed, making you come all over my cock and shooting my load way up inside your wet pussy."

His harsh words caress me as intensely as his fingers did when they were inside me a moment ago. I let out a moan.

His face tightens. "That's it. Fucking come," he says frantically, clearly on the edge of his own orgasm. "Come all over my dick."

I rub faster and my legs tighten as a strong orgasm seizes me.

Lance grunts through clenched teeth and the next thing I know I feel hot cum on my stomach. That sends me over the edge. I'm blown back by my own orgasm. I'm barely aware of all the cum that shoots out of him and how it sticks to my skin.

We're both breathing hard as we come down from our orgasms. I cover his penis with my hand, pressing it against me, smearing his seed on my skin with my fingertips. That's when I realize half of it went on my T-shirt which I'm still wearing and the other half is dribbling down my side onto my mattress.

There is cum literally everywhere.

Alarm bells go off in my head and I panic. I need to clean this mess or mom is going to find it. I'm sure she knows what cum looks like. "You have to get out of here!"

"Are you kicking me out of bed?" He smirks.

"Yes! Go before my mom wakes up!" I hate that I'm panicking, but this is serious. I push on him but he doesn't budge. All those muscles weighs a lot.

He chuckles. "Need some help?"

I giggle, "Get out!"

He sits up on the bed and stares at me for a moment before leaning down to kiss me again. His lips are forceful, desperate. He can't get enough. His hand runs through my hair and knots behind my ear. He breaks the kiss and bites my lower lip. "I fucking need to fuck you right the fuck now."

I desperately want him to. I'm just as scared Mom will walk in any second. I pull away. "We can't. You have to go!"

He stands up and slowly pulls his clothes on. "I'm not done with you. Not by a long shot. We're just getting started."

I hope not.

When he's dressed, he climbs out my bedroom window and leans his head in. "Get over here."

I jump up from bed and lean on the sill.

He kisses me one last time.

I squeeze my knees together and my thighs quiver all over again.

I'm about to ask him to take me with him when he breaks the kiss and says, "Laters."

He looks back and grins his devil's grin before hopping the backyard fence like a bandit and landing in his own yard.

A puff of summer breeze billows the loose flap of the torn window screen into my room. I hope Mom doesn't notice it in the morning. Or Lance's cum all over my bed. And my shirt.

What a mess.

I'll deal with it tomorrow.

I sigh dreamily and hug myself as I fall back into bed. The scent of Lance's sex all over me is intense. I turn and stare at my mirrored closet doors. I wish they were a secret magic portal between my bedroom and his and I could walk through mine like Alice through the looking glass. That way I could magically appear in Lance's bedroom any time I wanted. Or he could walk through his into my room any time he wanted.

Now would be good.

Speaking of magic, that's when I realize this is officially the best birthday ever and I'm only four hours into it.

But one thing has me worried.

I think Lance might really be the devil.

Chapter 5

CHASTITY

"Chastity! Get up! It's 8:30!" Mom pulls on the blankets at the foot of my bed.

At first, I think I'm being attacked. I'm barely aware of what's going on because I'm half asleep. Then my chest locks and I realize I'm still lying in my cum-soaked bed sheets and T-shirt. "Stop it, Mom! I'm awake!"

"We have a lot to do today to get ready for your party and the house needs to be cleaned."

"I know! Geez! Will you relax?!" I'm scared out of my mind she's going to see the sheets. Or smell them. Luckily, I must've pulled a blanket on top of me when it got cold during the night. That's when I realize my stomach and my sides and back are all crusty with dried cum. I must've rolled around in it while I slept. I have no idea how bad it looks. Worse, I'm not wearing any panties! I don't know where Lance tossed them.

If Mom pulls the blankets off, she'll kill me.

She tugs on them again. "Get up."

"Can I have some privacy? Please!"

"Get up." She wrinkles her nose. "Did you shower yesterday?"

"Yes."

"What's that smell?"

"B.O.! Will you leave me alone?! Gosh!"

She folds her arms and stares at me. "That's not B.O. I wash your clothes, remember?"

"It's B.O.!" Why is she so horrible?

"I don't know what it is, but it's not B.O. Did you forget to wear a tampon?"

"Mom!"

She sneers and shakes her head. "Just get up."

"If you give me a minute's privacy, I will."

"Why are you acting so strange?"

"Why are *you*?"

She rolls her eyes. "Fine. Hurry up or your sister is going to shower first and use up all the hot water like always. I don't want you waiting around until the water heater fills. We have a lot to do." She walks out.

I hate her.

She's ruining my birthday already. The weird thing is, she's ruining it because she's obsessed with making everything perfect. We can't just set out a bowl of chips and light some candles on a grocery store cake. Nope. Mom has to make it a birthday fit for royalty. Which I'm not. I'll never understand her obsession with appearances.

Nothing I can do about it now.

I have this mess to deal with.

I lift the sheet and grin.

I have Lance's cum all over me. When I climb into the shower, I'm reluctant to wash it off, but I do.

Today isn't going to be all bad.

I wonder when I'll see Lance again.

++++8++++

CHASTITY

"Look who decided to join us for breakfast," Mom smiles after I finish showering and dressing and walk in the kitchen.

Mr. McKnight sits at the kitchen table sipping from his AriZona Iced Tea bottle like yesterday. "Mornin'." He raises the bottle in a toast.

"Hey," I mutter.

Mom is busy making French toast in a cast iron skillet on the stove. She never makes French toast unless it's a special occasion. Usually it's cereal and milk.

I yawn. "I thought we had to clean house and get ready for the pool party."

"We have time," Mom grins like Susie Homemaker. "And you'll need a good breakfast to keep you going."

Mom is such a liar.

I open the refrigerator and pull out the carton of OJ. "You want some OJ, Mr. McKnight?"

"I'm good. Got my tea." He takes another sip. He really loves his tea.

Charity trudges into the room with her blonde hair hanging in wet coils right as Mom is ready to serve.

"Charity, your hair," Mom grumbles.

"What?" she grouses as she slumps into a chair at the table.

"Can you do something about it?"

"I washed it!" Charity barks. She has a short temper in the morning, just like Mom. But Mom is faking because Mr. McKnight is here, otherwise it would be a screaming match.

"Well, at least brush it or something." Mom makes a fluttery laugh, hiding her irritation. She's pissed.

"I did!"

"Charity, your tone."

Charity rolls her eyes.

"Can you at least put it in a pony tail? We have a guest."

"Fine." She slides out of the chair and walks out.

When she returns, Mom serves.

Charity is a zombie and eats in silence, staring off into space with a piece of French toast still on her fork while she chews. When she swallows, she takes another bite from the piece on her fork.

"Charity," Mom flutter-laughs, "please cut smaller pieces."

Charity's head turns slowly and she glares at Mom silently while she chews. She swallows hard then jams the piece still on her fork into her mouth and chews open-mouthed, snarling at Mom.

I hide my smile, waiting for the screaming match.

Mom flutter-laughs at Mr. McKnight, "She must've gotten up on the wrong side of the bed this morning."

Such a faker.

Mr. McKnight chuckles and sips his AriZona Iced Tea. "I know how that can go." He smiles at Charity. "Most mornings I get out on the wrong side too."

While chewing, Charity goes, "Grrg."

He chuckles.

I can't figure out if Mom invited him over or if he just showed up. I don't remember them saying anything about breakfast last night when he was here. Oh well. Mom chatters with him while we eat. Their conversation is so sickly sweet, I can't take another second.

I finish my French toast as fast as I can and wipe my hands on a paper napkin. "May I be excused?"

"Of course," Mom smiles. "After you brush your teeth, can you pull the folding tables out of the garage and clean them?"

"Oh, gosh. Thanks for reminding me about my teeth. I always forget to brush them and would've totally forgot because all I can think about is cleaning those tables." My sarcasm is obvious. I have a bit of Charity and Mom's morning temper too.

Mom tries to maintain a smile but I see her rage ticking around her lips. She stares at me. "Use Pine-Sol on the tables. They've been in the garage a long time. And clean the folding chairs too. There's a stack of clean rags on the dryer. After that, you can vacuum. Make sure you empty the filter first. It's full." Her smile ticks a challenge.

"Love to," I snark. I turn to walk out the room.

"And don't forget the pool."

I almost ask if Charity is going to do anything, but it's not worth it. Rather than give Mom the satisfaction of a reply, I don't turn around. I just roll my eyes and walk out of the kitchen.

"The pool!" she hollers when I'm in the hallway.

My shoulders slump and I stick out my tongue and make a nasty face for my own benefit. "I'll do it!"

"Don't yell."

Kill me now.

I thought my eighteenth birthday was supposed to be a fun celebration.

Oh, wait!

Mom.

She is an expert at taking the fun out of fun.

++++8++++

CHASTITY

"He snuck into your room and came on your stomach?!" My bestie Lark Barksdale gasps over the phone.

"Yeah," I whisper, standing in the garage with the door wide open. Daylight pours in. I hold my phone in one hand while I wipe down the folding tables with the soapy Pine Sol rag.

"That is so dirty! And creepy!"

"I know, right?" I'm so proud of myself.

"I am so jell, girlfriend. I've never had a guy cut a hole in my window and ravish me like that."

"Me neither." I'm sort of surprised because Lark has a lot of experience with boys. And men. She's not even sure where or when she lost her virginity anymore.

"When do I get to meet him?"

"I don't know. Maybe at my pool party tonight."

"Did you invite him?"

"No."

"How could you not tell him your eighteenth birthday was today?"

"I sort of lied and told him I was already eighteen."

"Chastity Shields! When did you suddenly become a lying slut?"

I grin, "Just this morning. Well, I lied yesterday. You know what I mean."

"Is this your first fib?"

"I think so."

"You're going to hell," she laughs.

"Don't say that," I fret.

"There is no hell, Chastity. How many times do I have to tell you? God isn't an asshole. She's kind. Good people go to heaven when they die. Bad people cease to exist. Or they get reincarnated as dog poop. Or something like that. I can't remember." Lark doesn't go to church. She makes up her own religion.

"Dog poop? Last time it was toilet paper."

"I don't know all the details. Yes, bad people are miserable after they die. But nobody tortures them with fire and pitchforks. Who would do that?"

"God?"

"I told you, she's kind."

"Okay. Anyway."

"Right. Back to your imminent corruption. When are you going to have sex with this guy?"

"Geez, I don't know."

"The sooner the better. If he's as hot as you say, don't wait. How big is his dick?"

My eyes pop and I check the door to the house to make sure no one is listening. "Big enough," I mutter.

"Is it donkey dick?"

"I've never seen a donkey dick!"

"Baby arm?"

"That is wrong," I frown. "Why does anybody ever say that? It makes me think it has fingers on the end."

"Eww. Good point. Some guy probably made that up. When should I come over?"

"Whenever you want. But I have to clean the house and the pool and the blah blah blah."

"Mmmmm, what time does the party start?"

"Eight."

"I'll be there at nine."

"You're soooo lazy, Lark."

"What can I say? Finch got all the hardworking genes." Finch is her older sister and she works at The Beverly Hills Resort as a concierge and busts her butt for tips on a daily basis.

"Come over whenever, Lark. I won't make you do any work."

"Your mom will."

"Good point. See you at nine?"

"No, I'll come over sooner. I want to meet Lance before everyone shows up."

++++8++++

CHASTITY

"Chastity, darling," Mom croons as if she calls me darling every day.

I'm busy vacuuming the living room. "What?!"

"Turn off the vacuum, dear!" She only calls me dear when we have guests. "I don't want to shout."

I kick the switch and the motor whines down. "What?"

"I don't think we're going to have enough paper plates and plastic cups for tonight. Can you run by Target and pick some up?"

"Don't we have like a hundred of each?"

"Well, you know," Mom giggles, "in case people don't reuse them. I would hate to run out."

"Fine. But why Target? Vons is closer and they have plenty."

"But they won't match."

I should've known. "Fine, whatever." I sigh and grab the keys from the key hook by the microwave in the kitchen.

"And take Charity with you," she adds.

Mr. McKnight is still sitting on the window bench. He's been talking to Mom all morning. By now, she's put away the dishes and cleaned the kitchen at least three times.

"Isn't she busy cleaning the bathrooms?"

Mom smiles in an odd way I've never seen before. "She could use a break."

"Didn't she just start a half hour ago?"

"The fresh air will do her some good." Her face says, "*Stop arguing with me.*"

"Okaaaay." I'm not buying it. She wants to be alone with Mr. McKnight. This is way too weird. I don't even want to think about why she wants to be alone with him. Unless I woke up in an alternate universe this morning. It's the only explanation.

Two minutes later, Charity sits beside me as I drive Mom's car to Target.

"Get your feet off the dashboard!" I bark at Charity. "Unless you want to clean it." I hate that I sound like Mom, but she will make someone clean the footprints if she finds any.

Reluctantly, Charity lowers her black and pink Skechers and sits up. "Mom likes Mr. McKnight," she says casually, looking out the side window.

"You noticed?" I joke.

"How could I not? I thought Mom hated men."

"Me too."

"What do you think they're doing right now? I bet they're kissing." She giggles with mild disgust. "Or they're doing it."

"Mom doesn't *do* it," I grimace.

"I know, right? What if Mom marries Mr. McKnight some day?"

"She'd never do that," I snort.

"Why not? He's hot for an old guy."

"I guess. Wait, what do you know about hot old guys?"

Sometimes Charity surprises me with the things she says. She's not a kid anymore. She shrugs. "Just sayin'. Mr. McKnight looks like Lance. They're both hot."

"Charity! What's wrong with you! You're fourteen!"

"I'm not blind," she smirks.

Suddenly my heart is hammering. What would happen if Mom *did* fall for Mr. McKnight? It could happen. Divorced people get remarried all the time.

Oh.

No.

Mom wouldn't actually marry him, would she?

If she did, that would make Lance my—

"Watch out!" Charity screams.

I slam on the breaks and nearly hit a motorcycle turning out of a strip mall driveway. For a second I think it's Lance and I'm about to run over my hot new neighbor, then I realize the motorcycle is bright green. Lance's is black. More importantly, I stop in plenty of time. But every muscle in my body is locked up tight. "Sorry," I mutter to Charity then hastily crank down the window. I stick my head out and yell at the guy on the motorcycle, "Sorry!"

He flips me off before speeding onto the road and driving off.

"Geez, Chastity," Charity grouses, "what the heck? You almost hit that guy!"

"I know!" I groan.

"All I said was—"

"Shut up!"

Twenty minutes later, we're walking through Target. Charity makes a beeline for women's underwear and starts rifling through black bras.

"Charity!" I gasp. "What are you doing?"

"Duh. I stopped wearing training bras at the beginning of summer. Don't you remember? Dad took me bra shopping in Illinois way back in July. Oh wait. You were here in LA working. Sorry, my bad."

"Dad took you bra shopping?"

"Yeah."

"I bet that was weird."

"Not really. He just waited outside the dressing rooms and paid for everything when I was done."

"He didn't let you buy *black* bras, did he?"

"No. I mean, I don't think he would've cared. But we both know Mom would've freaked if I brought home anything other than white. And blamed Dad. So I got white."

For a moment, I'm completely stunned. Charity is growing up *really* fast. Sometimes I forget she's not eight anymore.

"Let's go look at makeup," Charity grins deviously.

"Charity! Mom won't let you have makeup."

"I just wanna look."

"We're here to buy paper plates and plastic cups."

"Are you serious? Mom is completely gaga for Mr. McKnight. She's not gonna notice if we're late."

Why do I think she's right?

Wow, everything really did turn upside down yesterday when the McKnight's arrived.

"We can look at whore's paint on the way out," I say in my best big sister voice. That's what Mom calls makeup. Charity giggles. "Plates first."

"Hey, you're eighteen. You can wear all the whore's paint you want. Maybe you should wear some for Lance."

"What? Why would I do that?"

"Duh. Because you like him."

"No I don't."

"Liar. I saw the way you were looking at him all yesterday. You like him."

"So what if I do?"

"Maybe *you* should get a black bra. And a thong. Guys like thongs."

She's right. The granny panties Mom allows me to buy would never fly for a guy like Lance. "How would you know what guys like?"

"Don't be dumb. I go to public school and we have the internet."

I smirk, "If you keep talking like that, Mom'll pull you out and home school you."

Her eyes goggle. "No, please no. I would kill myself if she did that. Or run away." She chuckles casually.

I want to laugh, but something about her tone worries me. I don't think Charity would actually kill herself, but the very idea freaks me out. "Just don't talk about black bras and guys in front of Mom. Or makeup. Okay?" I sound like such an uptight big sister right now.

"I'm not an idiot."

"I didn't say you were. Just watch what you say around Mom."

She rolls her eyes. "Let's get those plates."

On our way to the cash registers, we pass the Family Planning aisle. Every time I buy tampons, I notice the boxes of condoms. I always steal secret glances at them, wondering what it would be like to not only buy them but also *use* them. If I'm going to have sex with Lance, I better be prepared. Can I sneak a box without Charity noticing? I don't mean steal it. I would never steal. But can I somehow bring them to the register and pay for them without Charity seeing? No, I can't risk it. I'll have to come back later.

"What are you doing?" Charity pries.

I realize I slowed to a stop while she kept walking. "Nothing," I gasp and start walking.

She turns and walks toward me. She'll figure out what I was looking at the second she sees the condom display. If she hasn't already.

I stride toward her, reaching for her wrist. "Let's go."

She pulls her arm away and walks right past me and stops, looking down the aisle. "You were looking at condoms."

"No I wasn't! Let's go. Mom is probably wondering what's taking us so long." Ever since Lance, I've been lying left and right.

"No she's not. She'll probably ask if she can borrow some of your condoms for Mr. McKnight."

"I don't have any condoms!" At least that's the truth. So far. "And would you shut up about Mom and Mr. McKnight already?!"

She turns down the aisle and emerges a second later holding a box of Lifestyle condoms. "I hear these are good."

"Geez, Charity! Are you serious?"

"Don't be stupid." She jabs the box toward me. "Mom would never let you get an abortion."

I'm stunned.

I buy the condoms, but pay for them with cash on a separate receipt.

I'm speechless the entire drive home.

Did Charity somehow hear Lance and me in my room last night?

The thought horrifies me.

What kind of an example am I setting for my little sister?

Chapter 6

CHASTITY

Mr. McKnight is still in the kitchen when we get home. Neither he nor Mom have mussed hair or rumpled clothes. They most likely did not have sex while we were gone. But you never know.

Mr. McKnight tips back the last of his AriZona Iced Tea. "All outta tea." He stands up.

"Would you like something else?" Mom offers. "I can make anything you'd like."

"That's okay. I'll get a fresh bottle from my fridge."

"Are you sure? I make a terrific sweat tea. I can whip some up in a jiffy."

"She does," Charity says. "But we all know how long a jiffy is."

"Charity," Mom hisses.

Charity smirks.

Mr. McKnight chuckles. "Thanks, Faith. I'll just hop back home and grab a fresh bottle."

Mom looks disappointed. "Okay." She walks him to the front door and returns a second later. "I don't know why he wouldn't want to try my tea."

"Because, he knows how long a jiffy is," Charity chuckles.

"Don't you have bathrooms to clean?" Mom prods.

I snicker.

Mom glares at me, "The pool isn't going to clean itself."

Out back, I scoop leaves from the pool with the skimmer. The sun is high in the blue sky and the summer weather is perfect. I'd love to be out here in my new pink bikini working on my tan, but with Mr. McKnight back in the house, Mom would say something, and I'm sick to death of her saying something. She's been doing it all day.

Sadly, she's like this every day.

I need to ask my boss Mr. Molton for more hours at Marble Slab so I can move out *yesterday*.

My thoughts drift to Lance as I lazily skim the pool.

I didn't see his motorcycle outside and his Dad didn't say anything about where he might be. What's he doing right now? Is he thinking about me while he does it? I wish I knew. Just because he broke into my bedroom last night and came all over me doesn't mean he'll be back tonight or tomorrow. He doesn't exactly look like the type. My shoulders slump at the thought.

I hope I'm wrong about him.

Grunting from Lance's backyard catches my attention.

I edge my way toward the fence.

The grunting continues.

I try to peek through the slits between the fence boards, but all I see is shrubs. I could start hopping to get a view over the fence and the tall shrubs, but I can imagine Mom yelling at me to stop snooping.

More grunting. It sort of sounds like Lance. But I can't be sure.

"Fuck yeah." *Grunt.* "That's it, bitch. Just like that." *Grunt.*

My eyes goggle.

He's got to be kidding.

"Fuuuuuck yeaaaaaah."

Is he having sex with someone? In his backyard? Hours after forcing his way into my bedroom?

This is ridiculous!

I'm going to kill him!

I work my way toward the fence, pretending to skim the pool. I still can't see ship through the fence and the shrubs. I move toward the side of the house so Mom can't see me unless she comes outside. Then I hop. I can't get enough height with the skimmer in hand, so I lay it down quietly on the patio and hop again.

All I see is the top of Lance's head and his bare shoulders. I hop again. His muscles flex impressively. Another hop. His body goes up and down rhythmically. So does mine, but only because I keep hopping like a pogo stick. I must look ridiculous.

"Fuck yeah," he hisses.

He is definitely having sex with someone but I can't see who. Up, down. Up, down.

I'm enraged. I have to know who he's with.

I try to get a better look. Hop. Hop. Hop.

I'm also a little bit turned on, which enrages me further.

So I stop hopping and grab the skimmer and scoop a wad of wet leaves from the pool and throw them over the fence at Lance in a wet lump.

"What the fuck?" he blurts.

Direct hit! I throw another netful of leaves. Serves him right.

"Hey!" A second later, his head hops above the fence between two shrubs. "Chastity?" *hop* "Is that you?" *hop.*

I almost laugh at how stupid he looks hopping up and down. But I'm too mad to laugh. "Yeah it's me." I scoop up more leaves and time my fling so it hits him in the face on the next hop. *Smack!* "Jerk!" Still too mad to laugh.

"What the fuck are you doing?"

"What the frick are *you* doing?" I've got another net load ready, holding the pool skimmer like a Valkyrie holds a spear before charging into battle.

Two shrubs suddenly shake above the fence like someone is climbing up them. Lance's face appears between them a second later.

I smack him in the face with the net. One wet leaf sticks to his face.

He stays where he is, eyes clamped shut, and spits the wet leaf off his mouth before glaring at me. "Are you insane?"

Why does he have to be so gorgeous? "No, but you are!" I circle around with the skimmer and dip it in the pool for another assault.

"Stop!"

"You stop!" I whip the skimmer around.

He drops from view as water flings over the fence, missing him. "You are crazy! You know that? Can you tell me what the fuck is going on?!"

"What's her name?" I've got the skimmer at the ready again, but I'm out of leaves.

"Whose name?"

"The girl you're having sex with!"

"What?!"

"I heard you! 'Frick yeah! That's it, b-word! Just like that! Frick, frick, frick!'."

He laughs. It's a wonderful sound that makes me hate him more. "You think I was having sex with someone in my backyard just now?"

"I know you were! I saw you!"

"No you didn't," he says calmly.

"Did too!"

"I wasn't. I promise." He sounds sincere.

"Then what were you doing?" I sound hurt and angry.

"Come over and I'll show you," he says calmly.

"I'm not coming over. Ever."

"Come over. Now."

Why does that make me pause? It shouldn't. It should make me look for something else to throw at him. "Fine," I huff and put the skimmer down beside the house.

"Meet me at the gate."

I walk along between the fence and the house and out my gate to the front yard.

Lance stands holding his gate open. He's shirtless and wearing nothing but black board shorts. Every inch of his skin is golden brown and glistening with sweat in the sun. Every single muscle is visible. Like, all eight hundred of them.

I would lick the sweat off of each one of those muscles if not for the fact I want nothing to do with philandering Lance ever again.

"After you," he nods into his yard.

I squeeze past him, determined not to touch any of his gorgeous, I mean gross, muscles.

"Have a look around. There's nobody here but me."

No one on the lawn. I check the other side of his house. No one there either. Just dirt along the fence. "So what were you doing? Pushups?" As if. A guy like Lance doesn't have to strain that hard to do pushups. He can probably do them for hours. While having sex with some random b-word. Yeah, there's a girl around here somewhere. I just have to find her.

"No, not pushups. Check this out." He kneels down on the grass and sets his hands in front of him like he's about to do a pushup. He slowly and smoothly extends his legs behind him, only they're not resting on the ground. They float a foot in the air. In fact, his entire body floats parallel to the ground, except for his hands, which hold everything up.

"How do you do that?" I marvel.

He doesn't answer. He just floats there, holding the pose. Then he does several pushups, still floating. His arms bulge and the veins pop like they're going to burst.

"Wow," I giggle. "That's amazing." It's also a total turn on.

"And fucking hard," he grunts. After the last pushup, he slowly tucks his knees back to his chest without touching his toes to the ground, then stands up. His entire chest is bright red and the muscles are pumped. "That's what I was doing back here. It's called a planche pushup."

"A what?"

"Planche. It's a gymnastics thing. Great workout."

"That is so cool. Can you do it again?"

"Sure," he grins and kneels down and does it again.

Although I wanted an excuse to see his muscles flex and watch his tattoos dance over them, it's also fascinating to watch. Who doesn't like hardbodies doing gymnastics? He does more pushups. He's grunting and shaking again and all I can think about is him grunting and shaking on top of me. While he's inside me. I'm getting wet. I better stop watching.

He stands up. "Had enough?"

"Mmmm, can you do it once more?"

He smirks, "Fuck off. You do it."

"Can you show me how?"

"Can you do a push up?"

"I can do twenty-five guy push ups."

He raises his eyebrows, impressed. "That's not bad. But guy push ups are here," he holds his hand level with his waist, "and planche pushups are up here," he lifts his hand above his head. "You have to work up to it."

"Okay."

"Are you serious?"

"You can be my trainer." Do I sound desperate? I hope not.

His slow devil's grin tugs at his lips. "It'll be a lot of *hard* work."

"I can handle it."

"You'll have to do everything I say. No questions and no arguing."

"Not a problem. You met my mom. I'm used to following orders."

"This is a different kind of order."

"Oh? What kind?"

His eyes glimmer wickedly. "My kind."

"I told you I can handle it." What am I agreeing to? I don't care. As long as he has his shirt off, I'll agree to anything.

"Be careful what you wish for," he drawls, his eyes afire.

"Chastity! I thought you were cleaning the pool!" Mom hollers from the other side of the fence. "Chastity?! Where did you go? You left the skimmer out! It belongs in the garage!"

I don't want her knowing I'm back here with Lance. With his shirt off. Even if I am eighteen. I whisper to him, "Come to my pool party tonight."

"You're having a party?"

"In my backyard. It's my birthday."

"Nice. Turning nineteen?"

"Ummm…" I consider lying but I've done enough of that already. "Nope. Eighteen." I grin innocently.

He narrows his eyes. "Yesterday you told me you were already eighteen."

"I am today," I grin. "As of twelve hours ago."

"Seriously?" He arches a doubtful brow.

"Yes. I'm eighteen."

His devil's grin returns and he snickers, "You dirty little liar."

"I'm full of surprises."

"Gimme your phone number. I might be late."

My heart hammers. He wants my phone number! "Where's your

phone. I'll put it in for you."

"That's what she said," Lance grins.

"What?"

"Just tell me your number. I'll remember it."

"Chastity!" Mom shouts. "Are you out here?! Where did that girl go?"

I tell Lance my number and he repeats it back to me. "Gotta go!" I whisper and jog out front. When I'm in my own backyard, Mom is staring at me, hands on hips.

"Where have you been, Chastity? We have a thousand things left to do."

"I was in the garage. Sorry."

I'm lying left and right again, aren't I?

I smile to myself. It's just white lies.

It's not like I'm killing anybody.

Slow and unnoticed is the slippery slope into sin…

++++8++++

CHASTITY

"I have to go to the bathroom." I slide past Mom.

"You have to clean the pool."

"It is clean." Doesn't she have eyes? I threw all the leaves at Lance.

Inside the house, I pass my room on the way to the bathroom and my phone beeps on my desk. I spin on the ball of my foot smiling from ear to ear and grab my phone before locking myself in the bathroom.

I turn on the fan for privacy, but I'm still standing up with my shorts on. Sure enough, Lance texted me.

Him: **It's Lance. Have you seen my dad today?**

Me: **He's here hanging with my mom.**

Him: **No shit?**

Me: **Yes ship.**

Him: **Lolls. Ship. What time is the party again?**

Me: **8. Wear a suit.**

Him: **Three piece or swim?**

Me: **Swim, duh.**

Him: **You gonna wear that pink bikini you were hiding under your clothes yesty?**

Me: **Wouldn't you like to know.**

Him: **I can wait. But it'll be HARD…**

Me: **Dirty boy.**

Him. **The more you tease me, the HARDER I'm gonna go on you**

when you start training.

Blushing, I smile from ear to ear and drop my phone to my side. I can't believe we're having this conversation. I giggle to myself.

Me: **You can go as HARD as you want.**

Him: **You keep this UP and I'm COMING next door to FUCK the shit out of you.**

I type out **Our parents are here** but the word Our in connection with the word parents freaks me out so I delete it and text: **Later.**

Him: **Promise?**

I remember the box of three Lifestyle condoms that is now hidden in the bottom of my desk drawer. Something tells me I'm going to use them. Soon. My hands shake so bad I can barely type my reply: **If you're good.**

Him: **What if I'm bad? Cuz that's all I know.**

My chest flutters. I'm shivering from head to toe and my wetness is pooling in my panties. I text: **I can be bad too.**

Him: **Prove it.**

Me: **How?**

Him: **Send me video of your pussy. Because I know it's wet right now.**

My eyes goggle and I press my phone against my chest. How does he know?

Him: **Send it.**

I can't do that! Can I?

Him: **I'm waiting.**

My index finger quivers as I slide through my apps to the video camera.

Knock! Knock! Knock!

I nearly have a heart attack.

"Chastity! You left the skimmer out by the side of the house!" Mom barks. "Don't forget to put it away in the garage."

"Okay! I'll do it! Can't I poop in peace?" I'm about to have a heart attack in here.

"Goodness. Don't forget to clean up your language after you finish with the pool." Her voice fades as she walks away from the bathroom door.

Him: **I knew you'd chicken out.**

Me: **Oh yeah?**

I unsnap my shorts and push them and my panties to my knees. The camera is set to face me, so I watch the screen as I frame a close up of my lady parts. Here goes nothing. I thumb the record button and it glows red.

I dip my middle finger inside myself, drawing out my wetness, sliding it around on my folds. I circle my clitoris several times. I'm snickering to myself when I thumb the stop button.

Should I really send this?

I should.

But first I text: **this isn't me.**

I send the video.

And wait.

My heart is hammering again.

Did he get it? Did I send it to the wrong number? Oh, geez! I double check that yes, I sent it to Lance. Why isn't he responding? Is he grossed out? No, he doesn't seem like the type. Is he forwarding it to his entire list of contacts with my name and address below it? No, he wouldn't do that. Would he?

I wait another three minutes. I'm freaking out.

"Chastity! How long does it take you to finish?" Mom hollers.

"Coming! I mean, almost done!" Geez. I hastily wipe myself clean and don't even pee. I pull my shorts up and button them.

My phone flashes on the counter. Another text.

Him: **I'm done.**

Done? My heart locks. As in, done with me? Did I gross him out? Scare him off? Oh, ship! What did I do?

A blank message comes in from Lance with an attachment.

It's a video.

Oh, no.

Do I even want to know what's on it? What if it's something that'll get me in trouble?

Better to know now than wonder all day.

I play it.

A close up of a big hand stroking an engorged penis. It might be Lance's, but it might not. It was dark in my room last night so I didn't get that good a look at his.

Grunting from the video.

The penis swells, the head red.

A pearlescent bead builds at the tip.

"Fuck yeah," from the tiny phone speakers.

I mute the audio in a panicked frenzy.

Semen shoots from the penis.

Lots of it. Rope after rope sticks to rippled abs.

Okay, those abs have to be Lance's.

The camera turns up to show his face, a sleepy grin from ear to ear. He starts talking. I can't read lips.

I back up the video and turn the volume up to minimum and cup my hand around the speaker and hold it to my ear as I replay the end of the video.

"That was me," video Lance says, "thinking all about you and what I'm going to do to you tonight when I tear your bikini off. But this time my cum will end up inside you. Every. Hot. Sticky. Drop."

Guilt.

I mean, gulp.

"Chastity!!" Mom hollers.

"Coming!" Or close to it. Because my lips are actually quivering.

Yes, *those* lips.

Wow.

Chapter 7

CHASTITY

"This scene is putting me to sleep," Lark says at my pool party that night.

The two of us stand off to the side in my backyard. Paper lanterns hang above the sedate crowd of guests standing around the folding tables with the appetizers. Calling this a pool *party* is completely misleading. It's more like a pool gathering of my frumpy friends from church and the few approved heathens from high school Mom allows at the house. Nobody is wearing their swimsuits except Charity. They're just standing around talking politely on the patio like this is post-Bible study tea and cookies.

Lark mutters, "Do you want me to spike the punch?"

"Good luck with that," I smirk. "Mom is hovering around the punch bowl like a hawk."

"I have my ways," Lark winks deviously.

"Yeah, but did you bring any booze?"

"Sadly, no. I figured your mom would frisk me at the door."

"Some help you are," I chuckle and sip the sparkling cranberry cocktail punch Mom made for the party. Not only does Mom not allow alcohol at my party, we don't even have regular soda or anything with caffeine. Just her fizzy juice concoctions. When Mom was making the punch earlier, I jokingly asked her if drinking sparkling water was a sin. Her response was, "No, but disrespecting your elders is."

The only thing remotely close to a party vibe in this place is Lark. Her shoulder-length wavy blonde ombre hair is as unruly as her outfit. Her cleavage revealing knit camisole and pink short shorts drew a double-take from Mom when she arrived. I'm surprised Mom didn't send her home to change. Lark is my only certifiably cool friend. The only reason Mom lets her come to the house anymore is because I've known her since pre-school.

Meanwhile, I'm literally wearing one of my church dresses. Mom insisted on it at the last minute and I didn't want to start a fight with her right before my party. She probably strategized that maneuver well in advance. Not that I have any outfits as racy as Lark's. Instead, I look like the kind of girl who marries a guy like Ned Flanders from the Simpsons. Mom would *love* that.

Okely Dokely!

I cringe.

I'd rather be a nun.

Lark says, "Maybe I should go home and get my Twister game. That might loosen up all your stiff friends."

"Are you kidding? Do you think *my* mom would let kids play a game that required everyone to get tangled up like that? We may as well ask Mom if we can have an orgy."

"Good point. How about Simon Says? Faith would totally let us play that, right? Or maybe Duck-duck-goose?"

I give her a smirk.

"Musical chairs? Freeze tag?"

"Shut up," I laugh, hating the fact that her suggestions are right on the money. I heave a sigh, nearly drowning in despair as I watch my hopes for an exciting and memorable eighteenth birthday go down like a sinking ship. Sadly, Lance never showed up. Or texted.

"What's all this racket?!" A baritone voice booms from the side of the house, startling everyone. All heads turn. The side gate clatters shut and the mystery voice continues, "If you people don't put a lid on all this noise, I'm gonna call the cops."

"Lance!" I blurt as he walks around the shadowy corner of the house.

He grins huge and walks over to me and Lark. "What up, ladies."

Without thinking, I throw my arms around his neck and hug him. A second later, I feel my mom burning a hole in my back with a judgmental stare, so I release him.

"Is this him?" Lark says bluntly.

Lance laughs. "Yeah, it's him. The man himself."

I giggle, "Lark, this is Lance. My new neighbor I was telling you about earlier."

"I thought you said he was a dork," Lark laughs.

"I did not!"

Lance chuckles, "She probably meant my dad."

"In that case," Lark's eyes glimmer at Lance, "howdy, neighbor," she purrs.

A flare of jealousy lights up my chest. I want to hiss, *He's not your neighbor. He's mine. So hands off!* I take a deep breath and remind myself Lark is always flirty like this and she would never try to steal my boyfriend, or whatever Lance is. Is he my anything? I don't know. I can't think straight because keeping my claws under control takes all my focus.

Lance grins his devilish grin and takes a long look at Lark. Perhaps too long.

She grins sensually.

Claws. I mean, *focus.*

He says, "What up, Lark the Spark?"

Lark coos, "Lark the spark. I like that. Nobody has ever called me that before."

She's telling the truth, as far as I know.

"No way," Lance says.

"Way," Lark chuckles confidently like they've been friends forever. She has no fear when it comes to hot guys.

Claws! Focus!

Lance runs his eyes up and down every inch of Lark's exposed skin. "Your friends must not know you very well, Lark. I picked up on your vibe the second I saw you."

"Really?" Lark flirts seductively.

Claws, claws, claws!

I huff, "Hey, Sparky. Do you two need a room?"

She rolls her eyes. "Don't be jelly, Chaz. I'm just window shopping."

"Who the fuck nicknamed you Chaz anyway?" Lance blurts. "It sounds like a dude's name."

"You think Chastity sounds better?" I challenge.

Lark asks, "Didn't you nickname her, Lance?"

"Nope."

Lark grins at me, "No wonder she's jelly."

"I am *not* jealous. *Sparky.*"

clawsclawsclaws

She rolls her eyes. "Uh huh. Give her a nickname, Lance. She won't chillax until you do."

Lance eyes me up and down. "How about Pink?"

I say, "Like the singer?"

"No fucking way. I hate that chick's butch hair cut. This is more my style." He runs his fingers through my long curly hair.

"Stop," I say bashfully. Not because I want him to but because Mom is around here somewhere and I don't want her seeing.

"You like it," Lance chuckles.

I pull my hair away and he lowers his arm. I ask him, "So... why Pink?"

"You really wanna know?" The look in his eyes says maybe I don't want to know here in front of Lark and the rest of the pool gathering.

"I do," Lark blurts.

Lance's slow grin spreads and he drills me with his hot gaze. "Ever since I saw you bent over your car flashing me your pink bikini and carrying that pink cake box, all I can think about is your pink pussy and how sweet it's going to taste."

I'm blushing and speechless.

"Oh. My. Fuck!" Lark laughs, her mouth agape. "Jesus, Chaz! This guy may be too much for you to handle."

I should be thinking *claws, claws, claws!* But they melted with the rest of me a second ago.

"That's for damn sure," Lance says. "But I'm gonna fuck her anyway."

Melt, melt, melt…

And… *drip.*

Lark is literally fanning her face. "Stud alert!" She laughs.

Mom glares at me from across the pool. That breaks the spell.

I hiss, "Can you guys not talk like this when my Mom is right there?"

"Sure," Lance grins. "But I'm still gonna fuck you. Tonight." He smiles at Lark, "It's her eighteenth. Every girl wants to get fucked by a hot guy on her eighteenth. Am I right?"

Lark is shaking her head, wide eyed and marveling at Lance. "You are the cockiest sonuvabitch I've ever met."

"And you haven't even seen my cock," he winks.

"I hear it's substantial," Lark giggles.

"Lark!" I hiss.

Lance grins. "You told her, didn't you?"

"No! I…"

"You told her. It's cool. Chicks always gossip about my dick."

Now my mouth is agape. "Are you for real?"

"Last night I was."

I laugh guiltily.

Lance just smiles.

Lark breaks into belly laughs.

Mom glares.

Apparently, my pool party is already running off the rails Mom laid down for it and it's quickly heading in the direction Lance planned.

And we all know where that is.

Sex Town.

Admission: one V ticket.

Does Lance always get his way?

I guess I'm about to find out.

++++8++++

CHASTITY

"You guys have anything to drink?" Lance asks.

"There's no booze," Lark rolls her eyes.

"That's cool. I'll take whatever."

I lead Lance over to the crowded food tables.

The church girls surround him. Lance is literally the finest fox in this uptight henhouse, so it's no surprise they drool over him. He looks deliciously dashing under the light of the paper lanterns. Mom gives Lance a minimally polite hello before ignoring him. But she makes sure to glare at him whenever his back is turned. She is so transparent. The few guys here don't know what to make of him. He's older than all of them. I think they're scared of his tattoos and muscles. But Lance is charming everybody. He's laid back and funny. Based on how he's acting, you'd think he had known everyone here for years.

Lance is the shining star lighting up my party.

After a while, he squeezes out of the henhouse and says to me, "Hey, Chastity, this may sound weird, but have you seen my dad around? He isn't at the house."

"Funny you should ask," I say. "He's still here."

"No shit?" Lance chuckles.

"Wait," Lark says, "that guy is Lance's *dad*?"

Mr. McKnight sits in the farthest corner of the yard on the prayer bench Mom built years ago. The bench is partially screened off by hedges. Mr. McKnight is in shadow, backlit by the low garden lights. He sips from his AriZona Iced Tea bottle, which I'm noticing he carries everywhere. He wears clean jeans and a brand new Harley-Davidson T-shirt with a metallic eagle on the front. A definite step up from his wife-beater. His hair is freshly washed and naturally rakish, like Lance's. In the dim light, he could be Lance's older brother.

"That's him," Lance sighs, disappointed.

Mr. McKnight notices us watching him and raises his AriZona bottle in a toast.

"You should go say hello," I encourage.

Lance's jaw muscles dance for a moment as he stares at his dad. "Later," he says with a tinge of agitation.

That's weird.

"Wow, Chaz," Lark says, "since you get Lance, do you mind if I take his dad?"

Lance grimaces.

So do I. "Um, I think my mom has already laid claim."

Lark's eyes pop. "I thought she was acting a little chummy with him. That is disturbing!"

"Don't remind me."

"When are you guys gonna double date?" Lark jokes.

Lance and I both recoil in horror.

Lark snorts, "Easy guys. It's just talk. It's not like your parents are gonna marry and make you two—"

"Stop!" I shout.

All conversation goes quiet and everyone turns to look at me.

"Sorry!" I wince. "Carry on! Lots of food and drink! Eat to your heart's content!" Everyone is still staring. "The pool is empty if you'd like to go for a swim!"

More Staring.

"Chastity," Mom says, "Is something wrong?"

"Nope! Everything is right! Go back to the party! Chatter chatter chatter!"

Slowly, people go back to what they were doing.

Lark is grinning.

"Geez, Lark," I hiss. "Change of subject, please."

"Okay. How about we light this party up? It's way too boring for your eighteenth."

"That's right," Lance grins at her. "Your lying friend Pink told me she was already eighteen when I met her yesterday."

"What?!" Lark gasps. "You did? No way! You're going straight to hell, Chaz. Lance, you better watch out with this one. She'll take you there with her."

He grins, "Where, to hell?"

Lark nods overly seriously. "Mmm-hmm. The City of Satan."

"Satan doesn't have a city," I mutter to myself.

"How would you know?" she challenges. "Have you been to hell?"

"No. And I don't plan on going."

Lance scoffs, "Don't worry about me, ladies. I booked a first class ticket to the City of Satan years ago." He winks at me. "Paid for it with my frequent flyer miles."

"You shouldn't joke about that," I grumble. No matter how much Mom likes to tell me and Charity that something as slight as running a red light or taking the Lord's name in vain will earn us a one way trip to eternal torment in the land of fiery cauldrons, and no matter how ridiculous I think she is, the jury is still out on whether or not people go to hell for minor transgressions. So my motto is play it safe.

Lark rolls her eyes, "I told you, Chaz. God is nice. She doesn't send people to hell for lying about their age."

"Still," I grumble.

"Fuck that noise," Lance says. "No more God talk. This is a party.

We're supposed to be having fun. We need some music. I feel like we're stuck inside that old movie *Footloose*."

"Foot what?" Lark asks.

"Nothing. Pink, your party needs tuneage. Now."

I frown, "My mom and I have a… *thing* when it comes to what music is allowed in the house. Or at my parties. The compromise was not to have any."

Lance gawks. "You can't have a party without music. This place feels like a fucking mortuary."

"Okay. What did you have in mind? All I have is the music on my phone."

"Don't worry. I've got shit back at my house that'll light this place up."

"What, a bag full of Molly?" Lark chuckles. "Because that's what you're gonna need to light up this crowd."

Lance smirks, "Who needs Molly when you got me?"

"What's that supposed to mean?" I demand. "Are you going to strip for us or something?" I clamp my hand over my mouth, surprised I said something so bold.

"I could," he grins and lifts his shirt, revealing his abs.

Lark's eyes bulge as she stares, pointing. "Happy trail!"

"Stop!" I knock her hand down.

"Let's go, ladies. I need your *help* over at my house." He says it with so much innuendo, my heart spins into overdrive.

What does he mean by help? Like, sex help?

From me *and* Lark?

Gulp.

"Let's go, Pink," he says. "Time's a wastin'."

I say, "Okay, but we have to be quick. Mom'll freak out if she realizes I've left my own birthday party." What I really mean is: *I may be interested in losing my virginity tonight, but not in a three-way with you and my best friend.*

He wouldn't try something like that, would he?

I'm not really sure but Lance isn't exactly the Ned Flanders type.

Lance reaches for my hand. "Trust me. You're going to enjoy this…"

"Enjoy what?" My voice quivers.

"Me, of course." He grabs my hand before I can stop him and sneaks me and Lark out the side gate.

I hope I don't regret this.

++++8++++

LANCE

Damn, this chick Lark is fucking tight. Between her and Pink, this is some serious Garden of Eden shit right here.

"I don't know if we should be doing this," Chastity says nervously.

"Relax," I say. "I do this sort of thing all the time." The living room in the rental house is dark. It's just me and these two hotties. I'm up to my elbows in sloppy boxes.

"My mom will kill me if she finds out," Chastity whimpers.

"It's okay, Chaz," Lark purrs. "Loosen up. What's the big deal? This is totally worth whatever shit your mom gives you later. If she even says anything."

"Believe me," Chastity squeaks, "she'll say something."

Lark rolls her eyes. "It's okay, Chaz. I mean, it's your eighteenth birthday. You *deserve* to let loose and enjoy yourself."

"If you say so." Chastity doesn't sound like she's into this.

She'll come around.

They always do.

"Yeah, that's it," I grunt as I pull my arm out of the nearest box. "I knew I packed my old headphones somewhere. Hold this."

Lark grabs the headphones and loops the cord neatly around her hand.

I ask Chastity, "Do you see my DJ turntable around here somewhere?"

"I have no idea what that looks like."

"It's a black box with two silver wheels on top."

"Wheels?" She's confused.

I walk over next to her and search through the pile of cardboard boxes in the corner, brushing my shoulder against hers on purpose. Now that we're alone, I kind of wish I hadn't brought Lark to help. But there's too much DJ shit for two people to carry. "Here it is," I say as I haul the turntable out of a random box and hand it to Chastity.

She smiles and cradles it like she's holding our baby or some shit.

Chicks. Sometimes, it's just too fucking easy. After I fuck her, I'll have to buy her flowers or whatever when I end things. She deserves that much.

Lark asks, "Lance, do you have a fog machine? All DJs have fog machines, right?"

"There's one around here someplace."

"Really? Where?"

"I don't know. Dig through some boxes."

Chastity says, "As much as I'd like to stay and look for the fog machine, my mom has probably already put out an Amber Alert for me. And if we bring a fog machine, she'll probably nix it on the grounds that it reminds her of Hades or brimstone or something."

Lark sighs, "She's right. We can have the brimstone machine next time. Hey, Lance, do you have any booze we can use to spike the punch back at the party?"

I want to say, *There's plenty in my dad's iced tea bottle*, but I don't.

"Are you crazy?" Chastity blurts. "I told you, my mom will go ballistic if we try. You *know* she'll find out."

"Don't listen to her," Lark says to me.

I don't know where my dad is getting more booze. He must've walked to a liquor store when I was out yesterday. I can never figure out where he hides his shit. If I did, I'd trash it. Sometimes I think he hides it up his ass. I'm not going looking for it there.

"Well?" Lark pushes.

I'm getting irritated. "Sorry, Sparky. I'm fresh out." I pick up the PA speakers and carry them to the front door. "Let's go."

"What happened to Mr. Bad Boy?" Lark presses, standing her ground.

I frown. "Are you kidding? You know that church camp back at Chastity's house is going to die a slow painful death if we don't do something quick."

Lark says, "You're old enough to buy booze, right?"

"Yeah," I sigh, "but I'm not getting any."

"Why not?"

"Cause I'm not."

"Why?"

I glare at her. I'm not about to explain that I won't contribute to my dad's alcoholism. That would require I tell her he's a drunk, and I hate talking about that shit. The fact that he is a drunk already makes me miserable enough. Going into it with strangers makes it worse because they always say encouraging shit like, *He can get help.* But I know he's never gonna change. It's in his genes.

Chastity says, "Drop it, Lark. He said no."

Silent thanks for that. I like Chastity's spunk. She's nobody's bitch. I smile at Lark. "Let's go, ladies. I can hear Chastity's party breathing its last breath. They'll probably start playing Bingo if we don't get back soon."

"Bingo?" Lark smirks and turns to Chastity. "This guy is totally perfect for you. Match made in heaven material."

"How again?" Chastity asks.

"After you guys have sex," Lark says to me, "you can go to Bingo night at her church together."

"Your church has Bingo nights?" I ask.

"Yeah," Chastity says.

I chuckle, "I love Bingo."

"You do?"

"Yeah. Why the fuck not? It's fun."

"I love Bingo too," Chastity blushes and hides behind her fuck me hair.

Yeah, yeah. She's falling for me. I knew that yesterday. There's worse things. I'll just have to explain to her I don't fall for anybody.

After we fuck.

And maybe play some Bingo.

Chapter 8

CHASTITY

"What's all this?" Mom asks, eyeing Lance's DJ gear suspiciously as we set it up on the card table Lark and I grabbed from the garage.

Lark says, "It's for the music, Mrs. Shields."

"What music?" Mom grumbles and aims a dangerous look at me. "I thought we agreed there would be no music."

Lance says, "It's cool, Mrs. Shields. I'll keep it low enough so the neighbors don't complain."

"I'm not worried about the neighbors," Mom says. Meaning, *she's* the one complaining.

Lance places his hands on Mom's shoulders. "Relax, Mrs. Shields. I won't play anything offensive."

"He's a great DJ," Mr. McKnight says. It's the first time he's come out of his corner all night. He takes a sip of his AriZona Iced Tea. Lance gives him a sharp look, a secret moment passing between them. What was that about?

"I don't know..." Mom says nervously.

"All set," Lark says, dusting off her hands. She just finished plugging in a long orange extension cord that runs to an outdoor outlet by the sliding patio door.

Lance slides behind the table and flips a bunch of switches and turns dials like he knows exactly what he's doing.

Mom watches Lance like he's setting the timer on a time bomb. She stares at the big speakers like the Devil himself might jump out at any second and start corrupting young impressionable minds left and right.

The first song to play is *Surfin' U.S.A.*

Mom smiles instantly. "I love The Beach Boys!"

It's a bit dated, as in pre-historic. But Mom is smiling.

"I told you I knew what I was doing," Lance mutters.

Mr. McKnight sets his AriZona Iced Tea bottle on the DJ table. Lance grimaces when he sees the bottle. Before Lance can say anything, Mr. McKnight grabs my mom and the two of them start dancing like imbeciles.

I can't believe my eyes.

Charity walks out of the house carrying a tray of appetizers and nearly drops it when she sees Mom. Then she hurries over next to me and sets the tray down. She whispers in my ear, "What the heck is Mom doing?"

"I have no idea," I giggle.

The next song Lance plays is yet another surf classic, *Wipeout!*

"I thought this was supposed to be a pool party, people!" Lance hollers. "Everybody into the water!" He peels his shirt over his head, revealing his crazy perfect body, kicks off his boots, and yanks his jeans down, leaving only his black boxer briefs.

Everybody gawks because he's stripping. Literally.

Beauty has a power all its own.

Lance dashes from behind the card table and leaps into the air, doing a slow front flip into the water, landing with a big splash that splatters the deck. The church kids jump back, trying to stay dry. Lance surfaces and whips his wet hair out of his face. "Come on, you guys, the water is fucking perfect! Quit standing around and jump the fuck in!"

I wince.

Mom winces.

Lark laughs.

Charity giggles and dives lithely into the deep end near Lance. They start frolicking and splashing each other like a couple of happy dolphins. Just what you would expect at a normal pool party.

Lark drops her pink short-shorts in front of everybody and peels her camisole off. A moment later, she is wearing nothing but the sexiest bikini ever. The bottom isn't quite a thong, but it's close enough and makes her butt look perfect.

Mom gives her a dirty glare.

The guys from church all look away bashfully, frightened by Lark's boldness. A few sneak polite glances. The girls from church smirk primly, eye-daggering Lark repeatedly. If they had a pile of stones, you know they'd start throwing them at the whore. Mom would be right beside them with a bullhorn shouting *Kill the harlot!*

Lance's eyes bulge when he sees Lark in her bikini, but he tries to pretend he's not staring.

Before I have time to be jealous, Lark dives into the pool and swims toward Lance and Charity.

Okay, I have plenty of time to be jealous. I push down my church dress, revealing my sexy pink bikini. The one that earned me my nickname. It's not as sexy as Lark's, but it'll do.

"Chastity!" Mom barks. "What are you wearing?!"

"My swimsuit," I grin as I dive into the pool to join the fun. I also want to make sure Lance doesn't get too close to Lark in her dental floss bikini.

For the next hour, a playlist of beachy surf music drifts from the speakers. My favorites are *Papa Oom Mow Mow* by the Rivingtons and *Good Vibrations* by The Beach Boys.

When *Hang On Sloopy* plays, Mom semi-slow dances with Mr. McKnight. They do a clumsy waltz together. They look stiff because Mom is making sure to leave enough room between them for the Holy Ghost. At least she's dancing.

It doesn't take long for the other kids to change into bathing suits and jump in the pool. Lance quickly organizes a game of Marco Polo. When that gets old, he directs the girls to climb on the shoulders of the guys for chicken fights. Charity insists on being on Lance's shoulders, which means Lark and I don't have to fight over him, so I'm fine with it. The two of them are nearly unstoppable because Lance is stronger than everybody put together and he does all the work for Charity. Despite that, everyone is laughing and giggling and having a thousand times more fun than I ever thought I'd have when this party started. When Lance and Charity are declared the chicken fight champions, we set up the swimming pool volleyball net and divide into teams. Everyone has a blast.

No matter how hard Mom tried to keep things boring, once again, Lance flipped the script.

++++8++++

CHASTITY

"Where's the birthday girl?" Mom smiles as she walks out of the house with the cake and the burning candles. Everyone stops what they're doing or climbs out of the pool to gather around Mom and sing Happy Birthday to me.

Lark wraps her arm around my shoulders. "You're all grown up, girlfriend?"

"Yeah," I giggle.

"And many more!!!!" everyone choruses.

I step forward to blow out the candles.

"Make a wish!" Charity cheers.

I stop short and glance at Lance.

"Hush, Charity," Mom hisses. "Witchcraft is the Devil's work."

Charity rolls her eyes. "Wishes aren't witchcraft."

"Hush."

Lark chuckles, "Make a wish anyway."

Mom eye-shoots Lark.

Lark wears a mom-proof vest that deflects the hate bullets.

Lance smiles his dangerous grin.

We lock eyes and a jolt of joy flashes through me. "I wish for…"

"Don't say it out loud!" Charity hollers. "You'll ruin it!"

People laugh.

I blow out the candles with one quick puff. I'm pretty sure that means my wish involving Lance and me and all kinds of naughtiness will come true. The only question is when.

Mom cuts slices of cake for everyone and Charity hands two to me and Lance.

"Thanks, Chair," I smile.

"Thanks, kid," Lance says, winking at her as she walks away.

He cuts into his cake with his plastic fork and slides a bite sensuously into his mouth, chewing slowly, enjoying every moment. His eyes burn into mine the whole time.

I'm mesmerized watching his mouth work. A dab of frosting is stuck to the corner of his full lips. I desperately want to lick it off. His eyes flicker suggestively. Just as I'm about to lean forward and suck off that dab of frosting with my own lips, his tongue snakes slowly out of his mouth and licks the frosting clean in a slow swipe.

I hide a pleasant shiver as a wave of sensations quivers through me, wondering what else he knows how to do with that tongue…

"You gonna make me eat your *cake* all by myself, Pink?"

Gulp. I can read between the lines. This is all so deliciously naughty. "Oh, yeah, right." I fork my own piece of cake and start chewing. I'm barely aware of the yummy flavor because I'm so focused on Lance's lips as he takes another bite. We stare at each other while we chew. It's like we're kissing. I work my tongue around in my mouth, imagining the cake is a piece of Lance.

He says, "I knew the cake in your pink box would be damn sweet, but I had no idea it'd be *this* good." He shovels more cake into his mouth and chomps merrily away.

At that exact moment, Mom catches my eye and glares at me, ruining my moment. As usual.

I suddenly feel guilty and glare at Lance like I wasn't just enjoying every second of our cake sex. "Will you stop!" I nearly choke on the gooey wad of Lance still in my mouth. Unable to swallow, I cough into my napkin, afraid chunks of frosting might go flying.

He laughs around a mouthful of cake, "Sorry. My bad."

"You're always bad," I laugh, dabbing cake-Lance off my lips with my paper napkin.

"That's what the ladies tell me." He glances over at the table where all my presents are stacked. "Hey, when you gonna open that huge stack of loot people brought you?"

"Later. Everyone's having too much fun. Tonight doesn't have to be all about me."

"Why not? It's *your* birthday."

"In that case, where's my present, Mister? I don't remember you bringing one."

"You kidding? I *am* the present."

I laugh. "Hush your mouth!"

"Oooh, dirty talk. Love it."

"That was not dirty talk."

"You sure? Cause I'm kinda turned on right now."

I stamp my foot, "Cheese us, Lance! Would you stop?!"

"Did you just say cheese us?"

I giggle, "So?"

"You have the dirtiest mouth I've ever heard, girl."

"Me dirty? You're the one who said the F-word in front of my Mom a hundred times today."

"Was that all? I thought it was more like a thousand."

"You're such a trouble maker."

"Only when I have a good reason."

"Oh? What's the reason?"

"You." His eyes burn into mine.

I flush from head to toe. I've never had so much fun flirting with a guy.

"Tell me something," he says.

"What," I mumble, staring at the lawn poking up between my toes.

"What do you want from me for your birthday?"

I laugh.

"I'm serious." He forks more cake into his mouth.

"You know what?"

"What?"

"I totally have to pee."

He snorts. "Is that your exit strategy?"

"I'm serious. I haven't gone since I don't know when. I'll be right back."

"I'll be right here," he chuckles.

I rush into the house. The door to the hall bathroom is locked. Someone must be using it. I consider using Mom's, but I hate her bathroom. She has all these religious plaques with religious sayings hanging on the walls and it creeps me out. So I wait.

Two minutes later, Gina from church walks out of the hall

bathroom. "Sorry," she smiles. "And happy birthday!" She throws her arms around me and squeezes me in a big hug which presses painfully on my bladder.

I break the hug as politely as possible. "Thanks."

"So, what're you gonna do now that you're an adult?" Gina has a really annoying voice, but she's sweet.

"Gosh, I haven't really thought about it."

"I can't wait until I turn eighteen. I'm thinking about going on a mission trip to Brazil. My brother did one last year and had an amazing time. His host family was really nice. They took him on a boat trip down the Amazon and everything. He said the rain forest is incredible and you have to go there to truly appreciate it. The exotic birds, the wildlife, even the bugs are cool! He even saw piranhas. Can you believe it? Real piranhas, like in the movies?" Her voice is twice as annoying when I have to pee.

I wince, "I sort of have to go pee."

"Oh! Sorry!" She blushes. "I'll see you outside."

I lock the bathroom door and barely get my bikini bottom off in time to sit down. Phew. What a relief.

I'm still going when there's a knock at the door.

Maybe they'll go away.

Another knock.

"Ocupado!" I call.

Someone jiggles the doorknob.

"Charity? Is that you?"

No response. Maybe she went to use Mom's bathroom.

When I finally finish, I wash up and open the door.

I gasp.

Lance fills the doorway.

He backs me into the bathroom and closes the door behind him, locking it. His eyes are wild, confused, animalistic. He looks almost... insane.

I'm suddenly more than a little scared. He's twice my size and can easily overpower me. "Is something wrong, Lance?"

He takes a step toward me. "Yeah."

I take a step back. The frosted glass window in the shower is open an inch and I can hear everyone on the patio outside chattering away. If I scream for help, they'll hear me and come running. But I can't decide if I should scream or not.

His voice is tight, catching in his throat when he speaks. "I was standing around outside at the pool waiting for you to come back and I was watching your sister and your friends and your mom. That's when

I realized you and me come from two different worlds, Chastity. You're all sweet and innocent and you have your shit together. I'm a mess and I'm not innocent. Not even fucking close." He looks pained, like he has more to say but doesn't want to.

My heart swells with sympathy. "What is it, Lance? You can tell me. I won't judge you."

He huffs a sigh. "My life is chaos, Chaz. Yours is organized."

I snort, "It's not as happy as you might think."

"I'm not talking about happy. I'm talking about problems. Real problems. You don't need me bringing my shit into your life. Trust me. You'll be better off if I leave you alone."

"What? You're not making any sense." Except he is. He's making perfect sense. I just don't want to hear it.

"I don't want to walk away, but I know it's the right thing to do. So I promised myself I wouldn't fuck you. If you weren't a virgin, I might think different, but…"

"Who says I'm a virgin?" My heart is spinning out of control. Lance makes me yearn to hold him and comfort him at the same time he makes me furious. I snarl, "And what makes you think I'll let you have sex with me?"

"Please," he snorts and runs his hand nervously through his hair. "Anyway, I promised myself I wouldn't, but I have to, Chastity. I *have* to fuck you. I *need* to fuck you. I don't know why, but I do. I never fuck virgins. But I have to fuck *you*, Pink. I have to." He sounds… desperate. Overwhelmed.

I am too. "Okay. I guess?" This is really weird.

He steps forward again and my calf thumps against the tub. I can't go back any further or I'll fall through the shower curtain.

"See, I don't *need* to fuck anybody. I never have. Anyone hot enough will get the job done. I don't care who they are."

"Am I supposed to be flattered by all this?"

"Don't you get it, Pink? It's you. You. I don't understand it. But I need to be inside your fucking pussy. I've been going crazy since I drove up yesterday." He hooks a finger through the left shoulder strap of my bikini and snaps it against my chest, right above my thumping heart. His eyes circle in their sockets for a second before roaming all over my body. "I'm going insane looking at you, Pink. I *have* to fuck you."

If this is his way of saying he likes me, it must be the weirdest way anyone has ever expressed it.

He pulls the cloth cup of my bikini over my left breast, exposing the nipple, which is already tight. The knuckle of his index finger skims across it. I feel an instant electrical connection and my heart races with a cocktail of fear and arousal. His face bunches. "I can't do this. You're a virgin. I can't."

"Can't what?" I'm as confused as he is but I'm getting wetter by the second. His big hand squeezes my breast, massaging it in complete contradiction to his words, pinching and twisting the nipple.

I'm breathless, my eyes half shut as I surrender to the pleasure of his hand. "Lance…" I whisper.

"I can't stop myself." He sounds almost full of regret.

My heart goes out to him. I place my hand over his, over my breast, over my heart. I stare into his eyes for a moment. "Then don't." I reach behind me and untie the string around my bust.

His other hand shoots up to my right breast and squeezes it too. "They're fucking perfect, Pink. Fuck. Perfect."

I don't think so, but my opinion isn't what counts right now and I'm not about to argue with Lance when he's gone off the deep end with lust. I untie the string around my neck and drag it out from under my hair and toss the top aside.

"Fuck, this hair," he marvels, combing his fingers up the back of my scalp and fisting it, pulling my head back. His mouth dives for my neck. His tongue glides from the pit of my neck to the tip of my chin.

I shiver and let out a little whimper.

He grabs me by the ass and throws me on the counter top next to the sink and stands between my knees. He wears only his damp black boxers and he bulges inside them.

I run my fingers across the head, stroking it through the wet fabric.

"I have to fuck you, Chastity. I have to." He pulls my bottoms down and I lift my butt to help. When they're down to my ankles I kick them off anxiously. He stares at my dripping center and chuckles, "You fucking want this as bad as I do, don't you?"

The pool between my legs is the only answer I give.

He squats down and his tongue attacks, bringing me instantly to the edge of climax. I slouch into his mouth, curling my back and lifting my hips off the counter with my arms. Then he—

Stops.

He stands frantically and rips his boxers off.

He plants both hands on the counter top on either side of my hips.

I press my knees out against the insides of his muscled tattooed arms, opening myself and coaxing him.

His head hangs between his shoulders and he sighs reluctantly.

I wrap my ankles around his back and tug him toward me.

His cock throbs between my legs, only an inch away. I can feel the heat as it nears.

We both stare at it.

He grabs himself by the base and lays his heavy length on my folds, pressing into them with the bottom of his cock, parting them.

He rocks forward and back, the bottom of his shaft rubbing across my clit.

We are skin to skin and an inch away from having actual sex.

He rocks back.

I pull him forward, digging my heels into his rippling back muscles.

"We—" His voice chokes.

He lifts his head.

Our eyes lock.

My mouth quivers, holding back the word.

"Should we get a..." he trails off.

I realize that Lance probably doesn't have a condom in his wet boxers. But I happen to have that box of Lifestyle condoms from Target in my bedroom. All I have to do is open the bathroom door and walk ten feet to get them. Well, and get dressed, or at the very least wrap towels around me and Lance before I open the bathroom door. But if I do that, someone might catch us and this moment will be ruined, our secret forbidden fantasy destroyed. There have been so many interruptions to my moments with Lance since we met, I'll be damned if I'm going to interrupt this one.

He rocks forward and back, unable to resist the kiss of our skin. His cock is wet with me. His foreskin rolls over his bulging head, covering it, then pops back, revealing it. His strokes get longer and his tip is getting dangerously close to entering me.

I am dying with pleasure.

He is too. His face is tight with agony.

Maybe we should...

I look down at his swollen tip. It pulses with pre-cum, ready to drip.

This is insane.

This is how people get pregnant their first time.

This is...

I don't care.

I need him inside me.

I don't care if I get pregnant.

I don't care if the condoms are in the next room.

I just don't care.

I want him to fill me up with his cum.

His hands grip my hips. His face is as red as the head. His jaw is locked, his teeth barred. A snarl hisses between them like he's in terrible pain.

I'm about to beg him to put it inside me, to come inside me, when...

He does.

He comes. Grunting.

All over me.

His semen hoses across my taut stomach.

I'm buzzing, my whole body sizzling with arousal and pent up heat. It's like I'm coming but I'm not. It's excruciating. So close to the edge of explosion, but everything is locked down.

I can't come.

It hurts. Actual physical pain.

I need to come so badly I can't stand it.

My whole body heaves with need.

His hard palm presses against my stomach, smearing his liquid seed up between my breasts, caressing me with his sticky hand.

His head hangs. His eyes burn under his dark brows. He's mad. "Fuck," he growls. "You didn't come."

Frustration blows through me. I want to scream.

His head dives between my legs, his hands squeezing the backs of my thighs, prying me open.

The second his tongue touches me, I come.

I drown in pleasure, slouching further down, pushing myself into his face, still coming, bucking, grabbing his hair with both hands like my life depends on it. My feet spasm in the air as the orgasm tears me apart.

I am in heaven.

His tongue circles slowly for at least another minute, lapping me up as I relax and rest my heels against his shoulders.

When his head lifts from between my legs, his mouth glistens in a satisfied smirk.

My eyes slit and I stare at him.

"What?" he mutters.

I reach down between my legs with both hands and drag my fingers through my soaking wetness and pull it up my stomach, across my navel and around my still sticky breasts. I massage them, mixing my fluids with his.

He chuckles, watching. "That is fucking hot."

Somehow, as good as that was, I am completely unsatisfied. Or just hungry for more. I can't tell which. "Fuck me," I whisper.

His eyes flash. "Did you just say fuck?"

I bite my lower lip in an evil grin and nod slowly. I whisper, "Fuck..." like it's the most beautiful word in the English language, savoring the taste of it in my mouth.

The devil's smile on *my* face slowly slides onto his.

"Nice," he says.

"Fuck me," I whisper. "Now."

Chapter 9

"Are you high?" Charity asks.

I sit on a lawn chair with my arms wrapped around my shins, resting my chin on my knees, staring at the electric blue glow of the empty pool like a grinning idiot.

Charity grabs a lock of my hair and wiggles it. "Anybody home? Earth to Chastity!"

"Stop!" I swat at her hand and pull my hair away.

"You look sprungover."

"I what?! What does that even mean?"

"It means you hooked up with Lance and you're basking in the afterglow."

"Where do you learn these words? And I did not hook up with Lance," I hiss.

"Liar. I saw you sneak into the house with him."

"I did not!" And that's the truth. He followed me inside. "More importantly, why are you stalking me?"

"I'm not. You can't stalk your own sister when you live with her."

"Whatever."

Although half the kids have gone home, those still here are lounging on the other lawn chairs while chatting or dancing to the surf music. Lance is now fully dressed, standing behind the DJ table with his headphones on. I think he put clothes on to cover up his hard on, which seems to have never gone away. I don't blame him. I've still got a girl hard on for him and my high beams are on too. That's why I have my knees up.

Charity asks, "You wanna see who can swim the length of the pool underwater the fastest?"

"What, in one breath?"

"Yeah."

I frown, "Aren't you tired?"

"No."

"I am. You do it. I'll time you."

"You don't have a watch."

"I'll count Mississippis."

"You're lame," she chuckles and dives into the pool.

Grinning, I shake my head. She can call me lame all she wants. I'm not getting in the pool. I need to stay right here with my high beams covered.

Mom and Mr. McKnight are still dancing together. When *Wooly Bully* ends, Mom says, "Let's sit this one out, Rod. I'm tired."

"One more song, Faith. The night is still young." His words are slurred. He grabs her around the waist, pawing at her as she tries to push him away. "Come on, Faith. We're still having fun."

Is he drunk? I don't know where he would've gotten any alcohol. We don't have any and he never left the party.

"I need to sit down, Rod. I've been on my feet all night." She's trying to get away, but Mr. McKnight won't let go.

I glance at Lance and remember his frantic speech about hidden problems. Is there something about his dad he's hiding? No answer comes from Lance because he has his headphones on and his head down, doing something on his turntable.

"Stop it, Rod!" Mom pleads.

"One more song, Faith." He is drunk.

I think. I don't have any experience with drinkers. But Mom needs help. I stand up and take a step toward them.

Mom barks at him, "Let! Go!" She pushes hard and Mr. McKnight stumbles back, colliding with Lance's DJ table.

"What the *fuck*, Dad!" Lance growls, ripping his headphones off.

Mr. McKnight flails and knocks against a piece of DJ gear on the table. When the black box of electronics starts to fall, he fumbles for it, trying to catch it. But he can't. The box tumbles from his hands and drops right into the pool.

Still plugged in.

"I! Can't! Move!" Charity mewls in a voice quivering with fear. "Some! One! Help! Me!" Her entire body jitters in the deep end of the pool as she attempts to stay afloat, her arms ratcheting through the water in spasmodic jolts.

Horrified, Rod twists around to face my sister. He's paralyzed with fear.

Mom spins around too. She didn't see the DJ gear fall in. She shrieks, "Charity!"

I forget all about the electrical cord and I'm about to jump in the pool to help when Lance grabs my elbow.

"Don't!!" He yells. "The water is hot!"

Mom takes a step toward the pool, but he grabs her by the arm too, restraining her.

"Let go of me!" Mom yells with a combination of hatred and

motherly fury.

For a moment, I'm totally confused and terrified. Somehow I forget all about the electricity. All I can think about is my sister in danger and why is Lance stopping Mom from saving her? I try to dive into the pool, but Lance wraps both arms around me, letting go of Mom.

"The water is hot!" he shouts.

What does he mean by hot? Hot like boiling? Is my sister *cooking* in the water? Oh my God, no!

"The power cord!" Lance shouts.

That's when logic returns. "Someone unplug it!" I shout, searching desperately for the cord.

Charity screams,. "Mom! Help!"

Mom reaches for the metal pool ladder, about to step into the water.

"Don't touch that!" Lance shouts. "You'll get shocked! Someone unplug the damn cord!"

Mom freezes, a pained look on her face, her hand one inch from the ladder. "My baby! Someone help my baby!!"

Lance whips his head from side to side, examining the mess of DJ gear. His dad is standing right in front of the table, frozen. "Get the fuck outta the way!" Lance yells, pushing him into the grass where he drops on his ass. Lance claws at the jumbled loops of cords until he finds the main orange cord snaking into the bushes. He yanks it free from the outlet with a pop, then whirls around and dives fully clothed into the water. He freestyles out to Charity, approaching from the side and hooking an arm around her ribs. He leans back, pulling Charity on top of him so her face is above the water. "I've got you. Relax. I've got you."

"Oh goodness, oh goodness!" Mom shouts, still afraid to touch the metal ladder. She drops to her knees, waving a hand toward Lance, trying to reach Charity.

Even though Lance has Charity, I'm overcome by the intense need to help my sister. I jump into the pool and swim toward them. "Charity! Are you okay?!"

She's coughing, her face pinched and red, her entire body shaking. For a second I think she's still being shocked, but Lance is fine. I'm not getting shocked either. Then I realize Charity must be *in* shock.

"Is the water safe?" Mom pleads, completely confused and oblivious to the fact that Lance and I are not getting shocked.

"Yeah," Lance says.

Mom jumps into the water in her dress and wades over to Lance and Charity. "Are you okay, Charity? Say something, Baby! Say something!"

"I called 911!" Lark shouts. "They're on their way!"

Charity coughs again, crying, "I'm okay."

"Are you sure?" Mom begs.

"I..." *cough cough* "think..." *cough* "so..."

"Can you stand up?" Lance asks. "We're in the shallow end."

"I don't know," Charity whimpers. She's acting like she forgot how to swim.

"Don't worry," Lance says calmly. "I've got you."

"I've got her," Mom says, reaching out for Charity, trying to take her from Lance.

"No!" Charity barks. "Don't let go!" She's talking to Lance.

Mom cringes and withdraws her hands, "Okay."

I give Lance a look.

He shrugs it off. "Charity, I'm going to carry you out of the pool. Is that okay?"

"Yeah," she mumbles.

He grabs the ladder with one hand. "Can you wrap your arms around my neck?"

"Yeah," she says tentatively.

I plant my hands on the deck and lift myself out of the water. "I'll help."

Lance climbs the ladder, holding it with one big hand while squeezing both of Charity's wrists around his neck with the other. The two of them drip all over the cement as Lance squats down and lowers her to her feet. She's way too big for me to cradle her like a child, but I try anyway. She ends up hugging me and I squeeze hard as we both sit down. She's shivering like it's freezing outside, but it's summer warm. She really must be in shock.

Soaked, Mom climbs the ladder and wraps her arms around both of us. "My babies," she whispers. "My babies are safe. Thank you, Lord. Thank you." She starts mumbling prayers under her breath.

I smirk. Lance is who she should be thanking. But she seems to have forgotten all about him. The three of us are somehow excluding Lance, who stands to the side, looking between us and the heap of his Dad on the lawn, who remains where he fell when all the drama started and Lance knocked him down.

Mr. McKnight looks sad and confused.

Charity starts rambling in half sentences, her teeth chattering. "I was— swimming and— my arms— froze and— I couldn't— swim and — I thought I— was going to— drown."

"I think she's in shock," Lance says quietly. "We should lie her down or something. And get some blankets."

I nod.

"I'll get some," Lark says, jogging into the house.

Mom hugs Charity. "It's okay, baby. The Lord is watching over you. You're safe. Everything's okay. You're going to be all right."

Lark rushes out of the house with blankets which Mom wraps around Charity. We lay her on a semi-reclined lawn chair, Mom by her side.

When the ambulance arrives, everything is chaos as the EMTs rush inside with a portable stretcher, but things calm quickly as they check all of Charity's vitals and assure us she's okay.

The head paramedic says, "We can take her to the hospital right now, if it'll make you feel more comfortable."

"I think that's a good idea," Mom nods vigorously.

"I'm tired," Charity groans. "Can we go tomorrow?"

Mom looks at the lead EMT.

"Her heart sounds strong and she wasn't burned. There's no sign of serious injury I can find. To be safe, I advise you to go to the ER tonight, but you don't need us to rush you there. Depending on your insurance situation, it could save you a thousand dollars. I'll tell the hospital I consider your daughter's case urgent, but without any burns or heart trauma, your provider might deny payment."

Mom winces and nods, trying to make sense of his words.

"I don't wanna go, Mom," Charity whines. "I just wanna go to bed."

"We'll take her," Mom says.

"I'll pay for it," Lance says.

"No," Mom grumbles, "I won't take your charity."

The irony that Mom won't take charity to help Charity is not in any way funny.

"Then take mine," Mr. McKnight says in a smeary voice. He's been hovering in the background this whole time.

"You're still here?" Mom snarls.

"I'll pay for it," Mr. McKnight insists.

"No," Mom barks. "I don't want *anything* from you. I don't need your *help*, and I don't want you on my property. Please go home." She turns her back to him and straightens the emergency blanket wrapped around Charity's shoulders for no reason.

Mr. McKnight sets his palm on her shoulder. "Now, Faith, I said I would—"

She twists away from his hand like it's on fire. "Don't you *ever* touch me again! Stay away from me and my daughters and this house!" Her eyes flash like she wants to attack him. "And keep your son away too!" Her cheeks shake with rage and impending tears.

"Mom," I hiss through gritted teeth. "Lance *saved* Charity. If he hadn't stopped me, I would have jumped into the electrified pool. You would've too."

She explodes. "If he hadn't brought his infernal stereo over here, none of this would've happened, now would it?!"

"Mom, you're missing the point," I whisper.

"No I'm not! It's his fault!" She snarls at Lance, then at Mr. McKnight. "And your fault too! Both of you get off my property! Now!" She throws her arm out like a sword. "I said NOW!!!!"

Dejected, Mr. McKnight mumbles, "I'm sorry. Really sorry."

Lance rolls his eyes, his jaw spasming. He grabs his Dad high on the back of the arm and shoves him forward. "Let's go, *Dad*," he grunts through gritted teeth.

Mr. McKnight stumbles, his free hand out to stop his fall, but Lance pulls him up before he hits the deck. When the man stumbles again, Lance hooks an arm around him and barks, "God damn it, can't you fucking walk?" Everyone stares. Before his dad can answer, Lance spins and squats in front of him like he's going to tackle him, but instead throws him over his shoulder like a sack of potatoes and carries him around the side of the house.

I dash to catch up. "Do you need help?"

"I've got it," Lance snaps as we melt into the shadows between the house and the fence.

"Are you sure?"

He stops and scowls at me, his face dark except for his burning eyes. "This isn't the first time he's fucked everything up and it won't be the last. So, no, I don't need your help. And I don't want it either. Your sister needs you. I don't." He starts walking.

I know he's angry. I won't let it get to me. He didn't deserve what Mom said. I want to reassure him, but all I can think to say is, "Do you want me to get your DJ gear? I can bring it over. Now or later. Whatever's easiest."

He doesn't stop or look back. "You can fucking keep it. Or sell it. I don't give a fuck." He kicks the gate open with his boot and it bangs shut after they're gone.

So much for my eighteenth birthday.

It ended with a bang, but it was the wrong kind.

++++8++++

LANCE

"You're a fuck up, you know that?" I grumble as I drop my dad on his air mattress. He falls in a heap and bounces once. After that, he doesn't move.

"Yeah," he sighs, his face buried in the bare mattress.

"You're not gonna suffocate, are you?"

He responds with a bubbling puff of air.

"Fucking waste of space." I grab his arm and roll him onto his other side and position his head so he can breathe. I slide down against the wall until my ass is on the floor. "How the fuck could you mess up tonight, dumbass?"

"I don't know." His eyes are closed and he's half-asleep already.

"Panty Shields was totally into you. But you fucked it up. In one damn night."

"Who?"

"Faith? Chastity's Mom? Who the fuck do you think I'm talking about?"

"Oh."

"Are you ever gonna stop drinking?"

"I don't know."

Same fucking answer every time. "You're gonna kill somebody sooner or later. I was hoping it would be you, but you almost killed Charity tonight. And you weren't even driving," I snort.

"Yeah," he sighs, his brow tightening with what looks like regret, but could merely be the onset of whiskey farts.

He's already been in jail twice for DUIs and his license is suspended for another year. If he keeps at it, it'll probably get revoked for good. The court would've made him use one of those Ignition Interlock Devices you have to breathe into to start your car, but he wrecked it. Beautiful 1971 Chevy GTO. It took him years to restore that thing to cherry and one night of drinking to demolish it. What a waste. The court did make him put an IID on his Harley back in Nevada. He looks like a dumbass when he blows on it. I always ask him if he likes sucking dick to get a ride. He always ignores the question or says at least he still gets to. I ask him how much he likes having to blow into it every 45 minutes to keep going. Same thing: at least he's still riding. I haven't broken the news to him that he can't use it in California. They don't allow them on bikes yet. Which means Dad's walking, riding a bicycle, or taking the bus.

Either way, I know he'll keep drinking.

Sometimes I want to ask him if he'd suck dick for real to get his next drink, but sadly I already know the answer is yes. Not that he ever has, to my knowledge, nor would he admit to it if he had.

It's so pathetic it makes me want to puke.

My old man is nothing but a washed up useless drunk.

"I miss your mom," Dad slurs, all weepy.

I scowl, "Shut the fuck up."

"I miss her so much."

I ignore him and dig a blanket out of a box and throw it in his face. It lands on his head like a little tent. He just leaves it there. I yank it off him and whip it open until it billows down on him. His boots poke out the bottom.

I shake my head and squat at his feet and yank them off. Each one thuds when it hits the floor.

I hit the lights on the way out. "Sweet fucking dreams, dumbshit."

He's snoring before I close the door.

Chapter 10

CHASTITY

Moonlight shines through my bedroom window.

I lie in silence under the covers. Tears streak my face. I sniffle and wipe my cheek. Tonight was a disaster.

We took Charity to the ER. Lark came along for the ride. The doctors said Charity was fine, but we should bring her in if anything strange happens in the next week or two. In other words, she's fine. But we didn't get home until 4:00am. Lark offered to sleep on the couch. Mom asked her to leave. She did.

Now I want to forget about everything.

Except Lance.

I can't stop thinking about him.

I stare at my mirrored closet doors, imagining Lance's mirrored bedroom next door. If they were magic like I wanted, I'd walk through right now and apologize to Lance for everything Mom said. She definitely over-reacted about him. But I'm not sure how I feel about Mr. McKnight. Some day I'll forgive him. But Lance? He's not a devil. He's a saint. He wouldn't even have sex with me. We sure came close, and we both came, but that was it. No penetration. I'm still technically a virgin.

I wish I was in his arms right now.

I wonder if he's asleep in his bedroom? Or is he awake thinking about me?

I crawl out of bed and place my palm against the glass. It's cool to the touch. I press my weight against it.

For a second, I swear to God, my hand moves a millimeter through the glass like it's liquid. When I push harder, nothing happens.

It must've been the moonlight playing tricks on my eyes.

I climb back into bed.

Maybe I should just climb out my window like a regular girl.

But Mom would totally wake up and grab me by the ankles when I was halfway out the window and pull me back into the room and cook me in her Gingerbread Oven like the witch that she is.

Sigh.

I can't wait to escape the religious cocoon that is life with Mom.

Maybe when I wake up in the morning, the zombie apocalypse will have happened and Lance and I will be the last two humans on planet earth. Then we'll have no choice but to start repopulating immediately. Charity can survive too, but she'll need to bring her own boyfriend.

What am I thinking? That'll *never* happen.

So what?

I'm eighteen.

I can do whatever I want.

I don't need a zombie apocalypse. I can start my own lifestyle apocalypse first thing tomorrow.

The idea puts a smile on my face.

After I drift off to sleep, I dream about Lance. Oddly, he has a sexy Southern accent like Daryl Dixon on the Walking Dead. He even has the shaggy hair and scruffy goatee.

++++8++++

LANCE

I am a fucking idiot.

Her pussy was right there! My cock was on top of it!

Why didn't I fuck her?

I yank on my hair and bash the back of my head against my pillow.

I've been tossing and turning on my bare-ass mattress since I put Dad to bed. I'm bare-ass naked and my rock hard dick points at the ceiling.

It's after four and there's no way I'm getting to sleep.

Whenever I close my eyes, all I see is Chastity's soaking wet pussy with my dick on top. I've jerked off twice thinking about it. Coming in my hand did nothing to relieve the need.

I need to fuck her.

If I *don't* fuck her, I'm not gonna be able to think about anything else until I do. And I have a lot of shit to get done tomorrow.

I need a release.

I grab my phone and scroll through my list of five-star LA booty calls. Eight gorgeous faces flash by:

Brooke.

Gia.

Jess.

Naomi.

Prue, who is kinky as fuck.

Raya.

Trysta, who would sneak out on her boyfriend to fuck me because she has before.

Yaz, best head I've ever had.

They're all nines and tens. Model hot. And all of them seriously know how to fuck. The kind of sex that is so over the top, it finishes you for days.

I drop my phone on the floor.

I don't give a shit about any of them.

I need to fuck Chastity. Until I come inside her, I'm not going to be able to think about anyone else. It *has* to be her.

The scary thing is my balls keep saying over and over, *Get her pregnant, Lance. Pregnant. Come inside her without a condom. As many times as you can. Pregnant, pregnant, pregnant.*

What the fuck? I've *never* wanted to get any chick pregnant. It's not worth it.

The good news is, condoms. And the pill. I'll just have to get Chastity on it quick.

Because balls be in control, yo.

I grab them and squeeze hard. I whisper out loud, "Why the fuck did you guys have to pick the god damn virgin?"

I chuckle to myself and drop my head on my pillow.

I roll on my side and stare at my reflection in the mirrored closet door.

Fucking Chastity Shields.

She's fucked my shit up but *good.*

I wonder if she's thinking about me right now?

Probably.

Wait a second.

What was I thinking?

I snicker to myself.

All the chicks in my phone are chicks I've fucked *before.*

I grab my balls again. "You want some strange? Is that it? Will that shut you the fuck up so I can get some sleep?"

They don't answer, but I know from experience.

It's all about the strange.

I need to go find me some.

Thank fuck for downtown raves. The after hours house party scene in LA is off the hook. Lucky for me I know where the best ones are at. I'm grinning as I stuff my legs into my jeans and get dressed.

I throw the garage door open and wheel my bike halfway down the driveway. I stop and stare at Chastity's house.

What the fuck am I thinking?

This is never gonna work.

I circle the GSXR-1000 around and roll it back into the garage.

God damn balls think they can tell *me* what to do?

Yeah, pretty much.

Fucking balls.

I punch the garage door button and trudge inside the house.

So much for sleeping.

++++8++++

CHASTITY

"Lance!" I scream. "Gimme your crossbow!"

He tosses it to me and I shoot a zombie right between the eyes.

"We gotta git outta here!" He yells it with a Southern accent and pushes me through a doorway in a random abandoned hospital, slamming the door behind us.

There's just enough light coming through the small window in the door to reveal a cramped broom closet full of dusty cleaning supplies.

Outside, hundreds of zombies lurch through the hospital hallway. We've been on the run through the vast maze of the building for hours. It's so big, I don't know if we'll ever escape.

Sometimes Charity is with us, sometimes she's not. But she always has an assault rifle and is always shooting from the hip at the hordes of zombies and yelling, "Eat lead, bitches!" I tell myself it's okay for her to curse since it's the apocalypse.

In the dark broom closet, I'm very aware of Lance's body pressed up against my back. Despite the chaos outside, this feels like the perfect intimate location for procreating. Since there's no one left alive to perform a wedding ceremony, not even a justice of the peace, I think it's safe to assume it's okay for us to have sex out of wedlock. I don't think God will mind because *someone* has to repopulate the planet

I turn around to face Lance.

The muscles of his bare arms ripple hypnotically. His devilish eyes flame as his mouth crashes into mine.

The sound of swelling violins stirs our emotions, fueling our desire. It's the passionate big screen kiss every girl dreams of.

Until one of the zombies claws at the window behind my head and gasps in a raspy zombie voice, "Chaz! Ti! Tee!" The sound is strangled and gurgly.

Torn from my moment with Lance, I twist around, prepared to put a crossbow arrow through the eyes of the zombie.

It's my mom.

She's the zombie.

A mombie.

I always knew she was undead. It explains everything.

I lift the crossbow, preparing to put her out of her misery. It'll do us both some good.

"Chazzzztiiiiiiiiiiteeeeee." She claws savagely at the glass.

"Do it!" Lance shouts.

I can't do it.

I lower the crossbow.

"Do it, Chastity! Kill your mom!"

I can't.

Mombie's withered face explodes with rage and she punches through the glass, grabbing me by the throat.

I scream.

She starts choking me, her grip impossibly strong.

I panic.

"Let her fucking go!" Lance growls, trying to break Mombie's grip, but it's too strong.

I start to black out.

I'm going to die.

In my dream.

A faint thought crosses my mind: if you die in your dream, you die in real life.

Fear takes hold and I fight for my life. I have to break Mom's grip, or this is it.

"Fight her, Chastity!" Lance shouts, his face full of emotion.

I'm trying, but she's too strong...

The color leaches out of my vision. My ears start to ring.

The world goes gray.

Then black...

"Chastity!"

I shoot up in bed like a sprung mousetrap, clutching my chest, convinced I have already had a heart attack and am now dying.

My bedroom is dark.

I can't hear my heart.

Every muscle in my body is frozen with panic.

All I hear is complete and utter—

"Chastity!" A voice hisses outside my window, scaring me half to death. Make that three-quarters since I was already halfway there. "Chastity!"

I stumble out of bed and whip my drapes open.

Lance.

He's sans crossbow and shaggy hair. But he still looks like Prince Charming knocking at my window, only this prince rides a motorcycle instead of a horse and is covered in tattoos instead of shining armor.

I sag with relief and pull the sliced up window screen aside. I stick my head out the window and whisper, "What are you doing here?"

"I can't sleep."

"I can," I frown, "Get out of here! I was having a great dream!"

"It was about me, wasn't it?"

"No!" What is it with men and their egos? "Would you leave already? My mom will shoot you if she sees you in our backyard."

"Does she have a gun?"

"No."

"Then I'm fine."

"She has a crossbow," I lie.

"Bullshit."

"Get out of here, Lance! I'm serious."

"Can we talk?"

"Not now! Try me in the afternoon." I don't know how much longer I can resist him. He looks incredible wearing nothing but jeans. I'm on the verge of inviting the sexy vampire inside once again.

"Why so late?"

"I have church in the morning. So if you would be so kind as to let me sleep, I might be able to stay awake. Mom hates it when I snore during the sermon."

"I can go with you."

"To church? You?"

He nods, "Sure. It might be fun."

"*Fun*? Church isn't supposed to be *fun*."

"Why not?"

I shake my head, "Would you quit arguing with me and let me go to sleep?"

"Please. I really need to talk."

"Really?"

"Yeah."

"You're serious?"

"Yeah."

I take a deep breath. "Okay. Hold on a second. I'll meet you out front. On the sidewalk." I grab a bathrobe and tiptoe out of my bedroom. I hesitate at the front door. What will Mom do if she wakes up and finds me outside talking to Lance in our driveway in the middle of the night?

Who cares?

I'm eighteen.

I grin as I open the front door as quietly as possible and pad onto the front porch on bare feet. It sure is warm out.

"Hey," he whispers from the shadows, sitting on the porch swing, his arm draped over the back.

There's room for me on that swing. My desire to curl up beside him is intense. I would do anything to sway under the stars with him, talking until the sun comes up. But it's too close to the house. "We can't talk here. It'll wake Mom. Let's talk in front of your house."

"Sure."

He grabs my hand without a thought and walks me to the street.

I'm floored he's holding my hand like we're... I don't know. But I like it. A lot. After last night's disaster, I thought he'd never touch me again.

"How's your sister? What'd the doctors say?"

"She's fine." I'm touched he cares. "Just needs to rest."

He runs his free hand nervously through his hair. "Good. I'm really sorry about what happened."

"Don't be. It was an accident. And you saved her." Images of Charity flailing spasmodically in the electrified pool prickle my brain. I shiver and bunch my robe together with my free hand.

"You cold?"

"Yeah," I lie. Right now, I just want to be held.

He pulls me against his chest and I melt into him. His naked pecs ripple against my cheek as his arms wrap around my waist. We're skin to skin. I feel his heat and hear his heartbeat and it's wonderful. I could stand here all night. Who knew the sidewalk could be so romantic?

"Anyway, sorry about what happened," Lance sighs.

"Your dad was drunk, wasn't he?"

"Yup."

"Where did he get the alcohol? We didn't have any and he was at our house all day."

"Did you see his AriZona Iced Tea bottle?"

"That's right! Was it full of alcohol?"

"Yup. Whiskey."

"I never would've known. With the label covering the whole bottle, you can't even tell what's in it!"

Lance nods, "He's clever like that. Too bad he's a total fuckup when it comes to everything else."

"It's not your fault. What he did, I mean. He's your Dad. He should be watching out for you, you know?"

His face knots into a sour snarl. "Yeah. Something like that."

"Chastity!" Mom hisses. "What are you doing out of bed?! It's the middle of the night!"

Mother *fluffer*.

I guess she didn't get the memo that I'm a legal adult and can do whatever I want now.

Lance releases me and we turn to face her as she strides down the driveway, belting her ankle-length robe around the ankle-length nightgown she sleeps in.

"What are *you* doing here?" Mom demands of Lance.

He smirks. "Doing where? We're on the sidewalk in front of *my* house."

"*Your* house. It's a rental," Mom scoffs with disgust and rolls her eyes. "Chastity, get inside."

"No," I bark.

Record needle screech.

Mom cocks her head, "What?" Somehow, she manages to enunciate every letter in the word.

"I said no." I say it firmly but calmly.

"You get in that house right now, young lady."

"I'm not young. I'm eighteen."

She whips her eyes at Lance. "This was your idea, wasn't it? Telling her she can do anything she wants now that she's all of eighteen?"

He shrugs calmly, "She can."

"Not while she's living in my house, she can't."

"Yes I can, Mom," I say stridently, struggling to stay calm.

Her eyes bug and a crazy smile wrinkles her mouth. "Ohhhhh, *that's* right. You're an *adult* now. *Alllllll* grown up."

"Well, no, but—"

She ignores me. "I imagine you know everything now. Your ignorant mother has nothing of value to add to your life. You probably have your own apartment lined up already so you can move out any day now and start paying your own bills and do everything else on your own. Does that sound about right?"

"What are you talking about, Mom? I'm not moving out. I—"

"You're acting like you're ready too. I would *hate* to do anything to stand in your way. I'm just your useless mother with her useless rules that you don't need to obey anymore. Isn't that so?"

"Mom, I—"

"I also imagine your job at Marble Slab will cover the cost of health care *and* rent *and* utilities *and* grocery bills *and*—"

"Mom! Stop!"

"Me stop? You're the one who won't stop." Her eyes dare me to disagree.

She didn't waste any time making me look like a foolish little girl in front of Lance. A grimace creeps onto my face. I can't help it. Mom is nuts.

"Go inside, Chastity. It's very late and you need your sleep. We have church tomorrow." She turns toward the house as if it's a foregone conclusion I'll follow her.

"No, Mom!"

She spins around. "No? No what?"

"I'm not going! We can skip church for once. Charity almost *died*. Luckily Lance saved her." I throw that in just to spite her. "It was a really long night and we should sleep in. For once. We'll go to church next week. When Charity is up for it."

"We will, will we? Now you're the parent too?" She gasps comically, pressing arched fingers to her chest, completely unaware of how prideful she's being. "I never realized eighteen automatically qualified you to do your mother's job."

"I'm not trying to do your job. I'm just trying to talk sense. You do what you want in the morning, but I think Charity will thank you if you let her skip church and sleep in. Come to think of it, you seem like you could use some rest yourself. You're acting a little crazy."

"Oh, that's just terrific." She shakes her head. "Are you parenting *me* now?"

I huff. "No. I'm just saying—"

"Then I suggest you not try and parent your sister either. And since you've been an adult for all of four hours, maybe you should leave the parenting to me for the time being. We will *not* skip church in the morning. Not after the mercy the Heavenly Father has shown us tonight. We need to show our gratitude. I'll allow your sister to stay home so she can recover after the... incident, but you and I should be there bright and early so *you* can pray for your sister and *I* can pray for you."

"For me? Why?"

Her eyes snap toward Lance, "If you can't see it, then all the more reason for you to be in the house of the Lord on *his* day so you can reflect on your latest transgressions and ask Him for forgiveness."

"What are you talking about, Mom? I didn't even do anything. You make it sound like I'm some sort of criminal."

"You may not be a criminal, but when you lie down with wolves..." She grins.

"Lie down? What's that supposed to mean?" I growl. She didn't find out about me and Lance, did she? Charity wouldn't have told her, would she? No, she would never do that. Besides, she didn't have time before she got shocked. Who else knew? Gina from church? Did she pass Lance on her way back to the patio? Did she follow him and listen in on the whole thing? She could have. Maybe she told Mom? I don't know.

A superior smile eases onto Mom's face. "I thought you were eighteen. I thought you knew everything." Her sarcasm is over the top. She snorts self-righteously, "Whose idea was the music anyway? It wasn't mine. I distinctly remember we agreed on no music. Was it your idea, Lance?" She glares at him.

I cringe. She's right on both counts. I jump in before she starts attacking him. It's the least I can do. "He may have suggested it, but I agreed to it. I said it was okay."

"You said it was okay," Mom nods gleefully. "Because you're the parent. I forgot. I'm just nothing, right?"

I chew my lip, gathering my thoughts. "If you're the parent, why didn't you make Lance take his DJ gear home?"

"Because you and Lark railroaded me."

"I thought you were the parent," I sneer. "And why did you spend all night dancing with Mr. McKnight? You could've sent him home too. Then Charity wouldn't have got shocked. But noooo, *you* were having too much fun dancing with Mr. McKnight, weren't you?" Now I'm just trying to hurt her.

She narrows her eyes, her face tight with fury. "Get inside. We're done. You're going to church tomorrow, and that's final."

I stand my ground. "No."

"Inside. Now."

"No." I fold my arms across my chest.

She lashes out, clawing at my arm. *"You get inside this instant!!"*

I jump back, "No, Mom! What is wrong with you?!"

She claws for me again.

Lance steps between us, "Easy, Mrs. Shields."

"Get your hands off me!!" Mom barks at him.

He didn't even touch her, but he holds his palms up and backs away cautiously.

"You did this to her," she growls at him, pointing her finger at him like a pistol. "She was never this *willful* before today."

"I didn't do shit," Lance chuckles.

"Watch your language! How many times do I have to tell you?"

"I'm not your kid, so you can shut the fuck up about the language."

Startled, Mom tucks her head into her shoulders like a turtle for a second before rabbiting at him. "Don't you talk to me like that!"

"I'm gonna talk any fucking way I want," Lance says. "You think I can brainwash your daughter in one day after eighteen years of parenting from you? You're nuts. Your daughter is stronger than that. You may not see it, but I do."

I swell with pride hearing Lance talk about me with admiration and dare I say respect? I try not to smile.

Lance continues, "She's not going to do anything she doesn't wanna do, no matter what I say. You can tell her what to do all you want, but she's eighteen and that means things are going to change. Get used to it, Faith. She's your daughter. Not your baby."

"What do you know about parenting? You're a child."

He raises an eyebrow with cocky confidence. "Am I?"

"You don't have any responsibilities. You don't know what it's like to take care of someone. You don't know—"

"Shut the fuck up, Faith. You're talking way outta line. You don't know shit about me."

She grimaces, "You call me Mrs. Shields!"

"I'll call you whatever the fuck I want." Lance looks ready to blow.

I'm suddenly worried they'll attack each other. "Stop it, you guys! This is stupid! We're fighting in the middle of the street at four in the morning!"

Mom sneers, "And whose fault is that, Chastity?"

I sigh and roll my eyes. I can't win and I'm tired of listening to her rant. She's going to keep harping away until I cave anyway, whether in front of Lance or in private. "I give up, Mom. You're right. It's all my fault. The party, the music, Charity, everything. We'll go to church tomorrow, okay? Bright and early." I stare at her, trying not to look as irritated as I feel. Someone needs to be the grown-up tonight. "But let Charity sleep in."

Finally, her face relaxes a fraction. "Of course," she smiles victoriously.

She didn't win anything. At least this way I'll get a few hours sleep before we have to get up.

Mom is already strolling toward the house, her body shaking between joy and rage. She stops at the porch and waits for me. "Say goodnight, Chastity."

Now she's being all polite and nicey-nice? What a hypocrite. Facing Lance, I grimace for his benefit, unwilling to obey Mom's orders. I'm half tempted to flip her off and stay outside with Lance. But I'm too tired. "Sorry about all this," I mutter.

"It's cool. I'll catch you later." Something in his cold tone tells me this most certainly is not cool, and he might not bother ever catching me again.

"Good night," I whisper, distraught.

Lance is already trudging toward his front door. If he heard me, he doesn't acknowledge it.

Chapter 11

CHASTITY

"We're late for church," Mom grumbles, startling me when she shakes me awake the next morning.

"I told you we should've skipped church!" I groan, my eyes still closed. I flop over in bed, giving her my back. Either someone stuck my head in a vise or I have a splitting headache.

"Get up and get ready to go. We're not *skipping church*," she mimics disdainfully. "And get a move on. You have ten minutes."

I shower and dress with my eyes closed. I'm not even sure what I'm wearing as I stumble to the car.

Mom drives. Halfway to church, she says, "I don't think it's a good idea for you to spend any more time with Lance."

Her words stab me awake. I cringe, my eyes half open. "I was asleep, Mom. Can we talk about this later?"

"No. We talk about this now." Her voice has that... tone.

I'm sick of that tone. I heard enough of it last night. I snap, "No, we fucking don't, Mom. I'm not having a fight right before church." I can't believe I just said fuck to my mom. I've never even said it out loud before. I mean, before last night.

The car lurches and she pulls over in a rush. A car behind us blares its horn. Mom parks in the first available space in front of an auto mechanic place on Vanowen Street. Cars whiz by.

"What did you just say?" She digs her fingernails into my wrist, breaking the skin.

"Ow!" I holler. "Let go!"

She shakes my arm, "You do not talk to me like that and you do not tell me what to do. Ever." Her eyes are knives.

I twist my arm free and rub the red half moons marking my wrist. I'm furious. "Do you really want to have a fight right before church? Because I will *so* go there."

"No you will *not*. I am your mother and you will treat me with respect."

I look out the side window, my face hot with rage. "Then treat me with some respect." I close my eyes, wishing she would go away.

Vicious claws yank my hair. "I'm tired of your defiance, Chastity!! If you want to live in *my* house, you have to follow *my* rules!!" She's pulling on my head.

"Let go of my hair, you bitch! I don't want to live in your house!" The words are out before I can stop them.

She flings her fistful of my hair in my face. "Then maybe you'd like to go live somewhere else!"

"Sounds like a great idea," I snarl.

"Fine. Then I'll expect you to start packing the minute we get home from church." She thinks she's calling my bluff.

"Why wait?" I kick the car door open and step onto the curb. "Have fun at church. Crazy bitch!"

"Chastity! You get back in this car!"

I slam the door in her face and start walking home. If she comes after me, so help me…

I listen closely, waiting for her to run up behind me.

The engine of Mom's car revs and fades into the distance.

I turn around and watch her drive off.

My stomach knots.

Whir.

What did I just get myself into?

I wasn't planning on moving out *this* soon.

Maybe I should call Dad. He would let me live with him. But that means moving to Illinois. Not unless I can take Charity with me. And Lance. Maybe I can crash at Lark's apartment. I'm sure her mom would understand. She knows how weird my mom is.

I look up and down Vanowen. Cars go by in both directions.

Unfortunately, none of them are going to stop and give me a ride and I can't call anybody because Mom insists I leave my phone at home when we go to church. Out of habit, I don't have it. But I need to get back to the house so I can pack.

Hmmm.

It's a long walk home.

Maybe I should wait for a bus.

I just don't know which bus to take.

Whatever.

I can walk. It's only a couple of miles.

My empty stomach burbles as I walk.

Whir.

I should've eaten something before we left. Or at least drunk some water. I'm dehydrated already and it's getting hot. Oddly, I'm getting clammy and chilled. No use crying about it.

I march toward home.

Mom is insane.

++++8++++

CHASTITY

I knock on Lance's front door. I didn't bother to go home first. When no one answers, I knock again. Footsteps thud behind the door. My heart fills with hope and starts to flutter. All I want right now is Lance. Now I'm the one who needs to talk to *him*. I probably woke him. Hopefully he won't tell me to leave.

The front door opens.

"Yeah?" Mr. McKnight stands there in sagging whitey-not-so-tightey underwear and nothing else. His hair stands straight up and he looks confused. Despite his dishevelment, his resemblance to Lance is uncanny.

"Uhhh… Is Lance here?"

"I don't know. Lemme check." He turns to walk away then turns back to me. "Charity, right?"

"No. I'm Chastity."

"That's right." Only he doesn't sound too sure of himself.

Did he forget my name already? He spent two whole days with us. A normal person would remember it. And what about Charity? Did he forget last night too? I don't see how. Last night, he was worried about her. Maybe he forgot because he was so drunk. I hear that can happen.

"Be right back." He leaves the door standing open.

I grimace when I see the hole in the butt of his underwear. I turn away until he's gone. I'm tempted to walk inside, but succumbing to temptation has gotten me in enough trouble already. I wait.

A minute later, he returns, hopping into view while trying to jam his leg into a rumpled pair of jeans. He starts to topple, on the verge of smashing face-first into the tiled floor.

"Careful!" I blurt, hands out.

He catches his balance by hopping several times, then hikes his jeans up, buttoning them without bothering to zip them. "You wanna come in?"

Not really. "Is Lance here?" Did he forget I asked?

"I don't think so."

The house isn't that big. I chuckle, "Uhhhhh, do you know where he went?"

"Hold on a sec." He walks away and returns a minute later holding a bottle of green mouthwash at his side. The bottle has no cap on it.

I wait for him to say something about Lance.

He stares at me sleepily. Believe it or not, he looks more tired than I feel. "What did you want again?"

"Lance? Do you know where he went?"

He looks up thoughtfully. "Not really." He lifts the mouthwash to his mouth and gulps some. He swirls it around for awhile then stares at me, his cheeks puffed out, his lips wet.

"Do you need to go spit that out?"

He closes his eyes and swallows it. "I'm fine."

I bite my lower lip, cringing. "I don't think you're supposed to swallow mouthwash."

"I didn't." he says, his voice hoarse.

"I just—" my voice fades to a whisper, "…saw you." Is he crazy?

"Lance isn't here."

"I know. You, um, said that already."

"Yeah."

This is really weird. "I should go. If you see Lance, can you tell him I stopped by?"

"Yeah." He just stands there looking at me.

"Oooookaaaaay. Bye." I back up carefully toward the driveway.

Mr. McKnight never takes his eyes off me. It's only weird because it's like I'm not even there. He looks right through me, not even seeing me.

It's the creepiest thing ever.

And somehow the saddest.

I've never known an alcoholic before, but I think one moved in next door.

Does that mean Lance is an alcoholic too?

The thought scares me.

Maybe Mom was right. Maybe I don't want anything to do with the McKnights.

No, that can't be right.

Lance isn't a drunk.

I mean, as far as I know.

Is he as clever as his dad? Does he just hide it better?

Oh, gosh. I have no idea.

But I can't escape the feeling that I just fell into something way over my head.

++++8++++

CHASTITY

"Where's Mom?" Charity asks, sitting across from me at the kitchen table eating a PB&J sandwich she made for herself. "She's really late."

I'm too nervous to eat. "Probably still at church. Eat your sandwich. I'm sure she'll be here soon."

The service ended two hours ago. Mom probably went to the luncheon afterward. We often go. There's really no reason to worry. But today is different because I'm dreading the conversation we're going to have when she gets home. If Lance had been home, I would've taken him up on that motorcycle ride he offered me the other day and insisted we make it an all day road trip. The last thing I want to do is face off with Mom again.

A text from Lance comes in on my phone.

Can I borrow your mom's crossbow? I need to use it to shoot somebody.

Me: **Who?**

I'm hoping he says my mom. Not really.

Him: **Long story. What r you doing later?**

Me: **I'm busy.**

Him: **Right. Me 2.**

Me: **No, I'm serious. I have to work today.**

Him: **On a Sunday? What kind of place makes you work Sunday?**

I hesitate for a second. I secretly think my job is as lame as my nickname, but I would never tell anybody because I'm grateful to have it. Oh well, Lance will probably find out eventually.

Me: **At an ice cream parlor.**

Him: **I'm totally coming by for a sundae, since it's Sunday. Can you hook me up?**

Me: **What, like a discount?**

Him: **No, like free?**

My bosses Mr. and Mrs. Molton own the shop and they aren't exactly rich so they discourage freebies. I type out: **Don't you have any money?** But I don't send it. Remembering the McKnight's lack of furniture and Mr. McKnight's weirdness makes me wonder if maybe they're really broke and Lance can't actually afford a five dollar ice cream. Maybe he can't. So I text: **Sorry. We don't do giveaways. But I think I can get you a coupon.**

Him: **No worries.**

After five minutes, he hasn't responded. Did I offend him? Maybe he really is broke? I'm about to bang out a quick explanation when my phone chimes.

Him: **What time you work?**

Me: **4-10pm. We close at 9.**

Him: **What's it called?**

Me: **Marble Slab Creamery. There's only one. You can Google it.**

Him: **Found it. I'll swing by before you close.**

My eyes light with joy. I was starting to worry Lance might never want to see me again after all the drama last night.

Me: **Ok. C u later.**

I set my phone down, ecstatic.

Mom's Toyota pulls into the driveway a second later, spoiling my mood.

"Mom's home," Charity says casually. I didn't tell her what happened in the car.

"Yeah," I sigh. I consider sneaking out the back door and hopping the fence and going anyplace but here. Keys jingle in the front door. My stomach knots. The front door opens. My chest locks, making it hard to breathe. Footsteps in the entryway. I swallow hard, my throat clicking. When is she going to explode? The dread is killing me.

Mom walks into the kitchen holding grocery bags, which she sets on the counter. "Hello, Charity. How are you feeling?"

"Fine," Charity says.

"That's wonderful. Do you feel rested?"

"I guess."

"How late did you sleep?"

It's totally weird that Mom is pretending I'm not here. Usually she just starts screaming at me.

"I don't know," Charity says. "Ten?"

"That's great. Have you had any symptoms the doctor told us to watch for?"

"No. Why aren't you talking to Chastity?"

I grin to myself. I love my sister.

"Who?"

Charity rolls her eyes. "Chastity. She's right in front of you."

"Oh!" Mom feigns surprise. "You're still here. I thought you had moved out."

My face sours. "Nope. Still here. How was church?"

Mom hikes her eyebrows. "Well, I don't know, Chastity. But if you'd gone, you would know, wouldn't you?"

It's nearly impossible not to roll my eyes.

Mom glares at me as she walks to the refrigerator and starts transferring groceries inside.

I get up to help.

"I've got it," she barks. "Since you won't be living here, I'll have to do it from now on, won't I?"

"I'll help," Charity sighs as she gets up from the table.

Again, love my sister.

Mom purses her lips and watches Charity unload the groceries.

Charity understands what Mom is doing and she's trying to defuse.

Mom plants her fists on her hips and stares at me. "I had a lot of time to think about our conversation while at church today."

I want to say, *Shouldn't you have been praying?*

"And it occurred to me, now that you're an adult, it's time you started living like one. You can either move out today or you can start paying rent. I was thinking four hundred a month. I did some checking on Craigslist this morning before church. That's quite a deal for a room in this part of the Valley. I won't even charge you for utilities."

Whir.

My stomach sours. I still haven't eaten yet but now I have no appetite.

I hate the fact Mom is one step ahead of me. After getting home and cooling off, I called Lark. She didn't answer, so I called her mom, who said Lark is at the beach all day. So I looked up apartment rentals online. Mom is right. I can barely afford the cost of living on my own with what I make at Marble Slab.

"Okay," I sigh. "I'll move out."

Mom is startled. She wasn't expecting that.

Neither was I.

Hopefully she doesn't expect me to move today, but if she's gonna be like that, I'll drive to Lark's and wait for her. Her mom will probably let me crash at their apartment long enough to find my own place. I hope.

Charity stops in her tracks, clutching a quart of half & half, "You can't make Chastity move out!" The panic and frustration in her voice is impossible to miss. She hates the idea of living here alone with Mom. We've talked about it more than once. But we might not have a choice.

Mom says, "Charity, this is between your sister and I."

Charity shakes the carton of half & half for emphasis. "No it's not! We're a family! You can't make Chastity move out!"

I want to cry because of how Charity is standing up for me.

"You're pushing her away just like you pushed Dad away!"

Mom looks pained. "I didn't push your father away! He—"

"You did too! You're always telling us how bad Dad is! Now you're pushing away Chastity too! Are you going to push me away next?! Maybe I should go live with Dad before you do!"

Silence.

Nobody says anything for a long time.

Mom is obviously shocked by Charity's words. She's not sure what to do. She shifts her weight to her other hip and blinks her eyes several times, frustrated, irritated, and probably a little bit hurt. She gazes up at the ceiling, her lips moving minutely, praying. After a moment, she closes her eyes, takes a deep breath, and glares at me. "Fine. We'll discuss this later. But until I make a decision, I want to make one thing *perfectly* clear to both of you."

We both stare at Mom, waiting.

"I don't want either of you having *any* contact with the McKnights." She shoots a look at Charity. "And I mean *none*. I don't want to see either of *them* anywhere near either of *you*, or this house. Am I making myself clear?"

I scoff, "Good luck with that. They live next door." I say it like she's insane, because she is, despite how calm she's acting.

"Mom, why are you being like this?" Charity demands. "Lance saved my life!" She's mad, her eyes on fire.

Mom is now twice as frustrated as she was a second ago. She shakes her head like her brain is popping like hot popcorn and she can't stop it. She yells, "*Just!! Don't!!*"

"Why?!" Charity demands.

"It doesn't matter why! I don't want you interacting with them! At all! Do you hear me?!"

"*YOU'RE CRAZY, MOM!!*" Charity screams, her voice shrill enough to shatter glass. She throws the carton of half & half on the floor. Cream blows out the end and sprays across the hardwood floor. She storms out of the kitchen and slams her bedroom door.

Mom is silent.

I hide a smile. *That happened.*

Mom shakes her head, completely exasperated, and almost turns to me with a look of commiseration on her face that says, "*Can you believe her?*" But she stops herself at the last second, ignoring me instead. She grabs paper towels and the trash can and squats to clean up the mess.

I slip out of the kitchen while Mom is distracted.

"We're not finished, young lady," she says to my back right before my foot touches down in the hallway.

"I have to get ready for work."

"Fine. We'll talk about this later," she warns.

"I'm looking forward to it," I whisper.

"What did you say?" she demands, her voice ice.

"Nothing."

Whir.

Chapter 12

CHASTITY

"Mr. Molton? Is there any way I can get more hours this week?"

He peels the lid off a fresh tub of mint chocolate chip and lowers it into the display freezer at work. "You've had twenty-five hours a week all summer. I was planning on cutting you back to fifteen starting next week."

"Oh, geez. Really?"

"With the summer rush over, that's all I really need. You know how things slow down once school starts."

"Right. Um, are you sure?"

He smiles, "You know I'd love to. But we can't afford it. I'll be covering your hours myself."

I sigh. "Okay."

"Is something wrong?"

Do I tell him? No. Can I hold it together and act like being on the verge of thrown out is no big deal? I doubt it. But I'll try. "No. Everything's fine."

He rests a comforting hand on my shoulder. His eyes are friendly. "You can tell me, Chaz."

I've known Mr. Molton since I was a kid. I got this job two years ago because he goes to my church. Mom knows him too. I blink back tears and look away. "My mom wants me to move out. We're fighting. It's serious."

"I'm sorry to hear that." He sighs thoughtfully. "Can you work it out? Maybe if you talk to her..."

"I really don't think so." I sniffle and wipe away tears. I grab a paper towel from the back and blow my nose before automatically washing my hands in the sink.

"I'll talk to my wife and see if maybe we have a little wiggle room on your hours. But I can't promise anything."

I nod vigorously, more tears threatening to spill. I sniff them back. "That would be great."

Luckily, an entire girls softball team pours in with their parents, distracting me from my thoughts. Serving twenty-five flavors of ice cream loaded with candy, cookies, chocolate chunks, peanut butter cups, jelly beans, gummy worms, gum balls, all drenched in five different flavors of hot fudge or caramel and topped with heaps of whipped cream to wide eyed kids for whom ice cream is heroin and cavities are an afterthought, always puts a smile on my face.

It's the simple things.

An hour later, the phone in back rings. Mr. Molton answers it and walks out a minute later, frightened of something. "Chastity, I have to go. Caden fell off his bicycle. Amy is taking him to the hospital." His worry is catching.

"That's terrible," I gasp. "Is it serious?"

"I don't know. I need to meet them at the Emergency Room. Can you handle things here?"

"Of course. Go. I've got everything covered. Give Caden a kiss for me. I hope he's okay."

He nods gravely, "Me too. Thank you, Chaz." He squeezes my arm. "You're a lifesaver." He throws a light jacket on over his Marble Slab polo shirt and strides out the front door, keys in hand.

When the softball team is finally gone, I busy myself cleaning tables before more customers show up. The team left a mess. I toss empty ice cream cups into the trash and sweep wrinkled napkins into the long handled dust pan.

Bing!

The front door chime.

Someone walks into the shop, but I'm busy using the tip of the broom to scrape up a stubborn ice cream soaked napkin that's glued to the tiles, so I don't check who it is. "Welcome to Marble Slab Creamery, I'll be right with you! What the—!" The someone just pinched my butt! I spin around, broom ready to strike.

Lance. Grinning. And already dodging back from the broom. "Easy, samurai."

"I should hit you." But he's too handsome to hit. So I shake the broom in his face as a warning. With a smile.

"I bet you're lethal with that thing, Pink."

"Care to find out?"

"No. I'll take your word for it." He stares at my chest. "You're pink again, Pink."

"Oh. The shirt. It's the uniform."

"Looks good on you. Love the shoes." He glances at my matching pink Keds.

I roll my eyes and rest the broom on the tiles like a spear. "To what do I owe this, *ahem*, pleasure?"

"Came for my sundae. On Sunday." He winks.

"That's right! What kind would you like? Oh wait. You have money, right?"

He smirks. "Of course."

"Perfect. What would you like?"

"You pick. Gimme something that'll blow my mind." His eyes flame and I'm instantly tingling.

Usually this place is my element, but with Lance watching, I'm all thumbs. I drop a scoop of ice cream on the floor, which I hastily clean up only to knock over the jelly beans. They clatter everywhere and roll off the counter, falling to the floor, rolling into every corner. "I can't believe I did that." I grab the broom and start sweeping.

"Relax. I'll help you clean them up." He walks behind the counter.

"Wait! You can't be back here. No customers."

"You sure?" He steps toward me.

"Stop."

He doesn't. He saunters forward until he pins me against the marble slab on the counter. It's chilled to a frigid 27 degrees, so it bites my back. But I barely notice because Lance is a hot wall of fire right in my face.

I grab an ice cream scoop from the bucket and hold it up to Lance's chin like a knife.

He arches an eyebrow. "You gonna cut me with that?"

"Try me."

"You're fuckin hot when you act dangerous."

My face bounces between laughter and irritation. "Okay."

"I'm gonna have to fuck you." He says it like it's punishment.

I jam the blade of the scoop into the crook of his jaw.

"You know I have a death wish, so go for it."

"Do you really?"

Rattlesnake fast he snaps the ice cream scoop out of my hand.

"Hey!"

He grins. Then he runs the dome of the scoop down my Marble Slab polo shirt, between my breasts. Then he cups my right boob with the scoop and lifts experimentally. "You really do have perfect fucking tits." He lifts the left one. "If I could eat them, I would." His devil's grin appears. "That gives me an idea."

"What?"

"In the back."

"Huh?"

"Get in the back of the store."

"We're still open!"

"You've got that doorbell thing. We'll hear if anyone comes in."

"No!"

"Yes." He slaps the scoop against my butt and jerks me toward him. He's already hard in his jeans. "Now turn around and march."

"Lance," I press.

"Now."

"Fine." I spin around. "Are you sure you'll hear the chime?"

"Yes. Now march." He slaps my butt with the scoop.

Why do I feel like I'm walking to my own ice cream execution or something? I don't know. But I trust Lance.

He grabs a whipped cream canister off the counter top.

"What's that for?"

"I'll give you zero guesses. Keep marching."

"You're weird."

"It's my key appeal."

I shake my head and my ponytail waves down my back.

"Take that stupid baseball cap off. It looks like shit."

Before I can remove it, he pulls it off and it sails across the back store room and lands on top of one of the industrial refrigerators behind some napkin boxes. "Hey!"

"I'll get it later." He kicks the store room door closed.

"Don't let it close all the way. I need to hear the chime."

He stops it with his toe, leaving it open a few inches. "That okay?"

"Yeah."

Lance may be considerate, but he is dangerous. Everywhere he goes, he disrupts things. There's this sense that whatever he touches goes bouncing off in a new and unpredictable direction, like a cue ball hitting a rack of billiard balls at a hundred miles an hour. There's no way to know how things are going to end up. For all you know, those billiard balls might jump off the table and shatter a window or roll right out the front door into oncoming traffic where they'll get pulverized under the wheels of a cement truck.

Yup, Lance is the walking incarnation of risk.

I'm game.

On a day like today, I need the distraction.

He heaves me onto the stainless steel prep counter and I land on my butt. He shakes the whipped cream can in his hand vigorously, grinning.

I smirk, "I bet you have a lot of practice doing that."

"Whacking off? Not really."

"Why not?"

"Because."

I'm waiting for him to make some joke about not masturbating because he has sex with thousands of woman on an hourly basis.

"Because…" I prompt.

"Because what?"

"You know." Why am I torturing myself like this? I don't really want to know his sexual history. Do I? Maybe I should. He did tell me his life is thirty-one flavors of crazy. Yeah, it's better I know. "Because…"

"Shut up." He squirts a fat dollop of whipped cream over my lips.

"Mmph!"

He leans forward and licks it, taking forever to get to my lips.

I stick my tongue out.

"Don't. I'm not done with the whipped cream." He smacks his lips. "This is some tasty shit. Better than the junk at the grocery store."

"I know, it's—"

Pblpblfft!

More whipped cream splatters my face.

His eyes sizzle. "Now I have to start over. Sit there and don't move."

I'm about to tell him I'm going to go get my samurai broom, but his gorgeous grin disarms me.

Standing between my khakis, he shifts his weight from boot to boot before leaning in slowly to lick the whipped cream and tickle my lips.

I wait patiently until he finally slips his tongue in my mouth. It's sweet with cream.

He grabs my ponytail like a rope and tugs on my head, exposing my neck. He sure loves neck.

Vampire.

He licks down one side and up the other before skimming along my jaw. He's really good at making out because it's a summer rain in my panties.

I let out a little moan when he circles my ear.

"Your hair smells like vanilla."

I giggle, my eyes closed, "It's the shop."

"Do your tits taste like caramel?"

"Um, I don't think so."

"Take your shirt off. And your bra."

"Lance! We're still open!"

"Nobody's here. It's dinner time. Nobody eats ice cream until after dinner."

"That's not true! We have—"

"I want you naked when I come back." He opens the store room door.

"Where are you going?"

"Stop asking so many questions." He closes the door behind him.

This is a really bad idea. But I am drenched and all that whipped cream kissing has me shaking with desire. I tear my polo shirt and bra off in a frenzy and set both down in a neat pile on Mr. Molton's desk. Geez, what would he do if he found my bra on his desk? I don't even want to think about it. I suddenly feel terrible knowing he's—

The door snaps open and I reflexively cover my breasts.

"Don't cover them." Lance holds a bucket of warm caramel sauce and a long handled ladle. He lifts the ladle high and watches caramel drizzle back into the bucket. "I'm going to have a Chastity sundae."

My eyes goggle. "You can't be serious."

"Get back on the counter."

"This is ridiculous, Lance."

"I know. On the counter." He kicks the door closed with the bottom of his boot.

I reluctantly hop on top.

"Lean back on your hands."

I do.

He drizzles caramel into the dimple between my collar bones, then drops the ladle in the bucket and sets it down. The caramel is hot but not burning. He plants his hands on the counter and leans forward, dabbing his tongue into the caramel pool at the base of my neck. A little rivulet runs down my breast bone. Lance catches it with his tongue, then licks his way back up. "Mmmm, that tastes fucking good. Salty caramel and a hint of... perfection." He straightens and licks his lips. "I had no idea you went so well with caramel."

"Me neither." But my neck is sizzling where he licked it and my own salty goodness drips into my panties.

He ladles more caramel on my chest, spiraling it around my nipples in thin trails.

This is so wrong.

We're in a family ice cream shop, for goodness sake!

When he grabs my breasts and goes to town with his tongue all over my nipples, my head rolls back and I moan long and low.

Why does this feel so incredible?

I don't know, but he can do it all day.

When I'm licked clean, he pulls me toward him by the waist and we kiss. Caramel never tasted so good.

"More," he grunts and coats my breasts again. He feeds me a drink from the ladle.

I hesitate, thinking about how I'll have to wash the ladle afterward. I'll worry about it later. If I remember. I drink it down and the sugar high hits instantly.

"I forgot the whipped cream." He spurts a fluff on each nipple.

I laugh. "I must look ridiculous."

He takes a step back. "You look like the yummiest sundae I've ever eaten…"

"But you haven't—" I stop myself.

He grins, "Eaten you?"

I nod. I can't believe I'm doing this.

He unbuttons my khakis and I help as he drags them down to my knees, pulling my white panties with them. The stainless steel is cool against my naked butt. Better remember to wash the counter top too.

"What's on your mind?" he asks. "You're distracted."

"It's just… I work here. I have responsibilities."

"Your only responsibility right now is…" His fingers find my folds. "…to enjoy yourself."

That won't be a problem.

"Fuck, you're soaked."

"Mmmm-hmmm." Eyes closed, I bite my lip and moan as his fingers make magic, erasing all my worries. This feeling of freedom and letting go overwhelms me. When Lance's finger slips inside me, all the stress of the past two days disappears. I am in heaven again. With my own dirty devil.

His thumb circles my clit and the fingers inside me find a new spot I didn't know I had. Unique sweet pleasure floods through me.

"What are you doing?" I gasp, breathless.

"My job."

His fingers fuck me and rub that spot and I start to come.

"Stop."

My eyes open. "What? Why?"

"I'm going to fuck you."

That should scare me but it doesn't.

He unbuckles his belt one handed and yanks at his jeans. Frustrated, he pulls his hand out of me to push his pants and boxers down to his thighs.

The emptiness I feel is instantly disappointing. I bite my lip, hungering for him to fill me up again.

A condom from his pocket appears and he tears it open, rolling it on his cock. He yanks me toward the edge of the counter top and plows my entrance with the bottom of his shaft, his fist wrapped around the base, seesawing up and down.

We watch my folds part and curl like water around the motion of his rock hard cock.

He hisses, "Look at that caramel pussy. Fucking gorgeous."

His tip teases my entrance.

He eases in.

Slowly.

He's a tight fit, but I relax and feel him stretch me to the max. I can barely take him, but he goes slow. I expect pain, but there is none. When he's all the way in and his balls press against my butt, I moan.

"Fuck yeah." He starts to thrust. Rhythmically. Slowly. Sensually.

I gasp, breathy, "Does this mean I'm not a virgin anymore?"

"Not till we come. Together."

We lock eyes.

I nod. "Together."

He continues slowly. In and out like he's revealing the secrets of the universe. It feels so incredibly good.

I want this feeling to last forever.

Him inside me.

Fucking me.

And like that, something happens.

I have had many orgasms in my life. In private. This is completely different. The level of pleasure is overwhelming and I'm not even coming. I can't form a coherent thought. I'm obsessed by the simple motion of the in and out. I don't want to think about anything else ever again.

Just.

Fucking.

"This is my pussy," Lance grunts desperately. His eyes are crazy again, like last night when he snuck into the bathroom. He is an animal trapped in the body of a man. Or a monster. Whatever he is, he just needs to fuck me. "Nobody else is gonna touch this pussy ever again. Nobody." He sounds furious. "My virgin cunt. All fucking mine."

I can't quite make sense of what he's saying. The in and out is scrambling my brain. But some vague corner of my mind mutters, *We're not even dating. I don't know what we're doing other than having sex. This isn't even making love. It's ridiculous. It's just meaningless slut fucking.* But somehow, I don't care. I'm loving every dirty word he says and everything his dick is doing to me.

"Only I fuck this pussy. Ever. Nobody else. You come for me and only me. You understand?" He's growling in my ear through fanged teeth, his voice low and dangerous, thrusting into me deeper and deeper. "Say it! This is my fucking pussy!"

"Yes!" I hiss. "Only yours. Just yours. Fuck me, Lance. Please fuck me hard." He does, building up speed in slow motion until my entire body is on fire with ecstasy. I whimper and start to come.

"Now!" He grunts. "Fucking come!"

We come together. Screaming grunting dying our little deaths at the pinnacle of climax. It's the most powerful orgasm I've ever had. It gives whole new meaning to coming.

I think I'm hooked.

If this is what sex feels like, I want to have it again and again every day and night until I can't think straight.

I grab the back of his head. He cups my cheek. We kiss blindly, devouring each other, breathing hard, coming down slowly, lost in our passion.

Oh my goodness.

That's when it hits me.

I'm not a virgin anymore.

I can't imagine a better first time.

I will remember this moment forever.

"*WHAT IN GOOD GOD ARE YOU TWO DOING?!*" Mr. Molton roars, standing in the doorway of the store room, his face red rage.

Oh.

No.

"*YOU HAVE WHIPPED CREAM ALL OVER YOUR NIPPLES!*"

I want to laugh because *that's* what he notices? Not Lance's condom covered cock inside of me?

Unfortunately, I don't laugh because this is a disaster.

Chapter 13

CHASTITY

"THE CASH DRAWER IS EMPTY, CHASTITY!" Mr. Molton screams. Lance and I are throwing clothes on while Mr. Molton has a meltdown. "Where is all the MONEY?!"

"I don't know!" I whine, jerking my pants up.

"Why the hell were you back here fucking! This is my store, God damn it! We got robbed!"

I wince, clutching my bra and polo shirt in front of my breasts. "For real?"

"NO! For FAKE! Yes we got fucking ROBBED! Because you were back here SCREWING!!!! What in HELL is wrong with YOU!! My son is in the hospital and I trusted you to cover the shop while I was gone!!!!"

"I—I—I—" can't think of anything to say right now. *Nothing can explain my actions. What I did is unforgivable. I am a terrible person. I am a sinner. An adulteress. None of this would've happened if I hadn't—*I block out the Mom thoughts before my head explodes.

"Chastity, this is the worst kind of fuck up I can imagine!! You're FIRED!!!!"

Sheer horror strains my face. "No! You can't, Mr. Molton! I need this job!"

"If you needed this God DAMN job, why did you FUCK this DEGENERATE in MY store room on MY time?!" He shovels both palms toward Lance.

"Easy, buddy," Lance warns. "I'm not a degenerate."

"Then what the FUCK are you?! A THIEF?! Did YOU steal the money?! Or did you have a friend help?! Was that your plan? Get Chastity in the back and seduce her while you ROBBED me?!"

Oh no. Leaden dread bombs my stomach. Is that why Lance closed the door when I asked him not to? Did he steal the money when he was getting the caramel sauce? I am so gullible! I totally fell for it!!

Mr. Molton grabs Lance by the T-shirt and twists it in his hand. Lance is way bigger than Mr. Molton, but Mr. Molton is so angry he doesn't think twice.

"Step off," Lance growls.

"My son is in the hospital! He won't wake up! The doctors don't know what's wrong with him! Who are you to tell me what to do?!"

Oh, no! Caden must've really gotten hurt. I really am a horrible person. A terrible, selfish, short-sighted idiot.

Mr. Molton's face crumbles. "My son!" His hand relaxes and he releases Lance's shirt. "Get out of here. Both of you."

"Can I put my clothes on first?" I have my pants on but I'm still holding my bra and polo shirt over my chest.

Mr. Molton doesn't look at me. "Get dressed in the bathroom. Then get out of here."

I grab the key from behind the counter and hurry into the women's room to dress. I don't check myself in the mirror, just throw my bra on over the remaining smears of whipped cream and caramel sauce and pull my pink polo shirt over my head before rushing back to the front of the store. Everything is happening too quickly. I need to do something.

But there's nothing I can do except watch Mr. Molton unravel.

He stands behind the counter and grumbles to himself, "Why are there jelly beans all over the place? And why didn't the thieves take the change? Fucking IDIOTS!!" He picks up the black plastic cash tray from the register drawer and throws it against the tiled floor. It cracks and spins chaotically, throwing coins in every direction in a pinging dance that takes forever to settle.

A lone penny spins on its edge on the cold marble slab. Mr. Molton stares at it, leaning his hands against the edge, unaware of the icy cold marble. When the penny finally comes to rest, he breaks into sobs.

A woman with two little girls at her side leans her head in the door and says, "Are you open?"

Mr. Molton stares at her, shaking his head, tears running down his face.

The brown haired girl says, "Mommy, why is that man crying?"

"You might want to come back later," Lance says quietly.

The woman hurries off with her kids.

"Get out of here," Mr. Molton sobs.

"How much was in the drawer?" Lance asks him.

"What? I have no idea! Now get the hell out of here!"

"How much do you think was in the drawer? If you had to guess."

Mr. Molton stares.

"How much?"

Mr. Molton shakes his head, frustrated and irritated. "I don't know. It was a busy day. I hadn't cleared the drawer since we opened. So, a lot."

"How much?"

"Why do you care?"

"Because I didn't steal your money. How much?"

"I don't know. If you minus the change, the charges and debit cards, at least six or seven hundred dollars."

Lance pulls out his wallet and starts counting out bills. "Here's eight hundred and eighty. It's all I've got on me." He sets it gently on the counter.

I don't even want to think about why Lance has that much money in his wallet.

"Why are you doing this?" Mr. Molton chokes out.

"Because you got robbed. Let's go, Chastity." He gestures for me. "Come on. I think your boss needs to be alone."

I hurry across the shop and take Lance's hand.

He walks me outside until we're standing in front of his black motorcycle. "I'm taking you home."

I wince. "I really don't want to see my Mom right now. She'll want to know why I left work so early."

"Fine. We'll go someplace else. You hungry? It's dinner time."

"Not really."

"Cool. We'll just go somewhere. Anywhere but here."

"I kind of want to be alone right now. I'm really confused."

He stares at me.

I wince. "Is that bad?"

He shakes his head. He looks hurt.

"I'm sorry. We can—"

"Where do you usually go when you need alone time?"

"My room?"

"We can't take you there. How about a park. Is there a park around here somewhere?"

"Yeah. It's "

"Put this helmet on." He hands me one.

"Don't you need one?"

"I brought a spare." He screws his own helmet on his head and adjusts the strap. "I figured I'd pick you up. You guys only have one car, right?"

"Yeah. My mom's Toyota."

"It was in the driveway when I swung by the house, so I put two and two together and figured you'd need a ride home. Let me help you with that." He gently squishes my helmet on my head, flips up the visor, and adjusts the chin strap. "Not too tight?"

"No."

He lifts me up onto the bike like a feather then swings his leg over the seat. "I'll go slow. Hold on tight."

I wrap my arms around his waist and hug him, vaguely aware of the muscles beneath his T-shirt.

"Where are we going?" he hollers at a stoplight, head turned back toward me.

"Uh, let me think. I never go to the park. How about that one in North Hollywood? On Tujunga? Do you know where it is?"

"The one at Magnolia, right?"

"Yeah."

The ride to the park is gentler than my mom drives, which is super careful. We may as well be on a bicycle. Bicycles make me think of poor Caden which makes me nauseous. I push down the guilt for now, but I know it'll come up later.

Whir.

When we get to Tujunga, he parks the motorcycle in a metered space next to another motorcycle already in it.

He lifts me off the seat. "You still wanna be alone?"

"I just want to sit some place. That picnic table in the grass looks good."

"You want me to sit with you? I won't say anything."

"Sure."

The 170 freeway is visible from the park and Sunday cars blow by. For a neighborhood park, this one is pretty big, but the surrounding streets and apartments are visible in every direction. Two guys play frisbee on a wide patch of lawn. A woman jogs past with a spotted dog on a leash. A Mexican family surrounds the next table over. Rapid fire Spanish and laughter billows into the air, wafted up by the meaty smoke coming from the rugged public grill. Kids circle a battered piñata hanging from a nearby tree, taking swings. By LA standards, we're as alone as we're going to get.

I sit on top of a square cement table, hunched over with my arms folded across my waist and my ponytail dangling from one shoulder, feet on the bench. Lance sits to my right on the next bench, legs outstretched, rocking the heel of one boot side to side in the tamped down grass.

My emotions are a jumbled mess. Too many extremes in too short a time. Too high and too low. I can't deal with all this right now. I stuff everything down as deep as I can and just sit there, numb. Numbing out is a trick I learned after one too many screaming matches with Mom. Rage is draining. I hate it. Numbness is easier. But it doesn't stop the dentist's drill in my stomach.

Whir.

Or my thoughts.

They go right back to Caden. I hope he's okay.

Whir.

And Mr. Molton. I suck.

Whir.

I'll have to see Mr. Molton in church next Sunday. Unless I don't go. Maybe I should quit going altogether. The low hum in my stomach blossoms into nausea. It's the stress. The price of numbness. All that anxiety has to go somewhere. Mine likes to destroy my stomach.

Whir.

I mutter, "I feel sick."

"Are we still not talking?" Lance says softly.

"You can talk."

"Have you eaten anything today?"

"I'm not hungry."

"But have you eaten anything today?"

"You know what? I haven't eaten a thing since last night."

"Maybe you should have some Sprite or 7 Up or something. You might be dehydrated."

"Shoot, I haven't dranken anything since I walked home from church." I said dranken. I can barely think. I do need food.

"There's a 7-Eleven right across the street. I'll go get you something."

"I'll come with you."

He stands when I do. He lifts his hand like he's going to grab mine.

I blurt, "Did you steal that money?"

He drops his hand. His eyes shift from side to side doing a whole lot of looking everywhere but at me.

"Did you?"

His fiery eyes land on mine. "You watched me count my money out for your boss."

"So?"

"What kind of bills did I give him?"

I frown, "Stop dodging. Answer my question."

"What kind?"

I shrug, trying to picture it. "A bunch of hundreds and some twenties."

"Eight hundreds and four twenties. It was all I had on me."

"Who carries that kind of money around?"

"I do."

I lose it. "You don't even have any furniture!! You have a thrift store couch and you live out of moving boxes!!!! How am I supposed to believe you just happened to have that much money?! If you subtract the stolen money, you would've had like one or two hundred in your wallet! *That* I'd believe. But not eight whatever!!"

"What sort of bills do you usually have in your register?"

"You're avoiding the question."

"What. Sort. Of bills?" It's a question and a command.

Irritated, I scowl, "Lots of ones. Always more than you need. Fives, tens, twenties under the tray. Oh, ship."

He nods, smirking. "How many hundreds do you get in an afternoon?"

"Not eight."

And like that, I believe him.

My stomach starts to settle. What a relief.

I lean forward and grab his hand and lead him across the grass holding hands.

We J-walk between moving cars on Tujunga. At the 7-Eleven, Lance opens the door for me. When I pass through, it chimes.

It sounds exactly the same as the one at Marble Slab.

Whir.

Lance notices and squeezes my hand. He gazes into my eyes while stroking the back of my hand with his thumb, but he doesn't say anything. He just leads me through the store as he grabs a bottle of water from the refrigerator wall. "Do you want a room temperature one?" He motions at a stack of them behind me.

"No, cold is fine."

He leads me to the soda machine and grabs a 64 ounce cup. "In case you're really thirsty. Ice?"

"Please."

Ice clatters and he fills the cup with Sprite.

He grabs a big bag of Peanut M&M's. "Protein. Everybody likes M&M's."

I struggle not to smile. He's right. I love them.

He pays with his credit card.

Outside, we sit on the curb like school kids.

He holds the Sprite up to me with a straw in it. "Sip."

I do.

He tears the corner of the M&M's open with his teeth then sets the bag between his crossed legs and pries out a brown M&M. "Do you like brown? They're always the last to go."

"I like brown best. They're more chocolatey," I grin.

"They're all the same," he chuckles then feeds it to me.

I chew. It crackles and melts in my mouth then crunches peanut. "No, the brown color adds a chocolate ambience. What about blue says chocolate to you?"

"You have a point." He drops the blue one he's holding back into the bag and pries out a brown one. He's smiling when he crunches into it.

I didn't realize Lance could be such a gentleman. And I never imagined eating M&M's and sipping Sprite sitting on the dirty curb at 7-Eleven could be so incredibly romantic.

As the sugar goes down, the dentist's drill in my stomach whirs faintly, reminding me hazily of the fact that my life is now upside down.

Fucked, fired, and fed by the hand of this gorgeous man in less than an hour.

With Lance, anything is possible.

What a crazy day.

Chapter 14

CHASTITY

"I don't want to go home."

"We can go wherever you want," Lance says as he tosses the wadded M&M's bag into the cement can in front of 7-Eleven.

I'm buzzing from a sugar high. I see the two shirtless guys at the park still playing frisbee. "I wish we had a frisbee."

"Those guys have one."

"What, are you gonna steal it? Oh, sorry. That didn't come out right. I meant we can't use theirs. It's... theirs." My idiot streak continues.

He smirks, "I knew what you meant. Let's join 'em."

"Can we do that?"

"We can ask."

I dash across traffic, J-walking. I wait on the other side.

Lance crosses casually, not even watching the cars.

"You're gonna get hit!" I holler.

He shakes his head, grinning, but doesn't go any faster. Just strolls up to me.

"You think the world revolves around you, don't you?"

"Last time I checked," he grins.

"Let's go." I grab his hand and drag him toward the guys with the frisbee. They turn out to be cool and we play for over an hour. Lance is a total show off, throwing the frisbee forehand, backhand, over his head, left handed, diving for the disc, rolling in the grass. I laugh constantly and forget about everything except frisbee.

Afterward, the four of us sit in the grass in a circle, leaning back on our hands, feet in the center, chatting about nothing and everything. Both guys are cute and cut. Not as built as Lance, who also has his shirt off displaying muscles and tats, but they're tan and plenty handsome. The guy with the bandana and the big smile says, "You guys wanna walk over to Tokyo Delve's for sushi and saki?"

I glance at Lance.

"Works for me," he says.

The four of us walk across the park to the stoplight.

Bandana, who is really tall, asks me, "What was your name again?"

Lance jumps in, chosing that moment to wrap his arm around my shoulder. "I'm Lance. This is Chaz." His smile says, "*Hands off,*

Bandana."

Bandana nods vigorously. "Cool names. I'm Scottie."

"Mitch," says the other guy with the puka shell necklace and wavy blond hair.

I grin to myself because I'm surrounded by cute guys. Too bad Lark isn't here. She could run interference with Scottie and Mitch. I can change that. I pull my phone out of my khakis and linger behind the guys and call her while we stroll down Magnolia. While I wait for her to answer, I realize my boobs itch. It must be the sweat from playing frisbee combined with the whipped cream and caramel under my bra. Gross. I need a shower.

Lark answers, "What up, bitch?"

"Do you know Tokyo Delve's in North Hollywood?"

"The sushi place?"

"Yeah. Meet me there."

"No! I just got back from the beach. I'm fried."

"Cute guys," I singsong.

"How cute?"

"You won't be disappointed."

"Wait, who is this? I think you called the wrong number. This is Lark Barksdale. My friend Chaz doesn't know how to pick up cute guys. So if you kidnapped her, be warned. I know ninjas and I will have them assassinate your ass."

I laugh, "Just get down here."

"I'll be there in ten. You better not be lying about the guys. Because, ninjas."

"I'm not!"

"Ninjas," she warns ominously and hangs up.

The front of Tokyo Delve's is all flashing Vegas lights and neon. Whenever I've driven by at night, there's always a line outside to get in. Not tonight. We're seated immediately. Lark walks in minutes later and I wave her over. She's basically naked in her pink halter and yellow mini. Her hair is perfect, her lips lush, and her smokey makeup pops her eyes. She sees Mitch and Scottie before they see her and she silently mouths to me, *"Nice."* She plops down between them on the other side of the six person table. "Howdy, boys."

They both smile at her, eyes all over her cleavage, which is highlighted by the yellow piping around her pink halter.

She scoots up her chair and smiles at me across the table, "I'll call off the ninjas." She holds up her phone and pretends to text someone.

Lance mutters, "What is she talking about?"

"Nothing," I giggle.

Lark asks, "Aren't you supposed to be at work?"

I roll my eyes, "Long story."

Tokyo Delve's buzzes with conversation. Half the tables are full already. Scottie orders saki bombs. I don't even know what that is.

The waitress cards the entire table. "No alcohol for these two." She points fingers at me and Lark.

"Me neither," Lance says to the waitress.

"You don't want a saki bomb, bro?" Mitch asks.

Lance shakes his head. "We'll have Cokes. That work for you, Lark?"

She smirks, "You're such a teetotaler."

Lance shrugs. "Thought I'd make you ladies feel at home."

I give Lance a thoughtful look. I'm thinking about his dad and his drinking. He probably is too.

Tokyo Delve's has raucous karaoke and an MC who leads the customers in hip hop line dancing. The waiters even get up on stage and do dance routines that include costume changes and backflips. It's craziness.

Eventually our waitress brings out four saki bombs and sets them on the table for Scottie and Mitch. Picture saki shot glasses balanced on two chopsticks on top of a beer mug full of beer.

"You sure you don't want one, bro?" Mitch asks Lance again.

"It's all you, man," Lance smiles. I can tell he's not exactly happy about all the alcohol.

When the waitress leaves, Scottie grins at Mitch across Lark, "You ready? One. Two. Three!" Both guys slap the table top and the shot glasses tumble into the beer. Before Mitch can pick up his glass, Lark grabs it and chugs it.

"Dude, where's mine?" Mitch grins.

"You have another one," she laughs.

By the time our sushi arrives, Lark has Scottie and Mitch eating and drinking out of the palm of her hand. I mean that literally. First, she feeds them sushi rolls from her hand. Then at one point, she wants to do belly shots, which she has to explain to me, but Scottie suggests we would get kicked out if she tried, and he clearly doesn't want Lark going anywhere. Neither does Mitch. I think they're thinking three way. Since they won't let her do a belly shot, Lark pours saki into her cupped palms and Scottie gladly sips it from her hands before she gives Mitch a turn.

Lark defies all expectations.

We're there for hours. Lark and I do the line dance, following along to the MC's instructions. Lark is wobbly from the saki bombs, but she's having a blast.

When we sit back down, Lance mutters in my ear, "We should go. Lark is hammered."

"What are you saying to my bestie?!" Lark slurs, grinning from ear to drunk ear. "I wanna know!" She stands up and tiptoes carefully around the table holding onto it and the chair backs for balance. It doesn't help. She stumbles into the table and it honks across the floor. Our drinks slosh and a Coke almost spills, but Lance saves it. Scottie grabs Lark's hips like she's his, holding her up. "Whoops," she giggles. She drops into his lap, her arm around his neck. "My hero!" She presses her cheek against his but doesn't kiss him. I can tell she's just flirting. A bit too hard for her own good, but flirting.

Scottie is clearly enjoying himself and might have other ideas. He rests his hand on Lark's thigh, caressing it. They stare at each other and his eyes glimmer.

She chuckles, "Don't fall in love with me, Scottie. I'm a naughty girl."

"I'm naughty too," he winks.

"How naughty are you, naughty Scottie?"

They tongue kiss.

I guess I was wrong.

Mitch watches, possibly jealous. It's hard to say.

Yes, Lark is a flirt. But I've never seen her this drunk.

Lance stands up.

I grab his hand. "Where are you going?"

"To pay the bill. Stay here. Keep an eye on Lark."

I watch him go to the sushi bar and flag down our waitress to pay. He returns, sticking his wallet back in his pocket. He grabs Lark gently by the arm and stands her up.

"No," Lark moans, "I was kissing Naughty."

"Say goodnight to Naughty. It's past your bed time."

Lark stands and coils her arms around Lance's neck. She smiles with sleepy eyes. "Are you taking me to bed? Do I get to see your lance, Lance? I don't mind sharing with Chaz. Unless Naughty and Mitch have lances too? Then we can have a jousting tournament!" She giggles at her own joke.

I grimace.

"Let's go, Lark." Lance puts his arm around her waist and turns her toward the front door.

I stand up to help.

Scottie shoots to his feet and puts a hand on Lance's shoulder. "Yo, bro. Where do you think you're going with her?"

"Sit down, dude," Lance warns.

"No, man."

"Sit. Down."

"She's not your girlfriend, bro," Scottie says.

"She's not yours either, so back off."

It's so loud with all the people dancing and the karaoke, nobody notices the tension between Lance and Scottie. Except Mitch. He stands up, backing Scottie's play. Both are buzzed on saki.

Lance looks at me. "Hold her?" I prop up Lark so Lance has his hands free. He turns to the other two. "Gentlemen."

They stare at Lance.

He says, "Lark is going home with us. You are staying here. If you follow us, you will regret it."

Scottie's face goes testosterone. "No, man. She stays with us."

Lance's hand flies up and he knuckles Scottie in the throat with one finger.

Scottie makes a "Gulck!" sound and crumples into his chair, almost falling on the floor, but his arm slams the top of the table, rattling glasses, and he stays in his seat. Barely.

"You should sit down too," Lance says to Mitch.

He does.

It's all over so fast, no one in the restaurant notices.

Lance helps me walk Lark outside.

"She can't drive," I say on the sidewalk.

"You drive her home. I'll follow on my Gixxer."

"What's a gickser?"

"Gixxer." He grins, "Sorry. Guy talk. It's short for GSXR."

"You're such a nerd. Gixxer sounds like a toy."

"Boys and their toys," he chuckles.

We walk to Lark's car, load her in, drive to the park where Lance's Gixxer is, then head toward Lark's apartment. We walk Lark up the stairs and ring the doorbell.

"Chaz! How are you?!" Lark's mom beams. Patience Barksdale is as pretty and blonde as Lark, but she's very granola and outdoorsy. She won't let me call her Mrs. Barksdale.

I smile, "Hi, Patience."

"Mom!!" Lark blurts. "I love you so much, Mom!"

Patience rolls her eyes at drunk Lark then says to me, "She didn't drive, did she?"

"No," I say. "I did."

"That's good. Did she do anything stupid?" she asks, taking Lark from me and Lance in the small apartment's main area, which includes the tiny dining room, kitchen, and living room.

"Almost," Lance says.

Patience narrows her eyes.

"It was nothing," I say hastily.

"That's good." Patience nods uncertainly at me. To Lark, "Why can't you be more responsible like your sister?" She chuckles nervously as she leads Lark to the couch. "I worry about you."

"Why can't she be more like me?" Lark muses sleepily as we all sit down.

"You're right. There's only one you," Patience smiles, patting her daughter's hand lovingly. She turns to me and Lance. "You two don't have to stay. I can take care of her from here. And thank you, Chaz. As always."

"No problem," I grin.

"Are you the new boyfriend?" she asks Lance.

My eyes bug.

Lance chuckles. "We're friends. I'm Lance."

They shake hands.

Lark giggles. "I told Mom you're going to marry each other."

My eyes butterfly.

"Remember," Lark chirps. "I'm the maid of honor."

Patience rubs Lark's thigh affectionately. "Lark likes to make up stories." It's obvious that it doesn't bother Patience. She accepts it because she loves her daughter unconditionally.

I'm jealous that Lark can come home drunk and her mom acts like it's business as usual. Not that Lark drinks often. She doesn't. But Patience is so mellow. Lark is so lucky. I've always been jealous of their relationship, and often dreamed of being adopted into the Barksdale family. Sadly, that's just fantasy.

Lark frowns sleepily. "They're totally getting married."

"Okay!" I blurt and shoot to my feet. "Time to go!"

We say our goodbyes before Lance and I walk down the steps to his motorcycle.

I say, "Thanks for helping me get Lark home."

"No worries. Where to now?" He hands me my helmet.

"Um…" I don't want to think about what is going to happen when Mom sees me tonight. And I'm not even drunk. Just jobless.

Whir.

Lance frowns, "Something bothering you?"

"Is it that obvious," I whine.

"To me it is. I should get you home."

In that moment I realize Lance is a special man with much more depth than meets the eye.

He is definitely boyfriend material.

What I can't tell is whether or not he feels the same way.

++++8++++

CHASTITY

Lance drives his motorcycle into his driveway and parks.

I grimace, "I should've asked Patience if I could crash at their apartment."

"You worried about your mom?"

"Yeah." I search Lance's gorgeous eyes, wondering what he's thinking.

"You wanna crash here?"

My heart jumps. "I would love to!" I clear my throat and try to act casual. "I mean, sure. Yeah. Whatever is fine." I know Mom will freak if I don't come home, but I'll worry about that tomorrow.

He smirks and nods toward the house. "Inside."

I wrap my arms around his elbow and he leads me to the front door, his keys in hand. He opens it and the TV blares in the living room. Some woman squeals, "Oh! Oh! Oh! Right there! Yeah! Oh! Like that! Give it to me!" Sounds like porn.

Lance frowns. "Fuck, sorry about this. Maybe you should wait here."

I'm totally fine letting him handle it. From what I saw earlier with Mr. McKnight drinking mouthwash in his saggy underwear, I'm afraid to think what he's doing in the living room while watching porn. I wait in the entryway.

The sound suddenly cuts off mid-squeal. Then, "Hey! Give me that! I wasn't finished with it!" Mr. McKnight grumbles drunkenly.

"You are now."

Splattering sound of liquid gurgling down the kitchen sink.

"Fucking waste of good whiskey," Mr. McKnight grumbles from the living room.

"Fucking waste of a good life," Lance grunts from the kitchen. His boots thud and he walks into the entryway. "Maybe you should go home."

"I don't mind."

"You sure?"

"Remember my mom? At least here she won't be yelling at me."

"It won't be pretty."

"It's okay. I don't mind."

He strokes the side of my head and sighs. "Are you sure? We might be up all night dealing with his shit."

"Yes, Lance. Yes."

He smiles at me. Not his devil's grin. Something else. The opposite. "Thanks."

"One thing."

"Yeah?"

"Is your dad, um, dressed?"

Lance snorts, "Yeah. He's dressed. Was when I came in."

I heave a sigh of relief. "Okay, good."

In the living room, I discover dressed means he's wearing only jeans. At least he's not, you know, hanging out. There's a stack of porno DVDs on the floor next to a dusty old DVD player. Yes it's weird. But I agreed to stay. When Lance sees me looking at the DVD cases, he dumps them in one of the many moving boxes still in the living room.

For the next two hours, we sit on the couch watching reruns of American Chopper. Lance sits between me and his dad.

At one point, I ask Lance if I can rinse in his shower because my boobs are really itchy from the caramel and whipped cream.

He leads me to his hall bathroom, which is the exact mirror image of my bathroom. Except it's completely empty. A single white towel hangs rumpled on the rack.

Lance winces, "I don't have any clean towels. But you can use mine." He pulls it off the rack and folds it into a wrinkled square. "Good as new." He looks apologetic. "It's all I have. Unless you want my dad's."

"No! I mean, yours is fine." I smile.

"I'll turn the water on for you. It's hard to set it so it's not burning or freezing." After it warms up, he gestures into the shower.

I smile coyly, "Are you going to join me?"

His face sinks. "I have to babysit my dad."

"Right."

He closes the door behind him when he leaves.

I strip and rinse. After, I grab Lance's towel and inhale deeply. So good.

I get dressed but leave my bra off. Should I wash it and leave it hanging on the shower or wait until tomorrow? I'll wait. I don't feel that familiar here.

I return to the living room, my arms folded across my polo shirt. I'm afraid Mr. McKnight will stare if he sees my nipples.

He never notices me. He just barks at the screen continuously, making all kinds of critical comments about the guys on American

Chopper and the shoddy custom work they're doing to the chopped motorcycles. Tonight, he's an angry drunk. He wasn't at the pool party. That's weird.

"That's not how you run a bead!" Mr. McKnight grumbles while one of the guys on the show welds a motorcycle part. "Guy doesn't know shit about stick welding. His drag angle is too steep. The slag is going right back into his weld puddle. That weld is gonna be full of slag holes. Put any pressure on that bracket and you'll crack it clean off."

"Instead of bitching about it," Lance says, "Maybe you need to open up a shop here in the Valley. Give you something to do other than sit around and get fat and stupid."

Mr. McKnight just grunts. Eventually, the comments fade to snores.

"Time for bed," Lance whispers. "Wanna help me with the grumbler?"

I smile, "Sure."

Lance grabs his father by one wrist and slings an arm over his shoulders. "If I trip, you catch both of us."

"I can't do that!"

He winks and carries his Dad to the master bedroom that is the mirror image of Mom's bedroom. Instead of all of Mom's frilly decor, all there is is an air mattress with a rumpled sheet hanging half off and moving boxes. I don't know why I was worried about Mom and Mr. McKnight getting together. She'll probably never speak to him again. Even if she does, I think once she gets to know him, he'll scare her off anyway. It's sad, actually.

I rush past Lance and straighten the sheet on the bed.

"Thanks," he says as he lays his dad on the air mattress, which flops up at the corners before settling.

"Why did you let her go?" Mr. McKnight mumbles sleepily. "You never should have let her..."

Lance freezes, his eyes alarmed.

"What is he talking about?"

"Nothing," Lance says, nervous. "Help me with the sheet." He picks up a wadded top sheet and we tuck his Dad in.

"You shouldn't have..." Mr. McKnight sighs, "let... her..."

Lance's face bunches for a second with distress. He turns toward the door. "Out. He needs his beauty rest." He's hiding something.

I don't want to pry.

When I walk past Lance, a high pitched squeaky fart whistles from his Dad. It's loud in the silent house. We both laugh.

"We better move before the smell hits us. His whiskey farts are worse than a sewer."

I stifle a giggle as he closes the door.

I head straight to his bedroom and sit down on his mattress. The curtains are open and the room is lit softly by the orange glow of a nearby streetlight and the LA night sky.

Lance kicks off his boots while staring at me, his face inscrutable but deliciously charming. He squats at my feet and pulls my pink Keds off.

"Pants," he says.

I unbutton my khakis and help him pull them off. I have my pink Marble Slab polo shirt over my head before he asks and my braless boobs fall right out.

"Whoa," he chuckles. "Tits." He stares at them for a while then grins. "Fucking perfect." He tugs his own shirt off and tosses it aside.

I'm surprised he doesn't have a hard on in his jeans already because seeing him shirtless makes me leak. Luckily I still have panties on. But he's nowhere close to trying to take them off. Oh well. Maybe we should just sleep. It's been a long day.

He unbuttons his jeans and pushes them down with his boxers. His cock grows quickly, lengthening, thickening, standing up, pulsing. He pulls my panties down without asking. I'm drenched before he finishes putting the condom on.

We make love slow and soft and silent. The low hum in my stomach from earlier today fades to nothing. All the stress and fear and guilt are pushed out of my body as Lance pushes in, filling me with his affection.

The moment is perfect.

In the soft amber glow of the LA lights, I fall asleep in his arms.

Chapter 15

I wake to the sight of Lance staring at me with his sleepy eyes.

It's morning and the world is quiet.

"You're gorgeous," he muses.

With his stubble coming in and his burning eyes, he wins that prize. I roll my eyes.

"You should shower. We have a long day ahead of us."

"What are you talking about?"

"It's Monday."

"So?" Did he forget I got fired? Not that I work Monday mornings, but still.

"So, get up." He climbs over me and stands, totally naked.

And totally erect.

Geez, that is a total turn on. How can he be thinking of anything other than sex at a time like this? I'm naked too. I pull my heels up to my hips, opening myself. I run my hands across my breasts, squeezing them. Then I slide them down between my legs, sinking my fingers into my collecting wetness, dragging it out to slicken my opening.

He closes his eyes and shakes his head. "What are you doing, Pink?"

The second he says my nickname, I know his effort to resist is useless. "Looking at you. And touching myself."

"Stop, Pink."

"Make me."

"I'm serious. We have a long day."

"Something is *long*..." I purr, massaging my clit and slide a finger inside me. "Fuck me, Lance. I know you're dying to."

His eyes are still closed. His cock jumps high and spasms for several seconds, like he wants to come but can't. "Fuck," he hisses and dives for me.

This time, our passion is intense. We fight each other silently, him pinning me on the mattress, me struggling against his powerful thrusting. But in the end I succumb, overwhelmed, overtaken, invaded. We come together, come hard, our bodies clenching one another, hissing, biting, burning, consumed by our fire.

After we shower and dress together, he mutters, "You hungry?"

"Are you gonna cook me breakfast?"

"My fridge is empty. I'll take you to breakfast." He slaps my khaki covered butt. "Now get moving! Long day, remember?"

"I need to go home and change. I can't go out in my Marble Slab uniform."

"You ready to face your mom?"

I wince. "Not even."

"So let's go. Nobody'll care about your outfit where we're going."

"Okay, but in that case, I really need to wash my bra." I give it a quick rinse in the bathroom sink. Luckily, Lance has a hair dryer which I use to blow dry my bra. When I'm finally dressed, I ask, "Where are we going? You still haven't told me."

"It's a surprise. Trust me."

"It better be a good one," I pout.

We walk into the garage and Lance hits the button on the garage door opener and morning light washes over the two motorcycles.

I ask, "Should we be worried about your dad?"

"I can only babysit him so much." It pains him to say it.

"Sure. Are we taking the Gixxer?"

He grins. "You remembered."

"Yup. When are you going to teach me how to ride?"

"You really wanna learn?"

I shrug. "Maybe. But after my breakfast surprise. I'm counting on you to make it good."

He grins and we put our helmets on. He rolls the motorcycle out of the garage and hits the door button before running out under the closing door, reminding me of Indiana Jones, except Lance has no hat to snatch from under the door before it slams shut.

We climb on the bike.

Right as Lance starts the engine, Mom comes running down our driveway, yelling. "Where have you been?!" She stops short at the low hedges between the two yards. "I waited up all night for you! I called the police! I called the hospitals! Charity was worried sick! She couldn't sleep!"

All of the peacefulness of my morning is burned away by Mom and by guilt. I'm speechless. I don't want to do this right now.

She continues, "Mr. Molton called and apologized and offered you your job back. He said you didn't answer your phone all night. Lord knows I tried calling you dozens of times! What happened, Chastity?!"

I lean my helmeted head against Lance's back.

"Chastity? Look at me!"

I roll my eyes before looking at her. "Can we talk later?"

"What?"

I holler through the helmet, "Tell Charity I'm fine. I'll call Mr. Molton later." If he really offered me my job back, that would be terrif. But I wasn't on the schedule until Wednesday anyway. Mr. Molton can wait. At least until I get away from Mom.

"You get off that motorcycle right now, young lady! You have gone too far this time! You have—"

VROOM!

Lance revs the engine loudly, drowning out Mom.

I giggle to myself.

"—If you don't get off that—" *VROOM!* "—I swear I'll—" *VROOM! VROOM!*

Mom is red in the face but she finally stops yelling.

"Are you done?" Lance asks her.

Mom's face knots and she shouts, "No, I'm not—"

VROOM! VROOM! VROOM!

I almost lose it laughing as Lance rides the motorcycle into the street and we drive off.

++++8++++

CHASTITY

Morning traffic on the 101 heading toward downtown is stop and go. It takes forever. At one point we're stopped so long I joke that I'm going to hop off his motorcycle and walk, not that I know where we're going. I don't.

When we're moving again, we take the off-ramp for the 110, then exit on 8th. We have breakfast at this really cool retro diner downtown called The Original Pantry Cafe. Historic photos of LA and old signs cover the walls. The place is packed, so we sit at the counter on stools and watch the guys frying the hash browns and flipping the pancakes. Lance pays because I don't have any money.

After, we ride his motorcycle to the Fashion District a few blocks away, stopping on a side street in front of an old brick building sandwiched between warehouses. He swings off the motorcycle and punches in a code on a keypad next to a small rolling steel garage door tagged with graffiti. The motor raises the door and we drive inside. The garage is small. It holds two parked cars and has just enough room for Lance's motorcycle and that's it.

"Where are we?" I ask, pulling my helmet off.

"My office."

"Your what?"

"My office. My workplace. Where I do my job."

What the fluff? "I thought you didn't have a job?"

"Not really. But it pays the bills."

Now I'm all kinds of surprised.

Lance has a secret life.

We walk through an interior steel door into a really cool room. High ceiling. Exposed arched beams. Skylights. Graphic screen print posters in vibrant fluorescent colors line the brick walls. In one corner stands a clothing rack and a glass display case full of blingy knickknacks. In another corner there's a lounge area with couches and a coffee table covered in magazines. Beside it is an air hockey table and a bunch of skateboards on hooks hanging from the brick wall. At the far end of the room is a wall of computers and monitors and speakers.

Two guys sit in front of the computers with their backs to us.

"Hey, guys," Lance says to them. "I got someone I want you to meet."

The guy on the right surrounded by stereo speakers turns around first. He has long dark hair past his chin and a trim beard. He's very attractive, but a bit skinny for my taste. His gray button down shirt is open over a white tank top. A gold medallion hangs around his neck. The rolled up cuffs on his skinny jeans stop at sockless ankles that dive into dress shoes. Leave it to a hipster to not wear socks with blue suede shoes. He leans forward in his chair and we shake hands. "Hey. I'm Micah," he says softly.

"Hi. Chaz."

"Nice to meet you."

Yeah, definitely cute. I try not to blush.

Lance says, "The nerd with no social skills is Beaver. But he's too busy to say hello."

"Hold on," Beaver says, his back still to us. His voice is thin and reedy and a little bit annoying. "I need to set this to render so I can go home." Make that a lot annoying. He clicks away frantically with his mouse in one hand while the fingers of his other fly over the keyboard. He finally spins around, looking completely disoriented. He has a puffy hair helmet, over-sized eyeglasses, and an 8-bit Atari T-shirt.

Lance asks, "Have you been here all night, Beaver?"

"Yeah. What are we doing?" His head volleys between me and Lance. After eight volleys he finally stops and stares at me. His eyes light up behind his glasses. "Hey! Who are you?" He jumps up from his chair and scissors his legs in the air before firing his arm at me to shake. His hand is warm and damp. He practically shakes my arm off.

"Easy, Beaver," Lance warns. "Don't break her arm."

I smirk, "I'm not fragile."

"Of course not," Beaver says. He turns my wrist and uses his other hand to pet the backs of my knuckles. He is super weird.

"Hands, Beaver. You only need one to shake."

Beaver's petting hand suddenly recoils like it just got burned.

Make that super duper weird.

"He's tired," Lance mutters. "He works vampire hours. Anyway. Guys, I don't want either one of you even thinking about putting the moves on Chaz. Especially you, Beaver." Lance points a warning finger at him.

I don't think Lance'll have to worry about Beaver. Ew.

Beaver scoffs. "Pfft. Are you kidding? She probably doesn't even know what Missile Command is." He pins his eyes on me hopefully, "You don't know what Missile Command is, do you?"

"No, sorry."

"Figures." Clearly, my Missile Command ignorance puts me out of the running for Beaver's affections.

Darn.

"I know how you are with the ladies, Beaver." Lance chuckles, "So keep your missile in your pants and your hands on your controller where it belongs."

"You mean my joystick?" Beaver snarls comically while grabbing his crotch and squeezing it while jack-rabbiting his hips up and down.

Lance laughs, "Fucking Beaver."

"I'm always fucking beaver," Beaver snivels, still thrusting at the air.

I grimace.

"Down, boy," Lance warns. "You're offending the lady."

Beaver rolls his eyes. There's a beep from the Mac behind him. He spins in his chair and grabs the mouse, instantly busy.

Lance must've been joking about Beaver. There's no way a guy like him has any luck with the ladies with behavior like that. Lance should be more worried about a guy like Micah. Not that I'm interested.

"Let's go into my office," Lance suggests.

"Nice meeting you," Micah says.

"Yeah. Likewise," I smile.

Lance's office is up a metal flight of stairs in a loft above the back half of the building. We walk through a glass door that closes behind us. A sizable A-frame skylight floods the office with natural light. A sliding window behind the big desk looks out over downstairs. Behind me, a wood framed glass door reveals a small outdoor patio dotted with potted plants.

Lance walks around the desk and sits in the executive chair in front of the sliding window. "Have a seat."

I drop into one of the chairs facing his desk. "Is his name really Beaver?"

"No. Bradley Wilson. Beaver is his scene name." Lance grabs a messed up Rubik's Cube off the desk and starts fiddling with it. He also puts his feet up. The boss gets to do whatever he wants.

"Scene name?"

"Music scene." Lance flicks the Rubik's cube with practiced skill.

"Oh. Um, do Micah and Beaver work for you?"

"Yup. Micah is my sound guy and Beaver is my video guy."

"Are you in the music business or something?"

"Yup."

"Really? What do you do?"

He points at the huge silk-screened banner hung from the brick wall behind him.

I read it out loud. "The three pee-aitch-four-tomb?"

"The Phantom."

I look at it again. TH3 PH4NTüM. "Oh! I get it! The numbers are vowels."

He fires a finger gun at me. "Smart."

"Who's the Phantom?"

"You don't follow EDM, do you."

"You mean electronic dance music? Not really. I mean, I listen to it sometimes, but I don't know any of the DJs or anything. So, who's the Phantom? Are you his manager or something?"

"Nope. He's me." He sets the Rubik's Cube on the desk, all the colors lined up.

"Did you just solve that?!"

"I'm full of surprises."

"Wait. Back up. What were you just saying about this Phantom guy?"

"I'm him. He's me."

"Oh. Oh, wait. I'm supposed to be impressed, aren't I? You've sold like a million records and you're famous and you've won Grammies and I've never heard of you, right?" I groan, feeling stupid and sheltered because of my weird Mom.

"No. But I'm working on it," he winks.

I feel much less dumb. "But you're seriously a DJ?"

He clicks around on the laptop on his desk for a minute then turns it around. A YouTube video plays in the browser.

The title reads TH3 PH4NTüM - Strapped & Capped. It's a synthy dance song with a hard-driving beat and a slurring baby voice that is completely catchy and nothing but nonsense. I like it immediately. The video shows a montage of different live outdoor raves crowded with audiences full of young people bouncing and waving glow sticks in the air. A guy with his shirt off and an incredible body that I immediately suspect is Lance stands at the DJ table twisting knobs and dancing in place. I can't say for sure it's Lance because he's wearing a shiny silver mask. "Is that you?"

He nods.

I watch as the video cuts back and forth between him and the crowd. He's either rocking along with the music, dancing on top of the DJ table, or waving his hands in the air while shouting into the mic to pump up the crowd.

"Wow, this song is really good, Lance," I smile. That's when I notice it has over two million views.

"Thanks," he says humbly.

"You are famous."

He rolls his eyes. "Not really."

"Does your music pay for all this?" I motion around the building.

He nods. "Yeah. Download royalties from iTunes, Spotify, Pandora, internet ads for the YouTube videos, live gigs, all that shit."

"That makes you the most famous person I've ever met. You're a frickin' rockstar, Lance! And you're my next door neighbor! Why the heck are you living in our dumpy neighborhood?"

"I needed to put my Dad someplace plain. No ties to his life back in Vegas." The way he says it hints at hidden pain and immense frustration.

I know enough to not ask more. I smile and look around the office. "It looks like you're doing just fine to me," I say encouragingly. "I mean, you've got your own office building! And employees! How awesome is that?"

"I lease this place and Micah and Beaver are freelance. I only pay them when I have something for them to do."

"What are they working on now?"

"Micah is mixing my latest track and Beaver is putting together an animatic for the video."

"An ani-what?"

"Animatic. Animated storyboards."

"And those are..."

"A bunch of drawings timed out to the music track to show investors what the video'll be when I shoot it."

"Investors?"

"Yeah. I've got a big idea for the new video that I can't afford out of pocket. It's pretty damn spectacular. But if I can get an angel investor to drop me some serious coin, I can shoot it exactly the way I envision it."

"Wow, that sounds amazing."

"Hopefully. You need a good track to put you on the map, but you need a killer video to launch your career into the majors. Without a video, your track won't go nowhere. But my man Skrillex—-"

"You know Skrillex?" I definitely have heard of him.

"His studio is downtown near here. I met him at a gig last year when Strapped & Capped hit a million views. Anyway, he took me on tour with him in Europe this spring for twenty-eight dates. I've got a lot of juice right now, but if I don't drop a hit video in the next few months, I could lose it and be back to where I was last year."

"What do you mean? Two million people have listened to your song! That's insane!"

"That was last year. In the music biz, that's a lifetime. Gotta keep hustling if I want to get to the next level."

"Oh. Sounds hard. I doubt I could do it. So, why did you bring me down here anyway?"

"To offer you a job."

"No way!" I nearly jump out of my seat. Mr. Molton's supposed call that Mom mentioned has been weighing in the back of my mind all morning. If he means it, I'll be totally grateful to have my job back. But can I stomach facing him after the way he caught me and Lance having sex in the back room of Marble Slab? I'll never look at that room or Mr. Molton the same way ever again. If Lance is actually offering me a job, I might just take it. "What do you need me for? I mean, besides moral support? All I know how to do is scoop ice cream."

"I need an assistant. I'm juggling too many things with prospective investors. I'm getting calls all the time, emails, meetings, it's insane. I barely have time to produce music tracks. I need a right hand woman." He winks and holds his hand up in this weird grip that obviously refers to fingering me.

"What's the thumb for?" I giggle.

"The other entrance," he chuckles, circling his thumb in the air.

My eyes pop. "No butts!"

He laughs. "Have you ever tried it?"

"Tried what? Butt sex? No! Of course not! I was a total virgin until you!"

"You're still partially a virgin. A butt virgin."

"Shut up!" I jump up from my chair, laughing nervously as I clap my hands over my butt. "There will be no butts!"

"Sit down. I'm just fucking around."

"Oh, good." I take a deep breath.

"For now." His devil's grin returns as he leans his muscled forearms on the desk and slays me with those burning eyes.

Why is it impossible *not* to wonder what he might do to my behind? And what that might feel like?

He holds up his hand in that weird fingering grip again and his thumb twirls in a slow circle.

I'm wet.

"But first," he mutters. "We go shopping."

"For butt toys?" I giggle. What am I thinking?

"If you want to…"

"No!"

"Joking. If you're gonna be my assistant, we need to get you a new wardrobe."

"Are you seriously offering me a job?" I'm having trouble believing all this is happening.

"Yeah. And a wardrobe."

"You can't do that," I snicker.

"Why not? Did you pay for that Marble Slab uniform you're wearing?"

"No, but…"

"Then I'm going to buy you a business uniform. Trouble is, you can't wear the same thing every day. You need at least five outfits, right?"

"Um," I laugh, "I guess?"

He stands up and offers his hand. "So let's go shopping."

Chapter 16

CHASTITY

The first place we go is Nasty Doll in the Garment District. Outside it's a glass walled stainless steel box. Inside all the outfits on the racks and mannequins scream cutting edge sexy. Lark and I have come here several times, but we could never afford anything accept accessories. Lark did steal a bra from here once, but that's it. Nasty Doll is well out of our price range.

Lance holds the glass door for me. "Go crazy."

"Wait, what do you mean?"

"Start grabbing dresses. Get whatever you want."

"Are you serious?"

He nods.

"Do I have a budget?"

"Sky's the limit."

My eyes goggle. "This isn't really happening."

He slaps my butt and I jump. "Feel that?"

"Yeah! Ouch!" I rub the backs of my khakis.

"You're not dreaming. Go shopping."

I step into the store with shining eyes and fast walk to the first mannequin I see, resisting the urge to run. The faceless mannequin wears what looks like a long sleeve white lace top with black lace mini skirt, but is actually a single piece A-line dress. The black velvet ribbon tie under the bust line gives it a sexy business look. The fishnet stockings and dominatrix platforms do not.

"You wear that to the office and I'll have to bend you over my desk and spank you while I fuck you," Lance muses behind me. His hands grab my hips and he yanks me into him, pulling my butt up like he wants to start right now.

I arch my back and my pussy clenches and I start to drip instantly. But I can't have sex with Lance in a clothing store. "Would you stop?" I whisper. "People are watching!" That's not exactly true. Although people are here shopping, it's not that crowded so no one notices us. I should be mad that he's pawing me in public like I'm his sex toy. But I realize it's turning me on. Which makes me more mad. Which in turn turns me on even more.

Okay, I need to stop and focus on dresses.

Because, shopping spree!

I gasp when Lance grabs the front waistband of my khakis and pulls it up snug against my folds and twists the pants left to right. The motion rolls the crotch seam across my clit, back and forth. I instantly forget the dresses. If he doesn't stop, I'll need to visit the ladies room before I try on any outfits. Good thing I'm wearing these khakis and not a dress. Otherwise, you'd have to follow me with a mop.

I break free from his grip and shuffle toward a round rack of tops. Everything is incredible. Lance watches from afar, leaning his elbow on a nearby rack. I hold a crop top up to my chest. "What do you think?"

"Perfect," he grins.

"You're no help," I chuckle.

I flip through more tops, not bothering to look at price tags because I know I could never afford any of it without Lance.

"Can I help you with anything, sir?" a sales girl asks Lance.

She doesn't see me because I'm behind a mannequin. I lean to the side to get a good look at her. She's a brunette dressed in a long sleeve black bodycon dress with diamond cutouts at the waist that reveal a taut stomach and a sheer upper that leaves nothing to the imagination. Her boobs and black mesh bra are totally visible. There is no denying she is bombshell hot.

Lance smiles at her, "I'm good."

"Yeah you are," she purrs, batting her eyelashes so hard they might fly off her face because they're obviously fake. When Lance says nothing more, she lifts one black suede ankle strap heel behind her and twirls her foot like it's sore, but she's really just showing off her toned leg. "These Jeffrey Campbells are killing me. They always make my calves so tight." What a humble bragger. Most girls would kill for a body like hers. And those shoes. And she's complaining? Total humble bragger.

Lance arches his eyebrows noncommittally.

She continues, "I don't know why corporate makes me wear *tight* outfits every single day." By tight, she obviously means her outfit *and* her body. "Sometimes a girl just needs to let loose, you know?" There she goes again with the humble bragging.

What a butt nugget. I repress a giggle.

Butt Nugget, a.k.a. the Humble Bragger, takes a dress off the rack Lance is leaning against for no reason and squeezes past him, rubbing her butt across his crotch before hanging the dress on a different rack. "Sorry," she giggles. "I didn't realize you were so... big."

What a witch! Now she's gone too far. I toss the top I'm holding onto the rack but it flops to the floor. Let Butt Nugget hang it up later. I stride toward them. "Ahem."

Butt Nugget pretends I don't exist. She's all eyes on Lance.

"Ahem."

She flashes me a superior smirk. "Can I help you?"

"I need to buy some clothes. I was thinking you could—"

"I'll say," she snorts as her eyes sweep up and down my Marble slab pink polo and khakis. "Please tell me you wore that to be ironic. Or you're a kids' party clown." She glances at my pink Keds like they're actual clown shoes and rolls her eyes.

I'm instantly furious. "No. I wore it because I slept at my boyfriend's last night and didn't have a change of clothes." I grab Lance's wrist and tug him toward me.

Butt Nugget watches with amused disdain.

I want to add, *We had sex last night and this morning and it was so good I can't describe it and you will never know what it feels like to have my man between your legs.* Lance seems to be enjoying all this, but says nothing. I think he's impressed I'm marking my territory. It fuels my confidence. "So maybe instead of judging me, you can do your *job* and help me pick out some outfits."

"Are you sure you came to the right store? Maybe you're more of a pink polo shirt kind of girl. There's a GAP Kids just down the street."

Total witch.

Lance's grin widens. He covers his mouth with his hand to hold back a laugh, still leaning against the clothing rack like a spectator.

I grit my teeth at Butt Nugget. "Maybe you could go find your manager and explain to her why you're being rude to a paying customer."

"I *am* the manager." Her lips flatten into a white line but she is no less sexy.

I really hate her. "Then maybe you could have one of your nicer employees help us?"

Lance turns his face fully away, snickering with wheezy laughter. He's loving this.

Butt Nugget rolls her eyes at me. "What do you need?"

"I need a whole wardrobe." I hope I'm not overstepping my bounds. Lance flicks a nod, giving me permission. "Like, a bunch of different outfits."

Butt Nugget's face sours. "I'd be glad to help."

It takes about twenty minutes to gather an armload of outfits with her help. Her irritation is obvious but she knows my size and her inventory and I can tell everything is going to fit fine. When Lance wanders off, she's even more irritated her eye candy is gone. Good. She leads me to a curtained dressing room along one of the walls. It's right out in the open. "Here you go." She practically throws the clothes at me.

I fumble to catch them as she storms off.

What did I ever do to her?

I sigh, pull the curtain closed, and hang the outfits on the rack. There's a full length mirror and the usual bench. I smirk at my pink polo shirt and khaki reflection. Yeah, not sexy. I can't strip my Marble Slab uniform off fast enough, but I fold it neatly on the bench. I'm down to my caramel stained white bra and boring matching white panties. With nothing but the flimsy print curtain between me and the Nasty Doll patrons browsing behind me, I feel vaguely exposed. Oh well. It's not like someone is going to sneak in here.

I examine my row of potential outfits. Some of them are pretty racy. I'm so irritated by Butt Nugget's dripping judgement, I go bold and grab the black bodysuit with the criss-cross side laces. I'm about to step into it, but it will look stupid with my bra and granny panties on underneath. Too bad I forgot to pick out some sexy new underwear. I'll grab some later. I twist and peek out the curtain to make sure no one is hovering close by. Then I quickly unsnap my bra and jump out of my panties before climbing into the body suit, ignoring the fact I'm buck naked in the full length mirror for several seconds.

The tight jeans and black leather belt with silver studs that Butt Nugget gave me to go over the bodysuit are the perfect fit. Wearing them lowers my anxiety because I don't feel nearly so naked. I stand on bare tiptoes twirling in the mirror to check out my butt in the jeans. I wish I had some nice shoes to see the complete ensemble. And I wish Lance was here so he could appreciate the outfit. Butt Nugget actually did good. I stick my head out the curtain looking for Lance, but don't see him.

A punker girl with a dress folded over her arm asks, "Are you done with the dressing room?"

"Oh, no. Sorry." Darn it. If she wasn't waiting, I'd go look for Lance so I could surprise him with this outfit. I don't want to be rude and make her wait. "Did you need to try on that dress?"

"No," she smiles, "I'll keep looking." She turns and walks off.

I feel bad because I have like ten outfits and that girl had one and I want to find Lance anyway. So I shimmy out of the jeans and peel them off my feet. I take one last look at myself in the mirror. I look pretty darn good in this black bodysuit. I smile as I peel the straps over my arms and push it down to my waist, revealing my breasts. A quick shiver tightens my nipples. It's chilly in the store from the A/C.

"God damn," Lance whispers, peeking through a crack in the curtain.

I almost cover my breasts, but don't. I stand there and stare at his burning eyes in the mirror. Something about Lance and the magic of mirrors turns me on in a way I don't understand and makes me bold. I smirk at him. "Do you like what you see?"

He pushes through the curtain and stands behind me, hands on my hips. He runs them up and down the outsides. Slowly. "These hips are fucking perfect."

I moan and lean my head against his chest, closing my eyes.

He kisses the top of my head. "You are so fucking sexy it kills me."

Through half hooded eyes, I smile at him. Without my panties on, I am soaking this bodysuit with my sex. I guess I'll have to buy it.

Lance's hands massage my breasts. "Look how fucking hot you are."

Mirror me is a knockout. I've never considered myself a knockout, but the mirror never lies. I credit Lance. He brought out this side of me. Without him, I'd still be in the clowny polo shirt and matching Keds. But I am a half naked goddess in a black body suit.

"I have to fuck you. Right here. Right now." His fingers slip beneath the V-line of the body suit crotch and slide down my stomach, tickling my trim pubic hair before hooking between my legs. "You can't get any wetter, can you?"

I shake my head. "Mmm-mmm." I can't even form words I'm so turned on.

His belt buckle tinkles and the leather tongue tickles my back as he loosens his jeans. He pulls the crotch of the bodysuit to one side and hooks it against the inside of my thigh. The head of his hot cock appears between my legs in the mirror. I arch my back and his cock disappears when he grabs it with one hand. I feel it brush languidly up and down my slick crevice.

The porno movie of us in the full length mirror is the hottest thing I've ever seen. I reach up behind me and cup Lance's cheek in my palm. He leans down and we kiss sideways for a moment, but we're both more interested in the magic mirror show in front of us.

I push my entrance against the head of his hard shaft.

"Fuck, Chastity. I need to be inside you. Your pussy feels so good on my dick." His fingers stroke my clit from the front as his fist works his hot head up and down.

It would be so easy for him to slip inside.

He pulls back, looking down behind me, between us, watching the action closely. "Fuck..." he groans.

I wish I could see.

He wants to be inside me as badly as I do. But he's just sliding up and down, teasing me. It's driving me crazy. What is he doing back there? What are we doing in here? We're in a clothing store, for goodness sake! Anyone could accidentally open the curtain and see us like this. The punker girl, Butt Nugget, anybody. Butt Nugget would definitely call the cops just to get back at me. Do I want to get arrested for indecent exposure or sex in public or whatever?

Believe it or not, I don't care.

The danger heightens everything.

I don't want to stop.

I whisper, "Are you gonna fuck me or not?"

The sudden pressure of him just inside my entrance shocks me. I suddenly thrust against him. I don't know if I did it on purpose or if he surprised me or pulled me into him, but I am intensely aware of the fact he is now halfway inside me.

Without a condom.

I am not on birth control.

This is insane.

He pushes forward.

All the way.

I am full.

Lance's cock is deep inside me.

Without a condom.

I am so scared I want to come.

Yes, come.

I want him to come too.

Our eyes lock in the mirror.

Both of us frozen with fear.

But Lance won't let go of my hips.

I don't want him to.

I feel him swell inside me.

Is he going to come?

I don't know, but I'm going to.

He yanks himself out of me. "Fuck, sorry." He hisses. "I shouldn't have done that. Fuck, fuck. That was stupid. Fuck. We should stop."

"Do you have any condoms?"

He nods.

"Put one on."

Lance takes a deep breath, staring at me in the mirror the whole time.

I mutter, "It's too late to do anything now." I can't believe my confidence. I sound like I've done this before. But I haven't done any of this before. Unprotected dressing room sex in front of a full length mirror? Not even close. I can change that right now. "Put on a condom."

The fear on Lance's face is burned away by his devil's grin. "Your pussy is all over my dick. I can still feel it." He already has the condom out and rolls it on. He pushes into me and groans. "Fuck."

Fuck is right.

With the condom on, I feel no inhibitions. "Fuck me, Lance. Fuck me hard."

His eyes flame and he walks me forward until my breasts and forearms press against the dressing room mirror. I spread my legs wide. I'm vaguely aware of the hum of customers shopping in the store. His cock slides slowly in and out.

It feels so good and so naughty I whimper.

Loudly.

"Shh," he teases in my ear. "They'll kick us out if they catch us."

I whimper again, not caring.

"Do you want to get kicked out or do you want to get fucked?" He punctuates his words with deep thrusts.

"Fucked," I moan. With his fingers stroking my clit and him filling me to the hilt with every thrust, all I can think about is sex and the need to revel in as much sex as possible.

Lance pulls on my hair and grabs my neck with his palm. For a second, I think he's going to choke me, but he doesn't. Just strokes me lightly, caressing my skin down to my chest until he grabs my breast and squeezes. His abs are hot against my back and I push into him, loving every second of this.

When I think it can't get any kinkier, he pulls away and something hard presses against the tight nub of my butt. At first I clench, resisting, but he's insistent. His cock is still throbbing inside me so it must be his fingers. Or that thumb of his. I relax. It eases in just a bit and pushes gently in and out. The pressure of being filled in both holes is the dirtiest thing I've ever done. Somehow this drives me crazier and everything tightens to maximum.

"Oh fuck," Lance whispers hoarsely. "I'm gonna come, Pink. Come inside your pussy."

He twitches and that throws me over the edge.

"Ma'am?" Butt Nugget asks through the curtain. "There are other customers waiting to use the dressing room. Are you almost finished with the outfits I picked out?" She knows it's me.

"No!" Lance grunts.

Considering this is a clothing store for women, and Lance has an unmistakably masculine voice, him saying No! is all kinds of wrong and every kind of hilarious. As tightly as I'm clenching through my silent orgasm, the urge to burst into laughter shakes through me and I blurt out once before clamping my mouth shut.

"Sir? There are no men allowed in the changing rooms."

"Yeah!" Lance laugh-chuckles. "Be right out!"

I snicker through clamped lips, near tears.

"Sir? Ma'am? I'll have to ask you to stop whatever you're doing and come out right now."

"I'm coming," Lance grunts. "Coming right now."

"Sir?"

Lance wraps his arms around my waist and hugs me from behind. He pulses inside me, emptying himself.

I push against him and moan loud enough for Butt Nugget to hear.

"Slut," she grumbles under her breath before walking off.

I'm secretly proud of myself.

Yes. She's right.

I am a slut.

Chapter 17

CHASTITY

"I need to change."

"No. Leave the bodysuit on."

"But it's soaked, Lance!"

"And it's gonna stay that way. I want you wet all day for me. I'm gonna have to fuck you again in less than an hour. No use cleaning up."

"You are a total pervert." Apparently, I am too because I leave the bodysuit on and put the jeans and belt over it.

Lance rolls up the used condom and is about to slide it into his pocket.

"Gross," I grimace.

"Did you want me to leave it here?"

"Good point."

He puts it in his pocket.

Butt Nugget is at the register when we pay. She grimaces the entire time she rings us up. The bill is almost $1,600 and that's for only six outfits. But they can be mixed and matched in two dozen different ways. I tell Lance it's too much, but he insists. I offer to take it out of my paycheck but he refuses.

Who am I to complain?

We walk outside with Lance holding four big Nasty Doll bags like he's my overburdened manservant.

"Give me some of those bags. I feel stupid with you carrying everything." I yank away the two in his left hand before he can stop me. I look at Lance thoughtfully.

The harsh sunlight somehow accents his rugged features. He is impossibly gorgeous in this light. Irresistible. His stubble makes me crazy. His eyes glimmer sun diamonds.

"Something on your mind?" he asks.

"I need to get on the pill. Today."

"I vote yes to that."

"I think I can go to Planned Parenthood and get it there."

"Consider it part of your job description."

"Um, that makes me sound like a whore."

"My whore," he grins and pulls me into him with his free arm.

"You're gonna be a kept woman. Get used to it."

Why does that not bother me?

We kiss for a minute standing in front of Nasty Doll. I hope Butt Nugget is watching.

I can't decide if we're a couple. We're acting like one. Sort of. But are we? Or is this just some sick game that Lance will get bored of next week or next month? I don't know. And I don't want to worry about it now. Now I want to enjoy myself. It's too beautiful a day not too. "Now what?"

"We have one more stop." He leads me down the sunshine sidewalk.

"Where are we going?"

"To the Fashion District."

I hold up my Nasty Doll bag. "I already have enough fashion to last me all year."

"You need shoes." Nasty Doll has shoes, but Lance wouldn't let me buy any. I thought he was trying to put a cap on the budget.

I shake my head and laugh. "You can't buy me any more stuff today!"

"You can't wear those shoes with these clothes."

Although I'm braless and pantyless in the black bodysuit and jeans, my feet glow pink. My Keds. "Fine," I grumble smile. "By the way, you never told me how much you're paying me. For the job, I mean."

"I was thinking forty."

"Forty what?"

"K."

"You mean forty thousand? A year?"

He nods.

That is way more than I made at Marble Slab. Today is too good to be true. "Wow! I'm rich!" I laugh. "I'll totally pay you back for all these clothes!"

He shakes his head, smirking.

"I'm not rich?"

"No. I told you earlier I won't be taking any money out of your paycheck. But you can pay me back in other ways." His eyes burn and his devil's grin sizzles.

If it wasn't before, my bodysuit is now officially soaked.

We walk into an old building in the Fashion District and ride the rickety old cage elevator up to the eighth floor. It has one of those accordion gates with the metal X's and it's layered with a rainbow of peeling paint beneath the most recent coat of gray. The gate rattles when Lance closes it.

I grin, "Are we gonna have sex in the elevator? It feels so… dungeony."

"Too short a ride for my taste. Plus, no whips or chains."

"You are *so* bad…"

"Yup."

The eighth floor hallway has no windows and the gray walls are dimly lit by bare bulbs hanging from the ceiling. It's a dank cave.

I step off the elevator first. "Where are we?"

"You're gonna love this place."

Not by the looks of it. It's too grimy.

At the end of the hallway, he knocks on a heavy gray steel door scuffed with black streaks.

After several minutes, the door creaks open.

"Lance, darling!" the man inside gasps. He wears a white and cream three-piece suit with an aqua blue tie, aqua blue patent leather shoes, and a matching wave of perfectly coifed aqua blue and blond ombre hair. "So good to see you!" He air kisses Lance with fastidious delight then turns to me. "May I presume this is your muse?" He looks me over. "She's not the hot mess express you usually prefer. This one has charm." His brows knit together. "But those shoes will never do." He turns his nose up at my pink Keds like they *actually* stink.

Lance grins, "Yeah. This is her. Sylvan, meet my girl Chastity."

He just called me his girl. I swoon but hide it.

Sylvan throws his head back and laughs. "Chastity? Please tell me a gorgeous thing like you does not live up to your namesake, otherwise I mourn Lance the loss of his treasured sex life."

Obviously, they know each other.

"Um…" I'm speechless.

"We're fucking," Lance smirks, his eyes flashing.

"Lance!" I smack his elbow, blushing beet red. "What is wrong with you?"

He shrugs. "What can I say? I want everyone to know I'm fucking the hottest girl in LA."

Okay, I'm flattered. But does the "we're fucking" comment downgrade the "his girl" comment he made a second ago? I hope not.

"Now that *that* is out of the way," Sylvan laughs, "let's do something about those gruesome shoes. Welcome to paradise." He sweeps his arms toward the interior of the brightly lit impeccably white studio.

The walls are lined with what looks like gigantic white honeycomb cubbies. More honeycomb pods rise up in the center of the room. Inside each white hexagonal hole is a different pair of shoes. There are hundreds of pairs, almost like this place is a gigantic walk-in beehive in white. Instead of storing honey, the honeycomb stores delicious shoes in every color and style. I've never seen anything like them, every last pair is a chic and sexy woman's shoe. From casual to dress, flats to stilettos, it's everything a shoe whore could ever want.

If Christian Louboutin has a cool secret showroom, I bet it looks exactly like this. Or wishes it did.

I'm blown away.

Lance says. "Hook her up with whatever she needs."

Sylvan grins at me, his eyes gleaming. "Where shall we start, my dear?"

I am in heaven.

++++8++++

CHASTITY

The rest of the week is a blur.

I spend nights at Lance's house because I can't bear to face Mom. I text Charity every day and call her when I can so she doesn't worry about me. And to lift her spirits. I feel like I've abandoned her.

I never talk to Mom. Maybe when I'm ready.

I've had enough of her drama for the time being.

Lance bought me a sexy leather jacket for our motorcycle commute. It goes perfectly with the pair of black boots I got from Sylvan. Yes, I officially look like a rocker chick. Lance and I always arrive early to the office. Beaver is usually leaving and doesn't return until late at night. Micah comes in at regular hours and I get to know him over lunches with Lance. The three of us always eat together. Micah lives with his girlfriend Shiloh. They've been together four years. She's an actress who's claim to fame is a Geico commercial and a few smaller ads for cable.

The first thing I do for Lance is help him organize everything. North Valley High had a Business Basics class that I took, so I know my way around Microsoft Office. Unlike my other classes, I aced Business Basics, so I have something to contribute.

I also take over Lance's list of contacts and his calendar, and answer phones. Calls come in all day long. What I didn't realize at first is that Lance runs a full-fledged business. Not only does he have songs for sale online, he sells merchandise of every kind imaginable. Vinyl records. Cassette tapes, which I never knew existed until Lance played me one on an old boom box in his office. I didn't even know what a boom box was until he explained it. Who knew? He also sells TH3

PH4NTüM branded shirts, shoes, jewelry, watches, skateboards, custom glows sticks, and my favorite: the pacifiers with little silver phantom masks with light up LED eyes. It also turns out Beaver does app development for Lance. Lance has his own TH3 PH4NTüM game. I joked he should do a men's fragrance and he said he's already working on one but hasn't yet worked out a deal he likes. He even showed me several actual glass bottle designs that incorporated various versions of his silver phantom mask. He does everything.

To my surprise, we're so busy all week, we don't have time for work sex.

We make up for it every night at Lance's house after Mr. McKnight is in bed. We use condoms every time. If Mr. McKnight hears us having sex, he never says anything, but he must know. I can't imagine what my Mom would be like if she knew we were having sex in her house. Actually, I can. She'd find a priest to exorcise me. People and their differences are fascinating.

Fortunately, my period comes on like clockwork on Friday. Lance and I breathe a sigh of relief and vow to be more careful.

On Sunday, I start the pills we got at Planned Parenthood. I also skip church. It's just a coincidence. I think.

Anyway, for the first time since Dad moved out, I don't go to Sunday Service with Mom and Charity. It feels really weird not to. I consider it. Lance even offers to go. But I just can't do it. I don't want to face Mom or Mr. Molton. Later that day, I find out through Charity that Mr. Molton's son Caden is okay. He had a concussion, but it wasn't serious. What a relief. I still don't want to see Mr. Molton. Or his wife Amy. He must've told her he caught me having sex. I know her. She works at the shop all the time and would want an explanation as to why he fired me. What else other then the truth would be believable? Even the truth seems ridiculous unless you were there. Amy probably didn't believe it at first. I hate to imagine the look on her pious face when she finally accepted it. Disgust. Yeah, no. Skip that.

The next week goes by just as quick. Working for Lance is non-stop work. Who would've thought? But I love every second of it. Lance is the best boss ever.

And the sexiest.

The following Wednesday, Lance walks in after lunch wearing an impeccable silver suit with a vest, no tie, and a white button down shirt open at the collar.

Sex beast! I didn't think Lance could do dress up. I goggle, "Where'd you get that suit?"

"Picked it up at my tailor today."

"It looks… incredible."

"I'd fuck him," Beaver says.

Lance smirks, "You'd fuck a knothole."

"That's why they call me Beaver!" He bucks his front teeth over his lower lip and makes this rapid fire beaver clucking sound with his tongue before turning back to his computer.

I laugh. After going on two weeks, I like the guy. He's sex obsessed, but he's harmless.

"You look fucking hot," Lance says to me.

"You told me to dress rock and roll." I'm wearing a sheer black crop top over a black bra, a black leather skirt, and my knee high black biker boots.

Lance says to me, "We have two presentations this afternoon."

"Is that why you're all dressed up?"

"Yup. You ready to meet your first investor?"

"*My* investor? I'm just your assistant!"

"You kidding? The more money I make, the more money you make. If we get an investor on board and my next video blows up, I'll double your salary."

"Double? That's eighty grand! I think that's more than my Dad makes."

"What can I say? You proved yourself last week."

"All I did was organize your office. Nobody gets paid eighty grand for filing and answering the phones."

"You can be the first. Anyway, that's all an if. If we get money for the video. If it blows up. If, if, if." His tone hints at the hidden stress he must be carrying.

I'm afraid to ask. I don't want to burst the fantasy bubble just yet. We're on a roll and I'd like to keep it that way. And besides, the outfits are real. The office is real. Lance is real. The work is real. So what am I worrying about?

"Anyway," he sighs. "We need to nail this meeting if we want to get money. We better leave now if we wanna beat traffic."

Micah drives us in his Mini Cooper. Beaver snores in the front passenger seat. Lance and I are in the back. Lance barely fits in the small seat, but he holds my hand the entire drive.

As we pass under the 405 heading west on the 10, I ask, "How come Beaver is here? He should be home sleeping."

"In case we have a problem with the video."

"And me? What should I do at the meeting?"

"Take notes. Listen. Watch people for anything I might miss. I don't know how many people will be in the room."

"I can handle that."

"That's why I hired you." His eyes drop to my cleavage. "And look hot."

I blush. "I'll do my best."

"You're doing fine from where I'm sitting. Mmm, mmm." He reaches over and taps Beaver's shoulder. "Hey. Beaver. You gonna be awake during the meeting?"

Beaver snorts, "Huff?" Then resumes snoring.

Lance chuckles. "Fucking Beaver."

I have the best job ever.

++++8++++

CHASTITY

No.

No, no, no.

No to Lance's idea for his video, no to the song, and no to the money. That's all we hear all day.

At the first meeting in Santa Monica at a major talent agency, the guys in suits with the manicured nails sitting across from us at the boardroom table in the meeting room aren't interested. They think Lance's song is derivative and the market is over saturated with EDM. If Lance had come to them with this idea a year ago, they said, then maybe. But not now.

"That went well," Lance grunts over lunch at the Third Street Promenade.

The second meeting is the opposite. A recording studio just off Wilshire Boulevard near the beach. The investors are casual, wearing shorts and T-shirts like they were just surfing and they all say "dude" a lot. They also say Lance's concept is too different. Too out there. They don't think the target demographic will get it. Not what I expected from their casual surfer attitude.

When we walk to Micah's car, Lance looks at me across the roof. "Really, dude? *Really?* Too out there? Dude?"

I snicker at how Lance is mimicking the investor's overuse of the word dude.

He flashes a smile.

Beaver says groggily, "Your video needs tits. Lots of bouncing tits."

"Shut the fuck up, Beaver," Lance laughs.

"Who doesn't like tits?" Beaver asks himself as we all climb into the car. "Do you not like tits, Chaz?" he asks me when we're inside.

"I like mine."

Beaver twists in his seat. "Lance, I'm telling you! Tits!"

"You can't have tits in a YouTube video." Lance is actually taking him seriously.

"Pasties. Like at a rave."

"America is afraid of bouncing boobs, nipples or not."

"America loves tits.They just won't admit it. Wait and see. The twenty-first century will be the century of the tit. Breasts everywhere. Look at what Chaz is wearing."

He's right. My new black bra is clearly visible beneath my short sleeve Lurex crop top.

"See?" Beaver says confidently. "Tits."

Lance grumbles, "Stop staring at her tits, Beaver."

"Just saying. Your video needs more tits. It doesn't have to be Chaz's tits. Any tits will do. Although hers are pretty spectacular..." He says it seriously, like he's solving a math problem, not lusting after mine.

I snicker.

Micah laughs, "Beaver, you need a girlfriend."

"I've got plenty." Beaver frowns and folds his arms across his chest before going to sleep.

Back at the office, Beaver goes home.

Micah says, "Do you guys mind if I mix on the monitors?"

"Um..." I don't know what he means.

Lance says, "He wants to use the speakers instead of headphones. I don't care. Raise the roof."

"Yeah," I smile. "Go right ahead."

Micah sits at his Mac and goes to work editing one of Lance's songs. The music is loud and the beat thumps through the floor, shaking the entire building.

"Office," Lance says to me.

I jog up the stairs.

When the glass door closes behind us, it mutes Micah's monitors, but the music still booms through the room.

"I need to fuck," Lance grunts, shrugging off his suit jacket and dropping it on his executive chair. He unbuttons his vest and rips it off. "Strip." His brutal tone is shocking and his eyes scorch me like I'm his victim.

Um, no? How is this in any way acceptable behavior? More importantly, why am I peeling my top off without a second thought?

"Now the skirt." He loosens his cuffs, removing cufflinks which he tosses on the corner of the desk.

His insistence fires my irritation. I throw my crop top in his face.

"Make me."

He catches the top and tosses it behind him. It bounces off the interior window and falls to the floor.

"Be careful you don't run over my top with your chair. The Lurex is delicate and you paid good money for it."

He snorts a laugh and practically tears his dress shirt off without unbuttoning it and throws it on his vest. "Strip, Pink. I'm going to fuck you until you scream."

Does he mean good scream or bad scream? I *should* hope he means the former but I *want* him to mean the latter. I am perverse. Why am I so turned on by his restrained rage? I bend down to unzip my motorcycle boots.

"Leave the boots on."

"Okay then." I stand up and unzip my leather skirt and shimmy it over my hips, stepping out of it. All that's left is my black bra, black panties, and black leather boots. I plant my hands on my hips and my elbows flare. "Now what, your highness?"

"Dance."

"Um, sorry. Not gonna happen."

"Dance, Pink. Now."

I fold my arms across my bra. "Sorry, your highness. I hate to break it to you, but I have zero experience. The only dance I know is the funky chicken. Or maybe the happy dance. So whatever sort of stripper fantasy your hoping to fulfill right now? Not. Gonna. Happen."

His eyes burn. "Don't make me come around this desk." He's not joking. He's frightening.

"How about square dancing?" I squeak, afraid. "I did that in grade school. I can do-si-do." I put my arms out in front of me in the do-si-do pose and step lively in a circle. Then I stick my elbow out and call, "Swing your partner!" I start giggling and stop dancing, bending over with my hands on my naked knees. I can't decide if I think he's ridiculous for acting this way or if he's scaring me with his glare. Probably both.

His eyes smolder with pent up fury. Then he *almost* cracks, a flash of a smile, but it's gone just as quick.

"Sorry," I laugh. "You're making me nervous. So I'm cracking jokes."

"Feel the music."

"Micah keeps starting and stopping it." At the moment, it's silent, but I swear he's played the same ten seconds over and over at least ten times.

Lance turns around and rips the indoor window open and yells downstairs. "Micah!"

"Yeah?" he hollers.

Lance stares at me as he continues yelling down to Micah. "Leave the music playing."

"I'm editing, Lance. Do you want me to put cans on so you don't have to hear it?"

"No. Leave it loud and take a break. I don't want you back here for an hour."

"You sure? I've got plenty left to do. I was hoping to finish before eight so I could take Shiloh out to dinner tonight. We won't have time for a movie after if I take an hour break now."

Lance is obviously frustrated. "Leave the fucking music playing and leave. Go take Shiloh out early. And see a movie. On me. Bring the receipts back so I can expense it. But I don't wanna see you here until tomorrow. Got it?"

"Yeah! Thanks, man!" Micah is obviously happy about it. "Shiloh will be stoked! Laters, people!"

"Bye!" I holler.

"Later, Chaz!"

The music booms through the studio a moment later, much louder with the window open.

Lance's face darkens like he's going to eat me alive.

Chapter 18

CHASTITY

"Dance," Lance commands.

"I told you, I suck at dancing."

"Feel the music."

I slump my shoulders for a second. "Okay. I'll try."

I start moving, picturing all the sexy dance videos I've watched in secret over the years. Beyoncé, Britney Spears, Shakira. But it's not like I studied their moves. Lark and I just jumped around to the songs like idiots. We weren't exactly trying to master dancing.

Lance sits in his chair, feet up on the desk, hands behind his head. Is he enjoying himself? Or is he just irritated?

Who knows.

I twist and gyrate and move my hips as best I can. The next thing I know I'm breathing hard from the effort. I'm so busy dancing, I forget about Lance, but I'm completely focused on doing a good job. I want to impress him as much as he's impressed me since day one. I don't want him to see me as the innocent church girl I am. I want to be dirty and slutty and his perfect fantasy. Too bad I have nearly zero experience in that department. Wait, that's not true. My mind drifts back to all the dirty things we've done since he first kissed me. I lose myself in the moment and I get a little bit turned on. I just hope Lance likes this.

When the song finishes and I plant my hands on the edge of his desk and flip my hair up over my head, he's sitting there glaring at me. Now his arms are folded across his chest.

I frown. "Are you even enjoying this? I'm trying to do a good job." And failing. Why does this make me want to cry? Because I feel like a failure as a woman? Oh yeah. That. It almost makes me mad, but I'm too confused to be angry. Just frustrated. "What am I doing wrong, Lance?"

"Stop asking questions." He sits up suddenly and I jump back from the desk. He steeples his fingers in front of him. "Touch yourself."

"I just was. When I was dancing."

"You're going to make yourself come for me. I'm not going to lift a finger."

"Don't be such a stick in the mud."

"Touch. Your. Self."

"Fine. Be like that. But you're not getting any of this tonight." I motion at my crotch with hands like blades.

His devil's grin curls. "I make the rules, Chastity. You do what I say."

I'm not your property, Lance!! I'm not your whore!! I'm not your possession!! You don't control me!! This is messed up!! You need therapy!! Like, years' worth!! What is wrong with you?! My chest heaves as I think these thoughts. But not one leaves my lips. I push my panties down and fight with them as they tangle in the buckles of my boots. Stupid panties! But I get them off and throw them at him. They miss. So I unhook my bra and throw that at him too.

He leans his head to the side, easily dodging my bad throw.

I snarl at him. "Fine! Tell me what to do! Fucking asshole!"

His slow smile spreads. "You realize that's the first time you've ever said fuck in anger? You're making progress."

"What, are you trying to turn me into you? A foul mouthed asshole who treats women like shit to get your jollies?" I'm so angry I forget the fact I'm arguing with him while naked. Well, except for my black leather boots which apparently give me the power to kick ass and take names because that's what I'm about to do.

"No. I'm trying to de-program you. Your mom turned you into a robot. You may not realize it, but you follow the script she beat into you."

"She didn't beat me."

"Maybe not physically. But mentally? That woman is a nightmare." He snorts, "And I thought my dad was bad."

Ouch. I should be hurt by his words. But I also know how sensitive he is about his dad. He means it in some strange way that makes sense, but I can't yet figure out how.

"Chastity, your Mom and all her bullshit is a part of you. That's what happens to anyone who has a parent. I was a fucking carbon copy of my dad for the longest time. It took a lot of work to not end up like him. I almost ended up where he is. But here I am."

"Well, you did good, asshole." My anger is half-hearted.

"All these sex games are for fun. For a release. But the only thing I really want from you is for you to find yourself. Get rid of all that shit your mom shoved down your throat. Become the person you want to be."

"That's exactly what I'm doing! We had sex in a clothing store, for goodness sake! My Mom would never do anything like that!"

"Goodness sake? You're still her daughter."

"Oh!" I stamp my booted foot. He's right. Nobody I know except

Charity ever says goodness sake or oh ship or cheese us.

"You may think you're your own person, but it takes a long time to wipe the slate clean. It did me, believe me. And some parts of you never change, no matter how hard you try." He lowers his eyes, shaking his head, probably thinking about his dad. "I'm just here to keep pushing you in whatever direction *you* want to go. What direction that is, I don't know. But you'll find it." He smiles to himself, "And if we fuck a lot in the process, so much the better."

"How do you know all this?"

"Experience."

Moments like this are a stark reminder that Lance is eight years older than me and didn't live a sheltered life with an ultra religious mother. He knows all about the big bad world and I know so shamefully little. But he's sharing his secrets, the keys to living a better life. With me. He obviously figured out how to build an awesome life. All I have to do is look around this office. He's not his dad. He escaped his humble beginnings and found success. And he's sharing it with me by making me a small part of it. Is that why him talking to me this way is such an incredible turn on? Obviously. But it's something else. I nod my head and smile. "You care about me, don't you?" I expect an evasive answer.

He smiles. "Yes."

"Why—"

"Shut up and touch yourself." He kicks his feet back up on the desk.

Now I want to touch myself. My pussy feels warm and wonderful and it's begging to be touched. "Can I ask one question?"

"One."

"Why do I have to touch myself when I totally want to have sex with you right now? Don't you want to have sex with me?"

"That's two questions. I'll answer the first."

I snort a laugh, "Fuck *you*, Lance." He is so irritating.

He smiles, proud of himself.

I hate him more. But I'm embarrassed to admit it's hate in a good way.

"I totally want to watch you make yourself come right now. For real. No faking. I'll know if you're faking. I want you dripping all over yourself. Got it?" He unbuckles his slacks and squirms them and his silk boxers down until his cock jumps out, hard as a rock.

"You are so weird."

"You think that now..." He grips his shaft and starts to stroke. "Start touching. Or you're gonna watch me come and I'll be all done for the night. So if you wanna fuck me, you better come first. That's how this game works."

"Game? What happened to me being my own person? You're controlling me more than my mom ever did."

"I'm not controlling you. You choose to leave or stay. The door's right behind you. Walk out any time you want. But if you stay we play it my way."

So I touch myself. Not because Lance told me.

I touch myself...

For me.

++++8++++

LANCE

Watching Chastity finger herself is the hottest fucking thing I've ever seen. She's bold. Brave. A fucking sex bomb.

She drops into a chair in front of my desk and hooks the heels of her boots on the edge. She pushes the chair back so her hot red pussy is in full view. I'm fucking hypnotized by the way the skin stretches as she slides four fingers across the surface. The corners of her lips pop out between them. That shit is fucking hot. I fucking love lips. And they are fucking wet and engorged with blood. The tight skin stretches and retracts as she works it. It takes everything I have not to jump over the desk and fuck her right now. She's been on the pill for more than a week. I could come inside her right now.

But I wait.

This shit is too good to miss.

The look in her narrowed eyes is total confidence. They challenge me with a threat. A dare. I don't know fucking what.

I am addicted to the witch's brew between Chastity's legs.

I stroke myself slowly, enjoying every second of this.

"You want this?" She sneers as she bites her lower lip and dips a finger inside her pussy and holds it there. "You can't have it. Look but don't touch, Lance." Her eyeliner, which she just started wearing a few days ago, is a little bit smudged, adding a sultry darkness to her eyes.

She pulls out and drags her finger around her clit in slow motion. Her head falls back on the chairback and she moans. She's not faking. Not some stripper or model chick pretending to get off so they can get in your wallet. This is the real deal.

Chastity is as turned on as I am.

"Taste it," I grunt.

"What?"

"Taste yourself."

Her dark eyes smolder. She's sneering again. She dips her middle finger into her pussy. Drives it deep. Slow. All the way to her knuckles. Fuck. She drags it out and flips me off. It's a wet lollipop of girl cum. "You want this, don't you? *You* want to taste it, don't you?"

Fuck yeah I do.

She snorts a laugh. "Well, fuck you. You can't." She licks her finger lollipop, savoring her sugar.

My dick twitches and I'm going to come. I instantly release my hand and try to relax, but every muscle in my dick and ass is locked up tight. A pulse runs up the shaft. Here comes the cum. I force out a slow breath, dropping all the tension in my dick and balls and manage to relax just in time to halt a full ejaculation, but a single bead of cum blooms at the tip as a wave of orgasm floods through me. God damn it, this feels good.

I stare at her, watching her suck on her syrupy finger.

I want to lick it clean. I want to fuck her till she screams.

I would never tell her this, but Chastity Fucking Shields is the hottest sexiest god damn perfectest woman I've ever had the pleasure to meet, to fuck, to eat.

Dinner time.

++++8++++

CHASTITY

Lance leans forward in his executive chair like he's about to stand up. "I'm gonna eat that sopping pussy of yours, Pink. Eat it till you come all over my face."

I laugh, "No you're not. Remember, no touching."

He eases back down in the chair and grins that devil's grin, entirely too satisfied with himself. He's loving this but he won't admit it. His hands squeeze the armrests of his chair like he has to hold on to that or he'll try to grab me.

To my surprise, I'm making the rules. Funny what playing with yourself in front of a man will get you if you're willing to try. Can you say, Shift in the Power Dynamic?

I tease, "If you want to touch something, Lance, touch yourself."

Between the V of my thighs, I watch him stroke himself slowly. I scoot my ass a little further down in the chair so he won't miss a thing as I resume touching myself. Then I sneer at him while I smear my fingers around my lips before returning them to my clit. With my other hand, I insert two fingers and start to fuck myself. It feels so damn good. I moan as my vagina tightens in a pre-orgasmic contraction. My eyes clamp and I moan long. "Nnnnnnn…"

"Fuck," he grunts, his face bunching. His hand suddenly freezes and squeezes the bright red tip of his dick. Only the very end of the swollen head pokes out. "I… can't—" Suddenly cum fires from his cock and he leans back in his executive chair, groaning loud.

I climb out of my chair and crawl onto the desktop, swiping a pile of papers out of my way. His legs are slack and I plant my hands on the seat of the chair on either side of his hips. He sits up when my weight tips the chair forward, giving me easier access to my target. My mouth dives at his cock, catching the last of him as he spurts onto my tongue. He's still large and I can't take him all the way in, but I try, kissing the shaft with my lips, swallowing cum down my throat.

"Lick the tip," he grunts.

I do, lapping him passionately. I have no idea what I'm doing, but he seems to like it.

"Fuck!" He tries scooting back in the chair but I won't let him escape.

I work his cock, cleaning the last of his seed.

"Ssssss!!!!" His entire body tenses.

I would say, *Now who's in control?* But I have his dick in my mouth. Even so, I start to smile, making it impossible to keep a tight seal around his girth. My drool drips out all over his lap. I try to suck it back, but it doesn't work so I do my best to relax my lips and focus on his pleasure.

He sucks air through his teeth repeatedly. "Fuck," *hiss* "fuck," *hiss* "fuck…"

I keep sucking.

After another minute, he sits up suddenly, laughing. "Stop, stop! You're gonna give me a heart attack!"

I release him but I lick my way up his stomach, tonguing the cum still stuck there.

"God damn, that's hot," he mutters.

"Mmmm-hmmm." I push up slowly, balanced with my hands on the seat of the chair and my knees still on the desk. My arms are shaking from holding myself up for so long in this position. That was a lot of work. But I don't let it show. I give him my sexiest pussy cat smile as I sit back on my heels on the desk and wipe my wrist across my mouth. "Mmmm. Yummy."

He's leaning back in the chair again, gazing at me through half hooded eyes. "You're telling me. Fuck, woman. Where did you learn to suck dick like that?"

"Just now. I just did what you said and went with it."

"Jesus Christ, you should give a blowjob seminar at the Learning Annex. You'd make a fucking mint."

"The Learning Annex?" I snicker.

"Or wherever they give BJ classes, I don't fucking know." He laughs softly.

"Hey, I thought you were supposed to watch me come," I tease, wiggling his cock. "You're a wet noodle."

"What can I say?" A slack smile eases onto his face. "You're too fucking hot and you dance like a pro and I couldn't fucking help it."

I smile, proud of myself, leaning my hands on my knees.

He stands up and his slacks fall to his ankles. He kicks them off with his boxers. "Now I'm going to fuck you."

"You're not even hard."

"Lie down." He looms over me.

I lean back on my hands and slide my boots out until they hang over the edge of the desk.

He squats down and grabs my thighs in his big hands and devours me. His tongue works miracles.

I'm already wet and charged from everything else. It takes seconds for me to fall back into ecstasy. "Oh, God, Lance, that feels wonderful."

He lifts his slick face. "Don't. Not yet." He stands and drops his cock on my crotch, hard once again. "You're going to come when I do." He fists himself and slides in slowly, staring down at our flesh connection.

He fills me and begins thrusting, holding onto my hips.

I don't know how long he pumps in and out, but I am flying the whole time. I try to wait for him, try so hard, but it's impossible. It feels too impossibly good. When I can't hold back for a second longer, I whimper, "Lance, I'm going to come." I coil my legs around his waist and pull him toward me.

He leans over the desk, chest to chest. "Not yet," he grunts.

"Please, Lance, I'm dying. Oh, God, it's so damn good. I can't take anymore."

"Not yet..."

"Please..."

"Not... Now—fuck—FUCK!—Come now! Now!!"

We both explode.

I float outside my body, or something, for several minutes. I'm brought back to reality by the tickling drip of his cum running down my butt crack. That's when I realize that having sex without a condom is light years beyond condom sex.

Wow.

I can't even put it into words.

It just is.

He weighs against me, slumped over the desk, his body hot and his muscles hard. He whispers in my ear, "*Now* you're not a virgin anymore."

I snort and whisper, "Just now? All that other fucking didn't count?"

"Nope. And you know what that means?"

"What?"

"You're mine."

My hearts swells and I wrap my arms around him and hug hard, squeezing with my legs too. "I love you, Lance," I whisper. "I love you so—"

He tenses.

Oh, ship!

What did I just do?

Chapter 19

CHASTITY

"What?! No fucking way!!" Lark is practically jumping out of her seat at the In-N-Out Burger in Burbank.

"Waaa-aaaay," I sing.

"Lance is the Phantom?" Her eyes are a mile wide.

"Yup."

"*The* Phantom? The one I saw on stage at Coachella last year when I got sunburned like a lobster?"

"Yes, the one with the abs and the mask."

"How did I not recognize those abs at your pool party? And, what the fuck! How could you not tell *me*?!"

"I just did," I giggle and pick up my double-double cheeseburger with grilled onions. We're sitting in one of the plastic booths in the middle of the restaurant, surrounded by other diners eating.

"So wait, your boyfriend is famous?"

"I guess."

"Is he rich too?"

"I'm not sure," I say thoughtfully. "But he's better off than either of us."

"That's not hard to do," she chuckles, swirling a french fry in her ketchup cup. "So, has he punched your V-card yet?"

I blush and take a bite of my burger so I don't have to answer.

"He did!" Lark gasps. "Where? When? How?"

When I finish chewing and dab my mouth with my napkin, I say, "Which time?"

"You fucking slut!" She grabs my wrist. "Give me the run down! I need to know every last detail! Body parts, bodily fluids, all of it!"

I look around In-N-Out. Fortunately, no one is paying attention. The constant drone of fifty different conversations creates a cocoon of anonymity. In a low voice, I relate an abbreviated version of events to Lark, smiling the whole time.

At one point, her eyes goggle, "He fucked you in the dressing room at Nasty Doll?"

I grin. "Yup."

"Did you get caught?"

"Sort of. Not really. The manager heard us but she didn't do anything."

She shakes her head. "Fuck me, Chaz. I haven't even done that! What are you doing topping my game like that?!"

I shrug and smile. "Just doin' my thang." I laugh.

"I'll have to step it up. Something with bondage. Yeah. Whips and chains. And airplanes."

"You mean like the Mile High Club?"

"You haven't done that too, have you?" she whines.

"No. Not yet." I smile at the thought.

"Okay. Phew. And you didn't do any of that fifty shades shit either, right?"

"No," I chuckle. Lark and I have both read the books and discussed them with her mom, who read them too. My mom thinks *Fifty Shades of Grey* is an interior decorating thing. I roll my eyes at the thought. "But you never know. Lance is really demanding."

"Guys like him always have whips hidden somewhere. Shit! That means I need to be more creative. What tops bondage?"

"Sex underwater in a shark cage, circled by a pack of great whites?"

Lark grimaces, "Is that what we've come to?"

"Afraid so. How about alien sex? I'm thinking octo-penis."

"What, like eight dicks on one hunky alien?"

"Yeah," I giggle.

"That's six too many."

"Why do you need two? Oh! You mean one for the... *mmm* and the other for the *mmm*?"

She nods, "That'd be the butt, Bob."

"The who?"

She giggles and shakes her hair, "Never mind."

"You know, when he was... fucking me, he—"

"Did you just say fuck?! Unholy shit, sinner! You said fuck!" She jumps up and stands on the red booth bench and points at me like I'm a cornered criminal. "Someone call the New York Times! Call CNN! My best friend just said fuck for the first time in her life!" Everyone inside In-N-Out stops and gawks at Lark, which is amazing because the place is busy and loud. Lark jams her hands on her hips and glares back. "What? *What?* I said fuck! Are you gonna arrest me?" Everyone stares silently, many mouths agape. One mother covers the ears of her young son. Lark smirks at everyone, "That's what I thought." She dismisses the room with a flip of her hand and sits back down. She folds her fingers calmly together on the table like nothing happened. "Hold up. You were going to say something about the fucking?"

"Mmm. When we were..." Now I don't want to say it lest Lark

make another scene.

"Fucking." she adds.

"Yeah, that. Anyway, he put his finger up my butt."

Her eyes pop and she gasps. Loudly.

People are staring again.

"What?" I mutter nervously.

"You're a *butt* slut!"

I grimace. "Shhh, Lark!"

"You liked it, didn't you, you dirty brown butt slut! You like ass play! I knew it!"

"Brown?" I'm blushing now. With both hands, I comb my long blonde hair over my face. I am blushing like crazy.

Fingers part my hair curtain. "Where does it end, Chaz?" She says it super seriously. "It's just a downhill slide to Slut Town from here, isn't it?"

I snort. "So be it."

She shakes her head. "Why am I not surprised? Uptight girls always like it in the butt. That's why it feels so good! Because you're butt tight!"

"I'm not uptight! Or butt tight! Or whatever!"

"So says your mom," she chuckles.

I have no idea what my mom might say about butt play, if she even knew what that was, but I'm very aware of the teenagers in the booth beside ours who are now laughing hysterically. At me, no doubt.

Lark doesn't notice. "How is Faith, bee-dubs?"

"I haven't talked to her in a while. She basically threw me out of the house."

She gasps. "Why didn't you tell me?"

"I've been staying with Lance."

"Oh, shit. Slow down your trip to slut town, GF! You're going to fall in love with him if you don't put the brakes on. Unless you have already. You haven't, have you?"

I hang my head and stare at the remnants of the fries on my tray. "I told him I loved him."

"What?! You've known him like what, two, three weeks?"

"I can't help it. That's how I feel."

"You feel that way because he took your virginity. How do you think I felt when that jerk Zack took mine? He even told me he loved me before we did it! And that fuckwad still joined the Army six months later!" She groans wearily. "Would you believe he has a kid now?"

"How do you know?"

"I Facebook stalked him. I'm better off without him. Never mind him. You gotta be careful with what you say to Lance or he'll join the Army too."

I chuckle, "I don't think he's the type."

"Truth. But fuck, seriously. Don't tell him you love him again. Maybe he'll forget."

"I wish."

"You never know. Guys have short memories. Just don't say it again."

"I know. It was stupid. But I said it. Because it's true, Lark. I love him." Fear twists my stomach in a knot and tears brim. "Maybe I screwed up. I knew it was a mistake the second I said it. I'm such an idiot."

"Whoa, GF. Don't beat yourself up. If loving him scares him off, and that's a big if, he's lame. Guys who run away because you tell them you love them are going to run away sooner or later anyway. Trust me on this," she chuckles wearily. "Anyway, what do I know? Maybe he loves you too and he's afraid to say it."

I gasp. "You think?"

"Easy, girl. Don't get your hopes up. Just play it cool."

"I don't know if I can."

++++8++++

CHASTITY

"Does it bother you I didn't say it back?" Lance asks out of the blue four nights later. We lie on his mattress, shoulder to shoulder, both of us staring at the ceiling. It's well past midnight.

I'm guessing he's talking about my I love you. Hope floods my body. Is he about to tell me he loves me too? Then I remember Lark's advice. Don't get my hopes up. So I stuff it down.

Whir.

Usually, when I stuff my feelings in my stomach, they're bad feelings. Not good ones. This is annoying. But I trust Lark more at this point than I do Lance.

Play it cool.

I sigh. "Do you want an honest answer?"

"Yes."

I collect my thoughts before saying anything. I may have zero experience when it comes to relationships, but when it comes to fights, I can see them coming a mile away, thanks to my mom, and I want to avoid one now because I should be sleeping.

As it is, things have been tense between Lance and I since I said it.

STEALING CHASTITY 181

We've been pretending nothing happened. The downside is that now nothing really is happening between us. We haven't had sex since. We haven't made out either. Nothing. It's like we're just friends and co-workers. We don't even sleep naked. He's wearing boxers and I'm in a T-shirt and panties.

What'll be next?

Him saying, *I think it's best for you to go back to sleeping at your Mom's house.*

The idea makes me furious.

I'm tired of pretending.

I'm tired of hiding my feelings.

If he's going to end this, let's get it over with. I hate wondering.

I take a deep breath and try to remain calm before I speak. "Yes, it bothered me. I felt really close to you in that moment and you didn't say anything. You just stood up and put your suit back on and left me hanging like I never even said it. For a minute, I remember thinking you had suddenly disappeared even though you were standing right in front of me. I felt completely alone. That's how my mom makes me feel when she gives me the silent treatment. How did you expect me to feel?"

I give him time to digest all that.

He says nothing. At least he's not yelling at me like Mom.

After a while, I start to worry again. Is he going to pretend I never said anything just now either? Is this his version of silent treatment?

I can't take this. "Lance?"

He's staring at the ceiling like I'm not even here.

That hurts more than I'd care to admit.

I'm not going to lie here like I'm okay with it. But I won't start a fight like he's Mom. I'm an adult. I'm going to act like one. For as long as I can manage it. "Lance? Please talk to me."

BLAM! BLAM! BLAM!

I jump.

Someone is pounding on the front door of the house. The doorbell rings a bunch of times really fast.

"What the fuck," Lance whispers, sitting up in bed.

I gasp, afraid for my life. "Something is wrong, Lance," I hiss, grabbing his elbow. "I can feel it."

"Relax. It's just someone at the door."

"In the middle of the night?"

He hops off the mattress and opens the bedroom door.

Mr. McKnight stands there in the hallway in saggy plaid boxers with his hair standing up. "What the hell is going on?" he mutters.

"I'll take care of it, Dad. Go to bed."

Mr. McKnight scratches his head. "It's Kane."

"Who?"

"Kane? From Vegas?"

"Fuck that guy," Lance growls. "He doesn't know where you live. Nobody does. I made sure of it."

That sounded weird.

Mr. McKnight says thoughtfully, "I don't know. Kane knows people. Maybe he tracked me down."

Tracked him down?

Lance grits his teeth, "It's not fucking Kane. How much did you fucking drink tonight?"

Mr. McKnight doesn't answer.

What are they talking about? Kane who? Do I even want to know?

The pounding at the door resumes. The whole house shakes. The doorbell rings several more times.

"Open up!" The voice is muffled but it stops my heart.

Lance charges around the corner toward the front door.

I catch up just as he grabs the doorknob in the familiar entryway, the one that is a mirror image of the one I grew up with. Rather than comforting me, the familiarity scares me to death.

Grunting, Lance rips the front door open wide.

"Charity ran away!" Mom sobs. She's fully dressed like it's the afternoon, not after midnight.

"What?" I gasp. "Are you sure?"

"She left a note! I found it in her room an hour ago! I have no idea where she went!"

"Oh my goodness. Maybe she's staying at a friends?" I can't escape the feeling that Mom concocted this story so she had an excuse to talk to me. Is she capable of that? Knowing how fake she is with everyone at church, yes.

"No. She texted that she was going to study at Sydney's after school. They had some big history project but she never came home. I called Sydney's parents, Becky's, everyone I could think of. No one has seen her." She jitters with panic.

"Are you sure?" I can't believe this is happening. More importantly, I don't want to believe it.

"Yes I'm sure!" Mom barks. "Do you think I'm crazy?"

Yes. I glance at Lance and he's hiding a smirk.

"This is all your fault, Chastity! Charity ran away because you did! She wants to be just like her big sister! Look what you did! My baby is gone! Because of you!"

Chapter 20

CHASTITY

"Maybe if you hadn't pushed me away, you wouldn't have pushed her away!" I yell.

"I didn't push you away!" Mom screams.

I snort, "Are you serious?"

"Yes I'm serious! You did this! You and your—" she sneers, "… boyfriend."

Lance chuckles and shakes his head.

"And you!" Mom fires a finger at Mr. McKnight. "You almost killed her! Ever since the electrocution, there has been something wrong with her! I think you hurt her brain!"

Mr. McKnight is clearly frightened and taking her seriously.

"Wait, wait, wait," I laugh. "I talked to Charity every day since then. She's fine. You're crazy, Mom. Mr. McKnight did not fry her brain."

He looks relieved. "I'm really sorry, Faith. I—"

Mom's eyes go feral. "Don't sorry me, Rod! Ever since you and your son waltzed into our lives, it has been a daily disaster!" She looks up at the sky. "What did I do wrong, Lord? Please tell me what I did. I will make up for it, I promise. Just tell me how to fix it."

I heave a sigh. "That's not going to help, Mom. We need to find her. Did you call Trish's house?"

"No, I… no."

"So call her. I don't know her number." Trish is a friend of Charity's from grade school, but ever since her family moved to Hermosa Beach two years ago, they don't get to see each other very often. But I know they text all the time and Skype nearly every week.

"Good idea. I'll do that right now." Mom jogs down the walkway outside and goes back home.

"What do you need me to do?" Lance asks me quietly.

"I don't know yet. But thanks for offering."

"Whatever you need, I'm here."

I nod, "Okay. Thank you. But she probably just took a bus to Trish's. Those two are super close. Charity is always telling me how awesome Trish's parents are. She probably wanted to get away from Mom for a while. I can't blame her." I put on a brave face, but something tells me it won't make any difference. "I'm going to see what's taking Mom so long. Wanna come with?"

"Sure."

"Put some pants on first."

He smiles, looking down at his boxers. "Right. You too."

"Oh yeah."

We throw on clothes in his bedroom and I grab my phone. When we come out, Mr. McKnight is dressed too.

"Can I do anything?" he asks.

I look at Lance for a second. He's inscrutable. I say, "You should stay here, Mr. McKnight. We'll let you know what we find out."

"Okay." He sounds sad.

I would invite him, but he shouldn't have to endure more insults from Mom.

Back home, I lead Lance into the kitchen.

Mom is on the phone. "Okay. Thank you, Linda. Yes. Please let me know if you see her. Thanks. Good night." She beeps off the cordless phone and stares at me with hollow eyes. "She's not there."

My stomach waves nauseously. "Did you ask if Trish talked to Charity?"

"Linda said not since the weekend."

"Hmmm. Maybe she's…"

"She's gone, Chastity," Mom says, frightened.

"We should go look for her," Lance says.

Mom stares at him like she can't decide if she hates him or needs his help.

"Shouldn't we call 911?" I suggest.

"I already did," Mom says. "An officer came by an hour ago. I gave him her picture. They're already looking for her."

I nod and think. "What did Charity's note say?"

She picks a folded sheet of notebook paper off the counter. Written in Charity's bubbly handwriting in purple ink is the following:

Mom-

I can't deal with you anymore. Don't look for me.

She didn't even sign it.

I've felt the same way a thousand times since Dad left. I feel her pain. I hardly blame her. At least I got out and had Lance waiting to catch me. Charity doesn't have anyone except… "Did you call Dad?"

Mom looks away nervously.

"Did you?"

She stares at me for a second before her face cracks. "No! I did not call your father, okay?!"

"Mom! Are you crazy? Dad is not the enemy! Call him! For all you know she's on a plane to Chicago already!" I pull up Dad in my contacts on my phone and call his number. The phone rings four times before going to voicemail. I hang up and call again. Same thing.

"He's not going to answer because he doesn't care," Mom scowls.

I glare at her and shake my head and dial again. While it's ringing, an incoming call from Dad flashes on the screen. I answer it. "Dad!"

"What's wrong, Chaz?" He sounds sleepy. It's two hours later there.

"Charity ran away. Did she talk to you?"

"What?! When?!" He's awake now.

"Today. Did she say anything to you?"

"No! I haven't talked to her all week. She hasn't returned any of my calls. Is she okay?"

"We don't know. I'm going to put you on speaker. Mom's here."

He sighs heavily. "Fabulous." His sarcasm is obvious. "Go ahead." I hit the speaker button. "Hello, Faith."

Mom doesn't respond. Her lips dance over her teeth, holding back her venom.

"Is your mother there?" Dad asks.

"Yeah, Dad. She's here."

"Faith, I haven't talked to Charity all week. What's going on?"

"She ran away, John," Mom sneers. "Were you not listening?"

I whisper, "Geez, Mom. Be polite."

She rolls her eyes. "She left a short note saying not to look for her."

"She what?!" Dad is still trying to process all this. "I can't believe she would do this. Chastity, did you notice anything wrong?"

I glance at Mom. "Something is always wrong around here. You know Mom."

Mom bares her teeth.

I shake my head slowly and glare back, daring her to say anything.

She doesn't.

"Have you called the police?" Dad asks.

I sigh, "Yeah, Mom did. I was hoping maybe Charity had decided to go live with you."

"I wish she had," Dad says, bemused and melancholy. He sighs, "Is there anything I can do right now?"

I look at Mom.

She shrugs and rolls her eyes, obviously not wanting to interact with Dad at all.

I smirk at her. "Probably not tonight, Dad."

"Do you need me to fly out? I can catch a plane first thing in the morning."

"Gosh, Dad. I guess it couldn't hurt."

"Hmmm. I'll make that call in the morning. Let's see what happens tonight. Maybe she'll come home. If she doesn't, I can be in LA by the afternoon."

Lance mutters to me, "We should go look for her. Now." He says it like finding Charity is a foregone conclusion. His presence is incredibly reassuring right now.

I can't imagine going through this with just Mom. We would be fighting the entire time. I'm so lucky Lance is here. Sadly, that makes me feel worse because at the moment, Charity has no one. She's all alone who knows where. I have to do something. "Dad, we're going to look for her right now. I guess we'll call you when we find her?"

"Good," Dad says. "As soon as we hang up, I'll call Charity's phone. Maybe she'll answer. If I talk to her, I'll call you right away. Call me if you hear anything, okay sweetheart?"

"Yeah, Dad. Love you."

"I love you too, Chaz."

The look of jealousy on Mom's face is obvious.

"And Faith?" Dad says over the speaker

"Yes? John?" she spits.

"She'll be okay. Charity is a smart girl."

Mom's face ripples with fear and rage. "She's fourteen and she's out on the street, *John!* She's just a child! Nothing about that is okay!!"

"Jesus Christ, Faith! That's not what I meant!"

Wow, only two minutes and they're fighting like they're still married.

"Don't you take the Lord's name in vain! This isn't his fault! It's yours for turning away from Him in your time of need! You left your daughters, *John!!*"

I roll my eyes in disgust. That's not true. Mom pushed him away, but I don't know if she'll ever see it.

Dad groans, "I have to go, Faith."

"Bye, Dad," I say cheerily.

"Bye, sweetheart. I'll call you if I find anything out."

"Okay. Bye." I hang up.

Mom hisses, "That *man*. Never taking responsibility for anything."

What a hypocrite. No use trying to tell her. "Calm down, Mom. You aren't helping. We need to find Charity. Not complain about Dad."

Mom snarls before turning away to sulk.

"How do you want to do this?" Lance asks. "I've got my bike, your mom has the car. We can cover more ground if we use both. You wanna come with me or go with her?"

That's a no-brainer. "Go with you."

"I can't look every direction at once!" Mom growls, spinning around. "You should come with me, Chastity."

Um, no?

Lance says, "Take my dad with you. He can help."

Mom folds her arms across her chest, "No, no, no. Never. He's probably drunk anyway. What good can he possibly do?"

"He's not drunk," Lance growls.

That's news to me. I thought he was. Is he?

"Says you," Mom scoffs.

I roll my eyes. I can't say for sure he hasn't been drinking, but he's not so drunk he can't help look. "Don't be stupid, Mom. Mr. McKnight isn't drunk. I just talked to him. He can help."

She huffs a sigh. "All right. Fine. But I'd rather go by myself."

"Mom." I prod.

She throws up her arms. "Fine! I'll take Mr. McKnight. But I'm driving. Who knows when he had his last drink."

++++8++++

CHASTITY

Before we leave, Lance gets our leather jackets from his house.

After that, Lance and I spend two hours cruising to every location we can think of on his motorcycle. Charity's school, the mall (which is closed), Marble Slab (which is also closed but she used to stop by to visit me when I was working all the time), the church (you never know), the nearby parks, everywhere. Mom calls repeatedly asking if we've found her. None of us have any luck.

I text and call Charity dozens of times, but she never responds.

I even text: *Chair, it's Chazzy Wazzy. I'm alone. I know you're mad at Mother Mather. Please talk to me and tell me you're okay. I won't tell her you talked to me. But I need to know you're safe. Please at least text me back. Okay?*

Charity is the only person who ever calls me Chazzy Wazzy. Mother Mather is a reference to Cotton Mather, the guy behind the Salem Witch Trials. It's what we call Mom behind her back when she has been particularly puritanical.

Not even that gets a response from her.

Is her phone off or her battery dead? Did she lose it or break it? Those are the only reasons I can think why she wouldn't respond to me. Unless she's in trouble. Or hurt. Or…

Gosh, I hope she's okay.

Dad can't get through to her either.

The whole time, I'm beating myself up in silence on the back of Lance's Gixxer while thinking every shadow I see is Charity hiding from us.

At one point we stop at the Valley Park skateboard park and talk to four street kids who are clearly under eighteen. They have grimy hair and haunted eyes and sit on top of a park picnic table. The one girl wears a torn army jacket. A guy wears a tattered leather jacket, another a dirty denim jacket with band patches, the other a ratty flannel. They look lost. Not literally. Emotionally. Spiritually. Like they're not sure who they are or where they fit in with the world. They don't even belong at the skate park because the park is closed at this hour. They just stare at the empty cement bowls behind the fences like they're watching the ghosts of skaters or perhaps wishing they had their own skateboards, but they don't. Just their shoes, which look thrashed. Wherever these kids may fit in, if they fit anywhere at all, it's not here or any place I would want to be, and definitely no place I want Charity to end up.

We show the kids Charity's picture but they don't recognize her. Flannel says he'd do her. Angrily, I say she's my sister. The girl in the army jacket says, "Fuck your sister." I'm about to scream at her when I realize their bravado is a thin veil hiding their fear. I can't really be mad at them because I feel so bad for them. When Lance and I turn to leave, the boy in the leather jacket asks if we have any weed. Lance says no and gives them eighty bucks and tells them to go buy food.

As we walk back to his motorcycle, I say, "They're probably not going to use it for food." I'm thinking about Mr. McKnight and how angry Lance gets when his dad has booze. Now Lance is giving weed money to street kids? It doesn't make any sense.

"I don't care what they use it for. The important thing is they realize there are people in the world who will help them. If they want it."

"Oh. Good point."

Just when I think I have a handle on Lance, he goes and shows how thoughtful he is. I should've realized his dad has him. Those kids looked like they had nobody. Nobody who could help, anyway.

We cruise the gloomy streets for another hour before stopping to stretch our legs and get gas at a Chevron station on Victory Boulevard. Sadly, we have no victory of our own to celebrate. We're the only people at the pumps this late. The cold fluorescent lights give everything under the overhang a grim cast.

I pull my helmet off, shaking my hair out. "How could I be so stupid? How did I not see this coming? I am such an idiot. I thought about running away a hundred times. I almost did twice. One time, I packed my stuff and everything. Why didn't it ever occur to me Charity might actually do it?"

Lance sets his helmet on the gas tank of the Gixxer. He leans his hands on the seat and shakes his head heavily. "Sometimes people hide things and you never know it." There is a deep sadness in his voice.

Is he talking about Charity or his Dad? Or someone else?

Probably all three.

He runs a hand through his hair. "Look. If it's anybody's fault, it's not yours. It's your Mom's. I'm not trying to be disrespectful, but that woman is way too extreme for her own good."

"I know." I shake my head morosely. "What are we going to do, Lance? Charity is out there all alone."

"We keep looking until we find her."

Lance hangs the gas hose back on the pump and we put our helmets on and climb on the bike.

Hours later, the sun is rising when we call it a night.

We pull into Lance's driveway a minute before Mom parks the Toyota in our driveway. She gets out of the car alone.

"Where's Mr. McKnight?" I ask.

"I have no idea," she grumbles.

Lance gives me a funny look.

I return it. "What the heck, Mom? Did you lose him?"

"No."

"Then where is he?"

"Pish. Probably at some all night liquor store."

Lance turns on Mom and grabs her arm in a strong grip.

"Let go of me this instant!"

Lance is pissed. "Did you leave him at a liquor store?"

"No! Now, let go!"

Lance shakes her. "Then where is he?"

"How should I know?"

Lance looks like he's about to bite her face off.

She whines, "Let go of me, Lance!"

"Where is he, Faith?" Lance's voice is deadly.

"Tell him, Mom," I grumble.

Mom huffs. "We had an argument. I made him get out."

"What?!" Lance is incredulous. "What the fuck, Faith?"

Mom growls, "You weren't there. We had an argument."

"About what?" I demand.

"About his drinking, of course." Her tone is superior and blameless.

"Mom?" I growl. "What did you say to Mr. McKnight?"

She smiles her superior smile. "I told him he was lost, that he only drank because he had turned away from the Lord. He said otherwise. I pressed my case. He let loose with a tirade of filth that I would not stand for. So I made him get out of my car." She is so proud of herself.

I want to kill her right now. "Mom! Now is not the time to be sermonizing! We need to find Charity, not save Mr. McKnight!"

She chortles. "I tell you, the devil is in that man and the Lord is punishing me for my transgressions." There she goes, making it all about her, as always. She smiles at Lance. "And your transgressions..." she turns to me, "and yours. I have no doubt the two of you are living in sin. Perhaps all three of you are to blame for Charity's running away. You're certainly setting a terrible example."

"Where did you leave him?" Lance demands.

"I don't remember. It was several hours ago," she chuckles like this is all a game.

"Where, Mom?!" I shout.

She rolls her eyes and tosses her hand. "Somewhere in Burbank. How should I know."

Lance looks like he wants to kill Mom too. Instead, he jumps on the motorcycle. "I have to go look for my dad." He speeds down the driveway before I can stop him.

"Lance! Come back! I want to help!"

He can't hear me over the scream of the motorcycle engine.

I'm heartbroken.

He left without me. Without a second thought.

I thought we were a team.

All night I had my arms around him on the back of his motorcycle while we searched for Charity like we were inseparable. It felt like the warm comfort of Lance and the smell of his leather jacket were the only things holding me together.

Mom says calmly, "Like all men, he will abandon you when you are at your lowest. Just like your father." She swells with hypocritical pride. Has she forgotten that pride is a sin? Or did she miss that lesson just about every single Sunday since forever? I'm not going to bother pointing it out.

She'll never learn.

I lose it. "Mom!! What the FUCK?! Are you crazy?!"

Her eyes pop when I say fuck. "Watch your language, Chastity! I taught you better! I can't believe how filthy you've become!"

"*You* can't believe? I can't believe you're so heartless! What the hell is wrong with you, Mom? You left Mr. McKnight stranded! He was trying to help! You're horrible." I grimace and lower my voice, trying to stay calm, but my hate leaks out with every word. "You give religious people a bad name. You disgust me."

"I disgust *you*? You broke one of the ten commandments." She is completely calm.

"No I didn't!"

"Honor thy father and thy mother. Or have you forgotten your commandments already? Living in sin will do that."

I sneer at her, "You don't deserve to be honored. Charity ran away because you're a terrible parent. She probably hates you as much as I do. If she gets hurt, it'll be your fault. You pushed her away."

Shock shakes Mom's face.

I turn and march down the sidewalk in the direction Lance went, away from the thin line of the rising sun behind me and into the last of the darkness. I'll never catch Lance on foot, because I don't have a car.

But I'll try.

At least this way I won't have to look at Mom for another second.

Chapter 21

"Where are you?" I say over the phone.

"I'm at the airport," my dad says.

"We couldn't find her, Dad," I sigh, sitting by myself on Lance's front step.

"We'll find her. As soon as I land in Burbank, we'll keep looking."

"I'd offer to pick you up, but I don't have a car. Sorry."

"Don't worry, sweetheart. I'll catch a shuttle. How is your mother handling this?"

"Screw her," I blurt, scowling for my own benefit.

He says carefully, "Did you guys fight?"

"Yeah," I groan. "She's crazy, Dad, I swear. She's trying to blame everyone but herself for Charity running away. How did you ever stand her?"

"She was different when she was younger. I don't know what happened to her. People change. But that doesn't matter. Let's stay focused on finding your sister. That's what matters. Oh, they're calling my flight. Gotta go."

"Okay. Call me when you land."

"I will. I love you, sweetheart. See you in a few hours."

I end the call and heave a sigh.

Although the sun is just up, the porch is still in the shade. I stand up from the cold cement because my butt is frozen. I gave up walking around the neighborhood looking for Lance after half an hour. It made more sense to wait for him here. I hope he finds Mr. McKnight soon.

I start pacing up and down Lance's front walk. I would pace in his driveway where the sun is, but I don't want Mom seeing me. For all she knows, I'm still out walking around. She certainly didn't drop everything to come looking for me.

I'm glad she didn't.

Some time later, a motorcycle turns onto our street and I immediately perk up.

I recognize the sound of Lance's Gixxer and walk onto the driveway.

He pulls into the driveway with his dad on the back. Mr. McKnight doesn't have his arms wrapped around Lance like I did. He's not wearing a helmet either. Or a leather jacket. Just a ZZ Top band T-shirt. He grips the tail of the motorcycle behind the seat. It looks awkward, like he could easily fall off if they went over a bump. I smirk to myself. Men. Always afraid they'll look gay.

"I'm glad to see you both," I beam.

Lance's helmet is still on, the reflective visor down. He busies himself helping Mr. McKnight, who doesn't really need any help.

Is he ignoring me?

My stomach twists.

They walk toward me.

"Everything okay?"

Lance flips his visor up, eyes cold. "Yeah."

Is he mad? He seems mad.

"Hey, Chastity," Mr. McKnight smiles. His lips are blue. He must be freezing in his T-shirt after that motorcycle ride.

Fricking Mom.

But at least I feel slightly better knowing Mr. McKnight isn't giving me the cold shoulder like Lance. "Sorry about my mom, Mr. McKnight." I hate that I have to apologize for her.

"It's my fault," he says. "I shoulda known better than to talk religion with her. That always pisses people off. Shoulda kept my mouth shut. Any sign of your sister?"

"No. But my dad is flying in from O'Hare today so we're gonna keep looking."

"Sounds like a good dad."

"Yeah," I smile. But I'm going nuts inside because Lance isn't saying a word. His helmet is now off, but he's not even looking at me. "Hey, do you guys want to go get some breakfast? I'm starving."

"Oh," Mr. McKnight glances at Lance. "We just ate. I didn't realize you wanted food. I woulda said something."

Lance is still avoiding my gaze.

I guess I need to go eat alone? Because there's no food in Lance's house. Ever. We always eat out. And there's no way I'm getting food from my Mom's. "That's okay. I can walk to the grocery store and get a bagel or whatever." I watch Lance. I can't blame him for being mad. Mom went too far, once again. I just hope Lance doesn't stay mad for too long.

Mr. McKnight says, "Maybe you should take her to breakfast, son. She's probably starving."

Is Lance going to answer? Or just glare at me? The knot in my stomach pulls tighter and the dentist's drill starts to whir, churning up all my hungry stomach acid.

Whir.

"Yeah," he grunts. "Want food?"

Is that the best he can do? Not exactly the kind of company I want at breakfast.

Mr. McKnight says, "I'm gonna crash. All that walking wiped me out."

I wince. "How far did you have to walk?"

"I don't know. The exercise did me good. Now I got a full belly so it's nap time," he winks. "You two should go. Chastity needs some food."

"Yeah," Lance grunts again.

Whir.

++++8++++

CHASTITY

"Where did you find your dad?" I ask as I pour maple syrup over butter covered waffles and sausages at Denny's.

"At a Yum Yum Donuts on Lankershim. He got sick of walking, so he called me. Had to pay the doughnut guy ten bucks to use his phone since pay phones don't seem to exist anymore." Lance glares at me. He isn't eating.

Whir.

I cut a triangle of waffle and start chewing. I'm going to drown out that dentist's drill with sugar and carbs. It usually works. "So he's okay?"

"Yeah. Like he said, exercise did him some good."

I'm still chewing, so I rush it and swallow a lump. Otherwise, I feel like I'm going to be talking to myself the whole meal. "I'm really sorry my mom did that. She's such a witch."

"Yup." He's still mad.

No need for more salt on that wound. Change of subject. "I think you'll like my dad when he gets here. He's cool. Nothing like my mom."

"Mmm." I expected him to say something like, *I can't wait to meet him,* or, *If he's anything like you, I'm sure he is.* But he's not speaking. His face says, *I don't give a shit about your dad, your mom, your sister, or you. So finish your fucking waffle so I can take you to your mom's house and never see you again. And, you're fired.*

"Um, do you want me to work today? Or is it okay for me to take the day off so I can go look for Charity?"

"No. We can keep looking. After we get some sleep."

"We?"

"What do you mean?"

"I mean, should I sleep at your place?"

"Of course." He's still frowny faced, but I'm starting to suspect it's not because of me.

Instant relief.

When I finish my waffles and sausage, Lance pays the bill and drives us home.

Our home.

"When does your dad get here?" he asks.

"After lunch."

"We should rest for a few hours. We've both been up all night."

"I'm not going to be able to sleep with Charity gone."

"You should at least lie down. Keep your phone by the bed. You can't run on no sleep forever."

He's taking care of me again.

It makes everything right.

We go inside and lie down together, me cuddling up against his side, his arm wrapped around me. I can't sleep, but I feel drowsy from the waffles.

It's as close to perfect as I'll get until we find my sister.

++++8++++

CHASTITY

"He's here!" I say, watching through Lance's living room window as a Lexus pulls up. I'm super nervous Lance won't like my dad. He already hates my mom, so odds are not in my favor.

I open the front door and trot outside.

Dad walks toward me, carrying his bags.

"Nice wheels, Dad! I thought you were taking the shuttle."

"I decided to rent a car so I wouldn't have to wait. This is all they had last minute." He sets his bags down on the cement and I jump into his arms. "Good to see you, sweetheart." He hugs me tight.

"I've missed you so much, Dad! You have no idea." All the emotions of my ongoing drama with Mom, and Charity's sudden disappearance, hit me in a rush. My exhaustion makes them come on stronger and I start to cry in his arms.

"I miss you too, princess." He tightens the hug. "We'll find your sister. I promise."

I believe him. I've always believed Dad. Why did Mom have to push him away? Why?

"You must be Lance," Dad says.

I turn around and Lance stands there with Mr. McKnight. "Dad, this is Lance and his dad, Mr. McKnight."

"Rod," he smiles. "Call me Rod."

They all shake.

"Let me take your bags," Mr. McKnight says, grabbing them before Dad can stop him.

"Thanks," Dad says.

Dad is blond like Mom. His hair isn't curly like us Shields women, but it's thick and wavy and looks good without even trying. Despite his good hair, in his striped polo shirt and Dockers he looks like any other suburban Dad. Next to a couple of motorcycle badasses like Lance and Rod, he looks soft, like the only exercise he gets is mowing the lawn on the weekends. But looks can be deceiving. Dad has been studying martial arts since he was a teenager and has two black belts. He can kick some serious ass. He was a bouncer at a bunch of LA clubs for a few years before he met Mom—not where he met Mom. They met at a bowling alley. Anyway, now he's an upper level manager at a credit card call center just outside of Chicago. But he shouldn't have any problem fitting in with these men. I hope. You never know when men will decide it's time to see who's the most manly and someone always ends up hurt by the results. I cross my fingers.

"We looked all night for your daughter," Mr. McKnight says.

"I can't tell you how much I appreciate that," Dad says.

"We're ready to head back out when you are," Lance says.

"I need to eat first," Dad says. "I skipped breakfast and all the airline had was peanuts. I'm starving and I didn't sleep last night and I can't think straight. Is there someplace quick around here? I need protein."

"There's a Subway down the street," Lance says.

Dad smirks, "Great. More crappy sandwiches."

"Do you want to go someplace else?" I offer. I don't want them arguing over something stupid like where to eat.

Dad snorts, "No. I just need food. And we can work up a plan of action for today while I shovel a sandwich down. While I'm doing that, you guys should make a list of every place you've looked and every person you've talked to so far."

"Smart thinking," Lance says, impressed.

I'm so glad Dad is here.

At Subway, Lance manages things so he ends up sitting next to me. There's a weird moment between him and Dad when Lance sits down beside me, but Dad is quick to pick up what's going on and lets it go, sitting across from us next to Mr. McKnight. We all unwrap our sandwiches and start eating. The men attack the food, but I pick at mine.

"So, no word from your sister?" Dad asks before taking his first bite of his hot meatball sub.

"No," I sigh. "I've called a hundred times since last night."

"When did you last try?" he asks around a mouthful of meatball.

"In your car on the way here."

Dad nods and grimaces, setting his sandwich down. "I should've gotten something light." Translation: *I have a dentist drill in my stomach too, just like my daughter, and it's whirring like crazy knowing my other daughter has disappeared.*

"I'll eat your sandwich if you can't handle it," Lance chuckles, halfway through his already.

"What'd you get?" Dad chides, rising to the challenge. "A six-inch veggie? If you're watching your calories, you could've ordered a salad and asked them to put the dressing on the side." Translation: *Women count calories and real men eat meat, so shut the fuck up.* He picks up his footlong meatball sub and chomps on it like he's starving. He'll probably regret it later. But you know, men.

I hide a smile.

"Yeah, so?" Lance laughs. "I like vegetables. And I had a big breakfast."

"Uh huh," Dad chuckles around his mouthful of meatball. "Was there any meat in your breakfast? Or did you have a bowl of Special K and skim milk? Or did you just have a Yoplait?"

I roll my eyes.

"I had the hash," Lance says defensively, chuckling.

"And he left half of it behind," Mr. McKnight nudges Dad with an elbow. "I had to finish it for him. Still can't keep up with the old men, can you, son?" He and Dad share a laugh at Lance's expense.

Grinning, Lance shakes his head and says to himself, "Buncha old farts is what you are."

Dad laughs, "All those greens'll make you the one doing the farting."

Mr. McKnight laughs too.

And like that, I know they're going to get along.

If only Charity was here, this moment would be perfect.

++++8++++

CHASTITY

The four of us spend the rest of the day looking everywhere and trying everything. The police haven't seen her. School hasn't started yet, so we can't ask the staff or teachers or the kids if they've seen her either. I try calling all of her friends again and nobody knows anything.

Charity just disappeared.

Poof. Gone.

For dinner, we order takeout Thai and eat in Lance's living room, sitting on the ratty couch and folding chairs with our food on moving boxes.

"What's the plan for tomorrow?" Dad asks. "You guys gonna be able to help again?"

"I can," Mr. McKnight says.

"I have some important meetings tomorrow," Lance says.

"You mean the—" I stop myself. He means more investor meetings. I know from talking to Lance that his dad doesn't know the full details of Lance's DJ business. He knows Lance is a DJ, and somewhat successful, but he doesn't know the full extent and I don't want to say too much. I'm not sure why. But something tells me there's a reason Lance took his dad out of Las Vegas and brought him here.

"Yeah, that," Lance says.

"Did you need me to come with?" I offer.

"If you can spare the time."

Dad asks, "Why all the mystery? Chaz, you never did tell me what Lance does."

"Um…" I trail off. At least he's not accusing Lance of selling drugs like Mom would. "Lance? Care to answer that?"

Lance nods. "I'm a music producer. I've got some big investment meetings this week. Trying to raise some capital for my next video shoot. There's a timing to these things. If I don't raise money now, it'll get harder to raise it next month. Harder and harder after that."

Dad looks impressed. "Gotta strike while the iron's hot, right?"

"Exactly."

"I get it. But the same thing applies to Charity. Anything could've happened to her. I don't want to assume the worst, but we need to prepare for anything. I need to set up a base of operations where I can make calls and stay organized. Chaz, what's the closest hotel around here?"

"Oh, I'd have to check."

"You can stay and work here, Mr. Shields," Lance says.

"Call me John."

"John. My house is your house."

"Shouldn't we be asking your father that?" Dad asks.

Mr. McKnight cocks his head toward Lance, "It's his place. He pays for it."

Dad raises his eyebrows. "Oh?"

"Yeah," Lance says. "You can set up here. Spread out however you want. I can bring in some work tables if you need them, and I'll pick up an extra air mattress for you today. Unless you're cool with the couch?"

"You don't need to do that. I can stay at a hotel."

Lance presses, "But then it'll be back and forth between here and there. It makes more sense if you're here with us."

"Yeah, Dad," I say. "Plus Mom'll be right next door."

Dad grimaces, "Splendid. But you know what? I think I'll take Lance up on his offer."

"Cool," Lance says.

The doorbell rings and everybody jumps.

I'm sure we're all hoping it's Charity.

Lance springs up and opens the door, "Hey, Faith."

Mom. Urgh.

"Please call me Mrs. Shields."

Dad rolls his eyes.

She sure knows how to ruin a party, not that we were having fun. But now we'll be having less fun. She'll make sure of it. She walks into the living room, followed by Lance, who stands behind her almost like a security guard waiting to restrain her if she gets out of hand.

"Hello, Faith," Dad says.

"Hello, John," Mom snips, trying not to roll her eyes.

"Any luck?"

"No. And you?"

Dad shakes his head. "I was thinking we should coordinate our efforts. We'll cover more ground that way."

"Is that what you think?" Mom snipes.

Oh, geez. What is she, twelve?

"Please, Faith. Let's not start. We need to find our daughter. Not fight about it."

"I agree," she smiles fakely. "Do you care to let us in on your master plan?"

"Mom! You're not helping," I groan.

"Your father seems to have this all figured out, so let's let him tell us what to do. Isn't that what you like to do? John? Order people around?"

Does she even hear herself? She's such a hypocrite it makes me sick. I want to tell Mom to leave. She's creating drama, not helping.

Dad stares at her. "Faith, can you try to calm down? I know you're worried about Charity. I am too."

"She's on the street, John! Or did you forget that already?"

I hate her. No wonder Dad left. She makes it impossible to have any sympathy for her.

"I understand that, Faith. That's why I dropped everything to fly out from Chicago. On top of that, I was up all night searching the internet for suggestions on next steps, so pardon me if I'm not handling things *exactly* the way you want. Now if you'll listen for a minute, I can tell you what I have in mind."

To my surprise, Mom shuts up and Dad refers to his pages and pages of notes on his yellow legal pad and explains to everyone his basic plan to organize, make fliers, create search grids so we cover the maximum territory, call runaway shelters, Child Protective Services, everything you could possibly think of. He also names off a bunch of non-profits that help families find missing kids and tells us we need to start making calls to all of them to get help. While he talks, Lance and Mr. McKnight both offer ideas that Dad likes and he jots them down on his legal pad.

When he finishes, Mom sneers venomously, "Aren't you three just as thick as thieves. I guess you don't need my help. You've worked out every last little detail without me."

Dad hangs his head between his knees where he's sitting on one of the folding chairs and shakes his head, muttering to himself.

"Are you praying, John? Because now would be a good time to start."

Dad lifts his head, exhausted like he just fought a war. "I'm not praying, Faith. Believe me."

"Then what *were* you doing?"

I turn to Mom. "Do you always have to be the center of attention? Is that it? Dad's ideas are better than yours so you're mad and you have to start attacking him and talking about church? Grow up, Mom. This is about finding Charity, not about you or church or anything else."

"Oh, it's not?"

"No, Mom. It's not."

"Hmph. Maybe if the three of you started praying, God would listen and bring Charity home," she says self-righteously. "I can't do all the praying on my own."

Lance starts talking, mostly to himself. "There's a thousand missing kids God never brings home, Faith. What about them? Doesn't God care about them?"

Mom's eyes fire. "That is the devil talking! You take that back!"

Lance stares at her. "It's the truth, Faith."

Mom's face knots. "I don't need to listen to your blasphemy! I'm leaving!" She turns and strides toward the front door.

Nobody rushes to stop her.

She takes her sweet time opening the door, like she can't figure it out even though it's the mirror image of hers next door. "Oh, this lock…" she grunts.

I scowl.

My phone rings, playing a Katy Perry *Dark Horse* ringtone.

Charity.

"Let me talk to her!" Mom shouts, grabbing for the phone before I can answer.

"Back off, Mom!" I wave her away and rush down the hall to Lance's bedroom, where I close the door. I answer the call, "Charity! Please tell me you're all right."

"What up, Wazzy."

"Are you okay?"

"Yeah, I'm fine. Don't tell Mom. Let her worry."

"Where are you?"

"I'm… at a friend's. For now."

"Are you safe?"

"Yeah," she groans. "Don't worry about me. I promise, I'm fine."

"Chair, people are freaking out. Dad flew in. He wants to start a nation wide manhunt for you. He's worried you're hurt or kidnapped. You really need to talk to him."

She sighs, "Maybe I should. But I'm not coming home."

Before I know what's happening, Mom opens the bedroom door and sneaks up behind me and grabs the phone from my hand. "Charity! Are you all right? Please, baby! Tell me you're all right."

I wrestle with her. "Give me the phone, Mom!"

She yanks it away and twists around.

Dad and Lance crowd into the room, followed by Mr. McKnight.

Mom runs on top of the mattress, kicking up the sheets and cowering against the wall like she's being attacked. "Charity! Where are you? Tell me so Momma can come get you. Charity? Are you there? Charity! Please, baby!" She starts to sob. "Please tell me where you are. Don't hang up! Charity!!!!" She screams and clutches the phone to her chest, curled around it like the phone itself is Charity.

I can't decide if it's the saddest sight I've ever seen or the most pathetic.

Chapter 22

CHARITY

The metal door of the tool shed slides open suddenly, scaring the crap out of me.

Steve holds a flashlight under his chin making him look all Halloween. "Bwah ha ha haaaa."

"Don't. You're freaking me out."

He lowers the flashlight and squeezes into the shed and closes the door. "Sorry." He points the light in the corner and it makes a dim glow inside the small space.

"What took you so long? I'm starving."

He sits on the dirt floor beside the pile of blankets I'm lying on and crosses his legs. "My parents talked and talked after dinner tonight. Sean was really hungry and he ate everything. So no leftovers. I had to wait until my parents went upstairs to make you a PB&J." He unzips his hoodie, reaches inside, and pulls out the sandwich which is folded in a paper towel. Then he pulls out a can of Mountain Dew. "We don't have anything diet. Mom says the fake sugar is bad for you."

"That'll work." I unfold the paper towel and gnosh on the sandwich. "Ew. This isn't grape jelly." I shouldn't be complaining, but it tastes super weird.

"It's orange marmalade. It's all we have."

"What's marmalade again?"

"It's jam. But with oranges." He shrugs. "I like it."

"I guess I'll learn." I take a careful bite and remind myself I like orange juice. Blech. Running away isn't a picnic. At picnics they have normal PB&J.

"I should probably go. I think my mom might be figuring out something is up."

"She probly thinks you come out to the shed to jerk off."

He smirks. "Ugh, I hope not."

"JK. Anyway, thanks for the sandwich."

"No prob." He stands and unzips his Affliction hoodie and hands it to me. "Here. You might need this. It's supposed to be colder tonight."

"Thanks." I put it on over mine and zip it up.

"Sorry I don't have a sleeping bag for you."

"It's cool."

He steps outside and slides the door closed. Then he opens it enough for me to see his face in the moonlight. "You can come inside, you know. I promise my parents are cool."

"Yeah, but they'll call my mom."

"Probably."

We stare at each other for a second. Steve is really sweet. Without him, I probably would've gone home by now. Sleeping outside sucks. I start to feel nervous with him staring at me. "What?"

"Nothing. Night."

"Night."

He closes the door and walks away. I can barely hear his footsteps on the grass and he makes zero noise going back into the house. Where it's warm.

Unlike here.

I pull the blankets up to my ears and shiver. The plastic painting tarp beneath the blankets crinkles loudly when I curl up. We figured out the tarp when I woke up this morning on top of damp blankets. Freezing. Steve found the tarp in his garage. At least today was hot enough to dry the blankets.

With any luck, I'll be warm tonight.

The shed is completely dark with the door closed. I know there's spiders in here with the lawn equipment and the garden tools, but they didn't bite me last night, so hopefully they won't tonight.

I hope there's no mice.

They're cute until they give you rabies.

I close my eyes and try to sleep. The smell of gasoline and motor oil from the lawnmower is annoying.

I'll get used to it.

It's better than Mom.

++++8++++

CHASTITY

Several hours later, Charity texts me:

Tell everyone I'm okay. I'll be home when I'm ready.

Dad is in Lance's living room talking quietly with Mr. McKnight because neither of them can sleep. Mom has already gone home. I show the text to Lance, who lies next to me on his mattress.

He says, "Better show your Dad."

I'm already in yoga pants when I rush into the room because let's face it, sleeping naked with your boyfriend when your Dad is talking in the living room is just weird.

"Dad! Charity sent me a text." I hold out the phone and he reads it.

His eyes light up with hope. "That's terrific. And you said she sounded okay when she called earlier?"

"Yeah. Same old Charity."

"I wish your mother hadn't've grabbed the phone like that."

"Me too. Should we tell her Charity texted?"

Dad snorts a morose laugh, "I don't want to go over there. Do you?"

"No."

"She can wait until morning."

"So, what's your plan, Dad? Are you going to stay until Charity comes out of hiding or whatever?"

"That's the plan. Hopefully she comes home soon. I only have so much vacation time. Maybe you can get her to meet up with me and you tomorrow?"

"That's a great idea. I'll text her right now."

Me: **Dad wants to meet up. Just him. No Mom. What do you think?**

Her: **Okay. Maybe tomorrow or the day after?**

Me: **I'll tell Dad. Stay safe.**

Her: **I am. Laters.**

Knowing that Charity feels safe, wherever she is and whether or not she actually is, removes enough stress from the equation that I'm actually able to sleep that night for a few hours.

The next morning, Lance whispers me awake. "Hey. I need to get to the office. You wanna come with or sleep in? Either is cool with me. If you need to spend time with your Dad, go for it."

"Oh. Uh, well, do you need me to come in with you?"

"It never hurts to have a pretty face in the room when you're trying to close six-figure investment money. But it's up to you. Your sister is what matters."

I'm touched that he's so understanding. But I want to be there for him too. He dropped everything to help me find her. The least I can do is go into the office with him. "Can I have a few minutes to shower and dress?"

"Sure. Meeting isn't until eleven. Take your time."

Two hours later we're on our way to Beverly Hills for the meeting. Once again, Micah drives his Mini Cooper and Beaver comes along. After we park the car and walk toward the office, I joke to Lance, "You really ought to consider getting your own car."

"Money is tight right now, otherwise I'd buy you one."

That catches me off guard. "Me? I meant you."

"I meant you too," he grins.

"Are you serious?"

"You need a car more than I do." He sounds serious. "I have the bike."

"That's sweet, Lance. But I seriously meant you. Your dad looked uncomfortable on the back of your motorcycle the other day."

"True. But you shouldn't be dependent on your Mom or whoever else for a car. Anyway, we can worry about that later. Now we need to focus on this pitch." He smiles, holding the glass door for me.

The modernist office building is on West Pico Boulevard near the Fox Studios and the Avenue of the Stars. The building is three stories, colorful and boxy. It belongs to a movie producer named Lou Buchanan who wants to expand his portfolio beyond feature films. So he agreed to take the meeting with Lance on the grounds that he could produce the video for Lance at cost in exchange for a hefty piece of the back end, meaning profits. I learned the term from Lance.

Unfortunately, Lou and Lance butt heads from word one. Lance has a very clear vision of what he wants. So does Lou, who is a silver haired guy who's at least sixty, but has the energy of someone much younger. He bulldozes Lance into a corner, wanting to change Lance's entire concept and asks for a much larger percentage of profits than Lance expected going in.

Lance is not pleased.

Lou smiles like the last-minute chameleon that he is. "With all that money coming out of my pocket, I need to make it worth my time. You understand."

Lance gazes out the huge picture window of Lou's third story meeting room at the golf course on the back side of the Beverly Hills Resort. He says thoughtfully, "Yeah, I understand." He smiles. "I don't think we see eye to eye, Lou."

Lou hops to his feet. "Suit yourself, son." He leans over the table and fires out his hand to shake Lance's. "I'm sure you'll find someone willing to take a risk on your idea." It's a subtle insult.

"No doubt," Lance grunts, pumping Lou's arm over the table.

"Pleasure meeting you, son. Good luck." He's out of the glass board room before I can even blink.

I whisper, "I think you insulted him."

Lance scowls, "I think anyone who says no to Lou Buchanan is insulting him."

"Good point."

"He sure has a hot secretary," Beaver says.

"Shut the fuck up, Beaver," Lance groans.

"You should ask her out," Micah says. "Since we have nothing to lose at this point."

"Great idea!" Beaver grins.

We make our way downstairs. As Beaver said, the secretary is indeed an attractive brunette woman who's just a few years older than me and looks like she belongs on a movie screen, not behind a secretary's desk.

Outside on the busy street, I ask, "So what now?"

"We ask another investor," Lance says. "And we keep asking until I run out of people to ask. Or someone says yes."

"Do you have any more meetings lined up?"

"Not yet. But I'll find somebody with money to throw around." He looks around. "Where's Beaver?"

The front door of the building opens and Beaver comes walking out.

"What the fuck, Beaver? Where'd you go?" Lance asks.

Beaver holds up his phone, "Digits! I got digits!"

"Bullshit," Lance chuckles. "The only digits you got are the ones you jerk off with."

"Huh?" Beaver says, confused.

Lance holds up a hand and wiggles his fingers. "You know, the ones attached to your hand?"

Micah and I both laugh.

I say, "Nice vocab, Lance."

He grins and winks at me, "You like that? I'm a fucking dictionary when I wanna be."

I nod, still giggling.

Beaver shrugs, "I don't care if you dicks don't believe me. I got digits." He jams four fingers at us like he's flipping us off with all four. "These and hers."

"We don't believe you," Lance chuckles.

I completely agree with Lance. The secretary was way too cute for Beaver, especially when he's wearing vintage high-waisted striped polyester pants and a faded Dungeons & Dragons T-shirt that is so thin you can see his pale skin through the material. He looks ridiculous.

We all climb into Micah's Mini and drive back to Lance's downtown office.

Lance doesn't mention the meeting the entire drive. He just stares out the window, lost in thought.

I think back to his comment about buying me a car. Especially the part about money being tight right now. I really don't know the details of Lance's financial situation. He keeps all that to himself. He could be teetering on the edge of bankruptcy and I wouldn't know it. I mean, I haven't even received my first paycheck yet.

Will it bounce when I try to cash it?

I don't know.

+++++8++++

LANCE

Fuck.

That bottom feeder Lou Buchanan the Douche Cannon was my last real shot at funding. I knew he was a long shot going in, but I didn't expect him to piss all over my idea like that.

Now the only people I have left to call are small money people. No one big enough to fund the entire project. If I can get enough of them to sign on, maybe I'll make my budget. The hard part is getting that first person to put their money on the line. No one small time wants to be the first investor. They need confidence that other bigger investors are willing to take a risk. So I'll have to play a shell game and hope no one figures it out.

The fucked thing is, I'm running out of money quick. If I don't find funding soon, I'm gonna have to close up the downtown office and work out of the house. I bet Chastity would love that. No more glamour. Just folding chairs and tables and the fucking cardboard boxes we still haven't put away because fuck, I don't have real furniture at home.

I think if I dig deep, I might be able to find one more big money guy who'll listen to my pitch for the video. He can probably fund the whole thing and then some. But he's a snake. No guarantees with him.

The only guarantee I have right now is if I get one more serious no, the house of cards that is my career comes tumbling down, all London Bridge and shit.

Fuck.

Why did I have to go and get Chastity fired from her job? Then trick her into thinking I had the yellow brick road all paved before her in gold? I'm sure it's too late for her to get her job back scooping ice cream.

I am such a dumbshit.

A real chip off my dad's dumb block.

Fuck.

I heave a sigh and stare at the band of pink and purple to the west as the sun sinks, standing on my driveway. I wonder if Chaz and her Dad are having any luck finding Charity?

"Lance?" Dad asks behind me. He stands in the garage, next to his

Harley, which is collecting dust.

Speak of the fucking devil.

The thing that really kills me about my cash flow problem is if things go south, I don't know how the fuck I'm gonna take care of his ass.

"Hey, Dad."

"Hey, Son."

Seeing him and his hog looking like nobody cares about either of them makes me want to cut my guts out. I hate his ass for what he's done to himself. He used to be my rockstar. When I was real little, he was sober. I was lucky enough to have a normal dad for a few years. Around first grade, when I was six, he started drinking. I don't know what happened that threw him off the wagon. Something between him and Mom. Maybe. I don't know for sure. I was too young and he never talks about it. I just see the effects. He's a run down wreck. Like his Harley. It used to be a diamond.

Fucking alcohol.

"Son? Can I ask a favor?"

"Yeah, what?" I sound more irritated than I feel. As it is, I feel like shit.

"I was wondering if I could borrow some money."

"Money is kind of tight right now, Dad."

"It's for something important."

"Yeah? For what?" I almost add, *You want whiskey, you old booze hound? How about a coffin instead. You're gonna need one soon anyway.*

"I need to buy a bicycle."

I hold in a laugh. "No shit?"

"Yeah. I found a good one on Craigslist for eighty bucks. It's a mountain bike. Looks good in the picture."

It makes me sad that my dad is asking me for eighty bucks. The fact it's eighty bucks for a bicycle is also pathetic. It's not something big like: *Son, that earthquake we had caved the roof in. Insurance won't cover it and repairs could run forty thousand easy and your mother and I can't cover it unless we take out a second mortgage.* No, it's: *Son, I'm a washed up drunk. I can't hold down a job since your mother ran off. I don't have a license because I drink and drive too much so I need a bicycle to get around. While you're at it, can you spot me an extra five dollars for a tire repair kit and a used bicycle pump? Nothing worse than getting a flat when I'm bicycling from here to nowhere.*

"What do you need it for?" I grunt.

"Thought maybe I could ride around town and keep an eye out for Charity."

I stare at him for a long time. I want to believe him. I really, really do. "John and Chaz are supposed to meet up with her for dinner tomorrow night. She'll probably come home then. You sure you need a bike?"

"What if she doesn't? What if she changes her mind? The kid already ran away. Who's to say she'll come back?" He's thinking about Mom and it makes me want to puke. "With a bike, I can keep an eye out for her all around town. And I don't have anything better to do anyway." That's for fucking sure. "Maybe I'll find her."

But he won't find Mom.

Fuck.

His story is good and he sounds so damn sincere. But he is so good at lying, I can't say for sure he's not going to use the money for booze. Fuck it. I open my wallet and hand him one-sixty, scowling. "Get a good bike." Today, I don't give a shit if he uses the extra money to buy booze. Maybe he'll surprise me and do like he says and he'll be the one who finds Charity. This entire moment is so sad and pathetic I just want it over with.

He takes the money but hands back half. "The bike is only eighty."

I almost tell him to keep it, but I can tell his sense of self-respect is on the line. I take the four twenties and put them back in my wallet. "If you need new tires or anything, let me know."

"Okay," he smiles meekly, "but I'll be fine with eighty."

I wish eighty bucks was all I needed to be fine.

Sometimes, I have to wonder what the fuck I'm doing with my life because it doesn't seem to be going the way I planned. Days like today I feel as fake as TH3 PH4NTüM.

Just a bullshit shell of a man who's nearly out of money and half way to being his washed up dad.

Fuck.

++++8++++

CHASTITY

"Do you think she'll show up?" Dad asks nervously.

"I hope so." I turn around in my outdoor seat, scanning the sidewalk behind us. Cars whiz by on South Glendale Avenue. Evening traffic. We sit near the walk up window of Taqueria El Tapatio, which is an old A-frame building in front of a laundromat and a Mexican market called El Pipil. Charity told us to meet her here. It's exactly the kind of divey place Mom would totally avoid.

Dad looks at the taqueria building thoughtfully, "I think this place used to be an old Wienerschnitzel."

"A wiener what?"

"Never mind. Do you think Charity took the bus? Maybe that's why she's late."

I shrug. "Who knows."

Dad starts drumming his fingers noisily on the table top. "Are you hungry? I'm hungry." He shoots to his feet. "You want some chips and salsa? Why don't I get some." He is super anxious.

"Sounds like a plan." I watch him while he leans down to talk to the Mexican guy through the walk up window. I can't hear what they're saying over the traffic on Glendale, but they're laughing at something. I think Dad needs to keep himself occupied. He walks to the table holding one of those red and white checked paper trays full of chips and a red ketchup bottle of salsa.

The second he sets them down, Charity walks up out of nowhere. She looks tiny and helpless but also tough and scrappy at the same time. She wears a black skirt I recognize, black leather boots I don't, and a garish Affliction hoodie with black and white graphics of skulls that I've never seen before. Mom would freak if she saw Charity dressed like this. The hood is up, covering her blonde hair even though it's warm out.

"What up, peeps?" She winks at Dad and does a sarcastic wave like this is no big deal. She's trying to act cooler than usual.

"Charity," Dad grunts, throwing his arms around her in a huge bear hug, picking her up off the ground.

"I'm choking!" Charity laughs, waving her arms. "Cough, cough!" She actually says the words cough, cough while patting Dad on the back.

He releases her and rolls his eyes while rubbing her back, "Such a comedian. Sit down with your sister, Chair. Have some chips and salsa." Dad motions to the seat next to me.

Charity looks at it warily. "Mom isn't waiting in hiding to jump out with a net and a Taser to catch me, is she?" Charity looks around in every direction.

I snort, "No. She doesn't know we're here."

She gives Dad a pointed look.

Dad looks hurt. "Do you think I'd tell her?"

"You better not," Charity warns.

Dad gives her a strange look like he doesn't know what to make of her attitude. But I think he's trying to keep the peace. "I didn't tell her, Chair. She has no idea we're meeting you. Please sit."

Reluctantly, she does.

I ask, "Did you cut your hair?"

"No. Why?"

"Cause you never wear a hoodie unless it's freezing."

She flips it back. "See? Still there."

Dad smiles when he sees her pile of blonde hair. Then he looks between me and her. "You two look exactly like each other. It's uncanny."

"Do not," Charity grouses. "I'm so much better looking than Chaz." She flips her hair and smirks.

I laugh, "Geez, Charity! Don't be so vain." I regret my words immediately because I sound like Mom.

"You're both beautiful," Dad assures. "What do you want to eat?" He stands up.

"Tacos," Charity says.

"Me too."

"Copy cat," Charity jabs.

"I'll get tacos for everyone," Dad says, "because I like the taste of cat."

Charity wrinkles her nose, "What?"

Dad shakes his head. "Bad joke. What kind of meat do you guys want?" he asks.

I say, "Make mine cat too."

"Nast!" Charity laughs.

Dad goes right up to the window to order because no one is in line.

"Dad is really glad you're here," I mutter.

"I can tell."

"How are you doing?"

She shrugs. "Mmmm."

"Sounds like you're having a party without me."

She sighs. "I'm fine. So glad I don't have to listen to Mom bitch about everything every single second."

"I feel you," I nod thoughtfully. "Sorry I bailed on you with Lance."

"I can't blame you. I would too. He's hot."

I blush. "I guess."

She snorts, "Don't be lame. He's gorgeous. Is he nice too?"

Despite the fact Charity and I talked plenty before she ran away, I didn't go into detail about my arrangement with Lance. I didn't want to make her more jealous. But I can tell her some of it. Assuming she comes home, she's going to find out eventually. "Yeah. He gave me a job."

"What happened to Marble Slab?"

Charity still doesn't know about Mr. Molton catching me and Lance and I'll probably never tell her. Maybe when we're both eighty. So I lie. "Oh, uh, Lance offered me a really good job. He pays better than Mr. Molton."

"That's awesome. What kind of job?"

"Oh, I'm pretty much a receptionist. I answer phones and keep the office organized."

"Sounds boring."

"I guess."

"But it was cool of him to give you a job."

I'm relieved she doesn't ask any more questions about Lance. What would she think if she found out Lance was a semi-famous DJ? She'd probably never come home.

Charity grabs a chip and squirts a ton of salsa on it and pops it in her mouth. Her eyes bug. "Hot!" She waves her hand in front of her mouth.

I laugh. "Eat another chip. It'll cool the burn."

She does.

Dad sits back down and we chat about whatever for a while. Charity polishes off most of the chips by herself in like two seconds.

Dad says carefully, "Chair, are you getting enough to eat?"

"It's only been a few days, Dad. I'm fine. But yes, I'm getting enough to eat. Do you know what marmalade is?"

I don't.

Dad narrows his eyes. "Isn't that orange jam?"

Charity nods. "It's disgusting."

"Please tell me you're eating something other than orange jam."

She rolls her eyes, totally exasperated. "Yes, Dad. I'm eating real food. Stop worrying about me."

Dad leans his forearms on the metal table. "Hey, I love you. I will always worry about you." He means it.

Charity feels it and nods solemnly.

Dad's eyes sparkle with impending tears. He cracks a smile, "I can't have my youngest daughter eating orange jam every meal, can I?" It's supposed to be funny, but it isn't really.

Oddly, all three of us laugh, overcome by emotion.

The Mexican guy inside calls out our order.

"I'll get it!" I bolt to my feet so Dad can have a minute alone with Charity. When I set the tray down, they're both laughing about something. "What?"

"We were talking about your mother."

"She's always good for a laugh," I say sarcastically.

We all laugh even harder than before even though my comment

wasn't very funny either.

I sit down and we fight over the tacos. "Which one is the cat?" I giggle.

"This one," Dad chuckles, handing me a Carne Asada taco. "I think it's still meowing."

Somehow, that's also really funny even though it's not.

Charity and I always have fun with Dad. Every summer with him has always been a blast.

He says to me, "We missed you this summer."

"Maybe *you* did," Charity laughs. I know she doesn't mean it. Unless she's trying to claim Dad all for herself. The important thing is that for a few minutes, everything feels normal and I don't want to shatter this fragile moment.

Dad says, "Remember how much fun we had at Raging Waves out in Yorkville?"

"It was awesome," Charity says.

Dad grins at me, "See? You missed out, Chaz."

I laugh, "You guys know Blazing Waters in San Dimas is way better. Too bad you don't live here in LA, Dad. We all could've gone." I stop myself, realizing I'm probably hurting his feelings. "Sorry. I didn't mean that."

Dad smiles, pretending. "It's okay. If I lived here, I would've bought season passes to the Blaze and taken you two any time you wanted."

Charity rolls her eyes. "Nobody calls it the Blaze, Dad."

"I do," he chuckles.

After the laughter fades, we all fall into uncomfortable silence.

I keep waiting for Dad to mention Charity's running away, but he keeps avoiding it. Maybe it's for the best. Talking about normal stuff feels so much better.

Dad says, "And speaking of living nearby, now that you're a high school graduate, Chaz, have you given any more thought to college?"

"I have terrible grades, Dad."

"They're not that bad. But that doesn't matter. You can go to a community college for two years and transfer to a four-year after."

"I guess." I'm not going to remind him that I've got a good job with Lance. For now. I'm still waiting on that first paycheck, but I want to believe it'll work out and I can forget about college and tests and grades for good.

"What do you think about the idea of moving out to Illinois and going to Oakton for two years? Then you can transfer to a university. Chicago has so many good schools to choose from. And you could live with me and save on rent. Your sister could live with us too."

Charity's eyes light up. "That would be awesome, Dad! Don't you think that would be super cool, Chaz?" She beams at me.

I grimace. That would mean leaving Lance. I don't want to do that, job or not. He may be evasive about saying he likes me, but the way he stepped up when Charity ran away has me seeing him in a whole new light. I mean, I'm *living* with him. *And* working for him. We're practically married, which secretly thrills me. I can't walk away now. I have to give Lance a chance to come around. As much as I would hate for Charity to move away to Illinois, maybe it's time. It would get her away from Mom faster than I ever could.

Excited, Charity says, "What do you think, Chaz? You, me, and Dad in Illinois?"

"We'll have to talk to your mother," Dad says, full of hope. "In light of the circumstances… who knows? Maybe she'll consider it." Notice he didn't say *change her mind* or *let Charity move to Illinois*. Nope. *Consider it.*

The idea makes me sick.

Whir.

There goes that dentist's drill.

"Please say yes, Chaz!" Charity begs. "We can both say goodbye to Mom for good! She'll be all alone like she deserves."

Dad smiles uncomfortably at that.

So do I. It's not like I hate Mom. Or do I?

Charity stares at me like I hold her future in the palm of my hands.

Whir.

"Yeah, that could be awesome," I say anxiously. Notice how I said could and not would?

Lance was right. I'm definitely my mother's daughter.

Whir.

Chapter 23

CHASTITY

Dad and I convince Charity to spend the night at Lance's.

We don't tell Mom and literally sneak her in.

Lance buys a sleeping bag for Dad who insists on taking the couch so Charity can have the second air mattress. It's like a sleepover. We stay up late that night talking about everything and nothing. Most of all, we laugh. It's amazing how well Dad gets along with Lance and Mr. McKnight. They trade jokes and friendly insults and share stories all night long while Charity and I mostly listen in awe. Without Mom around, we're both in heaven.

The next day, Dad convinces Charity to go back to living with Mom until he can talk to his lawyer and start talks with Mom's lawyer about moving Charity to Illinois. Nobody mentions it to Mom because we all agreed she would call in the Army and the National Guard if anyone tried to take Charity away from her.

That night is bitter sweet. I'm going to miss Dad. He makes having parents seem like a good thing, unlike Mom. With Lance and his Dad around too, it's perfect. There's nothing like having three strong men around protecting you and caring for you, especially when they all have a sense of humor that makes life seem like it's full of fun and infinite possibility instead of drab and dangerous. Not once does anyone mention heaven or hell or sins or damnation or blah blah blah.

Dad goes home the next day, optimistic about everything. Lance and Rod are both sorry to see him go. Not half as sorry as Charity and me.

A few days later, Charity calls me up at work.

"Hey, Chair. What's up?"

She groans, "Mom is freaking out again."

"What now?"

"She's making a huge deal about me being a freshman at North Valley. We had to go buy new clothes appropriate for my age. The outfits she picked out make me look like a dweeb. Then she lectured me about all the evil things boys will try to do to me. As if I didn't figure that out in middle school. She thinks I'm still twelve."

I snort, "Mom thinks *I'm* still twelve."

"Truth."

"How are you holding up?"

"Oh, you know. Mom. Has Dad said anything to you about moving us to Illinois?"

I wince when she says us. She's still hoping I'll go too. "No, not yet." It's the truth. "I'm sure it'll take some time for his lawyer to figure everything out."

"Yeah," she sighs. "Do you think Lance would mind if I slept on his couch again?"

"No, but Mom would."

"Yeah." She sounds miserable. "Oh, hold on. The wicked witch is summoning me. I have to go. Do you want to see a movie tonight or something? You can bring your date," she giggles.

"Who, Lance?"

"Yeah. But no making out if we're sitting together."

"Of course not!" I chuckle. "I'll have to ask Lance. He's been busy lately."

"Okay. Mom is about to burst a vein, so I better go. Call me later."

"Okay, bye!" I sound more cheerful than I feel.

I can't help but worry about what will happen if Charity ends up moving in with Dad. I don't want to leave Lance. I hate being forced to chose between him and my sister. Just thinking about it makes me nauseous.

Whir.

After a few days, I don't even notice the nausea. I get used to it. Work is a good distraction. There is a new flurry of calls from potential investors. We drive to a lot of meetings. This time, it isn't fancy entertainment offices and talent agencies. It's doctors and lawyers and real estate agents that Lance knows. One guy is literally Lance's dentist. Lance sells his butt off, doing his best to charm the pants off everyone. Unfortunately, we get nothing but no's. Lance acts optimistic, telling me and Micah and Beaver that the next one will be the one.

I can tell the stress is starting to wear on him and he's starting to doubt himself.

It's wearing on me too because I think it's making Lance more distant. Our sex life skipped the cooling off part and went straight to frozen. We still haven't had sex since before Charity ran away, since that time at his office when I told him I loved him. I can't help but think what I did ruined things between us. He doesn't even flirt. At work, he's still fun and irreverent, but that sexiness between us is long dead. I'm afraid Lark was right and I scared him off. Not literally. Just emotionally.

I don't know.

Whir.

It drives me nuts because I want to ask him what's wrong, but even I know guys hate talking about their feelings. I don't want to pry. I just want to take back telling him I love him.

Which I still do.

Sadly.

Maybe I need to stop loving him.

Can you do that?

I don't know.

Maybe I need to go back to living with Mom and Charity. Charity would like that. Then things would be back to normal. They'd be so normal it would be like Lance never moved in or turned my world upside down.

The only upside in my life is that my first paycheck clears when I cash it. I'm all smiles when I deposit it at the bank. $1,148.14. So many numbers on one check! I've never made a deposit this big in my entire life. I'm rich! But it doesn't make me nearly as happy as I wish.

I'd trade all the money I have in my savings and checking account if Lance would just look at me with that same fire he had in his eyes in the beginning.

That night, I make a move in bed.

Lance lies beside me in his boxers, his back to me.

I can tell he's not asleep. I peel off my T-shirt and panties and scoot up against him until I feel his sexy butt pressing against me. I kiss the back of his shoulders.

"What are you doing?" he asks in a low but friendly voice.

"Nothing," I grin, sliding my top hand around to caress his chest. Even relaxed, his muscularity is a total turn on. I slide my hand down his abs, still kissing his shoulders. My heart starts to hammer. I've never initiated like this before. I'm out of my element. But I think I can figure it out. I trace the V of his abs down to home plate. To the root. I'm surprised he's not hard. I can fix that. I take him gently in my hand, savoring the warmth of his softness. Feeling the heat pouring off his back against my chest. I stroke him slowly, hoping to coax him to hardness. I can take this all the way to orgasm, or he can take over whenever he wants. I don't care. I'm just happy to be holding the most intimate part of him, knowing I have access to this man who I have such strong feelings—

"Not tonight, Chaz," he says gruffly.

Chaz? He never calls me Chaz.

"I'm really stressed about the meeting tomorrow. Sorry."

Is he apologizing or is he sorry I tried to touch him?

I slowly release him. "Okay."

But nothing is okay. My voice hitches as I say it and I swallow hard, retracting my arm mechanically. As I roll over, I am heartbroken. That hurt. More than I thought possible. My entire chest collapses. I'm going to cry. I burrow into myself, trying to disappear from this bed, wishing I had someplace private to go right now.

I consider the couch, but Mr. McKnight is still watching TV. I can't face him right now. And there's no way I'm going to Mom's.

Maybe I should run away.

With my eyes clamped shut, I beat myself up.

Why did I do that?

I should've known better.

He was obviously not in the mood.

What was I thinking?

I am so stupid.

After this goes on for way too long, I pinch the bridge of my nose, trying to silence the self hate.

When my rationality takes over, I realize the sad truth:

You can't stop loving someone just because you want to.

No matter how much it hurts.

++++8++++

CHASTITY

"Isn't Julian Whittaker the guy who discovered Layce?" Micah asks from behind the wheel of his Mini Cooper. We're spiraling up a road into the Hollywood Hills to our afternoon meeting with none other than Julian Whittaker.

"Yup, Lord Julian," Lance says, tense.

Micah nods, "That's what I thought."

"Lord who?" I ask.

"His producer name is Lord Julian," Lance says like I'm a stranger.

"Oh."

For the first time, Lance sits in the front passenger seat next to Micah. He made some excuse about how small the car is when we left the office downtown. I got stuck in back with Beaver. I pretended it wasn't a major disaster. After last night, it's just one more example of how Lance is pulling away. I wonder how long this job is going to last. I'll probably have to suck face and call Mr. Molton after all.

For now, all I can do is pretend I'm not miserable. I smile, "Layce is way fresh. My sister plays her music all the time. I love her song *I Rise*." I start singing the opening lyrics, "*Your smile disarming, your eyes alarming, you're my very own Prince Charming…"*

"Stop!" Beaver groans. "You're making my ears bleed!"

I'm not that good of a singer so I stop instantly, embarrassed.

"Her music is awful!" Beaver growls. "Pop diva bullshit! Utter crap. Musical junk food for people with no taste."

"Wow, Beaver," I giggle nervously.

He grins, "But I'd still do her."

Lance smirks, "But would she do you?"

In a serious voice, Beaver nods eagerly, his glasses bouncing on his nose. "Oh, totally."

Lance bursts out laughing. "You are in deeper denial than anyone I've ever met, Beaver."

"Oh, I'm in deep, all right." He bites his lower lip aggressively, wrinkling his nose like he's all that. "Nnnn! Nnnn! Nnnn! Ride me, baby!"

After working with Beaver for weeks, I'm used to it and laugh it off. But he's still creepily disturbing. At the rate he's going, I suspect he'll never lose his virginity. Not that I know he's a virgin, but come on. Look at the guy.

Micah says, "I'd love to work with a producer like Julian. There's a rumor going around he's doing Taylor Swift's next album."

"But is he doing Taylor Swift?" Beaver says in a crafty voice.

I roll my eyes, "Okay, I'll say it. Fucking Beaver."

Lance snorts a short laugh.

I grab for that laugh like it's the key to Lance's heart and if I can only catch it, I can open him back up and he'll let me back in. But the moment fades before I think of anything else to say. It doesn't help we have no privacy because we're in the car with Micah and Beaver and I'm staring at the back of Lance's head.

Micah says, "I bet I'd learn more from Julian Whittaker in a single day than I would in six months working alongside anybody else. That guy knows recording inside and out. And the record business."

Beaver titters, "I hear he knows Layce inside and out too."

"Beaver," I groan. I wait for Lance to laugh.

He doesn't. Instead he says, "Didn't he win a bunch of Grammies for Layce's last album?"

"Yeah," Micah says. "*I Rise* won in four categories, including best pop video."

"I remember that!" I say. "It was beautiful. It reminded me of the Disney movie Maleficent. All dark and creepy. Totally cool."

"That was the one," Micah says. "If Lord Julian keeps killing it like he has been, he'll be up for Producer of the Year next Grammies."

"Wait," I say, "this Julian guy does videos too?"

"He does everything," Lance says.

"Could he do your video?" I'm full of excitement.

"Yeah. He could also launch my career into orbit," Lance says with real appreciation. "That's why we're going to meet him."

"And we're just going to meet this guy now?" I marvel.

Lance nods. "Yup."

"Why didn't we meet him first? It sounds like he can help you more than anybody else we've talked to."

Lance smirks, "Getting a meeting with Julian Whittaker is harder than winning the California State Lottery. Skrillex knows somebody who knows somebody who finally set this thing up. It took weeks to make it all happen. Now we just gotta make sure we don't blow it."

"No blowing it," I grin for emphasis.

"I'll totally blow it!" Beaver snickers. "Oh wait!"

"Aaaah!" Lance laughs. "Fucking Beaver. You'll fuck and suck anything that comes your way, won't you?"

Beaver is beet red. "No! No blowing anything! Eating and salad tossing only! I'm all tongue!" He sticks his out and waggles it, going, "Blahlah-lahlah-lah!"

"Beaver!" I laugh. "You are too much."

"That's what she said!" Beaver barks.

"More like he said," Lance smirks. "If you're lucky."

I giggle at that as Micah pulls to a stop in front of a gate set in a long row of tall hedges.

"Is this it?" I ask.

"Yup," Lance says. To Micah, "Hit the buzzer. Someone'll answer."

Micah reaches out the window and presses a button on a metal box inset into a square brick column.

"Yes?" a woman's voice answers.

Lance leans over Micah, practically climbing on top of him. "Lance McKnight to see Mr. Whittaker."

"One moment." After almost five minutes, the speaker crackles and the same voice says, "Please drive up and park to the side of the garage. He asks that you not block any of his cars."

"Will do," Lance says, excited. "I can't believe this is happening."

As we drive through the gate, I'm picturing some kind of tiny driveway, because we're in the Hollywood Hills and all the houses are crammed together. But as we circle up a long road to the house, it's obvious Julian Whittaker lives on a gigantic estate nestled away where you'd never know it. There's a six car garage set in the hillside below the multi-level mansion. A black Range Rover, black Mercedes, and a black convertible sports car with a red interior are all parked out front.

"Check it out," Beaver says, pointing toward the sports car. "Ferrari 458 Spider."

"Nice wheels," Lance says with admiration.

Micah parks off to the side and we get out of the Mini.

The house is even more impressive than Lord Julian's cars. It's like a scattered stack of white boxes with walls of glass, all balanced precariously on top of each other. Almost like a puzzle or Jenga tower or something. Not necessarily my style, but it's still impressive.

In a low voice, Lance says, "Beaver, don't say anything stupid and don't fuck this up. And that goes for you two, no fucking up. Got it?" Lance forks two fingers at me and Micah. "No fuck ups."

"Best behavior," Micah smiles.

I grin, "Not one fuck will be upped." I start giggling at my own joke and Lance smiles wide. It's the first genuine smile he's given me in days. After last night, it's feeble reassurance that we maybe sort of have a slim sliver of a connection remaining. Maybe. I press my doubt down.

Whir.

Stupid dentist's drill.

Whir-rr-rr.

My stomach grumbles audibly.

"Do you need a sandwich?" Lance asks, irritated.

"Sorry," I say, feeling stupid. "Won't happen again. That doesn't count as a fuck up, does it?"

"Don't worry about it," he says absently before turning and heading up the square stone staircase that leads to the front doors. He's annoyed.

Whir.

"Stop it!" I hiss at my stomach, shaking a finger at it.

Whir.

Whatever.

Nobody notices me talking to my stomach because they're all walking up the steps. As I trail behind them, I say to myself over and over: *No fucking up.*

No matter what happens when we walk inside, I will not fuck anything up.

I can't speak for Beaver.

But I will not mess this up for Lance.

Whir.

++++8++++

CHASTITY

"I'm Colette," a gorgeous woman says when the door opens. She looks like a supermodel in a business suit. "Please come in." We file inside and she closes the door behind us. "Can I offer you anything to drink?"

"What've you got?" Beaver says eagerly. His eyes roll over Colette like she's his own private pinup. Lance shoots him a look. "Oh, never mind. I'm fine."

Colette smiles at everyone. "How about water then?"

"Sure," Lance says.

Colette clicks across the tiles and out of the room.

"No fucking up, Beaver," Lance whispers.

"Okay. I won't say anything else." His regret is sincere.

Soft footsteps catch my attention. Golden blond hair rises up from a flight of stairs that leads downstairs. Followed by an excruciatingly gorgeous and impeccably dressed tan man. Holy cow. This guy just walked off the cover of the latest issue of GQ. He smiles when he sees us. His eyes lock on Lance. "You must be the Phantom."

"In the flesh," Lance smiles.

"Julian Whittaker. My brother Max insisted I listen to your last single this afternoon. I'm impressed." They shake hands briefly. Julian has shiny manicured nails that match the tone of his preppy dress shirt and slacks.

"Strapped & Capped?" Lance says.

"The same. Interesting use of the human voice. Was that an actual baby, or did you modify an adult?"

Lance is about to answer, but Beaver cuts him off.

"That was me," Beaver says, raising his hand. "I can sound really whiny when I try."

When he tries? How about always?

Lance glares at Beaver, who shrinks and puts both hands behind his back.

Julian's glittering emerald eyes dance between Lance and Beaver, as if he's trying to determine who's in charge.

I'll say it again: *Fucking Beaver.* He's not helping things any.

"Regardless," Julian says. "It was a strong song. The production was a bit compressed, but it was listenable. Very catchy. Excellent hook."

"Thanks," Lance says, nearly starstruck.

Micah is also starstruck and stares openly at Julian like the man walks on water.

Maybe they're overreacting.

Then Julian's eyes land on me. "And who are you?" He slides between Lance and Micah, who stand in front of me. He parts them like a gentle breeze has blown them out of his way. His magnetism floods the room and draws me to him. He takes my hand and kisses the back of it.

I giggle, "I'm, uh, Chastity." Why did I say that? I always tell people my name is Chaz.

And... Lance noticed. His eyes narrow with suspicion.

Oops.

"Chastity," Julian savors the word. "Do you taste as good as you smell?"

I laugh, "Uhhh-mmm-mmm."

Lance fires a warning glare at me that says, *Watch yourself.*

I guess I was supposed to utter an immediate no? What can I say? Julian is ten kinds of handsome, but in a way completely opposite to Lance. He's tall and tan, slightly slender, but the sheer physical presence of him in this mansion nearly sweeps me off my feet. I don't receive attention like this every day. Make that any day. And certainly not lately from Lance. So sue me if I'm speechless.

"Do you sing?" Julian asks.

"Not really," I giggle.

Beaver spatters, "She was just singing *I Rise* in the car on the way up."

Lance eye stabs him.

Beaver winces, "Sorry."

Julian is still holding my hand. Not like we're holding hands, but he's holding it in front of him like treasure. "I would love to hear your voice, sweet Chastity. Can you sing for me?"

My stomach flutters.

Everyone is staring at me.

The look on Lance's face says, *"You have already upped more than one fuck and are on the verge of upping every last fuck in the building."*

I giggle and smile politely at Julian. "Uhhh, I can't sing without any music playing. Aren't we here to talk about Lance?"

Julian smiles and releases my hand. "Of course. Shall we adjourn to my screening room?" He motions down the stairs.

"Colette was bringing us waters," Beaver says. "I'm really thirsty." Lance, Micah, and I all turn and glare at Beaver. He grimaces and swallows with an audible click. "It can wait."

Julian says, "I'll have Colette bring them to the theater. Please follow me."

I wince to myself as we go down the stairs.

At this point, between me and Beaver, it's safe to say every last fuck has indeed been upped.

At least I know things can't possibly get any worse.

++++8++++

CHASTITY

"I like it," Julian says after the presentation animatic of Lance's video idea finishes playing.

We all sit in Julian's dark screening room theater, which does in fact look like a miniature movie theater with four rows of seats in it. We're in the back row with Julian, except Beaver, who is in the projection room with his laptop running the video where he can't cause more trouble.

"This is just a rough concept," Lance says hastily.

"Of course," Julian nods while pointing a remote control at the front of the room. The lights come up to a dim glow. "But it has potential."

Tense silence.

We're all waiting to hear what Julian says next.

I expect him to now tell us how he wants to change things to his taste, just like that old guy Lou Buchanan. Lance will say, not a chance, Julian will say goodbye, and that'll be that and we'll be back to square one.

Whir.

"How much do you need?" Julian asks.

"What, cash?" Lance asks.

Julian nods.

"Uh, a hundred and twenty grand? Maybe less if I can call in a few favors."

"That's it?" Julian asks, surprised.

I'm blown away. Is he kidding? I can barely count that high. He's acting like it's dinner and a movie. But, based on this house and his cars, I shouldn't be surprised.

"Yeah," Lance says. "I know a lot of people who do good work cheap."

Julian smiles, "Let's say one-fifty to be safe. If you run under budget, so much the better."

"Yeah," Lance chuckles like he doesn't believe this is happening any more than I do. "What kind of percentage are you talking?"

"That depends," Julian grins.

I knew it. Strings are always attached if you look closely.

"On what?" Lance asks, sensing danger.

"On whether or not I get what I want." Julian's eyes swing over to me and lock on mine.

Oh. No.

I'm not for sale.

Lance follows Julian's gaze to me. He does not look happy. He looks pre-nuclear.

I was wrong.

There was one last fuck left on the table.

Apparently, that fuck is me.

And I just upped it.

++++8++++

CHASTITY

"Fuck that guy!" Lance roars as he strides up the stairs to the main level.

I shuffle after him, followed by Micah and Beaver. I'm totally confused. I think Lance was defending my honor, but I'm not entirely sure. He literally jumped out of his seat the second he realized Julian was looking at me. I mean, it's not like Julian came out and said he wanted to sleep with me. Sure, his eyes said it in plain English, but his mouth didn't. I don't know why Lance is all worked up. He doesn't even like me that much anymore.

"We never got our waters!" Beaver wheedles in a whisper. "I wanted to make a play for Colette! She's hot!"

"Fuck the water and fuck her, Beaver!" Lance barks. "We're outta here." When Lance reaches the front door and shakes the handle, it won't open. "What the fuck?" He shakes it again before examining the solid door like he's considering kicking it down with his motorcycle boots.

"It locks electronically," Julian says calmly as he steps purposefully up the stairs from below.

"Then fucking unlock it already."

"It requires hand print recognition." He says it like an arch villain who has us trapped like mice and is merely toying with us until he grows bored and decides to eat us or feed us to the sharks. "I need to actually touch it."

"Then hurry the fuck up."

Julian takes his sweet time strolling to the door.

Micah and Beaver are both stunned. Micah looks like he can't believe Lance is acting this way to the uber awesome Lord Julian Whittaker. Beaver looks anxious, like he's torn between chasing down

Colette to hit on her and not angering Lance.

Julian's hand halts a centimeter from the doorknob. He turns and smiles casually at Lance. "A word of advice."

"I don't wanna hear it," Lance bites.

Julian closes his eyes and shakes his head slowly, completely unafraid. "You'll never get your money, Lance. You're too impulsive. No one wants to invest in a loose cannon like you. Perhaps one day you'll grow up enough to realize that."

Lance squeezes his hands into fists and the knuckles pop. Julian doesn't look like the fighting type. Lance could easily tear him apart. Unless Julian has a bunch of thick-necked security guards waiting to pop out of trap doors and restrain him. Lance grunts, "Maybe one day you'll grow up and realize hitting on other people's girlfriends in front of them is a great way to get your teeth knocked out."

Wait. What?

Julian's casual smile turns coy. "I thought she was your assistant."

Lance growls, "She's my girlfriend, you fuck. So keep your eyes off her or I'll rip them out of your god damn skull. Now open the fucking door."

Oh. My. Goodness.

Stealth swoon.

Julian sniffs urbanely and turns the handle. "Good luck with your video." He sounds sincere.

"Fuck you, chump," Lance barks and grabs me by the hand, yanking me down Julian's square stone steps like a rag doll.

I float behind him, not because I'm literally being dragged along like a doll with my feet dangling in the air, which I basically am, but because manhandling never felt so good and I may as well be skipping in the clouds.

By the time we reach Micah's Mini Cooper, I do believe I've swooned all over my panties.

Chapter 24

"That guy doesn't know shit," Lance spits as Micah drives us down from the Hollywood Hills. He's been ranting non stop since we got in the car. This time, he sits in the back seat beside me. "I'm gonna raise that fucking money myself."

"How?" I ask.

"We're gonna hustle for it. Starting tonight."

"Hustle?" Isn't that what hookers do?

"Yup. Surprise rave. And I know just the place." Lance frantically dials his phone. "Hale, buddy! What up man?" Lance listens. "Awesome. Hell yeah, I did." Listening. "Totally. Hey, I need a solid, bro ... Is that warehouse of yours free tonight? The one on Industrial Street in the Toy District? ... Yeah. Uh huh. Yeah. Of course you're invited. You need me to set you up with a date?" Lance smiles at me. He better not mean me. "Well fuck, Hale! Why didn't you tell me you met someone! Bring her! I totally wanna meet her. I'll make sure she has a good time. Awesome. See you tonight, bro!" Lance ends the call full of excitement. "Micah, you think we can get my gear over to Hale's warehouse and wired up before midnight?"

"Yup. Just get me enough manpower to move the PAs out of storage, and I'll have it bumping by then."

"Sweet. Beaver, can you send out a blast to our insider list? Tell them to put the word out. I want that place packed. Anybody and everybody. Pull people off the streets if you have to."

"On it," Beaver says, thumbing away on his iPhone.

Lance looks at me. "I need smoking hot go-go dancers. I know a bunch, but this is short notice. You think you and your friend Lark could do it if I can't get anyone else to come out?"

"Um..." What happened to that protective side at Julian's and him calling me his girlfriend? Now Lance is offering me up like a piece of meat to whoever might need me. Maybe we should've stayed at Julian's to hear him out.

Am I being pouty?

I don't know. But the last half hour has been haywire and the crazy look in Lance's eyes is freaking me out. It's like I'm not even here. He has a way of doing that. Just like Mom. He's controlling like her too.

Am I making a huge mistake? The thought is nauseating in the extreme.

WHIR!!!!

Lance grins, "Don't worry, Pink. You'll be up on stage next to me. Any guy tries to grab you and I'll kick him in the face. You'll just be eye candy. It's good for dick morale."

I wince. "Dick morale?" Is that any way to treat your girlfriend? As dick bait?

"He's right," Beaver says, barely looking up from his phone. "Dicks need tits or they don't show."

I wrinkle my nose at Lance, "You want me to be your penis cheerleader?" Last time I checked, that's never in the girlfriend's job description. Maybe I should've read Lance's Terms of Service before I signed up for this. "I don't know, Lance…"

Lance laughs, "Only for tonight. After that, you can be my private penis teaser."

I grimace. "Penis teaser?"

"You need a penis teaser?" Beaver chuckles, "You having trouble getting it up for your lady?" He spins in the front seat and winks at me before his eyes drop to my breasts. "If he is, I'm always locked and loaded."

I wait for his tongue to do the waggle-waggle.

Beaver laughs a second later, and sure enough, his tongue *waggle-waggles*.

The maturity level in this car is down to nothing. I fold my arms across my breasts.

"Eyes up, Beaver," Lance warns. "Don't make me tear your eyeballs out."

Beaver rolls his eyes and faces forward. "Pfft, I don't care about Chaz. She's not my type."

He's turning his nose up at me? Whatever.

Lance snorts, "Beaver, you are high, man. Chastity is everybody's type."

Everybody's type? Am I the town pump now? Does anyone else feel like the levels of thoughtless self centered machismo and testosterone in this car have reached critical?

Lance nudges Micah, "Right, man?"

"Girlfriend," Micah deadpans, eyes on the road.

At least Micah is on my side. Or just staying out of it.

"Who is this Lark chick?" Beaver asks. "Is she a friend of yours, Chaz?"

"Yeah," I grimace sarcastically, "but you're not her type." I hope he likes how it feels.

Beaver goes, "Whatever."

Guess not.

Lance chuckles. "Don't even go there, Beaver. Lark will chew you up and spit you out."

"That's what I'm hoping," Beaver titters.

Why does it feel like Lance is having an entirely separate conversation from the one I'm having?

And why do I suddenly feel like a stepping stone for Lance to get what he wants and little else? Oh yeah. Because he seems to have forgotten I exist unless I can somehow advance his career.

I want to go home.

++++8++++

CHASTITY

"Do you want the JBLs?" Micah asks, referring to the gigantic PA speakers stacked in the storage garage beside a bunch of other big PA speakers crammed together.

"Yeah," Lance nods. "And the Sennheisers."

"You got it," Micah says.

Four guys whose names I think are Clay, Mitch, Adrian, and Jack help Micah load the speakers onto furniture dollies and wheel them to the freight elevator at the end of the hall so they can take them to the big white delivery truck waiting at a loading dock two floors down.

When the guys are gone, Lance stares at the remaining PA speakers and DJ gear, thinking.

And ignoring me like he has been since Clay, Mitch and blah blah blah showed up. That's when I became completely invisible to Lance. It's like he forgot I was here. I can't decide if he's doing it on purpose or just focused on the task at hand.

Does it matter?

I suddenly don't exist to the man I love.

I try not to let it get to me.

Whir.

"Is there anything I can do?" I offer. Despite how much I feel like Lance went from seeing me as his prize possession to his meat trophy in the span of seconds, I still want to be useful. I'm sure he's just stressing out about money or whatever. At least that's what I tell myself so I don't hate him. "Earth to Lance? Anybody home?"

He turns to me, blinking. For a second, he reminds me of Beaver, which is indescribably disappointing because it means either Lance has suddenly become repulsive to me or I haven't given Beaver enough credit. Neither makes me feel better. "Sorry," Lance mutters. "Got a lot on my mind."

"I was asking if I could help."

"You are helping." He turns to face me full on and squeezes both my arms affectionately. "Just having you here with me means more than I can put into words, Chastity. After Julian's thing today, I feel like I'm falling apart at the seams. But you're my glue, Pink."

"Glue?" I nearly laugh, but hold it back because I see he means it.

"Sorry. I can't think of anything that sounds less stupid. You know what I mean, right?" The earnest look in his eyes says it all.

"Yeah, of course," I say dismissively.

I was wrong about Lance.

He's not using me.

He's needing me.

Secret swoon.

++++8++++

CHASTITY

"I can't believe how many people showed up!" I holler in Lance's ear. The bass rumbles the old warehouse. Hundreds of people fill the floor and gyrate under the colored lights. Only in LA could you get this many people to show up out of nowhere for a surprise rave. *"This place is packed!"*

"For real!" Lance hollers back, grinning at me, twisting knobs on his DJ turntables while he bounces to the beat and holds his DJ headphones to one ear.

Equally impressive were the thirty-odd people who showed up earlier at Lance's office after we left the storage warehouse. They all came out to help. Lance knew all of them on a first name basis. Like a general marshaling his troops before battle, Lance organized them into a well-oiled machine in no time.

But none of that was quite as impressive as the way Lance is commanding the attention of his audience. Not only is the crowd hypnotized by his music, but the eyes of every woman (and quite a few of the men) are fixated on his incredibly sexy body and incredible stage presence. Mine are too.

A light sheen of sweat glistens on Lance's tan skin. He's shirtless, wearing only low-riding red sweats that reveal the waist band of white boxers. Dark letters on the boxers' waistband read *DJUI* (which I think is a pun that means DJing Under the Influence) and white letters stitched to the thigh of his sweats read *OOEE! SURE THING* like an invitation to rip his sweats off and see what's underneath. Matching white drawstrings dangle at his waist like symbolic penises, dancing against his obvious bulge as his hips keep time with the music.

It takes everything I have not to stare like a statue. Which is a problem, because I'm supposed to be go-go dancing. At one point, I actually did tug on his sweats. Lance merely grinned his devil's grin, daring me to finish what I started. Since there's a huge crowd of people less than ten feet away, I opted to ogle his body instead.

Am I horny?

Let's just say I'm glad I have this fringe belt on over the micro shorts I'm wearing because my arousal left a mark.

Geez, Lance is BBQ sex on a stick.

Too bad I have to share him with this crowded warehouse full of screaming fans all night. The good news is they're having a blast and they're spending money, which was the whole point of tonight. Many of them wear brand new TH3 PH4NTüM shirts of various designs which were purchased from the merchandise tables in the lobby. Another hot seller are the glowsticks of every shape you can think of, and TH3 PH4NTüM pacifiers with the silver mask and blinking eyes. Both girls and guys sport the pacifiers in their mouths.

"*Why do they have pacifiers?*" I holler.

"*It's a Molly thing,*" Lance hollers back.

"*You mean Ecstasy?*"

"*Yeah. They need something to chew on. The Molly makes them grind their teeth.*" He shrugs. "*It's part of the culture.*" It obviously bothers him. "*Forget about that shit.*" His eyes sweep over my nearly non-existent pink and black raver outfit: sequined headband and lace bikini top, skin-tight micro shorts (damp), fringe belt (hiding dampness), fishnet stockings, and knee high furry pink boots, all of it borrowed from Lark at the last minute this afternoon.

He hollers, "*You look hot as fuck, Pink. Why don't you shake that perfect ass of yours for the crowd and raise the dick morale around here? Otherwise I'm gonna bend you over my turntables and fuck you right here in front of everybody and forget all about the show.*" He grins and slaps my butt.

"*Ow!*" I jump before grabbing my behind and rubbing it.

Before I can protest, he whips his head forward, causing the silver mask tilted up on his head to tip down into place. Now he is TH3 PH4NTüM and he is focused on his turntables.

I'm tempted to tease him back, but something tells me Lance would *actually* have sex with me in front of everyone. I shiver pleasantly at the thought. I am literally dying for him to do me right now and I can't help but wonder if us having sex would drive the crowd wild, which is the purpose of this entire evening. But I don't want to screw this up for Lance. So he can screw me later tonight as many times as he wants. Besides, if we did have sex on stage, I have no doubt there would be video of me being fucked on the internet within the hour. I don't think I'm that adventurous.

Am I?

Another shiver.

Geez, I am turned on right now.

SLAP!

Another spanking from Lance. *"Start dancing!"*

"Okay!" If he keeps spanking me, I can't promise I won't do something stupid. It'll be his fault, so I won't have to take responsibility for it.

I watch Lark shaking it up on the other side of the stage, gyrating like a veteran stripper, totally uninhibited, teasing the guys in the front rows. She wears a similar raver outfit to mine, but hers is pastel yellow and lavender with furry purple boots. You'd think she'd been a professional go-go dancer for years based on how good she looks on stage.

I don't know if I can work it like that.

I almost fall over when Lance grabs me by the hips and pulls me in front of him, positioning me between his arms and the DJ turntables.

"You need to loosen up," Lance hollers through his mask.

"I'm trying!" I try to swivel my hips like Lark, but I feel way too clumsy to go-go dance.

"You did great in my office when you gave me that private dance. What gives?"

"That was private! For you not a bunch of strangers."

"So pretend it's just you and me."

"Yeah, right." He's got to be kidding.

The next thing I know, his hips push me up against the table, pinning me. He is rock hard. Between his sweats and my micro shorts, I can feel every inch of him pushing against the crack of my ass.

He is not helping me concentrate on my dancing.

But he is definitely making me drip. I should've worn a bikini instead because I'm literally swimming in these shorts.

"Relax," he says into my ear at the exact same time his big hand palms my stomach and slides right down the front of my micro shorts. He instantly finds my clit.

I melt into him, pressing back against his hot length. My thighs quiver and I want to sit down. Right on his cock. I don't care that this place is loud and crowded and jam packed with Lance's fans.

I just want Lance.

When his fingertip lifts and curls and pushes up into my pussy, I sink onto his hand, grinding against it, wishing it was his cock deep inside me and his hips pushing into me.

The bass beat thumps.

Lance thrusts. With his hips and his fingers.

He is fucking me. Not with his cock, but this is almost as good.

Fortunately, the DJ table is set up for Lance, who is much taller than me. The table top is nearly up to my boobs. The crowd can't see what's going on. There's a wall behind us with a flashing projection screen blocking anyone's view in that direction. To our sides, the backstage area is dark. There are crew people in the shadows, but they wouldn't film this, would they?

I hope not.

Because I can't stop.

"*All my ladies scream right now!*" Lance shouts on the microphone, his voice booming over the PA.

I'm gonna be screaming in a minute if he doesn't stop with his fingers. I brace myself against the edge of the table with both arms, arching my back and pushing against Lance's covered cock. I feel it throb against my ass, almost in time with the beat of the music. His fingers aren't as deep with me positioned this way, but he makes up for it by scribbling his finger against my clit in a way that makes it sing.

The women go wild.

So do I.

I come all over Lance's hand.

In front of everybody.

++++8++++

CHASTITY

"*Make some noise for me, LA!*" Lance yells on the mic.

The crowd cheers.

I feel like they're applauding my orgasm and I start to laugh.

"*Lemme see those hands up high!*" Lance withdraws his hand from me, which must be dripping with my cum, and throws his arms up in the air, spurring on the crowd. They throw their hands up in response as he circles the stage.

I'm still braced with my arms against the DJ table, catching my breath.

When Lance returns to his position behind me, he says in my ear,

"You relaxed now?"

All I can do is nod. My legs are jelly.

He slaps my ass again and waves of pleasure course through me. *"So go make that ass bounce for everybody! I wanna see you shake it!"*

I stand up and walk around to the front of the DJ table. It takes me a few moments to get into the dancing. I watch Lark for ideas and try to mimic her movements. I don't know if I'm doing a good job, but I don't really care because I just had a great orgasm.

As the beat gets ready to drop, Lance shouts, *"Here we go! On the count of three, everybody bounce! One! Two! Three!"* The beat drops in the song. *"Bounce! Everybody bounce!"* Lance starts jumping behind his table.

I bounce right along with the beat, getting totally into it.

The next thing I know, I'm having a blast and letting go. I switch between dancing in front of Lance and dancing with Lark. She wastes no time grinding on me. The guys at the foot of the stage love it. A couple of girls hold up their hands in heart shapes for us.

In my ear, Lark purrs, *"Let's give them a show!"*

I have no idea what she means but I don't care. *"Okay!"*

The next thing I know, Lark's hands are all over me. I can't decide if it freaks me out or turns me on. It's hard to say because Lance left me wanting him inside me. I know he's still hard. I can see his boner tenting his red OOEE! SURE THING sweats behind his DJ table. He looks so ridiculous I giggle every time I see it. I wonder what the crew backstage thinks.

Who cares.

This is rock and roll, people!

Lark's hands find my breasts and she starts massaging them. Am I surprised she knows exactly what she's doing? Of course not. She's a girl. Should I be doing this? I glance over at Lance and his silver PH4NTüM mask is up and his eyes are huge. I think I just blew his mind. I grind my ass against Lark. If her fingers go down my micro shorts, I don't know what I'm going to do...

Lance does. He bounces toward us but suddenly stops before he leaves the cover of the DJ booth. He quickly repositions the tent pole in his sweats to the side, then resumes bouncing toward us. Oh, geez. You can still see his cock in his sweats. It's bouncing too. Someone is bound to shoot video of that.

When he bounces up to Lark and me, he hollers, *"Yo, Lark! Hands off those titties! Them is my titties, girl!"* He's grinning when he says it.

"You're not doing your job, Lance!" Lark hollers. She twists both my nipples through my lace top.

I'm shocked by how good it feels. This is so wrong. I'm not a lesbian. I'm not even bi-curious.

Lark teases, *"Look how hard her nips are, Lance! You better do something about it or I will!"*

Holy cheese us. Lark is trying to corrupt me.

Lance smirks his devil's grin and grabs me by the arm, pulling me free from Lark and guiding me back behind the DJ table. I stumble after him. He traps me between his arms while he twists knobs and dials on the turntables. I am dying for him to twist my knobs and dials.

The music shifts to a hard driving sensual tribal rhythm.

"Time to get your freak on, LA!" Lance shouts on the mic. He grinds his hard-on against my micro shorts.

Then he rips them down.

Fuck.

I am totally exposed. And totally wet.

This is so hot I'm going to die from arousal.

I would run right out of here if Lance wasn't caging me up against the DJ table. What is he going to do? Where is his finger? And what is taking him so long?

He pushes my shoulders down hard, surprising me.

Then his fullness presses up against my entrance.

Yes, his hard cock.

I look down under my armpit and see that his red OOEE! SURE THING sweats weren't lying. They're down around his thighs.

His cock slides into me and starts a slow thrust.

I am being fucked in front of a rave crowd.

This is ridiculous.

But it's the hottest thing ever.

How is it that Lance knows what I want better than I do? He pushes buttons I didn't know I had, or if I did, he pushes them better than I ever could. It takes zero seconds for me to get lost in the pleasure of the moment. The loud as hell music, Lance's large as hell cock, and the crazy insane sensation of him sliding in and out in time with the beat.

I start to clench right away.

This is impossibly erotic.

I look up at the crowd and a girl on some guy's shoulders near the stage is staring right at me with a shocked look on her face. Pointing a cell phone at me.

My orgasm hits me before I even realize it. Lance pounds against my ass, working toward his own. I focus all my senses on what's happening between my legs. I can't hear anything except the music. If he's grunting or shouting, no one will ever know but him. I squeeze hard every time he pounds.

He swells and accelerates.

He's coming.

I can feel it.

Coming inside me in front of all his fans.

Someone is definitely recording this.

He slumps against me for a few seconds, his body heaving.

A few seconds later, *"Make some noise for me, LA! The Phantom in da house!"*

"The Phantom is inside me," I chuckle loud enough for him to hear.

He starts to laugh in my ear. *"That was a first!"*

"Sex on stage?"

"Yeah!"

"You too?" I laugh harder, feeling his cum dripping down the inside of my thigh. No one can hear me over the roar.

"Oh! My! Fuck!" Lark shouts, staring right at us, covering her mouth with both hands and laughing. *"You just got fucked on stage!!"*

That I did.

"You slut!" she cackles gleefully and shakes her fists. *"I always knew you were a fucking slut!"*

Yes indeed.

Chapter 25

CHASTITY

"How much did we make tonight?" Lance asks.

It's almost 8:00 a.m. and I haven't slept since yesterday.

Beaver is leaned over the pile of cash on the coffee table in the lounge area at Lance's downtown office. There is so much money it looks like we robbed a bank. Beaver glances at the pad of paper next to him where he is keeping count. "There's about twelve thousand eight hundred, give or take. If some of the bills weren't all sweaty and stuck together, I'd give you an exact number."

"You guys need a cash register," I smirk.

Lance chuckles and kisses my cheek, "We'll use your cash drawer expertise next time."

I'm curled up next to him on the couch, my feet tucked beneath me, still wearing my pink and black raver costume, trying to stay warm by snuggling up against him.

To my surprise, Lark sits next to Beaver. She's bumped her knee against his at least a hundred times, but he's been focused on counting all the money. Unlike the rest of us, he doesn't seem exhausted. I guess his night owl schedule is perfect for surprise raves. When Lark bumps his knee for the two hundredth time, I give her a look.

She grins and shrugs and silently mouths the words, *"He's cute."*

I have to hide a sudden scowl by biting my lower lip. She doesn't know him like I do. She met him last night at the rave when he was busy running all over the place helping set up. She doesn't know the first thing about him. The only explanation is she's too tired to see straight. I'm sure after a good night's sleep, she'll forget she ever met him.

"I still gotta pay everybody," Lance sighs. "Beaver, take out two hundred for yourself. And two hundred for you, Lark." He grabs a bunch of twenties and counts out ten and hands them to her.

She waves the money away. "Thanks, Lance. But you don't have to pay. I just came so I could hang with my bestie." She smiles at me. "I mean, free rave, right? And free sex show. I can't complain." She winks at Lance and he chuckles.

I goggle but say nothing.

Lance says, "Lark, you shook your ass like a pro tonight." He folds the bills and stuffs them in the top of one of her furry lavender boots. "You earned it."

"Thank you, Lance. Seriously," she says.

Lance stands up and grabs a huge handful of more twenties.

Most of the crew who helped with the rave still mill around the office drinking from beer bottles. Someone brought a case with them after we broke down the rave. Several stand around the air hockey table playing a game and talking trash about who is going to win. More are out in the garage or in the street smoking in the sunrise. I follow Lance as he goes from group to group, paying out everyone for the work they did, helping him count out money. He has to go back to the pile on the coffee table twice to get more. It shrinks a lot faster than I would've expected. I guess paying thirty people costs a lot.

The whole time, Beaver guards the money with Lark by his side.

At one point, as we walk away from the table, Lance whispers to me, "What the fuck is Lark doing with Beaver?"

"I have no idea. But she thinks he's cute. Fucking Beaver," I giggle.

Lance grins at that. "He's gonna fuck your friend's beaver if she's not careful."

I glance back at them and Lark is giggling at something Beaver just said.

Holy ship.

Lance might just be right.

++++8++++

CHASTITY

"I'm done," Lance mutters in bed back at his house, startling me awake.

"Huh?" My head is buried under my pillow on the mattress. I peek out from under it and see sun shining through the window. "What time is it?"

"I don't know. Three?"

"a.m. or p.m.?"

"Shit, I don't know," he yawns.

Probably p.m., because it's sunny.

What I can't figure out is whether it's today or tomorrow. My head pounds. I just slept for a long time and it feels like I didn't sleep at all. "What did you say before that?"

"Huh? Nothing."

"No. You said you were done." My first thought is he means us. He's done with us. My chest cements and I can't breathe. I try to calm myself. He can't mean that. After we had sex on stage last night? After he told Julian Whittaker off like that and called me his girlfriend? No, he can't mean us. I pull my pillow beneath my chest and turn my face toward him.

His fingers are laced behind his head and he stares at the ceiling, his face slack.

"Is something wrong?" I ask.

He closes his eyes, his brow knitting together. "Everything is wrong."

Now I'm worried. I push up onto my elbow, wide awake. "Lance, what's wrong? Is your dad okay? Did something happen while I was asleep?" Visions of us going to the morgue to look at Mr. McKnight's body flash through my mind. "Lance, tell me!" I whisper. "Please tell me."

He opens his eyes and stares at me. His irises are that same dark brown around a ring of orange that circles the pupil, but they're dull. The brightness is gone. The fire has died. "I'm broke, Chastity."

"What? You had eight thousand dollars left over last night! How can you be broke?"

"All my credit cards are maxed out. I'm already two months behind on rent for the office. Not to mention this house. I never should've rented this place on cash advances from my card."

"But what about the eight thousand? Won't that cover things?"

"For a month. But what about next month?" He's desperate.

"Take my paychecks back. You can have all of them."

He snorts, "I can't take your money. You earned it."

"But you need it."

"So do you. So quit pushing it," he barks.

I want to insist, but I don't want to start a fight. I've fought enough with my mom to fill a lifetime. I take a deep breath until I'm calm. I need to think, not lose it. A second later, my eyes light up. "What about throwing another surprise rave? You'd only have to do like ten more and you'd be able to pay for your video!"

"I wish it was that easy. You have a surprise show every night and it's not a surprise anymore. We'd have to hit up ten or twelve big cities other than LA. It costs money to take a show on the road. And I doubt we'd pull in the kind of numbers we did last night." He sighs. "I'm out of ideas, Pink. I already tried everything I could think of." His desperation is catching and more than a little bit frightening.

"What are we going to do?"

"We?" The sarcastic way he says it breaks my heart.

"Yes, we." I'm getting angry. "Aren't we a we?"

His face softens and he runs a hand through my hair. "Yeah. We're a we, Pink." He sounds sad. "But I'm doing a shitty job of providing for you."

"Providing?" I chuckle. "Be serious. I just found out we're a couple yesterday when you chewed out Julian Whittaker. You don't need to provide for me until we're—" *married*. I stop myself from saying it just in time. "I mean, unless we're—" I stop myself again. "Oh, I don't know what I mean!" Yes I do. I just hope he didn't figure it out. If telling him I loved him shut him down for weeks, what will the topic of marriage do?

"But I want to."

He wants to what?

Marry me?

My heart bounces all over my chest. He's been providing for me since the day we met, so that only leaves... Don't tell me he's really thinking about marrying me. If he is, I will literally die of happiness right here in this bed.

The fire in his eyes suddenly burns.

The girl sprinklers between my legs go off, ready to quench his flames. "Oh, Lance..." I purr.

He caresses my cheek. "Provide for you. That's what I meant."

I just fell in love all over again.

His face says the opposite. It drags and the fire goes out of his eyes. "Only problem is I can't even provide for myself. Julian Whittaker was the last chance I had. I've asked everyone I know to hook me up with every investor they know. Everyone has said no."

Julian didn't. But there were those strings... I heave a sigh. "Screw Julian. You don't need him. There has to be someone else. Or some other way. We can find your money somehow."

"There's no one left. I feel like an idiot, Chastity. You've had a front row seat to my failure. I fucked everything up. Right in front of the woman I love."

My heart opens wide for him, a blossoming in my chest that sweeps through me in a warm comforting wave. I cup his stubbled cheek with my palm. "Don't be an idiot, you gorgeous man. You just made everything right."

I snuggle into his arms and we kiss. Lips, tongues, everything is perfect. When I'm breathless from the exhilaration of it, I hold him tight. "I love you, Lance. Love you, love you, love you!!!!" I squeal with glee and shake a little happy dance in his arms.

He chuckles and hugs me hard.

That's when I realize I've been wanting to tell him I loved him since the day he moved in next door. At first, I thought it was just infatuation. Nothing more than a girlish crush. I mean, I was an innocent kid back then. I still am, but I know I can trust my feelings because he feels the same way.

I am on Cloud ten thousand right now, which is way *way* high up in heaven.

Lance grins at me, his eyes bright. Not with his devil's grin. This grin is different. This grin is innocent. Angelic. He combs his fingers through my hair. He whispers, as if he's afraid to say it out loud, "I love you too, Chastity."

We make love and the world is perfect.

Chapter 26

CHASTITY

"I can't believe I had to sell the air hockey table," Lance says morosely several weeks later. "I'm gonna miss this place,"

"Me too," I sigh.

Movers roll furniture outside on dollies. Lance's downtown office is half empty already.

"How long were you here for?" I ask.

"Two years."

"Wait, didn't you move here from Vegas a few months ago?"

"I didn't. Dad did. But I was back and forth between here and there all the time, keeping tabs on him. It got to a point where there was too much bullshit for him in Vegas and I knew it would be easier with him here. So I moved him. He didn't care. They sell booze in LA too." His face is grim.

"Oh." I say thoughtfully. "It seems like he's doing better."

He shrugs. "It's hard to tell. He hides it so well. I never know for sure and I can't babysit his ass twenty-four seven. He's not dead, so that's something."

"Yeah," I mutter. I can't imagine having to deal with Mr. McKnight like Lance has for who knows how long.

Considering we spend so little time at the house, there's no way of knowing what Mr. McKnight does when we're not around. It's not like he's a prisoner. He comes and goes whenever he wants and pedals to who knows where on that mountain bike of his. I don't really want to think about it because this day is dreary enough as it is. I look around the office for something that might cheer up Lance. "You know, we never got to have sex on the garden patio outside your office."

"Yeah," he says, depressed.

I wink, "We still have time."

"Let's wait till the movers are gone." He doesn't sound into it.

I try not to worry. We've made love every day since he told me he loved me. Not sex. Not crazy on stage fucking in front of crowds. We made love. Tender, wonderful love. Every single time. And we've told each other we love each other so many times I've lost count.

Despite the demise of this office, I am in heaven. As long as I have Lance by my side, the world could be crumbling around me and I'd be okay. Not that it is.

For the most part, things in my life are okay at the moment.

Charity has started high school. She seems to be adjusting. Things are mostly back to normal with her and Mom. Since I'm next door, I see Charity almost daily. She's holding up. I think half her problem is being in high school for the first time. I remember how hard my freshman year at North Valley was, and how long it took to get used to it. Charity will adjust. She's strong.

As for Mom, I avoid her. I talk to her now and then, but I feel like I'm done with her. Now that I'm eighteen, maybe I sort of am. Am I going to miss seeing her? I really don't think so.

"What now?" I ask Lance.

"After everything is sold or back at the house, I need to regroup. Figure out what the fuck to do next. You should probably look for a job." It pains him to say it.

"Do you think Mr. Molton would hire me back?"

He snorts, "I doubt it."

"I was just kidding. I'm done with serving ice cream."

His devil's grin curls. "You miss the hot caramel sauce, don't you?"

I flash back to the memory of our ice cream sundae Sunday sex. My first time.

"You're blushing," he chuckles.

"I guess I am." I try to only think about the good parts. Not the disaster that followed. *Whir.* "Can we talk about ice cream later?"

"Sure," he grins. "I'll have my banana waiting for your split the second you're ready."

"Your *what* for my *what*?" I giggle.

"Bananas? Splits? I think you can figure it out."

Despite the down mood of the day, I can't help but get wet.

Lance is perfect.

No matter what happens with his music career.

I'm never leaving him.

++++8++++

CHASTITY

"Mom is crazy!" Charity screams, barging right through Lance's front door, which apparently was unlocked. She slams it behind her.

"Jesus!" I jump off the couch and the course catalog from Pasadena City College that I was reading tumbles to the floor. "Please don't do that."

"Sorry." She's furious.

I pick up the rumpled catalog and set it on the couch. "What happened?"

"I can't do it, Chaz." She throws her hands up and lets them slap against her legs. She starts pacing, shaking her head and making her long blonde ponytail wave down her back. "I can't wait for Dad's lawyers. I have to go to Illinois now."

"Calm down, Chair. Sit down. Tell me what happened."

Lance comes walking out of our bedroom, which is now our office. Actually, office is a bit of an exaggeration. We added a folding table and a folding chair for each of us next to our mattress. It's cramped but it's cozy. Lance says, "Is everything all right?"

Charity throws her arms in the air again. "My mom is insane!"

Lance chuckles, "What else is new?"

Charity smiles and turns to me, "See? He knows."

I'm grateful Charity has stopped blowing her top. I hope she's just here to vent. I pat the cushion next to me. "Sit down, Chair. Whatever it is, I'm sure we can figure it out."

She slumps and trudges to the couch and plops down next to me. "Mom is so annoying."

"What happened this time?"

"I was studying in my room, listening to Katy Perry. NBD, right?"

"Right. I mean, if Mom didn't hear. Did she?"

"Maaaaybe I had the music a little loud..." she rolls her eyes and flicks her tongue on the L in loud.

I wince. "You know how Mom is about pop music."

"I know! But it's stupid! Katy Perry isn't Satan! I mean, what the fuck?"

I repress a laugh.

Charity catches it and smiles. "See? Mom is ridiculous!"

As long as Charity is smiling and not having a meltdown, that's all I care about. I would hate to think what would happen if she ran away again. Something tells me it would end much worse than last time. "Maybe you should wear headphones. So Mom doesn't know."

"Yeah, but then she asks what I'm listening to. I'm sick of lying and saying it's gospel music. I shouldn't have to lie about something so *stupid*." She spits out the word stupid. "You know?"

"Oh, I know."

"I can't deal with her any more. What's taking Dad and his lawyer so long?"

I sigh. "I don't know, Chair. It takes a while. Dad told me they have to get everything ready before they talk to Mom's lawyer. Cross their T's and dot their i's. You know she's going to freak when she finds out."

Charity groans. "I know. I wish we could just get this over with."

I don't. The sooner it happens, the sooner I'll be forced to make a decision between her and Lance because something tells me Lance needs to stay in LA to resurrect his music career, not move to the midwest. I sigh, "You just have to be patient, Chair."

"You should talk. You live here. With the cool people." She grins at Lance.

He sits down on the armrest next to her and smiles back, "Don't forget to count your sister."

Charity cocks her head to the side and narrows her eyes, "She's only semi-cool. And that's only because of you."

I roll my eyes and shake my hair.

She swats my knee. "JK."

I laugh, "No wonder Mom is sick of you."

"She's so sick of things, she's sick of herself."

"I never thought of that." I stop and stare at my kid sister, marveling at how smart she's getting. "But you know what? You're right."

Lance nods, "I've said it before. That woman needs to get lai—" He stops short when he realizes what he's saying in front of Charity.

"That's for sure," Charity sighs.

He chuckles nervously, "I meant, loosen up."

He's right on both counts. I sigh. "If only she would."

Bing-bong!

The doorbell.

"That's probably her," Charity groans.

Whir.

I hope Charity's wrong.

"I'll get it," Lance says, hopping up from the armrest.

Charity and I stare at each other, listening to the sound of the door opening.

"Hey," Lance mutters in the entryway.

"*WHERE IS SHE?!*" Mom shouts outside. "*I KNOW SHE'S HERE!!*"

"Who?"

"My DAUGHTER!! THAT'S WHO!! WHERE IS SHE?!!" Clicking heels on the floor tiles.

Here she comes.

Whir!

Mom marches up to Charity, her face boiling with rage, and shoots a finger at her. "You get back in the house RIGHT NOW!! You're GROUNDED, young lady!!"

Charity's face pinches into a scowl. "NO!"

"Get back in the house! RIGHT!! NOW!!!!" Mom is furious.

WHIR!!

My entire body vibrates in response. I think it's the adrenalin kicking in because I know Mom is primed for a huge fight.

"Calm down, Mrs. Shields," Lance says quietly behind her.

She whirls around and shoots him with another finger. "YOU shut up!! I don't want to hear anything from YOU!!!! YOU made this mess!! Every bit of it!!!!"

Lance is shocked silent.

Mom spins back on Charity. "Get back in the house before I make you!!" Her face twists in a horrid knot. She ignores me, which is good, because I barely recognize her.

"*NOW, CHARITY!!!!*" she shouts.

Charity stares at Mom, her face red, eyes wide, lips tight. "*No!! Get out of here, you BITCH!!*"

Mom's eyes pop with rage. "What did you call me?" Her voice is low and dangerous.

"*You're a BITCH! Now leave me alone! I HATE you! Get out of here!!*"

Mom lashes out and claws at Charity's arm. "*You do what I say, you little MONSTER!!*"

"*NO!*" Charity shrieks. "*Let go of me!*" She flails on the couch, kicking her legs at Mom.

Mom recoils, her face scrunched as she avoids Charity's Skechers. "*Stop FIGHTING me, Charity!!*"

I can't take it any more. "STOP, MOM!!"

She doesn't even hear me.

"*STOP!!!!*"

Mom wrestles with Charity, holding on tight to her ankles.

I dive between them.

Charity kicks me in the face, on accident. I see stars and clap my hands to my face. I fall back on the couch cushions.

Lance grabs Mom from behind in a bear hug, surprising her. When he pins her arms to her sides, she releases Charity. He walks her backward.

"*Let GO of ME!!*" Mom screams.

Charity is tipped back on the couch cushions, her feet still cocked to kick, breathing hard, teeth bared, ready to fight for her life.

"Ow!" I moan. "My nose!" I pull my fingers away and they're covered with blood.

"*YOU LET GO OF ME!!*" Mom shouts. Lance doesn't. She kicks the air, but she can't break free of his grip.

"Relax, Mrs. Shields! Everybody just relax!"

I touch my nose carefully. "I can't feel my nose!"

Charity's eyes goggle. "You're bleeding!"

"You kicked me!"

She winces. "Sorry." She reaches over to touch me.

I pull away instantly. "Don't! I think it might be broken."

"I'm so sorry, Chaz!" Her eyes are wet with tears. "I didn't mean it! Mom was—!"

"*Put me down, GOD DAMN IT!!!!*" Mom screams and everyone freezes. She stops kicking, but her legs dangle off the floor because Lance is so tall.

He says quietly, "I'll put you down if you promise to stay calm."

"*I will promise NO SUCH THING!! And the moment you put me down, rest assured I am CALLING THE POLICE!!*"

I scoff, "For what?"

"*For EVERYTHING!!!!*" She screams in ragged voice. She's not making any sense. But she's desperate because she lost control of this situation and herself. I can't believe she said God damn it.

She has never sworn in my entire life.

Something tells me today is doomsday.

"*You're INSANE, Mom!!*" Charity screams from the couch, crying out every word. Tears stream down her face. "*Look what you made me do to Chaz!! I can't live with you anymore!! I can't wait to move in with Dad!!*"

Mom's face explodes, yet she doesn't say a word.

I'm paralyzed with fear.

In a friendly voice dripping with dangerous calm, Mom says, "You can put me down now."

Lance releases her and takes a step back.

She smoothes her jeans and stares at the couch. Not at me or Charity, but the cushions between us, like she doesn't want to meet our eyes. "Have you talked to your father about this?" Her calmness is the scariest thing ever.

"*Yuh-huh-yes,*" Charity stutters, sniffling more tears.

Mom nods slowly and smiles creepily. "Okay then." She still isn't looking at us, just smoothing her blouse. "I will be at home. I have to make a few phone calls. Charity, please come home for dinner at six." She turns and walks silently out the front door without looking back.

I don't even hear the door close.

I knew it.

Doomsday.

And I'm stuck in the middle of it.

++++8++++

CHASTITY

"I'm so sorry, Chazzy Wazzy," Charity says sincerely. "I didn't mean to do it."

"It's okay," I sigh. "I blame Mom. But I still can't feel my nose."

"You will tomorrow," Lance grimaces.

"Great," I groan.

"I don't think it's broken," he says as he leans over the couch and delicately touches the bridge of my nose. "And believe me, I know broken. This looks like it'll be okay in a day or two."

"How swollen is it?" I ask anxiously, still holding a wad of bloody tissues under my nostrils.

He grins, "Looks like a bent red banana stuck to your face."

"More like a sweet potato," Charity adds. "All crooked and warty."

"Stop!" I giggle.

"You're laughing, aren't you?" Lance grins.

"I don't want to laugh," I pout and roll my eyes at Charity. "Does it look like a red banana or sweet potato or whatever?"

She giggles. "No. Sort of. Maybe a little?"

"Where's a mirror?!" I grumble, jumping up from the couch, which makes my nose pound.

"You don't wanna see it," Lance warns ominously.

Charity grimaces, "It looks terrible, Chaz, seriously…"

"You guys!" I whine, heading toward the bathroom. I'm almost afraid to look in the mirror. I slowly pull the bloody tissues away.

"See?" Lance grins behind me, his arm around me. "Straight as an arrow."

"It does not look like an arrow!"

Charity giggles, "I think Katniss used one just like it to kill Marvel from District One after he speared Rue."

"What?" I gasp, horrified.

She shrugs, "I just re-read Hunger Games."

Even Lance gives Charity a funny look in the mirror. After a moment, he turns me around and kisses my forehead. "It doesn't look like an arrow or a spear or a hot dog."

"Hot dog!" I whine.

Charity giggles.

Lance grins, "Don't worry. It'll be fine in a few days. But in the mean time it might feel a little better with some ketchup and mustard."

"Don't forget the bun," Charity snickers. "And the relish."

I growl, "I hate you both!" But I'm laughing, which makes me feel a little better about all of this.

Lance hugs me again. "Your nose is fine. I promise."

I sigh. "I hope so. In the mean time, we better call Dad and warn him about Mom. Who knows what she'll do now that she knows."

"Yeah," Charity shakes her head. "I wish I hadn't said anything to her."

"Too late now."

Whir.

The first thing Dad says when I call is, "Take a picture of your nose."

"Why?" I ask.

"In case I need it as evidence against your mother."

Whir.

"It was an accident," I say, defending Mom for some strange reason.

"I'm sure it was," Dad says. "But it wouldn't have happened if your mother hadn't lost her temper."

"Yeah." I hate that he's right. And I hate to see Mom and Dad fighting. Not that they are. Yet.

But they will.

Let the cold war begin.

++++8++++

CHASTITY

"So, if your mom and dad agree with what the mediator decides, this'll all be over today?" Lance asks two weeks later.

I shake my head. "Dad said the mediator doesn't decide anything. She just helps them come to an agreement on what they're going to do about Charity. If they agree, then yeah, it's all over today. Fingers crossed. They're sure taking a long time."

Lance squeezes my hand, which he has been holding for the past two hours. We sit in a lounge area in the office building where the mediator works. We're around the corner from the room where they're meeting. Dad flew into Burbank a few days ago. It's like he never left. Since Charity is fourteen, she gets to express her preferences for living arrangements. Since I'm eighteen, they don't need to talk to me.

Down the hall, a door bangs open. Mom's barking voice echoes up to the lounge. "This meeting is OVER! I knew mediation would be pointless!"

"Please, Faith," Dad says earnestly, "don't walk out now. We were making progress. Let's discuss this. We can figure this thing out."

"The only *progress* you want is to take Charity away from me. I will never let that happen. We can finish this *discussion* in court and let the judge *figure it out*." Her sarcasm is obvious. "Let's go, Charity." Mom's heels click on the tiled floor then stop. "I said let's go, Charity."

"No, Mom," Charity says calmly. "I want to stay here with Dad." Before we drove here, Dad made a big point to Charity that she needed to keep it together during the mediation. It sounds like she listened.

"Fine," Mom says. "John, make sure she's home by six o'clock for dinner." Her heels click and she storms toward the lounge area. She looks sharp in her gray power suit with her blonde hair up in a tight bun. Based on appearances, you might think she's the kind of woman every other woman wishes she was: beautiful, confident, capable. What a joke. More like bitchy, selfish and short-tempered. Looks can be deceiving. She doesn't spare a glance at me and Lance as she passes.

"Great," I whisper to him. "I knew she would do this."

Lance gives me a heavy look.

The past two weeks have been stressful on all of us. Charity has been at Lance's house almost every day for moral support and to get away from Mom. She even does her homework in Lance's living room. It drives Mom nuts, but I think she's just tolerating it so she doesn't look insane as far as the courts are concerned. I wish they could see her at her worst, not her best. But she's got the appearances thing down pat.

A few minutes later, Dad and Charity walk around the corner looking haggard and defeated.

"I don't want to live with her anymore," Charity says pathetically. She's near tears. "You know how crazy she is."

"Your mother is not crazy, Charity. She's just scared. And she deals with her fear by lashing out at everyone and everything."

"Isn't that the same as crazy?"

Dad doesn't know what to say.

Charity sighs, "What do we do now?"

Dad catches my eye briefly before running his hand through Charity's hair and placing it on her shoulder. "We do the best we can, Charity. With any luck, the judge will hear your side of the story and decide it's time for you to come live with me."

"What if he doesn't?"

Dad looks pained. "We'll cross that bridge when we come to it, sweetheart. But I promise, I will do everything I can to make sure things do work out. And whatever happens, I want you to remember I love you more than anything."

Charity glances over at me and winks. "Even more than Chaz?"

Dad smiles thinly, "Except that. I love you both the same."

"Okay," Charity sigh smiles. "I guess."

When they walk toward us, Dad trails behind Charity slightly. He looks broken.

Chapter 27

CHASTITY

"Where is she?" Mom growls in my face two weeks later.

"Not here," I grumble, holding Lance's front door open. She's obviously talking about Charity, who spends as much time here at Lance's house as Mom will let her. Ever since the mediation that went nowhere, it's not as much time as Charity would like, but she's back and forth so much, I don't give it a second thought when she's not around. "I thought she was at your house."

"She's not. She was supposed to be home an hour ago. Her dinner is getting cold."

"She's probably just avoiding you," I say with disdain. "Anyway, it's not my problem."

"She's your sister. Don't you care about her?"

"Don't you?" This is the first time Mom has said two words to me since the mediation. I was starting to think she'd forgotten I existed. Does she think I'm going to be on her side all of a sudden? Not gonna happen. "Charity wants to live with Dad."

Mom snarls, "Over my dead body."

"She cries about it to me every time she's over here."

Mom scowls but looks away.

I sigh, "Look, Mom. I don't know where she is. But she's not here. I haven't seen her since last night. She's probably at a friend's house. Have you tried calling her or texting?"

"She won't answer."

Big surprise. I roll my eyes, "Do you think she ran away again?"

Mom blasts me with a hateful look. "Don't you say that!!"

I shrug. "She did it before."

"How can you be so callous? Charity was supposed to come straight home from school! That was four hours ago!"

"How can *you* be so callous? You're completely out of touch, Mom. Charity hates you right now."

She smirks, "Tough love isn't a picnic. Maybe you'll figure that out when you're older."

I snort, "Is that what this is? Seems more like dumb love to me."

CRACK!

She slaps me across the face.

I hold my cheek. "What the hell, Mom?!"

Her nostrils flare, ready to hit me again. "You really ought to clean up that foul mouth of yours. Cursing is a sin. Or have you forgotten that?"

WHAM!!

I slam the door in her face.

Bing-Bong!! Bing-Bong!! Bing-Bong!!

I don't open the door.

I grab my phone and text Charity: **Did you run away again? Mom is looking for you.**

Ten minutes later, she responds: **No. But I shoe.**

Shoe? It must be auto-correct. I text: **Are you okay?**

Her: **I'm drugs.**

I really hope that was auto-correct. **Drugs?**

Her: **Drunk.**

Me: **For real?**

Her: **Yeppers** (followed by three drunk emoticons holding foaming glass beer mugs)

Me: **Where are you? Do you want me to come get you?**

Her: **No. Mom will kill me.**

Me: **Are you alone right now?**

Her: **With some boyz.**

Drunk with boys? That doesn't sound good. **Tell me where you are. I'm coming to get you. Don't worry about Mom. I'll protect you.**

While I wait for her to reply, I call Lark.

"What up, bitch?" she answers.

"Can you drive me somewhere?"

"When?"

"Now?"

"I just did my nails," she groans. "Can it wait an hour?"

"No."

"I did my toes too."

"Charity is in trouble. She didn't come home and she's drunk with some boys who knows where. I need to go find her."

"I'll be right over."

"I'm at Lance's."

"See you in five."

Ten minutes later, Lark knocks on my door wearing flip-flops, lavender board shorts and a half-zipped hoodie.

"Are you wearing a bra under that?" I ask.

"No. Too much boob?" She zips the hoodie up further, but leaves cleavage. "Are you ready?" Her keys jingle in her hand.

"I'm waiting for Charity to text me where she is."

"Is Lance here?"

"I just called him and left a voicemail."

She nods and sighs. "This is all so stupid. You know this is happening because your Mom walked out of mediation."

"I know. Don't remind me."

"Sorry. You know, if your sister needs a place to stay, my mom said she could stay with us. I told her what happened."

I smile at her. "Tell your mom thanks. But I don't think my mom would approve."

Lark sours. "Probably not."

My phone chimes when a text comes in.

Lark says, "Charity?"

"Yup."

"Where is she?"

I read the text. **Venison Boardwalk.** I smirk at the autocorrect. "Venice Beach. At the boardwalk."

"How the fuck did she end up there?"

"I have no idea. Let's go." I lock the front door and we jump in Lark's car. Someone pounds on the passenger window and I nearly hit the roof.

Mom.

"You're going to look for your sister, aren't you?!" She is such a snoop.

I crack the window an inch so she can't hit me again. "Yes."

"Where is she?!"

"Why don't you ask her yourself?"

Mom scowls, "I did. She wouldn't tell me."

I sneer at her, "And what does that tell you?"

Her upper lip starts to quiver angrily.

I roll up the window and mutter, "Let's go, Lark."

I watch Mom in the passenger mirror as we drive off. She's still standing on the sidewalk with her arms folded, holding in her rage.

Let her stew.

++++8++++

CHASTITY

Lark and I crawl through traffic on the 101. It's rush hour.

I moan and drop my head against the headrest, "We're going five miles an hour. It's going to take forever to get to Venice. Charity might be gone by the time we get there."

"Damn it!" Lark shouts.

"What?"

She slaps the steering wheel. "I knew I should've fixed the hover drive when I took this thing in for a tune up."

"What?!" I snicker.

She shrugs. "Just trying to lighten the mood."

"Thanks." I heave a sigh. I try calling Charity again. It's the eighth time since Lark and I left. Maybe she'll answer this time. I groan when it rings the fourth time. I'm about to end the call when it picks up.

"Chazzy Wazzy," Charity says in sloppy baby-talk.

"Whoa, Chair, you sound drunk."

"But I'm happy drunk," she giggles.

I put the phone on speaker. "Where are you right now?"

"Where are you?" she squeaks.

"On my way to pick you up. But I'm stuck in traffic. It might be a while."

"Boooooooo."

Lark winces and whispers, "She sounds loaded."

"Are you some place public?" I ask.

"There's publics everywhere."

"Where are you?"

"At the—" the sound breaks up.

"Where?"

"—the—"

"Shit," I hiss. "The signal keeps breaking up."

Lark says, "That sounds like the drum circle. The big one on the beach."

"You're right. Chair! Are you at the drum circle?"

"—beach—ocean."

"That's definitely the drum circle," Lark says.

"Chair, stay at the drum circle, okay? We'll meet you there!"

"—basketball—juggler—"

"Stay at the drum circle!"

The line goes dead.

I groan, "I wish we could get there quicker."

"Sorry," Lark says morosely. "I told you the hover drive is busted."

"I should call Lance." I speed dial him.

This time he answers immediately. "What's up, love?"

I never get tired of him calling me that. I smile slightly despite my low grade tension.

Whir.

He says, "I saw you called earlier, but I was in the middle of something."

I blurt, "Charity is in Venice with some boys and she's drunk. I'm driving there right now with Lark."

"Where in Venice?" His tone is immediately intense and focused.

"At the boardwalk. We think she's at the drum circle. As long as she stays there, she'll be easy to find. But with all this traffic, it's going to be at least an hour until we get there."

"I'm downtown. I can take surface streets on my bike and lane split the shit out of it and be there in thirty."

"You're not busy, are you?"

"I was, but this is more important." Random sounds like he's moving around flitter through the speaker. "I'm already out the door. I'll look for her at the drum circle. Text me Charity's number after we hang up so I can call her. And tell her to watch for me."

"Okay."

"I love you."

"I love you too."

I end the call, feeling ten times better than I did before talking to him.

"Lance is awesome," Lark says thoughtfully.

"Yeah," I mutter as I send Charity's number to Lance.

"Does he have an equally hot sexy brother I don't know about?"

"I don't think so." A few minutes later, I say, "Hey, I forgot to ask, whatever happened with you and Beaver? You guys were getting pretty cozy at Lance's office after he threw that surprise rave."

She grins coyly.

"What?"

She shrugs, "We're fucking."

"What?! You never mentioned that!"

"He has a big dick and knows how to use it. That boy is a human jackhammer. Who would've thought?"

I blurt a laugh. "Oh. My. Goodness. Lark, are you serious?"

She smiles slyly, eyes on the road. "Yup."

"And he doesn't have a tiny beaver sized dick?"

"Nope."

"How big is it?"

"We're talking donkey."

We stare at each other for a moment before bursting into laughter.

++++8++++

CHARITY

Drums.

Flashes of light.

Spinning, spinning.

Dancing on sand.

Can't stand up.

Legs not working right.

My ears hurt.

Ice picks.

I want to throw up.

The whole beach is going round and round and tilting crazily.

How much did I drink?

I don't remember.

Tipping, tipping, here comes the sand.

The spider catches me in his arms. All eight.

I think he has eight. I think I have eight too. Four arms and four legs. My four hands have twenty fingers. I smile at the spider and hold all twenty up to him. "Fingers," I giggle. "So many."

The spider smiles, "I see that."

"Where did gold mouth and his friend Joe go?"

"Who? You mean Antwan and José? They took off. You wanna go back to my van and get high?"

"Hi," I smile at the spider. What's his name again? He's cute. Really cute. Mom would hate him. Tattoos and leather. Like Chaz's boyfriend what's his name. I want my own bad boy.

"My van's real close," the spider says. "We can party there. Just me and you, fly girl."

At least two hands squeeze my boobs.

I'm fourteen, I say. Then I frown because the words didn't come out of my mouth. I try to say them again. *I'm fourteen*. It doesn't work. I forgot how to talk. So I try something simple, like friends. "Hi."

"All right, fly girl. I get you high. Let's go," he grins and picks me up with his spider arms.

I'm floating like a fly. The spider stares at me with all eight eyes like he wants to eat me.

"I like you," someone else says with my mouth.

"I like you too," he says, hungry.

++++8++++

CHASTITY

Parking in Venice is always terrible.

I have Lark drop me off on Windward Avenue, which is as close as I can get to where the drum circle usually is.

She says, "I'll go find parking. There's always spots down in the Venice Canals. You go look for Charity."

"Okay. Call me if you can't find me. But you know how loud the drum circle is, so if I don't answer, look for me there."

Lark drives off as I sprint down Windward, past all the booths selling cheap sunglasses, past the bike and skate rental shops, and toward the boardwalk.

Despite the cool fall weather and sundown hour, a scattering of street performers are still out juggling and doing magic tricks. A homeless guy with a sign that says "KICK ME $5" is wandering around near the palm trees, looking for customers but no one is buying. Numerous street vendors are still set up on the cement boardwalk, selling their spray-painted planet art or fresh sage or incense or greeting cards or hand-made jewelry. Plenty of tourists and locals are still out crowding the boardwalk, cycling by, rollerblading by, jogging by, strolling by.

Charity could be anywhere.

We're talking needle in a haystack.

My phone rings. It's Lance.

"Hey," I answer.

"I'm at the drum circle now." The drum sounds are audible over the phone. "You guys here?"

"I'm heading there now. Any sign of her?"

"Not yet. It's hard to pick her out with the sun already down. Do you have any idea what she's wearing?"

"No."

"No worries. I'll look for her hair."

I smile, "You can't miss that golden mop."

"Exactly," he chuckles. "Love you."

"Love you too." I end the call. Knowing Lance is already there is a huge relief. I try calling Charity again but she doesn't answer. I hope she's still at the drum circle.

"Chaz!" Lark shouts behind me, running to catch up.

I spin around. "Did you find a space?"

"Yeah. Some guy pulled out a block away and I snagged it." She's breathing hard from running.

"Awesome." I smile at her, "I'm so glad you're here, Lark. Seriously."

"*De nada*, bitch," she grins.

We hear the booming of the drum circle long before we reach it. It's on the beach sand out past the Venice Skate Park. When we step onto the sand, Lark kicks off her flip-flops and carries them in her hand. The circle is medium sized tonight. Sometimes the circle of people can grow as large as dozens of drummers and hundreds of spectators. Now it's definitely less than a hundred total. But in the twilight, and with everyone moving around, it's more than enough to make it difficult to pick out Charity.

If she's even here.

I text Lance: **We're at the circle.**

Him: **I'll look for you**

Me: **Have you found her?**

Him: **Still looking**

It doesn't take long to pick Lance's wandering head out of the crowd because he's so tall. And his black leather racing jacket with the two white stripes running down the left side sticks out against the tourists and skaters, and the hippies and granolas doing the drumming. He waves when he sees us. "Hey, Lark. What up?"

"Hey, Lance," she smiles.

Lance and I kiss briefly. He says, "I don't see her. I've circled twice."

"Maybe she has a hoodie covering her hair?" Lark offers, tugging on her own drawstrings.

"Didn't think of that," Lance says.

The three of us split up and scour the crowd for another twenty minutes. Some girls are so deep into their dancing it's hard to see their faces through their whirling hair without looking like creepers, but it's obvious from their hippie clothes they aren't Charity. At least, I hope not. For all I know, she bought a belly-dancer costume with her allowance money and is wearing it tonight.

"I don't see her," I say to Lance when we meet up.

"Call her."

I do. No answer. So I text: **I'm at the drum circle with Lance and Lark. Where are you?**

She doesn't reply.

Now I'm starting to worry. She could be anywhere. If she's still as drunk as she sounded an hour ago, she might not even know where she is. Or what is happening to her. I don't want to think about what kind of trouble my little sister might be in.

++++8++++

CHARITY

Black light.
Middle finger straight up.

Ty Dolla Sign *In Too Deep* poster.

"Your van is a red bedroom," I giggle.

"Something like that," the spider smiles as he closes the door.

No more outside.

Spider takes my shoes off.

I smile at my feet, "There you are!" I thought they'd disappeared.

Spider smiles, "I'm right here."

I meant my feet. I don't speak spider so he doesn't understand. But I have so many toes! Look at them! They wiggle all by themselves!

Spider crawls on top of me.

Did you know spiders have tongues?

They don't?

This one does.

I can taste it.

++++8++++

CHASTITY

"What do we do now?" I sigh.

"Keep looking," Lance says. "Do you have a good picture of Charity on your phone?"

"Yeah. Why?"

"Send it to me and send it to Lark. Then we can split up and show it to people up and down the boardwalk and ask if they've seen her."

"Good plan," I smile. "I'm so glad you're here."

Lark says, "I can go up and down Pacific Avenue and check the restaurants and coffee shops."

Lance looks at her. Then at me. "You two should stay together. It's dark."

Lark rolls her eyes, "Relax, Lance. I can take care of myself."

Lance puts a hand on her shoulder. "Do me a favor, Lark."

"Yeah?"

"Stay with Chastity, okay? Please? I can't be with both of you and I don't want either of you alone."

Lark nods, "Yeah, okay."

He smiles at me, "Send me that picture so we can start looking."

"Right." I swipe through my photos until I find a good one of Charity's face and send it to Lark and Lance.

"How drunk do you think she is?" he asks.

I wince, "I'm not really sure."

Lark says, "She sounded hammered."

He shakes his head, grimacing. "She'll probably be stumbling around. Keep your eyes out for that. How many guys did she say she was with?"

"She didn't."

He nods, "Well, if she is with a group of guys, they might be carrying her or helping her walk."

"You think of everything," I marvel.

"If I did, I already woulda found her." He sounds disappointed in himself. "You guys go south. I'll go north. We'll find her."

"Okay."

We split up and start asking everyone we pass on the cement boardwalk if they've seen Charity, showing them her picture on our phones. Everyone we ask shakes their heads. Some people sense our concern and they *want* to have seen her so they can help, but no one has. Not even the street vendors or the homeless people who've been here all day have seen her. I get more worried by the minute. It's almost like Charity was never here.

I text Lance now and then. He isn't having any luck either.

The crowds thin when it gets late.

I sigh, "She could be anywhere, Lark."

"Maybe we should try Pacific or the side streets? There's tons of food places. Maybe she's at one of them."

"Okay. Let's try that."

We snake up and down all the short streets that run between the boardwalk and Pacific Avenue, and along Speedway, which is more of an alley than an actual street. But Charity isn't anywhere and it's now completely dark and uncharacteristically cold for fall. I hope she has a jacket.

"I'm worried, Lark."

"We'll find her," she says with obvious doubt.

I text Lance: **Any luck?**

Him: **Checking basketball courts**

Me: **We're right near you.**

Him: **Where?**

Me: **Muscle Beach by the gym.**

Him: **Be right there**

The Muscle Beach outdoor gym is closed this late, the roll up doors shut down tight.

Lance looks hopeful as he approaches. "Did you find her?"

"No," I sigh.

He sinks.

"Charity still hasn't texted me back. Do you think something is wrong?"

"I hope not. We need to keep looking." He's insistent. "Are you two warm enough? It's getting pretty cold."

Lark has her hood up on her hoodie, which is now zipped up to her neck, and her hands in her pockets. "I'm fine."

"I'll be okay," I say. All I'm wearing is a T-shirt and jeans. I should've brought a jacket too.

"Here," Lance says, "take my jacket." He shrugs off his motorcycle racing jacket and drapes it over my shoulders before I can stop him.

"Thanks."

I notice the brightly lit T-shirt shop beyond the empty weight benches of the outdoor gym. Featured out front are rows of colorful striped knit Baja hoodies. Maybe I should buy one for Charity. If it gets any colder, she'll need it.

But we have to find her first.

Wherever she is.

Chapter 28

CHARITY

Spider is all over me.
Tasting me.
His tongue tickles.
Where did my pants go?
I don't care.
"Fuck," the spider says.
"Uh huh," I say.
"I'm all outta herb."
I smile. "He's funny."
"Huh? Who's funny?"
"Herb is funny." I giggle.
"Herb makes me funny too. Let's go get some, yo. You'll like it better if you're high."
"Hi," I giggle. "Are we friends?"
The spider smiles, "Yeah, we're friends, baby girl. Let's go."
I'm only fourteen!
Shhhhh. Be quiet.
Giggle.

++++8++++

CHASTITY

Lance's head drifts to his left, following something.
"What?" I ask.
Two street kids stumble up the steps leading into a shop two doors down from where we stand. They're inside before I get a good look. The sign over the door is yellow, green, and red and it reads WALL'S GREEN COLLECTIVE. There's a marijuana leaf in the center of the circled text. Below that the sign reads: MEDICAL EVALS - WALK INS WELCOME. It's obviously some kind of marijuana dispensary.
Lance strides toward the building.
"Did you see Charity?" I call out.
He doesn't turn around. "I don't know!" He's agitated.
Lark and I jog after him.
Lance jumps up the steps leading inside.

When Lark and I catch up, Lance is already at the end of a long white hallway with several plain metal doors on each side. He's walking toward us.

"Where did they go?" I ask, afraid to get my hopes up.

"All the doors are locked. They fucking disappeared."

Lark says, "I bet they went in here." She stands beside a door near where we came in and presses a small doorbell button.

Lance looks up and spots a camera watching the door. "Security check. Try to look friendly." At the moment, Lance looks anything but.

I smile and wave at the camera. "Say cheese," I mutter.

"Flash your tits," Lark snorts. "It usually works better." She unzips her hoodie half way, revealing cleavage, and thrusts her chest up toward the camera.

The door buzzes.

Lance grabs the handle, opening it. "Ladies."

I walk through first.

Inside is what looks like a waiting room that has been stripped clean. It's white and brightly lit with cold fluorescent lights. The receptionist's window is closed and made of black one-way glass that is probably bullet proof. More than a dozen people sit in several rows of cheap chairs in the middle of the room and along the walls. Everyone looks incredibly bored. I scan their faces. Two surfers. A guy in a business suit. Three hipsters with curly mustaches. A bunch of street kids huddled together along one wall. I concentrate on them. All have lip piercings or eyebrow piercings, earlobe stretchers, dyed hair, too much makeup, tattoos, boots, leather, ratty clothes.

Shit.

I don't see Charity.

Whir.

"Chaz?" The slurred word comes from a sleepy girl squeezed between two street kids. Sleepy girl's cheek is squished against the leather jacket covered shoulder of the guy sitting next to her. She lifts her head, revealing black lipstick and enough greasy black eyeliner to make Cleopatra laugh.

"Charity?" I stare right at her. I barely recognize her.

The hood of her purple hoodie hides her golden mop, but a few strands poke out. It's her. That's when I notice the guy she's leaning on. He has a chin-only blond goatee, pale pocked skin, and a bad tattoo of a spider on his neck. He's dirty and looks at least twenty and mad at the world. If he wasn't so grungy, he'd actually be cute. But he's way too rough for my sister. He watches me closely, unsure what to do.

I rush over to Charity, squeezing between a row of seats and nearly tripping over the three hipsters. "Sorry, sorry," I mutter as I pass.

Charity's face melts into a sloppy smile. She stares at me, her eyes struggling to focus. "What are you doing here?"

I lean down and shake her knee. "You were supposed to wait for me at the drum circle."

"I was?" Her eyelinered eyes are thin slits. She tries to sit up but is too weak and she slumps back in her chair. Wow, she's drunk.

"We need to get you out of here." I grab her arm and try to pull her to her feet.

The guy with the spider tattoo barks at me, "Who da fuck are you?" He projects a wave of hatred.

"I'm her sister," I hiss, tugging on Charity's rubbery arm.

She flops forward and her head tumbles between her shoulders.

Spider Neck stands up. "I don't care who da fuck you are. Get your hands off my bae."

His bae? Great. How much trouble has Charity managed to find in one afternoon?

"Let her go, yo," Spider Neck growls, fisting the shoulder of my t-shirt. "Fore I make you, bitch."

Out of nowhere, Lance slams him in the chest hard, knocking him back in his chair. "Sit the fuck down, buddy," he growls.

Everyone in the waiting room is now staring at us, eyes wide.

Spider Neck tries to pretend he's not scared shitless, frowning like he's tough. "Home boy don't know who he messin with."

"Neither do you, Emi-Ned. So shut the fuck up."

Spider Neck plays it off like he's tough, but he just sits there staring at Lance.

Lance glares at him, "Was it your fucking idea to take my girlfriend's kid sister to a pot shop?"

He doesn't answer.

Lance's eyes burn. "Well? Not talking?"

Spider Neck glares back switchblades.

"Drunk got your tongue?" Lance asks, pissed.

"Forget about him," I whisper.

He grunts.

After I'm sure Spider Neck isn't going to pull a knife or a gun, I say, "Lark, help me with her."

Lark grabs Charity's other arm and we both pull.

Charity leans forward in her chair like a limp doll. And throws up all over the white tiled floor. Vomit splatters everywhere like someone dropped a bucket of liquid pizza on the tiles.

"Aw fuck!" The people sitting close by are all instantly disgusted, lifting their shoes off the floor, scampering up onto their chairs and flicking off vomit or backing away from the stench which is like a punch in the nose.

I almost barf myself when the smell hits me.

"Breathe through your mouth," Lark gags. Her too.

We manage to get Charity to her feet. Warm puke stains the front of her purple hoodie. Lark and I get our shoulders under Charity's arms and walk her around the rows of seats, heading toward the door.

BLAM!

I turn and see Lance towering over Spider Neck who is lying on his back on the tiles. The guy slowly turns over on all fours, reaches into his leather jacket, then springs to his feet, a knife flashing in his hand.

"SIT THE FUCK DOWN!" Lance roars. He sounds so scary, he even scares me.

Spider Neck is considering his next move, eyes dancing between his knife and Lance.

Lance bares clenched teeth, "Don't make me tell you twice, dumbshit."

Spider Neck snarls.

"You gonna stab me?" Lance challenges. "Go right ahead."

Spider Neck is confused.

I'm scared out of my mind he'll do it.

"Do it," Lance growls. "Or are you too much of a bitch?"

"Lance!" I hiss.

Lance doesn't turn to look at me.

Spider Neck's eyes are wide with fear. Good. He lowers his knife and in a small voice says, "Sorry, man. I—sorry."

"Gimme the knife." Lance holds out his hand.

"What?" Spider Neck is confused.

"Gimme the fucking knife. I'm not gonna use it on you. But you're not gonna jump me when I turn my back either."

Spider Neck considers the gleaming blade.

I want to tell Lance he's going to get his hand cut open, but I don't want to distract him. My heart is pounding with adrenalin.

Spider Neck sets the knife gently on Lance's hand.

"Sit down and stay there," Lance commands as he closes the blade. "And put your hands under your ass."

"What?"

"Sit on your fucking hands."

Spider Neck nods and sits down slowly on the floor, on top of his hands.

"And put your feet out in front of you."

Spider Neck hesitates.

"Do it."

"Okay, okay," he whines then complies.

"Don't get up till we're gone."

"Yeah, dog," he mutters absently.

Lance turns and walks toward the door. There's a little waste basket near it and Lance drops the knife in with a clatter. He smiles at me and Lark. "Let's go, ladies."

I grin as Lark and I walk Charity outside into the cool night air.

++++8++++

CHASTITY

"Lance is a total fucking hero," Lark muses as we drive home and Lance follows behind on his Gixxer.

"Yeah," I smile.

Thankfully Charity doesn't throw up all over the inside of Lark's car on the drive home. But she did throw up once more while we walked her to it. When we get to Lance's house, I climb out of the back seat where I sat nursing Charity during the drive.

Lance pulls up on his motorcycle and parks in the driveway next to us. "Let me get her out." He peels his helmet and gloves off before leaning into the car. He scoops her up and lifts her out. "Whoa, that's ripe."

He's talking about the vomit on her hoodie. Lark and I had the car windows down the whole drive home. We did our best to clean her up before we left with some napkins and a water bottle Lance bought on the boardwalk, but the smell of vomit always lingers.

"What did you do to her?!" Mom yells, trotting up Lance's driveway. "Give her to me," she insists, waving her hands.

Charity is mostly asleep with her face buried in Lance's armpit, otherwise I bet she'd say no to the idea.

"Relax, Mom," I say. "She's fine." I asked Charity on the drive home if Spider Neck or anyone else did anything to her or gave her anything besides alcohol. I'm pretty sure the answer to all of the above was no, but she was so drunk and confused, I'm not entirely sure.

Mom tries to take Charity from Lance, but he won't let her. He gives me a look that says, "*Should I?*"

I wince and silently mouth, "*I don't know.*"

Mom turns Charity's chin side to side. "What did you do to your face, young lady? Where'd you get all this black makeup?" She pushes the hood back.

"Stop, Mom," Charity mutters, eyes closed, brow wrinkled as she waves her hand weakly.

Mom pushes Charity's hair back. "Did you get your ears pierced?"

Pierced ears? I missed that part.

"Charity, what did you do to yourself?" Mom grabs Charity's arm, which dangles over Lance's shoulder, and shakes it. "Charity? Why are your ears pierced?!"

"I don't know," Charity says sleepily. She reaches up to touch her right lobe. "Ow."

Mom laughs angrily. "Whore's paint and earrings all in one day. What's next? Prostitution?"

"Shut up, Mom," I warn.

She finally acknowledges me and growls, "Don't you tell me what to do! I'm her mother." She suddenly grimaces, "What's that smell? Is that vomit? Charity, are you sick?"

She doesn't answer.

I sigh, "She's drunk, Mom."

She glares at me "Great. Just great. And which one of you got her drunk? Was it you, Lance?"

"Are you kidding?" Lance scoffs.

"Certainly not! Your father is a drunk! I can only imagine how much alcohol you have lying around your house. It probably flows like wine. Charity spends plenty of time in your den of sin. She no doubt learned it from you. How many times has she seen you and your father get drunk?"

"Me get drunk?" Lance chuckles.

"Yes, you," she spits.

"Gimme a fucking break, Faith. For the last ten years, I've been the only thing standing between my dad and the grave. And for your information, your daughter was drunk when we found her. Right now you oughta be asking yourself why."

"How should I know why? And when did you become so concerned about the well being of my daughter?" It almost sounds like she means Charity *and* me.

"Don't be ridiculous, Faith. Charity is family."

"She's not your family," Mom spits.

"She will be when I marry your daughter."

Mom's eyes bulge. "You would never." It's a warning.

My heart swells. Did he just say what I thought he said?

"Get over yourself, Faith. I love Chastity. That means her sister is my sister. Got it? Why else do you think I dropped everything to go look for her? Twice?"

Mom's face wars with itself.

My heart is ready to burst. He did say it. He wants to marry me. How did this evening go from the worst I've had in weeks to the best of my entire life? And how does Lance manage to turn my life upside down over and over and over, in a good way? I have to hide my smile because now is not the time to celebrate.

Mom glares at me. "What are you smiling about?"

"Nothing," I say.

She narrows her eyes at me. "You know, ever since that sorry excuse for a father of yours showed his head around here, things have been a filthy mess."

Lance shakes his head and snorts. "You're ridiculous. John Shields is a good guy."

Mom sneers at him, "What do you know? Oh, I forgot. Now that you're taking my daughters away from me, you're the expert on everything, right?"

"John has been staying at my house off and on for the past few months. We've talked plenty. And I can tell you he's got his shit together and he's a great dad. I see him with Charity and Chastity and they love him. You should consider yourself lucky. There's a lot worse dads out there than him."

"You don't know what you're talking about. You're just a child. John is nothing but a—"

Lance cuts her off. "Open your eyes, Faith. I'm not a kid. I run a business. What do you do besides live off the money your ex-husband gives you every month?"

Mom's eyes pop.

It's true. She has never worked since I can remember.

"That's right, Faith. He told me all about it. The alimony, the child support, everything. When was the last time you worked a job, Faith?"

"I'm a mother! That's a full time job!"

"You're the mother of an eighteen year old who works for me and lives in my house and—"

"Your house? I thought—"

"Yes, Faith. I pay the rent. You think my dad can cover twenty-four hundred a month?"

Mom doesn't answer.

"I mean, fuck, Faith. Can you?"

She scoffs haughtily, "Well, I…" she trails off.

"Thought so. And Charity isn't exactly tied to your apron strings. She already ran away once. Maybe if you weren't such a controlling cunt—" Mom's face freezes "—you'd realize that you need to stop wasting John's money and blowing your daughter's college fund on all this court bullshit and do what's in Charity's best interests. Not yours. Don't you recognize a cry for help when you see it? Charity wants to live with her dad and she'll do anything she can to get away from you. Or kill herself trying."

Mom's face wrinkles with hate. "I don't have to listen to you! I don't have to listen to any of this!" Her eyes ping-pong between me and Lance.

"Instead of being a bitch about it and putting your daughter at risk, maybe you should help her. She's going to run away again and you know it. The question is whether or not she ever comes back. So you have to ask yourself: would you rather see Charity every now and then or never again? Think about what you're doing, Faith. You only get one chance to fuck everything up. Or make it right. Let Charity go live with her dad, Faith. If you love her, let her go. If she really loves you, she'll come back to you when she's ready."

Mom stares at him, her eyes jittering. "You have no idea what you're talking about! You're just a no good punk!"

Lance scowls half-heartedly. "Keep telling yourself that, Faith. But when you see Charity's face on the back of a milk carton, ask yourself if getting your way was worth it."

Touchdown! I want to jump for joy. Inside my head and heart, I do. But I remain silent so Mom can think this through. Is there any chance she was listening? Or will she block it all out and stick her head back in the sand?

"The Lord would never let that happen to my daughter!"

Sand, meet Mom's head. I sigh.

Lance smirks, "Are you sure? I've seen bad things happen to good people, Faith. It happens all the time. And if you hadn't noticed, *good* things happen to *bad* people. That makes zero sense. It makes me wonder if God is listening to you or anybody else or if he just doesn't give a shit."

"Blasphemy!" Mom shakes her head, astonished. "God has a plan for all of us! Even you! He will make things right! He will stop John from taking my daughter away from me!"

Lance shakes his head. "Stop worrying about what God is going to do, Faith. What are you going to do?"

Mom's chest is heaving like she just ran a marathon. Then it suddenly stops. She stares at Lance for several moments, confused. "You have no idea what you're talking about! You're just a child! You... you..."

Lance turns away, Charity still in his arms, and heads toward his front door. Over his shoulder, he says, "Think about what I said, Faith. Better yet, pray on it."

When Lance is halfway to the door, Mom screams. A shrill, loud, pained, blood-curdling wail:

"NOOOOOOO!!!!!!!!!"

++++8++++

LANCE

I can't believe I ever thought that Faith Shields was in any way attractive.

Dicks and balls are really fucking dumb.

Chapter 29

CHASTITY

"Are you going to fly out to Illinois for Thanksgiving so you can spend it with me and Dad?" Charity asks while packing up stuff in her bedroom. She's all smiles.

"I hope so."

"You can bring Lance."

I chuckle, "Thanks for permission. Did you mention it to Dad?"

"Yeah. He thinks Lance is awesome."

I smile, "Me too."

For the first time in months, I feel relaxed in my house. The one I lived in until Mom freaked out. I guess I still think of it as mine. My room still has most of my stuff. I only took what I needed to get by. It would be nice to chuck what I don't need and forget about it. Then again, why? Don't most kids leave stuff at their parents' houses after they turn eighteen? I mean, Lark still lives at home with her mom and they're pretty much besties. If only I were so lucky.

Charity zips up her knapsack, which is stuffed to bursting, and sets it on the floor next to her two suitcases. "Dad says you should buy your tickets now to save money."

"Good idea," I say. The question is, does Lance have money to spare? I have enough in savings to cover tickets for both of us, and I'll totally pay for Lance's ticket if he can't afford it. I'm not exactly sure what his financial situation is right now, but I can't ask him to spend money on a four day weekend trip when he has to worry about making rent so he and his dad can keep a roof over their heads.

Dad sticks his head in the door of Charity's bedroom. "We need to get to the airport if we're gonna make our flight."

"All packed," Charity smiles.

"You should say goodbye to your mother," Dad says, grabbing Charity's two suitcases.

Charity groans, "Do I have to?"

"You'll hurt her feelings if you don't."

"Fine."

"I'll be outside. Don't take too long. Chaz, are you gonna come with?"

I wince, "I wish I could. But I don't have a way to get home. Lance is working and so is Lark."

"Maybe your mother can follow and take you home?"

"Ummmm, she's too busy gardening in the backyard."

Dad nods knowingly. "Right."

The whole time Dad has been inside helping Charity pack what she needs for the move, Mom has been out back. It's like she's in denial that this is happening or wants to avoid Dad. I would've expected her to be inside overseeing the entire process so Charity wouldn't forget anything. That's how she always was in the past when she sent me or Charity off to church camp. I think she's licking her wounds because Dad won. Whatever.

Dad holds up a suitcase, "Help me with these?"

"Oh, right." I grab Charity's knapsack off her bed and we head outside.

Dad pops the trunk on the cheap Nissan he rented this time and puts the luggage inside. "Did your sister ask you about Thanksgiving?"

"Yeah."

"I'd love to have you and Lance come out."

"Yeah." I don't want to explain the financial thing to Dad.

"You know, I haven't had Thanksgiving with you and your sister in four years. I miss you guys." His eyes shimmer.

"I miss you too, Dad." I'm going to cry, but I try to hold it in.

"There's room for you too."

"What, you mean to live with you and Chair?"

Dad nods. It's obvious he doesn't want to get his hopes up.

I don't want to disappoint him but I can't say yes. "I don't know, Dad."

"I can get a bigger apartment, if that's what you're worried about."

I grin, "Big enough for me and Lance?"

Dad is about to say something but he doesn't. He just sighs hard. "I can't believe you're all grown up. My little girl. Just yesterday you were begging me for ballet classes. You cried when I said we didn't have the money." He scowls at himself and looks away. "I could've found the money somewhere." His eyes water. "I've been a terrible father, sweetheart. I want to make it up to you."

A tear drips down my cheek. "Oh, Dad." I reach out for a hug and he squeezes me. "You're the awesomest father ever."

"I love you too, sweetheart." He breaks the hug, but holds my arms. "You'll come out for Thanksgiving?"

I smear my wet cheek. "Promise."

"And bring Lance. He's a good man."

"I know."

Chapter 30

CHASTITY

BANG!!

A gunshot goes off in Lance's garage and I jump out of the folding chair I'm sitting on in Lance's bedroom. My heart races and I trot through the house into the kitchen right as another gunshot rattles the windows.

BANG!!

I vaguely recall Mr. McKnight passing by the bedroom door earlier and telling me he would be out in the garage. Then I suddenly remember that cryptic conversation Mr. McKnight had with Lance the night Charity ran away, the one about some guy in Vegas named Kane who might come looking for him. I forgot all about it until just now. When I reach the door between the kitchen and the garage, I freeze. Gunshots. Not the sound of another one, but the idea of one. Did someone just shoot Mr. McKnight? If I open this door, will there be some scary guy in a trench coat on the other side, pointing a gun at Mr. McKnight, who will be lying on the cement floor of the garage in a pool of his own blood, slowly dying?

My heart literally stops. So does my breathing.

I'm scared out of my mind.

What do I do?

If Mr. McKnight is laying out there dying, I can't leave him to bleed to death. But I don't want to get killed either.

BANG!!

That's when I realize it doesn't quite sound right for a gunshot. It sounds kind of like…

I slowly open the door to the garage, wincing, convinced I'm about to be shot in the face or the chest by whoever Kane is any second.

BANG!!

It takes a second for me to make sense of what I'm looking at.

Mr. McKnight stands beside his Harley with a smile on his face and his hand on the throttle. Sun pours through the open garage door, bouncing diamonds off the motorcycle chrome. It looks so clean, like he just washed and waxed it. The engine of the motorcycle is idling, but it leans on its kickstand. He thumbs a button on the handlebars and the engine rumbles to a stop. "Backfire. My bad. I think one of the O-rings on the fuel injector is shot."

"Geez, you scared me," I gasp, my heart still thumping.

He winks, "I could tell. Sorry about that. I shoulda rolled her out of the garage and started her on the driveway."

"It's okay."

A BMW drives up outside and parks beside the curb. The driver door opens and a woman steps out. She's very attractive and wears a knee length maroon business dress that looks expensive. She clicks up the driveway on black pumps. "Are you Lance McKnight?"

Mr. McKnight walks out of the garage, smiling casually. "I'm his father, Rod McKnight."

She's grinning, obviously affected by Mr. McKnight's charm. "Do you live here with your son?"

"Yeah. What's your name?" He holds out his hand to shake hers.

She pushes an envelope into it. "I'm with the rental company that owns this house. Please make sure Lance receives this letter."

That doesn't sound good. The woman turns and walks away, whipping her long dark hair behind her as she climbs in her BMW and drives off. I guess I was wrong about Mr. McKnight's charm.

"That was odd," I say.

"Sure was." Mr. McKnight stares at the envelope in his hand. The rental company logo is printed on the top left. Lance's name and address are in the middle.

I wonder what's inside?

Mr. McKnight opens the envelope without a thought and reads it. "Three day notice to pay rent or quit." He stares at me. "Why didn't he say something?"

Whir.

++++8++++

LANCE

I feel like a total tool.

"I'm broke, you guys," I mumble across the kitchen table. The letter from the rental company lays in front of me. Dad and Chastity sit facing me like this is an intervention. Not a booze hound intervention. A broke-ass loser intervention.

"Why didn't you say something?" Dad asks.

I scoff, "What, do you have a bunch of cash stashed somewhere I don't know about?"

"No, but I could sell my hog. It's worth at least ten grand now that it's cleaned up."

I shake my head and sneer, "You're not selling your bike, Dad."

"I have money," Chastity says earnestly.

I roll my eyes, hating every second of this. "I told you before, Chaz, I'm not taking your money. You earned it. It's yours."

She smirks, "That's why I can do anything I want with it."

"I'm not taking it to pay my rent."

"Your rent?" she smirks. "I live here too, you know. What if I mail a rent check to the rental company and pay them myself?"

I reach across the table and take the envelope and letter and jam them in my jeans. "No. You're not doing that."

"You can't stop me." She's smiling.

I force a grin. "Thank you. But please don't. Okay?"

She sags. "Why won't you let us help, Lance?"

Dad says. "Yeah, son. You're not alone in this. You understand? We can help."

"Thanks, Dad. But this is my mess. I'll fix it."

Somehow.

Too bad I'm all outta ideas.

That night in bed, Chastity asks, "What do you think about moving to Illinois? I was looking at rent online and it's cheaper than California by a lot."

"You want to be close to your sister and your Dad, don't you?"

"Well, yeah. But I want to be close to you too." She rests her hand on my bicep. "Seriously, Illinois might be good for both of us. I mean, living next door to my Mom is weird."

Why does it feel like everything I worked for is falling apart? If I leave LA, it will fall apart. I can't keep the DJ thing going from Illinois. All my juice will drain away and I may as well get a job at a gas station. I mean, what the fuck else am I gonna do? The fucked thing is, I already feel Chaz slipping away. Women always love you when you've got your shit together and money coming out your ass like a golden fucking goose. But once the golden shit dries up and you're nothing, they leave. Look what happened to Dad. "I have to stay here with my dad, Chaz. If you need to move, I get it. Family is important."

"Do you want me to move?" She sounds hurt.

"No, it's just... Fuck. I don't know." This is killing me. What kind of man can't pay his own fucking rent? I am such a fuckup.

"Let me pay rent this month, Lance."

"It's too much."

"I told you I can cover it. We can figure something out next month. I'm sure there are cheaper places here in LA that will fit the three of us."

"Fuck, Chaz. I told you I'd figure it out."

She looks hurt. "Why won't you let me help you?"

"Because you shouldn't have to." I am such a douche.

"That's ridiculous. People help each other. And I'm going to help you whether you like it or not."

"Don't pay my rent."

"I'm not going to."

Why does that freak me out? "Then what are you going to do?"

She rolls over on the mattress, turning her back to me. "I don't know. I'll figure something out."

++++8++++

LANCE

The house is dark when I come home the next night.

"Dad? Chaz? Anybody here?"

Silence.

I flip on the lights and stare at the thrift store couch and the folding chairs in the living room. Man, this place is a fucking dump. I'd buy better furniture, but fuck. I'm broke.

I smile to myself, but there's nothing happy about it.

I drop on the couch and stare at the sleeping TV.

I fucking hate TV.

But the silence in this place is driving me fucking nuts.

I call Chastity on my phone. She doesn't answer. I text her: **Call me.** She doesn't.

That's not like her. She always answers the second I call or text. At first, it was kind of weird that she did. Most chicks I've hooked up with always played hard to get. I saw through that bullshit so I didn't care. Chastity isn't like that. She's straight up.

But she's not answering.

Now I'm worried.

Why wouldn't she be answering?

If she's hurt, I'll fucking—

I don't know what I'll do. You can't kick the ass of a car accident or whatever. Fuck, it kills me she doesn't have a car yet. Maybe she's with Lark. I don't have Lark's number otherwise I'd call. Fuck.

I'm going nuts wondering where Chastity is.

An hour later I'm still sitting on the couch waiting for her to call. My mind bounces between where she might be and what the fuck I'm going to do next. I don't have rent money. And I doubt my credit card will front me a $2,400 cash payment at this point. I've already run up enough debt as it is. These days when I call them they aren't nice like they used to be. Missing payments will do that.

Technically, I'm not broke. I have some semblance of credit left. But my cash flow dried up a month ago and that means I'm heading straight toward broke like a runaway train.

If it was just me, I'd crash on a couch somewhere and live off mac and cheese. But I have to think about my dad. And Chastity. I would never ask her to live with her mom. That'd be torture. If she moves to Illinois, I won't have the money to fly back and forth between here and there to see her.

Fuck.

I hate this.

My boots bounce on the carpet.

I spent all fucking day trying to figure out a plan of action to dredge up some investment cash. Sadly, I don't got shit. It's getting to the point people won't return my calls. I'm quickly becoming a nobody. One thing's for fucking sure. I'm not going to beg. I say fuck to that shit.

Now my boots are practically jumping up and down. I'm going nuts. If I sit here any longer, I'm gonna pop.

I call Chastity again.

I really need to talk to her right now.

Still nothing.

Fuck it.

I need some relief. With Chastity gone, I can't fuck away the stress.

That leaves one thing.

One thing that always works.

Am I doing this?

I'm doing this.

I grab a backpack out of one of the cardboard boxes still in the living room and head out the door to the liquor store. I don't even bother searching the house because Dad is fucking Houdini when it comes to hiding his shit. Twenty minutes later, I'm sitting at the kitchen table in the dark house.

Alone.

The cheap chandelier over the table shines down on a bottle of Jim Beam.

Fuck, I want a drink so bad. I can taste that shit in my mouth. Feel the burn and the sting when it goes down. I swallow dry, wishing it was whiskey.

Just one drink.

I don't need the whole bottle.

I'm not like my dad.

I can control it.

Fuck, I haven't drunk a drop in more than five years.

I'm rock solid.

Just one shot.

Just one.

That's all I need.

My boots dance under the table.

I reach for the bottle and stop.

No.

I sit back and rest my elbows on the table and crack my knuckles. I don't need a fucking drink. I jump up from the table and pace the kitchen, staring at that fucking bottle of Beam like it's my enemy and my savior.

I don't need it.

Yes you do.

Fuck no I don't.

Yes.

I grab the bottle and twist the cap off and throw it in the sink where it clatters like a hockey puck. I hold the bourbon up to the light. Look at that fucking color. Like liquid caramel for adults. So fucking sweet.

Just a sip. That's it.

One sip.

Yes.

Fuck, no, I don't—

Yes...

"What are you doing?" Dad asks quietly.

"Fuck!" I blurt, every hair on the back of my neck standing up. "Where the fuck did you come from?"

"Didn't you hear me calling your name when I walked in?"

"No." I frown. "You did?"

"Yes." His eyes are locked on mine. Somehow, there's a fight to the death going on between us right this very second, but we're both just standing here motionless. "What are you gonna do with that?" He's talking about the bourbon.

I picture him walking to a cabinet and pulling out two shot glasses and pouring some for both of us. Then we can get drunk like two washed up fucks. "Why?" I bark defensively. "You want some?"

"No."

"The fuck you don't," I scoff.

"Okay. You're right. I do want some. But I'm not gonna drink any." He stares at me for a long time. "Are you?"

I'm waiting for him to do something dramatic like grab the bottle from me and pour it down the sink like I did that time, or throw it through a window. Then we'll fist fight until neither of us can stand up. It wouldn't be the first time.

Dad looks so fucking calm. His eyes never waver from mine. "The choice is yours, son. Don't let the alcohol make it for you."

"What the fuck do you know," I spit. "You're an alcoholic, Dad. All you do is drink. I mean fuck, I pay your goddamn rent every month!"

He sighs heavily. "You're right. These days, I don't know shit, son. But I know I love you. And I don't want to lose you like I lost myself."

I'm stunned by his words.

He reaches into his pocket and pulls something out, setting it on the table with a clink.

A gold-plated aluminum Alcoholics Anonymous coin.

Two Months.

The curved inscription reads:

TO THINE OWN SELF BE TRUE.

The three sides of the triangle read:

UNITY - SERVICE - RECOVERY.

I flip it over and read the inscription.

God grant me the serenity to accept the things I cannot change, the courage to change the things I can, and the wisdom to know the difference.

I say, "This is yours?"

He nods. "I've been going since... Since..." He looks away and mutters, his voice thick, "Since that night next door. At the pool."

"Charity."

"Yeah." He nods slowly while staring at his feet. "I almost killed her."

I say nothing because it's true.

The kitchen is quiet. Just me and him. He looks at me again. "You've got a lot to live for, son. You've got a beautiful young lady who loves you. You've got your health, and you've got me. For whatever that's worth," he grins. "Don't make the same mistakes I did, son. Be a better man than I was. Be the man I wished I was."

A flood of painful memories from childhood slam through me. Dad drunk. Dad yelling at Mom. Dad yelling at me. Mom disappearing. Dad and me fighting, punching each other in the faces like sworn enemies. Why the fuck were we always fucking fighting? The rage builds up inside me until I'm a bomb ready to blow. "FUCK!!!!" I shout and hurl the Jim Beam against the kitchen wall. It shatters and the booze rains down the paint.

Dad smiles quietly, "I'll get a broom."

I smirk, "We don't have a broom."

"You're right," he chuckles. "Don't worry, son. I'll clean up your mess." He stares at me for a moment. "You've cleaned up enough of mine. About time I returned the favor. Oh, by the way. I found this." He reaches into his pocket and pulls out another coin.

A bronze five year coin with a Roman numeral V embossed in the center circle.

My five year coin.

"Where'd you find it? I thought I'd lost it."

"Remember that old acoustic guitar of mine I gave you way back when? The one you never play anymore?"

"Yeah. Didn't Mom buy that for you?"

"Yup. Before you were born. I decided to start playing it again since you weren't. Your coin was in the case."

"That's where it went?"

He nods. "You must've left it there for safe keeping. Anyway. You wouldn't want five years of hard work going to waste, would you?"

I stare at that bronze five year coin for a long time. He's not talking about guitar playing.

"No," I mutter.

I take it from his palm and slide it in the front pocket of my jeans.

For safe keeping.

++++8++++

LANCE

"I'm fucking broke, Dad. I mean, I've got nothing."

He drops the wad of newspapers holding the glass shards of the bourbon bottle into the trash.

I grab a fresh roll of paper towels and unwrap a bunch.

"Gimme those," he insists, taking the wad from my hand. He's down on hands and knees, wiping up my mess. "I don't know much about what you do, but I know you always have options. You can always solve a problem if you stop and think about it."

"I've tried, Dad. I went to every investor I know and asked for money. Everyone said no for one reason or another." I can't believe I'm talking business with my dad. It feels too good to be true, but it's happening. It doesn't matter that he doesn't have any easy answers. It just matters that I'm talking and he's listening and he's trying to help. Trying. That's the important thing.

"Then you gotta find someone else with money. There's lots of rich people in the world. I know a few in Vegas."

"Fuck that crowd," I snort. "The interest they charge is murder."

Dad smirks, "Ain't that the truth. Don't you know anybody else in LA who'll help? I can't believe everyone said no to you, son."

"One guy said yes."

"Who?"

"A record producer named Julian Whittaker."

"Why did you turn him down?"

I wanna punch something. "Because sometimes yes costs too much." The way that fuck was eye raping Chastity makes me fucking pissed even now. I don't know why I was surprised. That shit happens all the time in the record business. Either way, my answer to him would've been and will always be no. Julian Whittaker can go fuck himself if he thinks I'd trade Chastity for his money.

Dad stands and drops the wet paper towels into the trash. "You hungry?"

"Yeah. Why? You wanna get some food?"

"I'm starving. But we should wait for Chaz. Do you know where she is? She's usually here around dinner time."

Chastity.

That's when I figure it out.

"Fuck, Dad. I gotta go. I think I know where she is."

I run out of the kitchen and grab my keys and helmet.

I sure as fuck hope I'm wrong.

Chapter 31

LANCE

My GSXR screams as I lean into the hairpin turn, heading up into the night dark Hollywood Hills.

This is ridiculous.

I don't know what I'm thinking.

Chastity would never do something this crazy.

Would she?

I hope not. She's not that kind of girl.

Is she?

Let's see. I fucked her at her ice cream job. I fucked her in a dressing room with people right outside. I fucked her on stage in front of a crowd. She's crazier than I ever woulda thought. Who knows how crazy she really is.

Fuck.

I grit my teeth inside my helmet and toe the shifter and crank the throttle as I go up another hill. Mansions whip past on both sides of the windy road as I fly by, their lights blinking through the trees.

As I make the final turn, I try to calm down.

She's not gonna be here. Once I know for sure, I'll realize what an idiot I'm being and laugh at myself the whole way home.

Then I see Lark's car parked near the gate to Julian Whittaker's mansion.

Then I see red.

I can't get off my Gixxer fast enough. It nearly falls on me as I lean the bike on the kickstand and tear my helmet off. I pound on Lark's driver window.

She jumps in her seat before cranking the window down. "What the fuck, Lance? You scared the shit out of me!"

"Did Chastity go in there?"

"Yeah. She walked through the gate an hour ago and told me to wait for her."

"Fuck. How could you let her go in there?"

"Let her?" Lark challenges.

"Yeah. What were you thinking?" I'm pissed.

Her brows tighten. "Bite me, Lance. I'm not her Mom."

I don't have time to argue. I sprint past the front of her car to the intercom at the gate. I hit the button a bunch of times. No one answers. This is bad. I run back to Lark's car. "Has anyone come out since you got here?"

"Some woman drove out after Chaz went inside, but that's it."

"Shit. When?"

"Right after Chaz went in."

"Fuck, fuck, fuck."

"What, Lance? Is Chaz in trouble?" She's worried.

"I don't fucking know." I turn around and eye the gate. Vertical black bars and an arched top. I jump up and grab the arch, swinging my leg over and dropping to the other side.

"What are you doing?" Lark asks, running up to the gate.

"I'm gonna go get Chaz."

"Should I be calling 911?"

"If Chaz is hurt, yes. If I kill someone, no."

Lark looks at me like I'm crazy. "Um. Okay."

Right now, I am.

I turn and jog up the curving driveway in a crouch, listening for sounds of security. A place this big has to have something. To my surprise, I make it all the way up to the six car garage without hearing a sound, going right past a big black Range Rover and that Ferrari 458 Spider parked out front.

Then I hear it.

I turn and scan the dark lawn that rolls down the hillside.

Two loping silhouettes bounding up the grass.

When they start to bark, I run.

Fucking Dobermans.

I sprint up the square stone steps to the front door.

Nails click behind me.

If this was a martial arts movie, I'd either use some ninja shit to subdue the dogs, or do a flying kick through the front door of Julian's house and land on the broken door like a surfboard. But I have zero experience fighting dogs and this front door is definitely kick proof. Luckily, there's a flat overhang to the right. I run down the short slope of dirt beside the stairs, hopping bushes. I jump and grab for the overhang, catching it with one hand. I swing the other up and do a pull up.

Barking Dobermans nip at my heels.

Lucky I'm wearing motorcycle boots. I kick up and get both forearms on top of the overhang.

Something snags my jeans.

I kick as hard as I can.

A yelp and the dog lets go.

I heave my legs up and roll onto the overhang, which is covered in fine gravel. I guess this is a roof. One of many on this place. I stare down at the Dobermans. They bark like crazy. One of them is a jumper, but he doesn't come close to reaching the roof.

"Fuck you guys," I whisper.

How am I going to get down?

Or in the fucking house?

I roll onto my back and stare at the night sky.

This is insane.

I wait for a minute, listening for someone to open the front doors and call the dogs off. When that doesn't happen, I look down and see the dogs just sitting there staring up at me. At least they're not barking.

I wish I'd brought meat. That'd keep them busy. But I used up all my steaks the last time I snuck into some rich asshole's mansion to rescue my girlfriend.

I chuckle to myself.

If this wasn't actually happening to me right now, I wouldn't fucking believe it. Oh well.

Time to get Chastity.

She's somewhere inside this huge house.

I stand up and look around. Since all the walls on this place are glass, it shouldn't be hard to find her. Unless Julian's got her locked up somewhere in a sex dungeon with the whips and chains. He totally seems like the type. No worries. If he does, I'll chain his ass up and whip the shit out of him.

I creep quietly across the roof, on a mission to find the woman I love.

++++8++++

CHASTITY

"I think it's time for me to go," I say to Julian over the bed that stands between us in one of his mansion's many guest bedrooms. Like the rest of his house, the decor of the room is minimal and precise. Shades of gray on white with an accent of red stitched on some of the rectangular furniture. I set the glass of wine Julian poured me on the window bench.

"Already?" He sounds bemused, sipping his own wine.

"I shouldn't have come here."

"Then why did you?" he asks, arching a thoughtful brow as his eyes glide over the curves of my off-the-shoulder dress. "And why did you come dressed to play?"

I suddenly feel like covering up or hiding behind something. Julian's predatory tone makes me nervous. "I don't know. I thought maybe... I don't know what I thought." I want to leave as fast as possible, but Julian stands between me and the bedroom door. I wonder if I can run past him and down the stairs and outside before he can catch me. Then I remember how his front doors have hand print recognition locks. I wouldn't be able to get out. I'm screwed. Coming here was a horrible idea.

THUD!

My heart jumps at the loud sound behind me.

Julian frowns. "What in the world?"

THUD!

Someone just kicked one of the bedroom windows. Twice. With the lights on inside, it's impossible to see outside into the dark.

Julian walks up behind me.

THUD!

We both stare out the window.

THUD! THUD! THUD!

Fists and a face come into view.

"Lance?" I mutter.

He screams something through the window, his face a ball of fury. The thick glass mutes his words to a vague bass rumble. He pounds the window again and again.

"One second," Julian says impatiently, setting down his wine next to mine on the bench and reaching for several levers on the heavy frame. When he finally opens the window, it pivots a quarter turn in its steel frame like a revolving door. That is one big window.

"Get your fucking hands off her!" Lance shouts, diving through the narrow gap. His torn pant leg catches on the corner of the frame and he tumbles to the carpeted floor. He twists and kicks his leg until the jeans tear free. Then he's on his feet in a flash, looming over Julian, ready to kill.

Julian chuckles casually, unafraid. "You certainly have a flair for the dramatic, Lance. Did my Dobermans give you any trouble?" He picks up his wine glass and sips it.

Lance glares at him then flicks his eyes at the second wine glass. "What the fuck were you thinking giving her wine? She's eighteen, dumbfuck."

Julian shrugs dismissively. "I thought she would enjoy it." He steps past Lance and runs his hand across the window glass. "I was told by the agent who sold me this place that the previous owner was obsessed with security. A sultan's son or some such. According to the agent, all the windows in this house had been bulletproofed and could withstand a rocket propelled grenade. At the time, I thought she was exaggerating to close the sale. Perhaps I was wrong." He turns and smiles at Lance and me. "I presume you came for Chastity?"

"Fuck yeah I did," Lance grunts, throwing a protective arm around my bare shoulders. "Are you okay? Did he hurt you?" He eyes my tight fitting dress.

"No," I sigh. "I'm fine."

"Did you drink any of his wine?"

"No. Yes. A little. I'm fine, Lance. It was just wine."

"It better be," Lance growls at Julian.

Julian chuckles, "It's a rather fine '88 Richebourg Grand cru. Do you think I'd sully a sixteen hundred dollar bottle of wine with Rohypnol? The bitterness would destroy the flavor." He lifts my glass from the sill and offers it to Lance. "You should taste it. The end note of violets is sublime."

I don't remember tasting any violets. Not that I know what violets taste like.

"Fuck you, Julian," Lance grumbles.

The truth is, I'm relieved he showed up when he did. Julian seriously creeps me out. It doesn't matter that he's really good looking and super rich and knows all about wine. He is weird with a capital *What the fuck*? I never should've come here dressed like this. Or at all.

"Let's get the fuck outta here," Lance says, leading me toward the bedroom door.

"You won't be able to get out the front door unless I open it," Julian teases.

Lance spins around. "So go fucking open it. Before I open up your head."

Julian looks at Lance thoughtfully, then walks toward him gracefully, stopping a foot away, looking him straight in the eyes. He's Lance's height, but not quite as muscular. "Lance, do you recall when I said that you were too impatient for your own good?"

"You're about to find out how impatient I am in about half a second."

Julian closes his eyes and snickers. "Calm down, Lance. Not everything in life is a show of strength and bravado."

"It's not a show, motherfucker."

"Never underestimate an opponent, Lance," Julian says almost apologetically.

Oh, geez. What is Julian going to do? Whip out mad ninja skills? A gun? Two guns? Ten? Or maybe a hundred security guards with ten guns each? Based on his complete confidence, probably all of the above.

"Is that a threat?" Lance fires.

"Merely an observation." Julian brushes past Lance and me without looking back. He stops in the hallway. "Are you two coming?"

Lance and I are both speechless.

"Feel free to use the bed," Julian says as he heads toward the square staircase.

Lance and I goggle at each other.

I want to say to Lance, *Did he mean now? For, you know... you and me to have sex? In his house?* Then I realize Julian probably has cameras in every room so he can film people having sex. And probably jerk off to it later. He seems like the type.

Julian talks over his shoulder as he descends the stairs, "I never intended to bed Chastity." He stops after two steps and turns to face us. "Not that I would turn down the opportunity." His eyes rake over my dress.

Lance tenses. I squeeze his wrist, trying to soothe him.

Julian flashes a quick smile before continuing down the steps. "I merely wanted to insist you include her in your video. Your concept begs for an ingenue like Chastity to play the part of Christine." Julian's voice recedes below us, "When you didn't suggest it yourself during our first meeting, I thought I'd insist on it. It's my money, after all. But you were too quick to..." His voice fades until he's too quiet to hear.

Lance and I stumble over each other as we rush down the stairs to catch up with the man with the money.

++++8++++

CHASTITY

"I can't believe he said yes!" I whisper to Lance as we walk down the square stone steps outside of Julian's mansion, a huge smile on my face.

"I hope those fucking Dobermans are inside or I'll tear their throats out with my teeth." Lance is furious. He's not even listening to me.

"He said he had them brought inside."

Lance doesn't hear that either. "Did you see the way he had his eyes all over you after we went downstairs to talk money?! He totally wants to fuck you!!" Lance's anger is white hot.

"But he didn't and he won't."

Lance stops on the steps, squeezing my hand hard. "And what the fuck were you thinking coming over here?! You were ready to fuck him, weren't you?!"

"No!"

"What was with the wine?! You should've known better!! And what the fuck were you doing in his bedroom?!"

"He poured me a glass without asking and offered me a tour of the house! So what?" I'm getting angry because he's angry.

"A tour?!"

"Yes, a tour! I thought if we were walking around, he wouldn't be able to get too close! And I've never been in a mansion before this place! Who wouldn't want to see the rest of it?!"

He glares at me, trying to make sense of my words. "If you wanted to tour a mansion I could've taken you up to San Simeon for the weekend to tour the fucking Hearst Castle! You didn't have to come here!"

"I came here to get *your* money! And I got it for you, so shut up!"

"I told you I would deal with the money situation myself!"

"Well, I helped, so suck it!"

"And what's with the fucking dress?! Your tits are practically falling out!" His brows are dark. His eyes burn. He grabs the off the shoulder strap near my arm pit and yanks it.

My boob pops up and jiggles. The half moon of a nipple shows above the material.

We both stare at it, hypnotized.

He pulls again on the dress and my nipple pops all the way out. In a menacing voice he says, "You were gonna give him this?"

"No! I would never!"

He grabs my boob from the bottom and squeezes hard. "You better fucking not. This is my fucking tit."

Now I'm furious because of his sexist comment and that he would ever doubt me. "Who do you think I am, Lance?!"

He growls through sharp teeth, "You're fucking mine." His possessive fury is oddly erotic.

"Oh yeah? Prove it."

His eyes flash fire as his mouth dives for my nipple and bites.

I moan and curve into him. His hands dig into my ass, smashing my hips against his. He picks me up roughly and carries me down the steps, his tongue attacking mine. My arms lock around his neck and my legs wrap around his waist, which pushes my dress up to my butt. I vaguely wonder if Julian is watching all this through the windows. There's no way to know. More importantly, I don't really care because I'm soaked.

When we're on the big driveway, Lance tears away from the kiss and growls, "Nobody fucks you except me, got it?" I reply by squeezing my thighs. "Fucking nobody." He lays me down gently. Cold metal buckles under my back. That's when I realize I'm lying on the trunk of Julian's black Ferrari.

"Lance! You're gonna dent the—"

"Shut the fuck up," he hisses as he tears my panties off. "No back talk from you. Got it?"

I nod silently.

He growls, "You're gonna come all over Julian's car."

"I don't think I can come on command, Lance."

"I told you, no back talk." He grabs my ankles and pushes my knees up, opening me. He strikes like an anaconda, his tongue all over my clit and my slippery lips.

The pleasure is instant and intense. "Oh, Lance," I moan.

On the second floor of Julian's house, the lights in one of the rooms go off. The ghost of a face hovers at the window. Julian is watching. Let him. All I care about is the man between my legs. "Oh, God, Lance, I'm gonna come," I whimper. The moon floats high in the sky, a big glowing O. I would reach out and touch it but my own big O is so intense I melt all over Lance's face and come all over Julian's Ferrari.

As I heave in deep breaths, Lance rips his belt open, the buckle tinkling as he shoves his boxers down to his thighs and stabs me with his hard cock. He fucks me hard and fast. I'm so wet he glides and slides, filling me up.

How is it that he knows what I want better than I do? He pushes buttons I didn't know I had, or if I did, he pushes them better than I ever could. He gives me things I can't give myself. It makes me feel dependent in a way I can barely comprehend right now and that frightens me. But it also thrills me because I want to be dependent on Lance. I want to be bound to him forever.

"This is my fucking pussy. Mine. My. Fucking. Cunt. Nobody fucks you but me. Say it."

"Uhhhh…"

"Say it!" He roars.

"Your fucking pussy," I gasp. "Your cunt. Only yours." A second orgasm builds as Lance swells inside me. I tip my head back onto the cold metal of the Ferrari and glance up.

Julian is right at the window.

Jerking off.

His eyes are locked on mine.

Because of the angle, I can't see his penis over the window sill, but his arm is moving and it's totally obvious what he's doing. I can't decide if it's weird and creepy or a total turn on. Julian is dashingly handsome. His button down shirt is hanging open, revealing his own set of chiseled abs. Not that I care because—

"Fuck, Chastity, you're fucking coming. That's it. Fucking come all over my dick." Lance hovers over me and I claw his muscled shoulders as he pounds me.

"Oh, fuck, Lance, it's—" My orgasm explodes and I scream.

"Fuck yeah," Lance grunts.

Right when I think he's going to come he pulls out.

"Lance," I gasp, "What are you—"

"Shut the fuck up."

I guess he's going to come on my stomach, which is partially covered by my dress. The idea makes me smile. Having Lance shoot his semen all over me is so porno. So slutty. I love it.

But he doesn't. He shoots his load on the back of Julian's Ferrari. "Fucking asshole," Lance hisses.

I sit up suddenly and look between my legs. Cum drips down the Ferrari logo onto the back bumper. "Lance! Don't! He won't give you the money if he finds out!"

"Fuck him and his money. He can fucking keep it. If he thinks he can have you, I'll fucking murder him." Semen still pours from Lance's cock in big bursts. He pushes me back down onto the Ferrari and jams his dick inside me, thrusting hard. "Nobody is going to take you from me. Nobody."

He pounds hard and, oh, does it feel so incredibly good. I'm not even coming but I want him to keep driving into me like this forever.

I languish on the back of Julian's priceless sports car, enjoying every moment of this. It doesn't take long for Lance to get hard again. He just keeps fucking me. Drilling me. Destroying me.

"You're fucking mine, Pink. This pink wet pussy is all mine."

"Yes, yours," I moan, relaxed, raising my arms over my head languidly. "All yours, my love."

He grunts and fucks me harder.

As another orgasm starts to build, I arch my back and open my eyes, looking at Julian's window. Right as Julian comes. His face is tight as his hand pumps furiously along his cock. The head of it is literally pressed against the window. A frothy white stream dribbles down the glass. He thrusts his hips like he's trying to fuck his way through the window to my pussy. But he can't.

Because only one man gets my pussy.

The one throbbing and thrusting inside me right now.

"Fuck!" Lance roars, shooting himself into me as we explode together.

Chapter 32

LANCE

"I can't believe this is actually happening," Chastity marvels.

"Me fucking neither," I chuckle.

We stand inside the ginormous interior of the historic Orpheum Theatre in downtown LA looking at rows of red velvet seats from the back of the main floor. This place has everything you could ever want in an old time opera house: the gold, the columns, the curlicues, the balcony, the box seats, the giant red curtain the size of a movie theater screen, the vaulted ceiling that looks like it took a million skilled man hours to carve and paint. It's the fucking perfect location to shoot the video for my new track *Opera*.

"Julian really came through," Chastity says.

"Yup."

He pulled some strings and got us access. Nobody gets access to the Orpheum on short notice unless you know somebody important. In this town, Julian knows everybody important. He also helped me land the best video DP a guy could want. Jens Nilsson. Guy has already won three VMAs and a Grammy and he's just getting started. I don't know shit about cameras, but Jens does. As Director of Photography, his job is to help me set up all the shots and handle the technical stuff so I can focus on directing the story. Beaver and Micah are on hand to keep an eye on things, along with a huge crew of people I know personally, people Jens works with, and Julian's crew. Shit, even my dad is here in case there's any last minute welding work that needs to be done. If anything metal breaks, he'll know how to fix it faster than anyone else in town.

For all of one day, this place is an A-list feature film movie set for me to do with as I please. My own fucking playground.

For one day.

That's all Julian could get and that's all he's paying for.

One day of shooting to bounce my career out of the toilet.

Getting all the shots I need for the video in less than twenty four hours is going to be tight as hell. But we've been here dozens of times since Julian inked the deal, scouting all the camera locations in the lobby and the main theater, analyzing the backstage and rafter rigging for wire and lighting options, and planning our shots down to the last detail.

A guy with a headset mic walks up to me while flicking his finger on his iPad. "Lance, we need you down on the main stage in five."

"Got it."

"Now or never," I mutter to Chastity.

She hugs my side and pats my chest. "You're going to rock this place, Lance." She takes a step back to look me over. "You look gorgeous in your costume."

"You like it? It's not too frilly?" I'm wearing a billowy unbuttoned white shirt to showcase my abs, a blood red cummerbund, and skin tight black tuxedo pants that hug my junk like bicycle shorts. The outfit has a few added belts and buckles that give it a bit of a goth touch for that bondage vibe.

"Nice cock," she giggles.

"You can totally see it, can't you?"

She winks, "Don't get hard on camera. Unless you want everyone to know how big your dick is."

"It's gonna be tough not to with you looking like Angel Slut."

Chastity is in a tight lace wedding gown that has a cleavage cut down to her navel. She had to be taped into it but it still shows plenty of underboob in the middle. Her long hoop skirt is cut so high in front it shows her legs in white garters and stockings and a tight white thong so small it looks like a shoelace in front. She had to wax her bush down to a landing strip for the shoot. "How you liking the wax?"

Her eyes flare. "It makes me horny just thinking about it. Every step I take in this thong rubs me just right."

"Fuck, I'm already hard."

She stares at my dick.

"Oh, geez, Lance. Sorry." She leans into me, pressing her palm against my rager. "Do we have time for a quickie?"

We drove here at 2:30 this morning so we could both start makeup. After two hours of that we spent another two hours in wardrobe getting sewn into these costumes. "Not dressed like this. Don't wanna pop a seam. After."

"I don't think I can wait." She shimmies her hips and runs her hands between her thighs.

My dick twitches uncontrollably. "Fuck, Pink. I love you. You're a crazy fucking slut. But we have to wait. I'm begging you."

"Okay." She grins and tiptoes up to kiss me, "I love you too, Sir Cocks-A-Lot."

"Sir what?" I chuckle.

She slaps my ass. "Let's go. You're supposed to be on stage."

We walk up the center aisle toward the front of the theater.

"Do you think my mom will show up?" Chastity asks.

"She's invited. We'll see."

"I'm so glad Charity flew out. She's like a kid in a candy store being on a real live movie set."

"It's not a movie set."

"That's what she called it. She totally couldn't sleep last night. Thanks for letting her come."

"Are you kidding? She's practically my sister at this point. She had to be here."

We both turn and wave to where she sits way up high in the back of the balcony with John Shields and a few of the crew. She and her dad both wave back.

Chastity says, "Your Phantom makeup is perfect, by the way. Just enough to be creepy but not enough to get in the way of your good looks."

"You're giving me a swelled head, Pink."

Her eyes flick to my dick. "I can see that," she giggles.

Yeah, I'm still hard. Chastity just does it for me.

The costume guy meets us at the foot of the stage with my silver Phantom mask in hand. This is a special one I had made by a guy in the Valley named Jordu Schell who has a shop that does monster shit for huge movies like Avatar and Hellboy. Like my face makeup, the silver mask is a balance between handsome and scary while maintaining my brand image. Jordu does awesome work and he's worth every penny. The costume guy says, "Are you ready for the mask? You'll need it for the first shot."

Before I can answer, another guy hollers from up on stage. "Lance, you got a minute?"

"Hold on a sec," I say to the costume guy.

The guy hollering my name from the stage is Codie Bennett. He's the stunt coordinator for the shoot and he's a good guy. Like me, he's pretty damned ripped and his arms bulge out of his T-shirt almost as big as mine, but with no ink to speak of. All the women on the crew have been staring at him almost as much as they've been staring at me. Almost. I notice Chastity's eyes are all over Codie. I lean over and whisper, "Keep your eyes off that guy. I only want you looking at me like that. Got it?"

She smirks and whispers, "Are you kidding? I know what I'm doing."

"What are you doing?" I chuckle.

"Making you jealous," she winks. "I'm just getting you worked up for later. I don't want you forgetting to fuck my brains out after this is all over and done."

"You can count on that, Pink. But if you keep staring at Codie, I'm gonna fuck you right in front of him." I glance at the costume guy who is hearing all of this. Whatever. "Don't think I won't."

"Mmmmm…" Chastity moans, "I know you will."

I laugh. "Fuck, Pink, you are the sluttiest woman I've ever known."

She grins and walks her fingers down my chest. "And don't you forget it."

I'm fucking harder than I was a minute ago.

++++8++++

CHASTITY

Lance doesn't have to worry about me.

But there's no denying that this Codie guy is an extra large bottle of hot sauce. I met him briefly during makeup when he came into the dressing room downstairs this morning to discuss the stunts with Lance. He's funny too. I never would've thought a guy as good looking as him would have a personality, but he does. In fact, it's kind of hard to miss. His white T-shirt has big block letters that read COCKSURE and in smaller letters, Entertainment, which I found out is the name of Codie's stunt company. It didn't take long for me to realize his shirt is also a statement of fact. Too bad Lark couldn't be here today. She'd probably love a guy like Codie. Then again, I think she and Beaver are still a thing. She can't quit her human jackhammer.

Lance and I walk onto the stage.

Codie says to Lance, "Dude, I'm straight as a hard on, but with this pirate shirt you're wearing, even I'd fuck you." Codie reaches out and tugs on Lance's open tuxedo shirt front in a brazen alpha male display.

Lance smirks, "So you admit I'm so good looking you can't help but wonder if my abs make you a wee bit gay for me?" Lance holds up his thumb and finger a millimeter apart.

Codie chuckles and lifts the bottom of his COCKSURE Entertainment T-shirt without a second thought, revealing incredible abs of his own, which he flexes impressively.

Lance and I both look, because it's sort of hard not to stare when someone peels their shirt up right in front of you.

Codie taunts Lance, "Who's a wee bit gay now?"

"I don't know, man. Looks to me like you manscape the shit outta that shit. Do you do your nails too? You know, get a mani-pedi on the weekends with all your bros at your favorite West Hollywood spa?"

They both laugh, completely enjoying the verbal sparring like old friends. They only met once before when they came here to the Orpheum to plan out stunts, but they totally hit it off like best buds.

"Pfft," I snort. "Men. You two are a bromatch made in heaven. My dressing room is empty right now if you guys need a moment alone."

Codie lowers his shirt hem and grins at me, "Speaking of fucking, is this guy fucking you?" He hooks a thumb toward Lance.

My face glows red and I chuckle. "Ummm…"

Lance just smiles, amused.

Codie says, "Cause if he's not, I totally will."

"Not if I don't let you," I laugh.

"You will," he chuckles.

"I will what?" I press.

Codie smirks, "Where's the fun if I have to tell you?"

"Easy, Codie," Lance says casually, unworried. "She's mine."

"That's right," I say. Although I'm completely in love with Lance, I'm glad he's beside me. Codie is magnetic and difficult to resist. He just needs a reminder I'm off limits. I lean into Lance and cup his balls through his tight tuxedo pants and smirk at Codie. "You see this package?"

Codie nods appreciatively. "Damn. Nice dick, dude. Almost as big as mine." He winks at Lance. "Almost, as in not even close."

Lance chuckles, "Dude, you need glasses."

Codie points both index fingers at his COCKSURE *Entertainment* shirt. "Did you not read the shirt?"

Lance rolls his eyes and laughs, "Okay, enough with the comparing dicks. I call a dick truce. We've got work to do."

I giggle.

"You got it," Codie laughs. "Dick truce." The two of them bump fists. "We're here to work, right?"

I can't resist one last joke, so I say, "You two can hold each other's dicks later."

They both roll their eyes.

I smirk, "I mean, that's what you two are dying to do, right?"

They both snort laughter.

"You two look really guilty," I joke.

Codie says, "Back to the stunts." He takes a deep breath, still snickering at his behavior. "Right, stunts. I don't want anyone getting hurt today." He's all business now. "When that chandelier falls on the audience, it's going to be dangerous no matter how much rigging we have supporting the breakaway pieces. By the way, the way your dad designed the frame for that thing is genius. I need to get him working for me. Anyway, it'll be controlled chaos with everyone jumping out of the way and tumbling over theater seats. Lot of chances to catch ankles or break wrists if people don't fall just right. So we need to coordinate everyone's exit path from the chandelier."

Lance nods, "Of course."

Lance and Codie talk in detail about the placement of the stunt performers and how the action will be choreographed. You'd think they were laying out plays for a Super Bowl game or an actual battle based on how many moving parts the chandelier scene will have.

Jens, whose name I found out is pronounced "Yenz" when he taught me how to say it earlier, walks up to Lance and Codie and says in his Swedish accent, "Guys, are you ready for first shot?"

"Yeah man," Lance says, "Let's make this shit happen." He grabs the bullhorn from the assistant director who is standing next to us on stage. *"Places, everybody! Time to get this show on the road!"* Then he motions to the costume guy, who carefully places the silver mask on Lance's face.

++++8++++

CHASTITY

The day is a blur of activity. Everything moves so fast, I barely have time to think. I do my best to be where I need to be when I need to be there. Since it's a music video, I don't have any lines to memorize. My job is simply to emote, which I can do, and look pretty, which Lance convinced me I would be a natural at.

In the video, I play the part of Christine, the young opera singer the Phantom could never have. The visual story of the video follows the classic Phantom of the Opera novel fairly closely. I know, because Lance made me read his tattered copy, which was full of his notes scribbled in the margins.

Lance's depth never ceases to amaze me. He knows the classic tale inside and out. What struck me most about the tragic novel was that the Phantom was sometimes called the Angel of Music, and that young Christine believed the Phantom was her own musical angel, sent from heaven by her father to guide her singing career. That's not exactly what Lance did when he came into my life, because I'm not a singer, but he brought with him the music of our love.

I don't have any acting experience except a few grade school plays, but it's easy for me to emote because I bring my real emotions for Lance to all of our scenes as Christine and the Phantom. Even with a camera in my face and all the blaring lights, all of my focus is on Lance and the love I feel for him.

With Lance foremost in my heart, I get lost in the romance of it all.

The day is long and the work is hard, but I love every second of it. Before I know it, we've worked late into the night and we're down to the final scene when Christine and the Phantom kiss for the first and only time.

Between our costumes, the ambience of the Orpheum Theatre, and the on-set fog (which mutes my awareness of the ever-present steadicam operator), all of it feels real.

When Lance and I kiss, it's electric.

I forget that this is make believe.

It feels real.

Like I am living the classic fairy tale.

The moment Lance gets down on one knee as the Phantom and removes his mask, baring his soul, it nearly breaks my heart. I don't see a monstrous devil. I see the angel inside his eyes. He looks deeply into my soul, staring up at me as if he is in terrible pain, his sadness so great that his heart is on the verge of bursting from an explosion of joy and love and imminent rejection because the Phantom knows he can never spend forever with Christine. His eyes shimmer with his desperate love. I feel deeply the Phantom's hidden pain as if it is Lance's own and therefore mine. It overwhelms me and I nearly lose it in front of the camera and start sobbing, wanting desperately to break character and smother Lance with real kisses of real love and eternal reassurance, but I manage to hold myself together. Even so, real tears pour down my face as I lean down to kiss him, my hands gently cupping his makeup-deformed jaw as our lips touch. The kiss makes me feel like we're both floating toward heaven, lifted up by our love.

But as everyone knows, the story of the Phantom is a tragedy, and Christine's kiss must come to an end.

I break contact with Lance's lips and my world comes crumbling down. It takes everything I have to hold myself together in front of the camera and not collapse on the floor.

After an infinite moment of terrible sorrow, Lance finally breaks character and yells, "Cut!"

The crew starts wandering around and chattering, doing whatever they need to do.

I'm still lost in the moment, overcome by sadness, feeling the Phantom's loneliness as if it is mine.

"Are you okay?" Lance whispers, his hand on my costume-covered shoulder.

I shake my head, holding in tears. "Yeah, I'm fine," I sniff.

"No you're not." He wraps me in his arms without hesitation. As busy as Lance has been since we started filming this morning, directing everybody, answering thousands of questions, making last minute decisions, he steps away from his role as leader to focus on me, to focus on his role as lover, as the one man in my life who matters above all others.

I cherish this man.

I hug him back fiercely, disappearing into his warmth and love, feeling the intimate connection of our souls. A real and special connection of complete and timeless love that the Phantom of the novel will never know. I weep in Lance's arms as I grieve for the fictitious Phantom and all the lost souls of the world who will never know the kind of special love that Lance and I share.

Lance kisses the top of my head gently.

He whispers, "I love you, Chastity Shields. I love you with all my heart."

I finally break down and sob against him.

"I love you too, Lance. I love you so much…"

+++++8++++

CHASTITY

Everyone crowds around the monitors backstage to watch the video playback of the scene we just shot: The Kiss.

"*Va coolt*," Jens says, grinning from ear to ear. "This video is going to be incredible, Lance. I'm telling you."

"You said it, Jens," Lance nods, also smiling. "That's a wrap, people!" He holds his hands up and starts clapping. The crew joins in, applauding and cheering. "Time for the champagne! I want everyone down here for a toast!"

A crew member wheels over a craft services cart loaded with champagne glasses and unopened bottles. Several people help pop corks and pour. The rest of the crew scattered around the opera house make their way backstage. It's so late, Charity and Dad have already gone home.

Lance puts his arm around me.

We both hold champagne glasses filled with Martinelli's sparkling apple cider. Mr. McKnight holds one too, as do several of the other crew members. But everyone else has regular champagne.

"You guys did a fucking awesome job today," Lance says, holding up his glass.

The crew cheers.

"We couldn't have made it through this long ass shoot without all of your dedication and hard work. I'm fucking impressed."

More cheers.

"I have to thank some people for today. Julian Whittaker, where the fuck are you?"

Julian steps out from behind a row of crew members and holds up his glass.

"Julian paid for all this shit, so round of applause."

The crew claps and hoots.

Julian grins and raises his glass.

Lance then runs down a thank you list of everyone on the crew, thanking nearly all of them by name. I don't know how he remembers them all because I sure can't.

"And I want to thank my Dad."

Mr. McKnight chuckles.

"Even though we didn't need your expert welding skills today, you welded the shit out of that chandelier during pre-pro. It was an honor to have you be a part of this thing."

"It was an honor to help, son" Mr. McKnight's eyes are obviously wet. "I'm so proud of you."

"Me too, Dad. Me too." Lance's throat is tight. He clears it several times, looking at his feet, the emotion of the moment getting to him.

The crew starts to mumble.

"Don't drink yet," Lance chuckles. "One more person to thank. The most important of all. Karen?"

One of the assistant directors named Karen, who I do remember, squeezes through the gathered crew holding a huge bouquet of roses. She puts it in my hands.

The plastic wrapping crinkles as I hug it to my chest. I mutter, "Oh, Lance, you shouldn't have."

"Too late. Already did," Lance winks at me. To the crew he says, "We literally would not be here tonight if it wasn't for the love of my life, Chastity Shields. She made this shit happen, guys." Scattered applause and a whistle. "I've never met anybody like her." He starts to choke up, tears near. He sniffs them back. "So let's give her a huge hand."

The crew erupts with loud cheering and I gaze deeply into Lance's eyes. I absolutely love and adore all of his devilish qualities, but there is an angelic sweetness to him that I never would've imagined lay beneath his dangerous exterior. He really is the most amazing man in the world.

There is no one like Lance McKnight.

And I love him with all my heart.

"Quiet, everybody! I've got one more thing I have to say." Lance puts his arm around me. "They say behind every successful man is a good woman. In my case, that is absolutely true. When I thought everything in my life was falling apart, this woman right here stepped up to the plate and did what she had to do to keep me on track." He winks at me. "When I had given up, she went to bat one more time. She succeeded where I failed. She was willing to risk everything to make my dream come true. *My* dream. Without you, Chastity Shields, I would be back to..." He glances at Mr. McKnight, who is quietly crying. Then he closes his eyes for a second, overcome by emotion. "Without you, Chastity, I probably wouldn't be here."

There's an ominous quality to his words that frightens me to death. So I wrap both arms awkwardly around his waist and hug him as hard as I can, never wanting to let go.

He hugs me back and kisses the top of my head, then separates us. He reaches into his open tuxedo shirt.

He pulls something out.

He gets down on one knee.

He opens a pink velvet box.

He looks up into my eyes. His sparkle with the same brilliant clarity as the small ring in the pink velvet box.

"Pink," he winks, "I mean, Chastity Shields, will you do me the honor of being my savior, my lover, the woman of my dreams, the woman who saves me from myself, the woman who is my everything? Chastity Shields, will you marry me?"

My entire body shakes.

I physically can't speak.

Can't.

Say.

A.

Word.

Epilogue

CHASTITY

EIGHT MONTHS LATER...

"Damn, that is one fucking view," Lance chuckles.

We stand on the very top of the Eiffel Tower. Not the one in Vegas, which Lance took me to several months ago. I'm talking the real one. In France.

Before I met Lance, I had never been any place outside California other than Illinois to visit my dad. But here we are in Paris, high above the City of Love.

It's almost closing time at the tower, but the outdoor summit deck is still active with tourists. The moon is full and hovers high overhead in the midnight sky. Across the river *Seine*, the *Arc de Triomphe* glows in the distance, floating like an island oasis of light in the dark twinkling ocean that is Paris at night. To my right, the *Cathédrale Notre Dame*—the most famous church in the world—stands proudly in the heart of the city.

"Oh my goodness," I sigh. "It sure is beautiful."

"So are you," he grins his angelic grin.

We kiss quietly, trying not to attract too much attention from the crowd.

Ever since Lance's video for *Opera* went up on the internet, life has turned upside down. At first, the video languished. We thought it was a dud. Then something happened. It shot up to eight million views in one week. We were checking the view count every hour. Then the song was playing on the radio. We heard it in Micah's car one afternoon coming back from lunch. That night, Beaver told us it was all over internet radio. When it hit a hundred million views, Julian Whittaker threw a party at his mansion. Lance didn't want to go, but I told him he didn't have to worry about Julian and that we deserved to celebrate and owed Julian our thanks at the very least. We went and had a blast. Julian really knows how to party. The things that went on at that mansion... I can't even begin to tell you. Hot, wet, electric. The memory of it makes me shiver pleasantly.

When the video hit two hundred million views, Julian called about booking an international tour immediately.

And here we are, eight months later, on tour with some of the biggest names in EDM.

Lance's song *Opera* now has over eight hundred million views.

His shows are packed with screaming fans.

Lance is a celebrity.

I am too. Because I'm featured in the video.

Almost everywhere we go, someone recognizes us. It's overwhelming. Despite all the makeup I wore in the video, I've been photographed at Lance's side a million times. My face is all over the internet, just like Lance's. More insane is the fact that I'm officially on the tour payroll. I go on stage every night with Lance, in costume as Christine, to reenact some scenes from the video when he closes his set with *Opera*. I can't get over how crazy the crowd gets when they hear it and when Christine and TH3 PH4NTüM kiss.

Sadly, Lance and I haven't had sex on stage since that time at the surprise rave in downtown LA, but we make up for it by having sex backstage in Lance's dressing room after almost every show. And did I mention I'm a member of the Mile High Club now? Many times over.

And lest I forget, yes, there is video of me being fucked on stage by Lance at that surprise rave. I mean, it's not like you can see Lance's dick going in and out. But the look on my face when I come leaves nothing to the imagination. The video *is* grainy, so I could just be having a muscle cramp that Lance is massaging with rhythmic hip thrusts from behind me. Yeah, right.

I'm an international celebrity slut.

I smile at the thought.

"I am the luckiest man in the world, Chastity," Lance sighs as he hugs me from behind and we gaze out at the view of Paris.

I hold up the engagement ring sparkling on my finger. Not the ridiculously expensive eight-karat one Lance tried to buy me yesterday at Cartier on the *Rue da la Paix*. Which, by the way, is a five minute walk from the Paris Opera House, a.k.a. the *Palais Garnier*. Before going to Cartier, we toured the opera house and saw the Phantom's fabled Box Five, the falling chandelier, the catacombs, and even the real lake beneath the opera house, just like in the book. It was incredibly romantic and beyond anything I imagined while reading it.

When Lance took me to Cartier afterward and tried to buy me that ring, I said no. Not because it cost some ungodly amount of Euros. With the ad revenue alone from the *Opera* video, Lance is set for life. With the royalty payments he insists I accept because I'm in the video, I am too. The reason I said no to the extravagant ring at Cartier was because I wanted to keep the small ring he bought at the mall in Glendale before the money started pouring in. The ring he presented that night at the *Opera* video shoot. The ring that came in a pink velvet box. I smirk at the thought. The ring I haven't taken off once since I said yes and he put it on my finger. This is the ring I want, the ring I'll treasure forever. All the money in the world can't buy the love that Lance has given me. "Me too," I sigh, overcome by the romance of the moment.

"You're the luckiest man in the world?" Lance jokes.

I turn around, grinning, "You know what I mean."

His angelic eyes lock on mine. "I love you, Pink. From the day we met, I've never loved anyone like I love you, and I'll love you ten times as much in a year, and a hundred times as much in ten years."

"How much will you love me in a hundred years?" I giggle.

"I can't count that high," he jokes. "Now we just have to plan the wedding. Maybe we can have it at the Paris Opera House."

I laugh, happier than I've ever been. "Do they do that sort of thing?"

"I have no idea," he grins. "But we can ask. I mean, I'm the PH4NTüM and the managers of the opera house have to do my bidding, right?"

We both laugh and gaze out at the opera house to the northeast, which is clearly visible in the distance.

I haven't spoken to my mom more than a few times in the past year. She's always cold and distant when I call. I feel bad for her, but she doesn't want my help or good wishes or anything like that. Sometimes when I call, she doesn't even bother to answer, but I know she's home.

I guess not every ending is happy.

As I expected, Mom never showed up at the *Opera* video shoot, and she turned us down when Lance offered to fly her out to visit us in London recently. She's never been but I know she's always wanted to go and see Buckingham Palace, the Tower of London, Westminster Abbey, all that stuff. But she skipped it. I think she's still grieving Charity being in Illinois.

Charity loves living with Dad. I'm happy to report that she hasn't worn whore's paint once since she moved out there. When I asked her why not, she shrugged. She also told me she isn't running around with any more random boys. To everyone's surprise, she asked Dad if she could take Krav Maga classes. Krav is a self-defense thing. It wasn't good enough for Charity that Dad has two black belts, although neither are in Krav. Dad offered to take Krav classes with her, but she said no, she wanted to do it herself. She's fourteen. It's normal. She also surprised everyone by joining the photography club at Palatine High School. Go Pirates! Charity hates organized sports. She says they remind her of church. But she loves the photography club, and none of the boys in it have neck tattoos.

Anyway, she and Dad flew out to see us in London. They even took the Chunnel under the English Channel to see Paris, but that was weeks ago and they've since flown home. I know they had a ton of fun on the trip. Charity is in love with Paris and can't wait to come back and spend more time at the *Louvre*. The thing that struck me most about Charity when she was in London was that she just seemed so light and happy and not nearly as crabby in the mornings like she used to be. I asked Dad if she was like this at home, and he said she was. He also said she was seeing a therapist every week, and she seemed excited about continuing. What a relief.

As for Mom not coming to London, my guess is that she didn't want to make the trip because of Dad and maybe partially because of Lance, who she still blames for Charity's move to Illinois. Maybe one day, Mom'll let go of her need to blame everyone else and control everything and accept that life is full of surprises and you have to just go with it. Maybe she'll realize that Dad isn't her enemy and Lance isn't either. It would make her a lot happier.

Who knows.

But I'm happy.

Because I have Lance.

"Let's go back to the hotel, Pink," Lance says right before slapping my ass.

"Hey!" I laugh and glance at one of the uniformed gendarmes who smirks at me and Lance. "People are watching!"

"So? I've been dying to fuck you since we came up here. Something about standing on top of a giant steel dick makes me think I need to show it who's boss."

I laugh at the image of straddling the Eiffel Tower like a steel dildo.

"What?" Lance asks.

"Forget it," I giggle.

"Tell me you wouldn't want me to bend you over the railing here while I fuck you from behind in front of the most romantic view in the world?"

"How about we go back to the hotel? It has a pretty good view." I glance over at the gendarme, who is still watching us closely and possibly eavesdropping.

Lance grabs my hands. "As long as I'm looking at you, Pink, the view is always perfect."

I fall into his fiery eyes and my heart melts like it's the first time.

He gestures toward the elevators. "After you."

"Such a gentleman."

"No, I just want to stare at that perfect ass of yours."

"You're too much, Lance," I laugh.

"Wait'll you feel my cock inside you. That'll be too much. You'll be begging me to stop because it feels so damn good you think your pussy is gonna explode. But I won't stop. I'll just keep fucking until the orgasm tears your pussy apart. The French do call orgasms *la petite mort*, right?"

"What?"

"The little death. How close do you think I can take you to the edge without killing you?" His devilish grin returns. His smokey eyes burn with the promise of exquisite danger.

Okay, I'm wet.

What else does a girl need?

I mean, other than her very own *little death* machine?

++++8++++

That night, after we die our little deaths in each other's arms, while I lie beside Lance in the rumpled hotel bed, I can't help but thank goodness for sending him into my life.

++++8++++

LANCE

For the first time in eighteen years, my heart is finally wide open.

++++8++++

Fin.

We all know Rod McKnight and Faith Shields have some unfinished business. Want to know how that time bomb blows up? Sign up for my mailing list, and you'll find out! You'll receive a short novella that dishes all the dirt!

Sign up here:

http://eepurl.com/B7crf

IF YOU ARE ALREADY ON MY MAILING LIST, THE NOVELLA WILL BE IN YOUR INBOX ON

JANUARY 16TH, 2016!

I only send out emails to announce new books or give you freebies like Rod and Faith's novella.

Personal thanks from Devon Hartford:

Thank you so much for taking the time to live with Lance and Chastity and their families for a while. If you enjoyed *Stealing Chastity*, please leave a review wherever you purchased this ebook, on Goodreads, or any book blogs you frequent. Be sure to tell your friends about it!

Contact me and let me know if you want to read more about

Lance & Chastity!!

Like me on Facebook

Friend me on Facebook

Follow me on Twitter @DevonHartford

Follow me on WordPress at devonhartford.com

ABOUT THE AUTHOR

Devon Hartford spent most of his life in Southern California frequenting many of the locations in Cover Model. Devon is an artist and musician, and drew upon his experiences with both while writing his previous romance series The Story of Samantha Smith and The Story of Victory Payne.

OTHER BOOKS BY DEVON HARTFORD:

ROMANTIC COLLEGE COMEDY
Fearless (The Story of Samantha Smith #1)
Reckless (The Story of Samantha Smith #2)
Painless (The Story of Samantha Smith #3)

SCORCHING HOT ALPHA MALE ROMANTIC COMEDY
COVER MODEL
Stealing Chastity

ROMANTIC HIGH SCHOOL COMEDY
Stepbrother Obsessed

BILLIONAIRE ROMANCE
ONE YEAR LOVE - Part One
ONE YEAR LOVE - Part Two
ONE YEAR LOVE - Part Three
ONE YEAR LOVE - Part Four
ONE YEAR LOVE - Collected Edition (Parts 1-4)

ROCKER ROMANCE
Victory RUN 1 (The Story of Victory Payne)
Victory RUN 2 (The Story of Victory Payne)
Victory RUN 3 (The Story of Victory Payne)
Victory RUN 1-2-3 (The Story of Victory Payne - Collecting Parts 1-2-3)

ACKNOWLEDGMENTS

A HUGE thanks to all my passionate and fantastic beta readers:

Neicy Cassidy, Steffini Walker Texas Ranger, Rosanne Triegaardt, Her Highness Samantha Sheeley (Queen of All Typos), Stephanie Svajgl, Natasha Slater, Elizabeth Pawelczyk, Bethanie "The Typo Hammer" Melander, Mandy Jamerson, Miss Constanza from Puerto Vallarta, Mandy Karsa, Maria Combee, Nicki Hewitt-Hart, Cyndi, Megan C Christmas, and The Ever Special Mel Bushell for invaluable feedback and encouragement! You guys rock the typo sauce!

Jackie Barnett for her last minute genius and much needed content editing comments.

Hayley Picknell for slick Brit Pimpin' and awesome reviews everywhere!

Michele McKenzie for equally all-star pimpin' and typo-snyping.

Amy Cossio for always rocking the Awesome Saucio.

Everybody's ever luvin' cowbag, Lindsey Melia for ghetto ghood pimpin'.

Chrissy Zent Sharp for awesome book pimpery via The Book Whore-der's Delights. Be sure to check them out if you're a Romance reader.

And last but not least, for last minute typo-snyping of the highest order and in the face of great personal danger, I award a Typo Heart to **Colonel Melanie Starr**, the one and only **Comma Bomber**, who saved this mission from certain disaster at the 11th hour, but not without significant personal sacrifice on her part. Colonel, I salute you!

Thanks to everybody else who has helped make this book a reality!